Praise for the Love and Honor Series

"Hallee writes with such authentic detail that I felt the sweat drip off my brow, heard the buzz of the African jungle, and ran for dear life with Cynthia and Rick. A rich story of courage and seeing the world with new eyes. Riveting, this book will get under your skin and into your heart. Absolutely fantastic."

Susan May Warren, *USA Today* bestselling author,
on *Honor Bound*

"What a fabulous story with perfectly crafted characters who grab your heart from the opening page. I loved everything about it—from the witty dialogue to the breath-stopping suspense to the tender romance. Once I started, I couldn't put it down. I highly recommend this book and can't wait for the next one."

Lynette Eason, award-winning, bestselling author of the Extreme Measures series, on *Honor Bound*

"Hallee Bridgeman weaves a military suspense with romance for a fast-paced adventure. *Word of Honor* kept me turning pages all night long."

DiAnn Mills, author of *Concrete Evidence*,
on *Word of Honor*

"This book has something for everyone—action, adventure, romance, and true-to-life sadness and grief. Hallee crafts a complex story infused with spiritual truth, wrapped around intriguing lead characters with complicated personalities and backgrounds. Phil and Melissa will have you rooting for them the whole way through."

Janice Cantore, retired police officer and author of
Breach of Honor, on *Honor's Refuge*

HONOR BOUND

LOVE ★ HONOR
BOOK 1

HONOR BOUND

HALLEE BRIDGEMAN

Revell

a division of Baker Publishing Group
Grand Rapids, Michigan

© 2022 by Hallee Bridgeman

Published by Revell
a division of Baker Publishing Group
PO Box 6287, Grand Rapids, MI 49516-6287
www.revellbooks.com

Library of Congress Cataloging-in-Publication Data
Names: Bridgeman, Hallee, author.
Title: Honor bound / Hallee Bridgeman.
Description: Grand Rapids, MI : Revell, a division of Baker Publishing Group, [2022] | Series: Love and honor ; 1
Identifiers: LCCN 2021056319 | ISBN 9780800740207 (paperback) | ISBN 9780800742256 (casebound) | ISBN 9781493438853 (ebook)
Subjects: LCSH: Women missionaries—Fiction. | Missionaries, Medical—Fiction. | Special forces (Military science)—Fiction. | Rescues—Fiction. | Jungle survival—Africa—Fiction. | LCGFT: Thrillers (Fiction) | Romance fiction. | Christian fiction.
Classification: LCC PS3602.R531375 H66 2022 | DDC 813/.6—dc23
LC record available at https://lccn.loc.gov/2021056319

Baker Publishing Group publications use paper produced from sustainable forestry practices and post-consumer waste whenever possible.

22   23   24   25   26   27   28   7   6   5   4   3   2   1

This book is dedicated to the men and women who have served in the United States Army Special Forces branches. Specifically, to my father, Bill Poe, who was in the 2nd Battalion 75th Ranger Regiment, and to my husband, Gregg Bridgeman, who served in the 20th Special Forces Group (Airborne). Your selfless service and warrior spirits served as an inspiration for many of the characters in this book.

Be devoted to one another in love.
Honor one another above yourselves.

—Romans 12:10

Glossary of Military Terms and Acronyms

AO: area of operations

B-7: life preserver

BIRD: helicopter

BOUNDING OVERWATCH: a military tactic of alternating movement (leapfrogging) of coordinated units to allow, if necessary, suppressive fire in support of offensive forward movement or defensive disengagement

CAP: Captain

CHU: containerized housing unit (a small, climate-controlled container)

CRRC/CRICKET: combat rubber raiding craft

COMMISSARY: store on military base that sells groceries and household items

DFAC: dining facility

DV: distinguished visitor

EVAC: evacuate

EXFIL: exfiltrate (withdraw)

FEET DRY: at the target destination (in naval aviator lingo, it literally means "no longer over the ocean but now over land")

HQ: headquarters

HIGH SIDE: the SIPRNET

INTEL: intelligence

KLICK: kilometer

LZ: landing zone

MEB: US Army Marketing and Engagement Brigade

MERC: mercenary

MIKES: minutes

MRE: meal ready to eat

ODA: Operational Detachment Alpha

OPCON: operational control

PCS: permanent change of station

PR: personnel recovery mission

PX: post exchange (a department store on a military installation)

RECON: reconnaissance

ROGER: understood and acknowledged

ROGER, WILCO: understood, acknowledged, and will comply

SCIF: sensitive compartmented information facility (a secure location where classified information can be reviewed)

SIPRNET: secret internet protocol router network (a network the Department of Defense uses to transfer classified information)

SITREP: situational report

CHAPTER
★
ONE

KATANGELA, AFRICA

Captain Rick Norton crouched near the edge of the dirt road. Ears still ringing from the intense firefight, the smell of gunpowder burning his nose, he looked around, counting team members. Gerald "Jerry Maguire" McBride and Daniel "Pot Pie" Swanson came out of their hidden and elevated sniper-spotter positions. They both threw him a silent thumbs-up.

Travis "Trout" Fisher crouched nearby with his carbine pointed downrange and his radio rig tucked away. He also offered a thumbs-up. Jorge Peña "Colada" and Bill "Drumstick" Sanders glided backward toward his position with rifles at the ready. "Up!" they said in unison.

Rick scanned the jungle around him. "Ozzy, position?"

No response.

His gut tightened, and he motioned for the men to regroup. Tension flowed through the team like electricity, then came a measure of relief when they found their combat medic, Phil "Doctor Oz" Osbourne, lying under a banana tree. He was trying to patch up his own thigh with a surgical clamp and a threaded needle below his hastily applied field tourniquet. Rick slid on his knees toward him and took the clamp from him.

"Caught one, Cap," Ozzy said, his voice hesitating as shock started to overtake his body. "No way I'm getting out of this jungle on my own two feet."

Wordlessly, Rick clamped Ozzy's artery despite its best efforts to worm up and out of sight, then wrapped a fresh field dressing bandage around his thigh, securing the clamp and protecting the wound.

"You don't know that, Doc," Sanders said. "I'd want Daddy patching me up if you were otherwise occupied."

Despite his tension, Rick internally rolled his eyes at the "Daddy" nickname. Sanders had drawled the words in an Alabama accent just to make them sound sweeter. Rick would address his mockery in a more appropriate manner, maybe with a bucket of ice water in some idyllic moment of downtime. For now, he let it slide and listened to Fisher calling headquarters for their extraction. He looked up expectantly as Fisher ended the radio call.

"They can pick us up twenty klicks from here, azimuth 26."

Twenty kilometers? With a quick calculation, Rick translated that distance to just over twelve miles. He scratched his red beard, estimated the amount of blood already lost, observed the rate it continued to soak into the field dressing, and concluded that Ozzy wouldn't make it two miles, much less twelve. He would lapse into hypovolemic shock before they could get halfway there, and he would undoubtedly expire soon after.

The team's military intelligence asset, First Lieutenant Peña, retrieved and studied the laminated map that hung from a snap ring on his pack. In his fascinating mind, Peña carried all their mission details. He had an olive-green bandanna tied close around his head but kept his curly black hair uncovered, and his heavy black beard was shaved close to his face. "There's a village two klicks east. Near the river. They have an American doctor, Cynthia Myers, in residence."

Rick pressed his lips together. He knew all about the American doctor. At least, he knew all about her father. "Any other options?"

"Drop packs," Peña said. "Four-man carry to the exfil LZ. Bounding overwatch. Rotate out every five to ten mikes."

Rick considered how long it would take for them to carry Ozzy through the jungle. Even after dropping their heavy packs and rotating in shifts, they would move too slowly. "It would take too long."

"Have them move up the exfil time or relocate the LZ. This is a PR, after all," Sanders said. Personnel recovery missions merited an elevated priority over routine combat operations and could require a more accessible landing zone.

"No-go on that one, Daddy," Fisher said. "Limited resources. Politically sensitive area and such. Azimuth 26 is the best we got."

Rick glanced at the blood-soaked bandage and nodded. Making his hand into a blade, he gestured toward the tree line. "Village it is. Maguire, Colada—fashion a stretcher. Trout, tell HQ to save their fuel for now. Pie, go collect some visibility on the AO until we're ready." He turned to Sanders. "You're on point with me, Drum. First leg."

"Check," Sanders said.

"Go get yourself a little recon while we partake of this incredible good fortune."

"Medals, Cap," Ozzy interjected, his tone dry. "Thanks of a grateful nation, for sure."

"You concentrate on stopping yourself from bleeding so much, Doc. I will take this time to plan our exfil, secure in the knowledge that this mission will doubtless earn us all legendary chest candy and fruit salad."

His team snickered. They did not do their jobs for recognition. Green Berets had a reputation as the "quiet professionals" for a reason.

Using a nylon-poncho liner and some cut-down saplings, they fashioned a makeshift stretcher and carefully lifted Ozzy onto it. Sanders returned with a nod, indicating a clear path.

"Trout, toss your rig and Doc's pack on there too," Rick said. "You and Jerry Maguire make like Sherpas for Doc Oz. Pie, take overwatch for the first klick. Drumstick and I got point out of the gate." He focused on the tall Black man with the thick black beard and shaved head slicing an apple with his razor-sharp K-BAR knife. With the name Daniel Swanson, everyone called him Pot Pie. "Pie, when we arrive, stand to. You and Colada establish a home base close to the village. Bring silence to bear if the situation screams for it."

"Roger, wilco, Cap," Swanson said with a nod.

"Any questions or suggestions?" Rick searched his men's faces in the ensuing silence. "Right. Let us know if your little arms get tired, ladies. Let's roll."

★ ★ ★

Doctor Cynthia Myers had made her way to a remote village in Katangela to run an OB clinic and was the only doctor within several kilometers. Women came from villages all around for care. In the five months she'd been here, Cynthia had witnessed people dying of everything from infection to sickness to mortal wounds sustained in a hippopotamus attack.

As she stood in the dirt courtyard in front of the clinic, she watched a chicken with a fat grub clutched in its beak strut from the edge of the jungle. "You're going to get in trouble, Amelia," she said. The hen had become known as Amelia Egghart because she tended to explore the outside world as often as possible. "Tadeas doesn't like it when you escape from the coop."

Suddenly, ominous sounds interrupted her. From somewhere in the distance came the faint but unmistakable sound of automatic gunfire. Despite the isolation of the remote village in the wild of the African jungle, she had heard that sound all too often since her arrival.

The sounds escalated, a set of low, thunderous cracks alternating with short but sharp high-pitched bursts, like a distant percussion section warming up for a marching band concert at halftime. Something about these cracking reports sounded very different and threatening.

Her nurse, Tadeas, came out of the hospital building. "Apparently, there are more than just Kalashnikovs in the jungle today," he said.

"Pistols?" Cynthia asked.

He shook his head. "ARs. American rifles. Western mercenaries love expensive black rifles. The locals favor AKs. Those are cheap, and so are the bullets."

She felt her eyebrows knitting together as she listened to the now-sporadic gunfire. "That sounds close."

Tadeas turned his eyes toward the tree line. "Actually, that sounds very close."

Though they were nearly always fatal, the American-made 5.56 caliber rounds—much like the Kalashnikov 7.62 caliber rounds—created overwhelming trauma whenever patients survived the gunshots.

Meeting Tadeas's eyes, Cynthia saw her own worry reflected. "I'm going to go find something to eat," she said. "See if you can relieve Ayo. She may not want to leave Gamila yet, but she needs to eat something."

Gamila had gone into labor at four that morning. For six hours, Cynthia and Ayo, her midwife-in-training, had ministered to the teenager as she progressed through the labor. Having witnessed the growing infatuation blossoming between Tadeas and Ayo, Cynthia had no doubt that he would see to her trainee's needs now.

"One of the villagers brought your dinner, Doctor. I covered it and put it in your pantry," Tadeas replied.

He ducked into the doorway of the clinic, and she walked across the dirt courtyard into her own simple one-room home. She poured some water into the washbasin and wet a clean rag, then scrubbed her face, neck, and arms with the soap. As she rinsed with the cool water, inhaling the lavender scent, she felt ready for another five or six hours of work before she could safely call it a day.

Cynthia rebraided her hair, put a fresh bandanna around her neck, and unbuttoned her shirt, then slipped it off her shoulders. Wearing just her tank top and jeans, she sat on her cot and bowed her head. "God? Thank You for bringing me here, even amid the circumstances that perpetuated my decision. And thank You for the life You brought into the world today. Be with Gamila and give her wisdom in parenting."

As she lifted her head, her stomach gave an audible growl. Remembering Tadeas's words, she opened the cupboard above her sink and found some fried bread and a mango beneath a napkin of cheesecloth. She bit into the bread and closed her eyes, enjoying every flavor. Just as she put her knife to the skin of the mango, she heard the unmistakable sound of a truck engine revving high, followed by gunshots and a woman's fearful cry.

Stomach twisting, Cynthia jumped to her feet, slipped the knife into her pocket, and threw her shirt back over her shoulders. Stepping out into the courtyard just as a truck came to an abrupt halt directly in front of the clinic, she shielded her eyes and nose. Dust thrown up by the truck tires swirled around the vehicle, momentarily obscuring it in a powdery reddish-brown cloud.

As the dust settled, a man yelled out, "Where is the doctor?" He stood in the bed of the truck, wearing an unbuttoned olive-green uniform shirt with brass ammunition belts crisscrossed over his chest like bandoliers. In his hand he clutched a nasty-looking rifle with a drum-sized ammunition magazine. Out of the corner of her eye, Cynthia saw villagers ducking into the nearest buildings.

Angry at the violence that had once again permeated her peaceful home, she pushed back any fear she might have felt, stepped forward, and lifted her chin. "Hey, you! I'm the doctor."

Using the side of the truck as a brace, he vaulted to the ground and approached her, looking her over from the top of her braided hair to the toes of her size 4 brown leather boots. "You? You are the doctor?" he asked with a snarl.

"Yes. I am." Despite the fear that made her stomach clench, she held his gaze and waited.

Finally, he stepped back and gestured toward the truck as the driver got out and walked to the back. He opened the tailgate, reached in, and pulled something forward. "Save this man's life."

"Tadeas!" she yelled, walking toward the back of the truck. "I need gloves!"

As her nurse emerged from the clinic, the two men leveled their weapons in his direction. Rounding on the apparent leader, Cynthia said, "You want my help? I need my nurse."

Speaking in French, he granted Tadeas passage. Tadeas handed her two pairs of gloves and her stethoscope. His eyes screamed at her to use caution with these men. She didn't know how to reassure him or if she even should, so she thanked him.

Without warning, the driver kicked Tadeas in the back of his knees, bringing him to the ground. Before she could even gasp, he put the muzzle of his rifle against the back of Tadeas's head. Knowing that the man would not hesitate to kill him, she decided not to react as she slipped one pair of gloves into her pocket and put the other pair on.

When she approached the rear of the truck, she saw a young man lying atop a pallet on the open tailgate. Spent shell casings littered the truck bed. The smell of gunpowder mixed with blood filled her mouth with a metallic taste and almost overwhelmed her. Inspecting the patient, she saw his olive-green shirt soaked with blood. When she pulled the knife out of her pocket, the warlord put a hand on her wrist.

Cynthia looked into his wild brown eyes. "You can hinder me or stay out of my way. The choice is yours."

"Be very careful, Doctor. I have the power to kill everyone here. Their lives are in your hands." He released her.

She stripped the gloves off and dropped them to the dirt. She retrieved the second pair and carefully put them on. "Please don't touch me again. I have no intention of hurting your man here. But by interfering, you have just delayed my examination and put his life in further danger."

The man snorted but took a step back. She turned to the patient and ignored the fact that the man watched with bald suspicion as she cut the bloody shirt away. When she set the knife down, he picked it up and closed the blade, setting it far enough away that she couldn't easily grab it, and of course contaminating it. Cynthia shook her head in frustration at the man's stubborn stupidity.

Trying to put him out of her mind, she examined her patient. Two bullets had penetrated his right lower abdomen. She suspected the rounds were 5.56 caliber based on the size of the entry wounds and the trauma. Even in a stocked hospital with trained emergency staff, she couldn't see saving this man. He bore a brand on his inner wrist—the bull's-eye mark of Chukuwereije, a warlord who had grown in strength over the last five years. If she did not give the appearance of trying to save him, Tadeas would die. And likely Ayo. Maybe even her.

Heart pounding, she put her stethoscope to his chest. Shallow breaths, thready heartbeat. Moving the stethoscope down, she listened. No bowel sounds. He was so close to death. Without God's hand, nothing would change the inevitable.

Even as that thought crossed her mind, he took his last rattling breath. Had they noticed? Pushing her fingers against his neck, she searched for a pulse but found nothing.

Could she pretend he was still alive for a few minutes, stall them until she figured out a way to get Tadeas out of this mess? Probably not. These men had likely seen more death in their young lives than she would in her entire life. She had no options. Just as she took her stethoscope out of her ears and prepared to tell these warlords that their friend had died, she heard a commotion.

From out of the woods on the edge of the village, two soldiers emerged wearing camouflaged uniforms. They held their weapons at the ready and walked in a surprisingly fast crouch, though their upper bodies remained perfectly stable and the muzzles of their rifles perfectly vertical. They moved with practiced skill, looking like little tanks rolling across a smooth countryside.

The Chukuwereije soldiers started screaming orders. The driver lifted his weapon and fired twice. One of the oncoming soldiers fired a single shot, and the man fell at Cynthia's feet. Before she could react, the leader grabbed her and put a pistol to her temple. The hot gunmetal pressed painfully against her skin.

Out of the corner of her eye, she saw Tadeas dash into the clinic. He likely went in to protect Ayo and Gamila. Once he was out of the way of any danger, she felt a sense of calm replace her rising panic.

CHAPTER

★

TWO

With the doctor at the forefront of his mind, Rick stepped out into the clearing and stopped in his tracks. Chukuwereije soldiers held the doctor at gunpoint. It took a moment for his brain to kick into gear, for the focus of the adrenaline to come into play—just in time for his team to catch the attention of the Chukuwereije soldier on watch.

The soldier yelled something, and Rick and Sanders froze, weapons ready. Out of the corner of his eye, Rick watched two women sneak out the back of one of the buildings. One clutched a bundle to her chest, and the other had her arms around her as if supporting or shielding her.

The man yelling at them lifted his weapon and fired two rounds before Sanders dropped him with a single shot.

"Could have done that a little sooner, Drum," Rick said.

"Really? Seems like you had your weapon pointed in the same direction as me, Cap," Sanders replied.

The other soldier grabbed the doctor and put the barrel of a pistol to her head.

The two men dropped to one knee in a synchronous movement and carefully aimed their weapons.

"That's Duong," Sanders said in a low tone. "Not like him to be away from the crowd and out in front."

"We must have clipped someone pretty high up for him to be out here all by his lonesome." Rick scanned the area, but he saw no other evidence of activity.

Rick could practically hear the shrug in his friend's whispered reply. "We took out a truckload back there. Think they're alone?"

"One way to find out," Rick said. He pulled down the bandanna that covered his mouth and, in French, yelled, "Let the woman go!"

Duong screamed back, "I will kill her!"

In English, Rick quietly asked Sanders, "You got him?"

Sanders focused, aimed, and calmly brought Duong into his sights. The hostage considerably complicated his odds of a clean shot. "Not so much," he drawled. "Maybe keep him entertained until Maguire can show him the money?"

"Help me help you," Rick murmured.

Keeping his right hand on the pistol grip of his M4 carbine and his finger on the trigger, Sanders dropped his left hand and surreptitiously signaled for the sniper team to take the shot as soon as they safely could.

Rick yelled, "Sure you will, Duong. You're a killer. So you kill her, then I'll kill you. Where will you be then?"

"Laughing, because then your doctor would be dead. And we both know you need her."

Rick's blood froze as Duong cocked the pistol. Doctor

Myers wouldn't get out of this situation alive if Duong got his way. He needed to stall.

"Let's play this out without any more bluffing, Duong. You kill her, then I kill you slowly. See, I'm a killer too. Trained by the very best."

"No shot," Sanders whispered.

Rick made no sign that he had heard. "There're medical supplies here. We'll revive you just to kill you some more. I promise you, Duong, it will hurt the entire time you're dying. For days. Understand? Or you let her go right now, then maybe you live. Or maybe I make it quick and painless."

In truth, Rick would never torture anyone. But he had also seen what the men in this warlord militia would do to entire villages. He needed Duong to hesitate, so he needed him to feel some fear.

"No shot," Sanders whispered again.

Rick nodded and shouted, "So think it through and make your choice."

Duong yelled back, "I'm dead either way. At least I take her with—"

Even knowing it was coming, Rick failed to hear the suppressed subsonic sniper round when McBride fired. Duong went down, and the doctor came through it with nothing worse than a stain on her shirt.

"Jerry, you had me at hello," Sanders said as he and Rick rose from their crouch.

They moved forward, weapons still at the ready, head and eyes moving everywhere, peering into every corner and shadow. They walked quickly—almost a crouching run—with knees bent to absorb any uneven ground beneath their feet, prepared for unknown attacks coming from any direction.

The doctor stood shocked, with two dead Chukuwereije soldiers at her feet, Duong's blood spattered on the side of her face and a little in her eye.

Ignoring her for the moment, Rick checked the dead to ensure they weren't just playing possum, then his men cleared the immediate area. Sanders threw him a thumbs-up and turned his back, weapon at the ready downrange in the direction of possible hostility. Rick flipped his selector switch back to *safe*, then dropped his rifle to hang on his sling harness. In the same motion, he stripped the bandanna from his face.

The doctor stood still exactly where he had left her. She looked like she might hyperventilate at any moment. She had blond hair pulled back into a ponytail, and the low heel of her boot might have pushed her toward the five-foot mark.

"Doctor Myers!" Rick said in English. When she didn't even look in his direction, he gripped her upper arms. "Are you okay?"

She blinked up at him with big blue eyes but made no answer.

"Hey!" Rick gave her a little shake. She appeared to notice him for the first time. "Are you injured? Did they cut you? Or shoot you? Or hurt you in any way at all? I need you to answer me."

"I'm not hurt," she said. "I'm okay."

Her voice sounded soft but eerily calm. Rick had heard this exact tone of voice on the battlefield before.

"Okay, good." He took her at her word. Her breathing had returned to something close to normal, and she didn't look too freaked out. He reached into his field pouch and retrieved a set of surgical gloves. "Listen up. We need your help. They got our medic. We did what we could, but it's a little beyond our skill set. Or his."

He checked behind him and made sure McBride and Fisher followed with Ozzy. As they approached, the doctor assessed their situation, stripped off her latex gloves, and accepted the fresh pair he offered. She pulled the gloves on even though they swallowed her small hands. He couldn't help but feel impressed at the way she handled herself in such an intense situation.

His hands dropped back to his rifle. With angry eyes the color of a stormy sky, she snapped at him, "Put your guns away. You don't need them."

He didn't blame her aggression in the wake of two men getting shot dead right at her feet. He could help redirect her anger to the proper place. "Anymore, you mean."

She gave him a look of incomprehension.

"We don't need them anymore."

"Anymore?" Fisting her hands, she rounded on him. "This is a peaceful village. Put your guns away."

"It didn't look so peaceful when we arrived." He walked over to the truck bed and looked inside. Jalil Chukuwereije stared lifelessly back at him.

With a snarl, Doctor Myers asked, "And whose fault is that? Huh? Whose bullets killed that boy in the back of the truck?"

Nodding, his voice intentionally calm, Rick gestured to Jalil. "That 'boy' is Jalil, the oldest son of Chukuwereije, the vilest warlord I've ever had the displeasure of encountering. That 'boy' has murdered hundreds of people as lieutenant to his father—entire villages, in fact. I won't bore you with the number of people he has personally raped and maimed." He bent down, nearly touching her nose with his. "Hundreds, Doc. Now, you have your tools? We have ours. In case any more of these 'boys' show up, we'll just keep our tools close at hand, if it's all the same to you."

Her jaw muscles tensed as she clenched her teeth. She stared into his eyes for several seconds before looking back to the men carrying the stretcher.

Rick scanned the dirt streets of the village, looking for any further sign of trouble. He didn't like standing out in the open in the middle of three dead Chukuwereije soldiers.

Just as he started to redirect his men into one of the buildings, the doctor gestured to the building behind them. "My supplies are in there."

He let McBride and Fisher precede him into the mud hut. A very tall man wearing blue scrubs emerged from a nearby building and attempted to follow them inside.

Sanders stepped in front of him. "Just the doc," he said quietly in passable French.

The man had nine inches on Sanders and looked like he might try to bodily move him out of the way. Instead, he simply said in clear English, "I am with the doctor."

"Uh-huh. Sure you are," Sanders said. He coughed, and a strange look crossed his face. Before Rick could ask what had happened, Doctor Myers spoke.

"That's my nurse. Let him in." She didn't even look up as she examined Ozzy's leg.

Rick nodded at Sanders, who leaned against the wall to allow the larger man to rush by him.

Rick started toward Ozzy. Doctor Myers glanced up. "I can try to suture the artery, but I'm no vascular surgeon."

"We appreciate anything you can do," he said. They had no choice. Ozzy wouldn't survive if they didn't try.

He heard a strange gargling sound and looked behind him. Sanders stumbled fully into the room, crashed into a cart filled with supplies and equipment, and landed on the ground.

CHAPTER

THREE

Cynthia gasped and rushed over to the man who'd fallen. His body armor vest—in addition to the thick ceramic armor plates in pouches to the front and rear of it—had straps, belts, Velcro fasteners, clips, and pockets that obstructed anything she might do to examine him. She ripped the fasteners off, pulled at the straps, and pushed the clips aside. The armor plates were astonishingly heavy. She finally spread open the vest, seeing the blood spreading along the left side of his uniform shirt. She could also see his Adam's apple getting pulled to the right as if from some internal force.

Within seconds of her stethoscope against his chest, she diagnosed him. "Tension pneumothorax."

The red-haired man with the thick red beard who had argued with her outside pulled a kit out of his backpack. "I got this. See to our medic, please."

"What does a mercenary know about relieving a tension pneumo?"

The man looked confused for a breath, then he nodded once, as if having assimilated all of her assumptions to formulate his reply. "Ma'am, we are not mercs or any other kind of criminal. We're soldiers in the US Armed Forces, and we are here legally. That's all I can tell you about our mission and way more than you need to know." He gripped her wrist and studied her with intense green eyes. "Doctor, I can rig a four-gauge valve in the intercostal space between the third and fourth ribs for Sergeant Sanders here, but I cannot suture an artery. Let me help Sergeant Sanders and leave you to Lieutenant Osbourne."

Not mercenaries? She looked at the group through new eyes. She didn't like not taking full control of all her patients. However, she knew enough about the American military to realize that this man would indeed know how to correctly install the valve. "Yes. Okay." Ripping another pair of gloves off, she caught Tadeas's eye. "I need a suture kit. And the ultrasound machine."

"Yes, Doctor," he replied, then headed to the back of the room, where he opened the supply closet.

She rose to her feet and went back to the table. The medic had his eyes open. "Hello there," she said, putting a hand on his forehead. "Can you tell me your name?"

"I'm Phil Osbourne. Ozzy. You Doctor Myers?" His dirty-blond eyebrows furrowed over his gray-green eyes.

"That's me. Okay, Ozzy. I'm going to see what I can do to suture your femoral artery. Good thing it's so big, huh?"

His body quaked with shock. She wished she had a way to warm him. "I t-t-tried t-t—"

"Shh," she said, needing him to conserve his energy. "It's okay." She stayed calm because if she didn't attempt to do this, he would die. And if he died while she tried, at least she had tried. With her hand still on his forehead, she closed her eyes and whispered a quick prayer.

Tadeas handed her a fresh pair of gloves, then rushed out of the room. She knew he'd gone outside to start the generator.

"You know, Ozzy, most people get on this table to deliver a baby. You're not going to surprise me, are you?"

He smiled, but before he could reply, his eyes rolled back in his head.

Tadeas returned and washed his hands. As soon as he reached the table, Cynthia said, "I need light." He adjusted the overhead light until she nodded her approval. Humming her favorite praise song under her breath, she began repairing the artery.

"Doc's an actual doctor," one of the men said. "He's like a mouth surgeon."

"Oral surgeon," the soldier with the curly black hair and close-cropped beard corrected. He smiled with gleaming white teeth.

"We have a surgeon who comes through here monthly to do scheduled C-sections and tonsillectomies and what have you," Cynthia said. "He usually stays three days then leaves. Anyone else who isn't an actual emergency, we transport out of here." Doing her best imitation of a surgeon's knot, she snipped the thread and looked at the two men on the floor. "How's it going, Grizzly?"

One of the men against the wall snorted, and the man on the floor looked up from taping the tube to his friend's chest. "Was that meant for me, Doctor?"

Feeling a flush crawl across her cheeks when she realized

what she'd said out loud, she looked back at Ozzy's artery, trying to decide if she had the courage to release the clamp. "Your beard makes you look like a mountain man. Grizzly Adams was my first thought."

He tossed the tools he'd used into a nearby basin with a little more force than necessary. "I see. It also makes my face unrecognizable to most facial detection software. My name is Captain Norton." He gestured toward his friend. "Where do you want him?"

She released the clamp and watched as the sutures held. Silently, she thanked God for His guidance. "Tadeas will get a bed ready for him. I want to check him out first." She dressed the thigh in a clean bandage, wishing she had blood to give him. "I saw letters on Ozzy's boots. Is that blood type?"

"Yes," Captain Norton confirmed.

"Are any of you also O neg?"

A man with light-brown hair and beard nodded and stepped away from the wall. "I am. Gerald McBride, ma'am. What do you need?"

"At least a pint if you can spare it." She looked at Tadeas, who had finished setting up the ultrasound machine. "See about getting me two cots. We'll put Ozzy here on one and McBride there on another, and do a direct transfusion." Looking at the leader, she said, "As long as there are no objections, Captain."

He unclipped his carbine and set it against the wall, loosened his body armor, and took a long, slow drink from his Camelback. Then he retrieved his rifle and took up a post alongside the door, his eyes scanning for any movement out toward the tree line. He held his weapon loose and low. What he did not do was dignify her attempt at sarcasm with so much as even his notice.

She looked at the gear and ammunition he carried and idly wondered how the men could move with such ease and grace under the weight of all that equipment.

Tadeas enlisted the help of one of the other soldiers, and they left the building to go get the cots.

"Take all you want, ma'am. Anything to help Doc Oz," McBride said. He unfastened his armored vest and set it gently on the floor before he stripped off his sweat-stained outer blouse.

She smiled, impressed at the camaraderie as Tadeas and the other soldier returned, each carrying a cot. "He must be a good man to have all of you so worried about him."

"They're all good men, Doctor Myers," Captain Norton said without looking in her direction. "The best, in fact."

Feeling a little defensive and outnumbered, Cynthia said, "Tell me something. How do you all know my name, Captain?"

His expression didn't change, but he did turn his gaze in her direction. Under all his gear, she thought she saw his shoulder make a small movement. "You know my name, ma'am. Only seems fair."

"It may be fair, but it doesn't answer my question."

He turned his gaze away, staring at the tree line. "Can you keep a secret, Doctor?"

"Yes. Of course I can."

"Good." He nodded. "So can I."

After a few seconds, she realized he didn't plan to confide in her. "That's not an answer either."

The tone of his voice remained even. "It'll have to do."

She wasn't going to get anything else. As she slipped on

yet another pair of gloves, she watched Captain Norton clip his weapon back onto his sling harness, then move it around behind him. On her count, they lifted and moved Ozzy to one of the cots. In no time, she had a direct transfusion going between the men.

She turned and found that her mountain man had already lifted Sanders onto the table. When she caught his eye, he said, "I don't want Chukuwereije's men finding this village, Doc. Fisher and I are going to go handle that truck and the bodies."

The thought of the warlord made her hands tremble. Taking a deep breath to still her emotions, she turned on the ultrasound machine as the men left. Somewhere inside Sanders, a bullet had collapsed his lung. She needed to find it. Without risky exploratory surgery, which she didn't even know if she could perform under these conditions, she thought using ultrasound technology was the next best thing.

In no time, she had the wand out and slowly ran it along Sanders's skin. After several minutes, she spotted the bullet. It sat precariously near his heart.

"Tadeas," she said, "come look at this." Pointing to the screen, she showed him the bullet.

"Right next to the pericardium," Tadeas said.

"Like a little bird egg in a nest."

"You aren't going to try to get that out, are you? There's no way I'd play around with that thing."

"I don't see that I have a whole lot of choice. One shift and he dies."

"Good to know, Doc," Sanders said.

Cynthia met the gaze of her grinning patient. "Try not to shift. Sanders, right?"

"Bill. Call me Bill." He nodded slowly. "I will abstain from even shifty thoughts."

Cynthia printed several shots of the bullet at different angles before shutting down the machine. "Let's get the operating room prepped."

Tadeas nodded and started to walk away.

"When you move him, do it very gingerly," she said. "Get McBride to help you so there is minimal movement."

"Yes, Doctor."

Rick lifted his left hand in a fist, and Fisher froze. Soundlessly, the two men lowered to a crouch. A rustling in the bushes got closer, and Fisher silently raised his weapon. Snorting mixed in with the rustling. Rick signaled to wait just as a wild boar burst out of the brush. They sat perfectly still as the animal went by, never even glancing in their direction. Listening intently, Rick waited thirty seconds, then ninety, and finally rose to his feet and kept walking.

The constant diligence exhausted the mind. He would usually have two sets of men take turns on point, giving the group in the back an opportunity to give their brains a break. With only two of them, they had to be extra careful not to let their tired minds relax too much and put each other in danger.

By the time they made it back to the village, night had set in. The forest around them came to life with the sounds of croaks, screeches, humming, and rustling. Most of the buildings looked like blackened rectangles in the night, but they could see the flicker of candlelight in a few of the windows. Two women sitting in front of an outdoor oven stopped talking as they walked by, staring at them with dark eyes that reflected the hot coals smoldering in the oven.

Rick took their stares in stride. His firefight with the Chukuwereije rebels had brought the warlord's men to the village, placing these women and their families in danger. These women probably didn't consider his team different from the butchers, murderers, and slavers who had terrorized this land for hundreds of years. But they didn't realize they would face far more prevalent danger without the presence of his men.

For weeks they had pushed the notorious warlord back, away from the remote jungle villages, back toward the industrial areas near the river. They had successfully interdicted and suppressed his intended inhumane activities, including and especially the harvesting of young boys from the villages. This particular village would have held great interest to the warlord because of the obstetrics clinic. Some women traveled for days to see Doctor Cynthia Myers, bringing their other children along with them. Young children filled the huts of expectant mothers. Many of the men in this village fished, which gave the villagers good nutrition, resulting in stronger boys—exactly what Chukuwereije looked for in his conscripted private army.

Silently, Rick and Fisher reached the center of the village. Dark windows in the hut where the doctor had worked on Sanders and Ozzy greeted them. Even so, he checked inside. Someone had spotlessly cleaned every corner and reorganized every shelf. Next door, in a long rectangular wooden building, Rick could see light. They crept over and peered through the window, inspecting the three rows of beds. Four had patients. Sanders's black hair stood out against the white sheets. As he opened the door, Doctor Myers stepped into his path.

"Captain. Glad to see you made it back," she said, handing a clipboard to a female nurse. "But if you wish to come inside and visit your friends, you're going to have to leave your weapons outside."

A dozen retorts froze on his tongue. She had already made her feelings about firearms clear. He didn't think his responsibilities included schooling her in the realities of life, which often trumped high-minded philosophies when it came to matters of survival.

"Yes, ma'am," he agreed smoothly. "I can do that."

He caught Fisher's eye before he unclipped his carbine and propped it up against the outside wall. "But Doc, I don't want you to imagine for even one second that you have the authority to keep me from seeing to my men. You don't. Not in any country on this earth." He slid his pistol from the holster at his chest and handed it over grip first to Fisher, who secured it in the load-bearing belt at his waist. "I'll play nice, but it's just playing. I hope we understand each other. I'll just leave Fisher out here to guard our weapons against any idle curiosity."

"This is a peaceful village. I doubt your weapons would hold any interest for long."

"If you say so." He kept his voice even and amicable.

"The knife too."

"Oh, now, Doc." Rick raised an eyebrow as he gave a very unfriendly smile. "You have sharper knives than I do. That right?"

Fisher helped the conversation by wisely adding his own silence to it.

"Your knife is a weapon, Captain," Doctor Myers said. "My knives save lives. Your knives take lives."

36

Amused by her hubris, he gave a genuine smile. "Look, Doc. I respect what you're going for here. I do."

"Don't patronize me, Captain."

His expression turned puzzled. "I'm not sure I would know how, ma'am. I honestly do respect you. Okay?"

She took a breath with her eyes closed, then schooled her features. "Okay. If you respect me, you will leave all of your weapons outside of my clinic."

"I get your point." He nodded. "You should take this into account, though. The real weapon isn't the rifle or the pistol or the knife. It's me. The truth is that every single object within reach of my hands is a potential weapon. Comes down to it, I could strangle you with my boxers or smother you with my socks. You want me to leave them outside too?"

Her nostrils flared and her cheeks flushed. "Fine." She gestured, and he stepped up into the wooden structure, his knife still firmly sheathed.

The sharp odor of industrial disinfectant assailed his nose, and he saw a few damp spots on the floor where someone had scrubbed the tile clean. Shelves of supplies stood neatly organized and labeled. A water cooler took up a corner next to a green metal desk that had probably seen the last world war.

As the doctor turned to look at him, he caught the faintest scent of lavender. "Lieutenant Osbourne regained consciousness about an hour and ten minutes ago. He's in a lot of pain, but the sutures have held, and his volume is good enough that his BP is safe. Now the question will be whether I can keep infection at bay. I'm afraid intravenous antibiotics are not readily available here. I have given him some orally, and we'll keep the wound clean."

Rick nodded. "And Sanders?"

She hesitated and glanced away before looking back at him. He wondered whether she had just prepared herself to lie to him or to give him bad news. As if of their own accord, his eyes went to where Sanders lay on a bed across from Ozzy's. He appeared asleep. A clean white bandage covered his chest.

She cleared her throat. "The bullet that punctured his lung entered through the armpit and was dangerously close to his heart. I had no choice but to operate on him and remove it." She gestured to the end of the room, where double doors stood closed, guarding whatever lay beyond. "We have a sterile operating room. I went in, found the bullet, and closed him as quickly as I could. His lung will heal. He just needs a chest tube for a while." She stuck her hands into the pockets of her jeans and rocked back on her heels.

He waited, processing the notion that his best friend in the world had just undergone open-heart surgery in the middle of the African jungle.

Finally, she said, "Again, I have no IV antibiotics. At this point, all we can do is pray." She hesitated. "Hard."

She didn't speak again. He stared at her upturned face without really seeing her while he contemplated the facts, thinking of logistics, the mission, communications. "I guess we do that first."

"What?" she asked.

"Pray." Rick took a knee and folded his hands over it, then bowed his head and closed his eyes. He silently appealed to God to protect his men, to heal their bodies, and to keep the village safe from the enemy. "Amen," he said out loud.

"Amen," Doctor Myers echoed.

Rick looked at her sharply, searching for any hint she

might be mocking him. When he didn't detect any evidence of it, he asked, "When can we move him?"

"I'd be afraid to move him for at least a week. I don't know if he could handle the pain of transport at any time in the next three or four days."

"And Osbourne would do well to be still for a week too?" She nodded. "I think I would be comfortable with that."

He studied her, trying to read her body language and facial expression. "Are you willing to keep them here?"

He gave her credit for not immediately answering. Instead, he could see that she carefully considered his words and thought about her answer. "I'm fine with them here. I'm fine with you here. I am not fine with you walking down the center of the village brandishing your weapons." When he opened his mouth, she cut off his sarcastic retort with a raised hand. "I get that you saved my life. But understand, I would have given my life and given it gladly. Instead, three men are dead, and you took two lives to save my one. Those statistics don't add up."

He took a breath and smiled. "Guess you took statistics at Berkeley?"

"Stanford, actually."

He nodded. "I took statistics at the Citadel. By my count, I took two lives and saved this entire village. But I guess statistically it's open to interpretation. New math and all."

"Any loss of life is too much," Doctor Myers said.

He felt his teeth grit together and forced his jaw to relax. He'd never come across anyone so closed-minded. "Fine," he bit out. "I'll take my men, and we will stay in our camp. Likewise, our weapons will stay in our camp. Meanwhile, I can try to get you IV antibiotics or any other medications or supplies you need. Can you give me a wish list of your specific needs?"

Her eyes widened, and she nodded, clearly ignoring his evident dissatisfaction with her demands regarding firearms. "I'll make a list."

After glancing at his men lying in their cots, he closed his eyes and took a deep breath through his nose. The smell of the pine cleaner took him back to the Infantry Basic Officer Leader Course he'd attended in the backwoods of Fort Benning, Georgia. He'd cleaned that latrine one too many times with industrial pine cleaner.

He opened his eyes, feeling the weight of his fatigue as he slowly let out his breath. "Don't be afraid to ask for anything at all," he said, feeling his beard shift as he smiled. "We may not be able to get something, but the answer's always no if you don't ask, Doc."

In the quiet of the night, Cynthia typed patient notes into her laptop, detailing the surgery she'd performed on Sergeant Bill Sanders. She'd had to crack his chest. A part of her had hoped the bullet would just make its way to her when she went after it and the surgery would require little effort or know-how. Instead, she found herself repairing an artery and then patching him back up. It had taken every ounce of skill and not a small amount of prayer to keep him alive on the table. Thankfully, Tadeas had his blood type, which allowed her to replenish some of the blood lost with whole blood instead of just saline. She honestly would rather face more warlords than ever again hear the sound of a chest cracking under the force of her own hands.

Now to keep him from getting an infection.

She prayed Captain Norton would have the opportunity to fill her supply list. Then she would feel far more confident in Sanders's survival.

After she typed the last sentence, she turned the laptop off. She used the generator to charge it once a week, and the notes piled up when the battery died in between charges. As she closed the lid, she jumped at the screech of a milky eagle owl right outside her window. Thinking of the critters that enormous owl would eat, she didn't mind the noise it made in the late evening. The spiders here grew to the size of house cats.

As she prepared for bed, exhaustion washed over her like a tide. A middle-of-the-night wake-up, followed by a delivery, followed by the emotional trauma of acting as a human-shield hostage for an insane man, followed by vascular surgery on one member of the US Army Special Forces and dangerously-close-to-the-heart surgery on another, had absolutely exhausted her. Her time here was nearly up. She needed to make a decision in the next two weeks about whether she intended to stay on for another six months or go back home and . . .

And what?

Reenter the life of a privileged American from a wealthy family? Go back to driving her luxury German-made car from her suburban home to her private-practice OB clinic on the correct side of the James? She'd come here to hide and heal, to escape life and all of the baggage that came with it. She'd learned, after five months, just how much life she could pack into one backpack.

When her fiancé, in an inebriated state, had arrived with another woman to a White House dinner she'd also attended, and very publicly and thoroughly destroyed her life, she'd fled to Africa instead of facing the daily mass of reporters who camped outside her home and office. Her father's people had fought her, but in the end, she'd won. What did it matter if her father was a senator from Virginia? It didn't affect her out in the jungle.

While she'd suffered deep humiliation and heartbreak and been in misery for months, she'd never considered death an option. Analyzing the events of the day, she felt confident that her readiness to face death didn't have anything to do with any lingering heartbreak.

In the five months since she'd come here, she had healed, and her heartbreak had gradually diminished. The thought of her fiancé with another woman being broadcast over every possible news media no longer brought her to her knees in sorrow. Now it just caused a twinge of discomfort in her heart, making her briefly question what might be wrong with her that he would seek out the company of another woman, seek to so publicly humiliate her and laugh the entire time. When those thoughts tried to destroy her emotionally, some rational part of her brain would engage, and she would remind herself that the problem lay with him, in his heart, and not with her. Those moments of discomfort had happened less and less lately.

Now her desire to stay had more to do with her relationship with God than it did with a desire to lay some past emotional pain to rest. She had grown ever closer to Him while here. In this jungle, He had become real to her—no longer some mystical, unseen, and largely uncaring force occasionally referred to but never accessible. He had spoken to her, comforted her, and directed her in more ways than she could have ever imagined possible.

When that evil man had cocked his pistol, when she'd known with unshakable certainty she would die today, she had searched her heart and discovered that if God had planned it this way, then she felt prepared to follow His plan and meet Him.

The man's death affected her more than she cared to admit. Despite his actions leading to the final conclusion, she couldn't help but feel like maybe the only reason he'd died was that she'd been close enough to grab. Silly, she knew, to take the burden of blame from the murderer and put it on her own shoulders.

She thought of Captain Norton and his team. An armed detail did not bother her. She'd attended an exclusive girls' boarding school from the age of twelve. Some of the girls there had personal security, and the school itself had armed security. As her father rose through the ranks in Congress, eventually her parents employed an armed personal protection security company. Cynthia didn't object to the presence of the weapons themselves. She simply objected to the kind of violence that brought men to use those weapons to take lives. While she did mostly appreciate the saving of her own life, she abhorred the thought of the death of two men in exchange for it.

Just as she put toothpaste on her toothbrush, a rapping on her door startled her. She knew of no women close to their due dates. She crossed the room, still clutching the toothbrush, and opened the door, suspecting Ayo. Her eyes widened when she saw Captain Norton.

"Captain," she said, a question in her voice.

"Doctor."

When he said nothing more, she slipped out of the building

and shut the door behind her, not wanting insects to fly into her room. "How may I help you?"

"I'm sorry to intrude, Doctor Myers. I just wanted to thank you for helping us today. I don't think I remembered to thank you, what with everything that happened and all. I wanted to get that said before another day started. I know you resented helping us. Even so, I'm grateful. We all are."

Her eyebrows drew together in a frown. "I don't resent you or your men, Captain—simply the violence that brought you to me."

He opened his mouth to speak, and she held up her hand to stop him. Her cheeks heated when she realized she was holding up her toothbrush, appearing to wave it at him like a wand. She dropped her hand to her side.

"I think a lot of my anger was a delayed reaction to what happened to me and around me," she said. "And because I misidentified you as mercenaries, that really put my defenses up. What I'm trying to say is that I owe you an apology. I understand your job. I really do. More than you know."

"Oh, I know," he said. "You were part of our mission brief."

"Me?" She asked the question even though she probably wouldn't like the answer. "Why? Because I'm an American?"

"This jungle is full of Americans." He leaned against the wall and crossed his arms over his chest. "You're the daughter of Vice President Randal Myers. I have a file on you."

As if in denial at his words, she shook her head. Two months after she'd arrived here, the previous vice president of the United States had suffered a major heart attack and died on the way to Bethesda. Before the month was out, her father had raised his right hand while a representative of the Supreme Court swore him into office as the new vice president.

"No," she said. "He wasn't the VP when I got here, and he wouldn't let people know where I am regardless. He knows how much I value my privacy out here."

"Would you like to see the file, ma'am?"

"That's how you knew about Berkeley." A strange feeling of betrayal overcame her. As surreal as the idea was, her father was one heartbeat away from becoming the unelected leader of the free world. But why would a Special Ops unit have a dossier on her? Had it come from her father, or from the Secret Service? Why couldn't she find any peace, even in the middle of the jungle? Headlines, pictures, and gossip magazine covers flooded her mind. "I have to go to bed," she whispered as she battled the humiliation and anger that rose in her. "Good night, Captain."

"Doctor Myers," he said, laying a hand on her wrist and effectively keeping her from fleeing back inside. If he noticed that she clutched her toothbrush a little tighter at the feel of his calloused fingers, he gave no indication. "If it's any consolation, there are only two of us who know." His fingers slid away as gently as feathers.

With a dry mouth, she said, "I'd appreciate it if you kept it that way."

"Of course, ma'am. And for what it's worth . . ." He paused, and his eyes met hers. "That man was an idiot. And a jerk. You deserved better, and I'm not the only one who says so."

She looked down, knowing the rush of heat in her face made her cheeks red. She didn't look at him again until he stepped backward. "Have a good night, Captain."

CHAPTER

FOUR

Sunlight shone through the palms and danced across the floor in a soothing rhythm. Cynthia lay in her cot and watched the light and shadows form patterns, listening to the sounds of the village outside her window. As she gradually came awake, it took her a few moments to remember the events of yesterday. When it all came flooding into her mind, she moaned and rolled over, seeking escape.

She had certainly had better beginnings with people than she did with Captain Norton. The circumstances had overwhelmed her until she made him a target. Thankfully, he didn't seem to have taken it too personally.

When she rolled out of bed, her sore muscles screamed in protest. No wonder she'd slept so long this morning. If she had a fully staffed hospital on her hands, she'd take the morning off. However, she had patients to check on, and no one could do it but her.

She pulled on her last clean pair of cargo pants and a white tank top. On her way out of the hut, she slipped on a cotton shirt and grabbed her laundry bag. She stepped into the bright sunshine and shielded her eyes, gazing down the dirt road at the line of huts going toward the river. Two women walked up the road, water jugs balanced on their heads. She looked in the other direction, up the hill toward a tighter cluster of huts. A kid dashed by on his bicycle.

Nothing appeared out of order. Chukuwereije's men hadn't attacked during the night. She rubbed the back of her neck and crossed the road to the clinic ward.

She stepped into the building, appreciating the pine smell of disinfectant. Tadeas sat with his feet on the desk, the chair inclined as far back as it could go, his head back, softly snoring. She let the wooden door slam shut, and he simply raised his head and looked at her. She could tell when he got his bearings as his eyes cleared, and he pulled his feet down and sat up.

"Good morning, Doctor. I left you an egg." He held out a little plastic bowl that contained a blue-green speckled egg.

"Oh, wonderful," Cynthia said, taking the bowl from him. "You had some, right?"

"Yes. Three." He patted his stomach. "And I made some for the patients."

Cynthia stopped at the shelf and filled her cargo pockets with gloves. "Anything last night?"

"No. I gave Sergeant Sanders more pain medicine at seven, and Doctor Osbourne wants to speak with you."

"Okay. That accounts for our new guests. How about Hermand?"

Tadeas glanced at the schoolteacher who had fallen prey to a button spider during lunchtime yesterday. "Antivenin appears to have done its job. He seemed less restless around three this morning. Vitals are normal. As soon as he wakes up, he can probably go home."

"And Mireille?"

He shifted a piece of paper on the desk and picked up the chart for the forty-six-year-old woman with pneumonia. "Her fever broke at four this morning. I gave her another dose of acetaminophen. Her IV site was bothering her, so I started a new one in her other hand. She's due for another dose of antibiotics at ten."

"Perfect. I'll release her after that last IV dose and give her tablets to finish her treatment. Go home. I'll let you know if I need you today."

"Is Ayo coming in?"

She smiled at his affection for her student. "She is doing house-call rounds in villages today. But she'll be here around sundown to restock supplies."

"Okay. I'll be back at seven."

"Thanks."

After he left, she grabbed her stethoscope, blood pressure cuff, and two clipboard charts and walked down the row of beds until she reached Lieutenant Osbourne. "Good morning. Nice to see your eyes."

He sat propped up on pillows. His bloodshot eyes had dark circles under them, and his blond beard barely stood out on his pale face. "Doc." He gestured at his leg. "Nice work."

"Well, I'm not a vascular surgeon, so it will need patching up when you get to civilization." She glanced through his chart. "You refused pain medication?"

He shook his head. "Narcotics tend to alter me."

"Hmm. That used to happen to my grandmother. Doctors thought she had dementia, then they took her off medication and suddenly she had full use of her faculties." She set the clipboard on the bed and pulled on some gloves. "I've given Captain Norton a medical wish list that includes some intravenous antibiotics. I'm hoping he's able to secure them for me today. I am giving you pills, but I would feel a lot better if we could do it through IV."

She lifted the bandage on his thigh and felt along her incision. The skin around it had turned an angry red color and felt hot to the touch. "Did Tadeas feed you?"

"Yeah. He gave me some boiled eggs and some very not bad fried bread."

"Ah, yes, the woman who cooks for us can do incredible things with wheat and cardamom. It's like a gift from God." She replaced the dressing and put a hand on his forehead. "How's the food sitting?"

He shrugged. "Nothing to complain about. I could use some ibuprofen if you have it."

She glanced at the top of the chart. "Doesn't look like Tadeas gave you any last night. Is that right?" Using her stethoscope, she listened to his chest. No sign of pneumonia or an irregular heart rhythm. She slipped the blood pressure cuff onto his arm.

"I was fine until I sat up to eat. I think moving it as I shifted brought the pain."

"I'll get you some. Need anything else?"

"Do you have a way to get a message to my team?"

After she noted his blood pressure in the chart, she slipped off the gloves. "No. But I have a feeling they'll be here soon. Captain Norton was here until after midnight."

He looked over at Sanders. "How's Drumstick?"

With a chuckle, she asked, "Drumstick? Is that because his last name is Sanders?"

"Well, yeah. Finger Licking Good was too long, as was Eleven Herbs and Spices."

She grinned, enjoying the man's sense of humor despite the seriousness of his wound. "Were those the only options?"

He gave a small shrug. "Well, Colonel was out for obvious reasons."

Her grin transformed into a smile. "Right. What do they call you?"

"Doc Oz."

"Clever." She shifted to the second clipboard. "I had to get a bullet out of his chest in an operating room designed to do planned C-sections, and with only the blood my nurse could provide." She glanced at him. Worry etched lines into his face. "If we can keep him still and your man can get me IV antibiotics, I think he'll be fine."

"Daddy will get it done."

She had started to turn away but paused. "Excuse me? Daddy?"

"Yeah. Team Daddy. It's just what we call the team leader."

"What an interesting culture," she said. "I'll bring you some ibuprofen as soon as I check on Chicken Leg over there."

"Thanks." He closed his eyes.

She knew he had to be in tremendous pain right now. A shot of morphine would make him feel better, even if it did alter him slightly. She would readdress it later in the morning.

At the next bed, she pulled on another pair of gloves. Sergeant Sanders lay with his eyes closed, breathing evenly.

She set the clipboard down and reached for his bandage. As soon as her hand touched his chest, he snatched her wrist faster than she could process the movement. A gasp escaped her, and she froze. He opened his eyes much slower than he'd grabbed her. His dark brown eyes and black beard provided a rich contrast to his pale face.

"Sorry," he said in a hoarse voice. "Reflexes."

He closed his eyes again. This time when she touched his chest, he didn't move. She inspected his incision. It looked good. "Did you eat anything?"

Without opening his eyes, he said, "No."

"Do you want something? I can get you some broth."

"No thanks." He opened his eyes again as she listened to his heartbeat. "What happened? Last thing I remember was getting Ozzy into your exam room."

She noted his pulse rate on the chart and said, "I talked to you some last night, but you were just coming out of anesthesia. You got shot." She carefully lifted his arm and prodded the bullet entrance. She didn't like the angry look of the skin around the sutures. "Bullet went in here and lodged itself right next to your pericardium. If you had sneezed, it probably would have penetrated your heart. I can tell you that you're alive today because God wants it that way. I can't imagine how you lived."

"Well," he drawled, "I'm a special little snowflake. Ask anyone."

"How's the pain?"

"Not bad, actually. It only hurts when I breathe."

She chuckled and slipped the blood pressure cuff on his arm. "You're not due for another dose of pain meds for a while yet." She frowned as she measured the high blood pressure. When she got a bead on his systolic, she asked, "Think you can sleep some more?"

"Probably."

She double-checked his chart. "Okay. I'm going to go ahead and have someone make the broth in case you wake up hungry. Try to sleep."

★ ★ ★

Swanson and McBride stepped into the clearing carrying a tough box between them. As soon as they set it down, Rick broke the seal and opened it. Among the food packets, called MREs, and the ammunition to replace what they'd used yesterday, he found the medical supplies requested by Doctor Myers.

"I'm going to go check on Drumstick and Ozzy," he said, stashing the medical supplies in his rucksack. "Peña, you're with me." He set his weapon against a tree. "Leave your weapon. Apparently, firearms are bad, even when they're used to shoot the bad guys."

Peña snorted. "There's all sorts of ways to get rid of bad guys. I don't need no stinkin' gun."

"I tried to tell her." He looked over at Swanson and Mc-Bride. "I know you're tired from ten klicks of wilderness. But stay alert. Chukuwereije is going to have scouts all over this jungle looking for his son."

"Roger." McBride grabbed an MRE and read the packet. "Mmm. Pasta in tomato sauce. Just like Mama used to make."

"No wonder you left home," Swanson said. He sat on a camp stool and looked at Fisher. "Hey, Trout, got any more of that hot sauce?"

Fisher dug into his cargo pocket and pulled out a thin

bottle of Louisiana hot sauce. "This'll fix anything." He tossed it toward Swanson, who smoothly caught it in the air.

Rick and Peña left the camp, and the green undergrowth of the jungle enveloped them. They moved swiftly and silently, and in about a hundred yards they walked out of the tree line and into the clearing at the edge of the village. It felt strange to traverse down the street without the weight of his weapon. Rick didn't like the way it made him feel vulnerable. He might have to rethink his agreement with Doctor Myers.

When they arrived at the clinic, he glanced in the window before going to the door. Both of the beds that had been occupied last night sat empty, their mattresses bare.

The screen door squeaked as Rick opened it. They stepped into the building. No one sat at the desk. He slipped his rucksack off his back and set it on the floor against the desk. As he crossed the room, Doctor Myers came through a doorway in the back of the building, carrying a laundry bag. She paused when she saw him, then resumed walking.

"Good afternoon, Captain." She glanced at Peña. "Lieutenant? Is that right?"

He smiled. "Yes. First Lieutenant Jorge Peña."

"It's nice to meet you."

"Doctor," Rick said by way of greeting. He paused at Ozzy's bed. Doctor Myers set the laundry bag down and joined him. His medic lay with his eyes closed, not moving. "How's he doing?"

"There's infection setting into his leg. The oral antibiotics are not strong enough to combat it."

He gestured at the rucksack. "Looks like your list got filled."

"Oh!" She put a hand on Ozzy's shoulder. "That will be a tremendous help."

Something about the way she touched his medic softened the part of Rick that had reacted to her and made him argue with her yesterday. He could see her care for her patient, could tell that she had made him entirely her charge. The simple movement totally reversed his opinion of her.

He walked over to Sanders's bed. Seeing his best friend lying so still and pale hurt his heart. Fresh anger coursed through his veins. "How's Drumstick?"

Doctor Myers smiled at him, a smile that reached her eyes and transformed her face. "I heard about those names, Daddy," she said.

Heat flushed his cheeks, and he was glad his beard covered the blush. Before he could reply, her face sobered again.

"He's in a lot of pain, which makes sense. I powered up my laptop last night and sent an email to a colleague at Walter Reed, seeking confirmation of care. They're six hours behind us, so I'm hoping to have an answer late afternoon."

"Would a sat phone help?" Peña asked.

"That's a thought." She raised her eyebrows. "I can send him another email and give him a time I can call. I have one here that was given to me for emergencies, but I don't think it's charged."

Rick looked at the oil lamp hanging from the wall. "How do you have email?"

"I have a small generator. I used it last night when we operated on Sergeant Sanders. But fuel is precious, so I only charge my laptop once a week. I can connect to a satellite interface during certain hours. My father made some arrangements for me when I first got here."

He put a hand on Sanders's shoulder. His friend didn't move. "Will he be okay?"

He focused on her face as she formulated her answer and got the impression that whatever she said, it would be the truth. "I am an OB, Captain. I have facilitated thousands of births. I am neither a thoracic nor a cardiothoracic surgeon. I drew from my experiences as a medical student and can promise you that they've received my best care. Beyond that, I don't know. God will have to intervene."

He processed that affirmation along with what she'd said last night. "The longer we sit here, the more likely Chukuwereije finds us. Are you still thinking a week before we can move them?"

The pleasantness slid off her face, and her eyes hardened. Suddenly he was facing the woman he'd sparred with last night. "Can you keep them out of the village?"

He lifted his hands out to his sides. "Or die trying, Doctor."

With a huff, she started to walk past him, but Peña stopped her. "Doctor, it's important that only you take care of these men while they're on narcotics."

She gestured at Ozzy. "He's not on narcotics."

"Fine, then we'll discuss Sergeant Sanders alone," Peña said. "He has knowledge, information. You never know exactly how someone will respond to medication, and we're in the middle of a highly sensitive mission. A word here, a word there, and the balance of power in this nation will shift in a direction that would hurt everyone involved for years to come."

She waited for several moments, just staring blankly at Peña, then said, "I am one person. Sergeant Sanders requires twenty-four-hour care. If you don't want anyone but me taking care of him, then you need to have someone else here with me. I can assure you that my nurse Tadeas—"

"Could very well have ties to Chukuwereije, even remotely."

Doctor Myers closed her eyes, shook her head, and took a deep breath, clearly gathering patience before she spoke again. "—is not from this country. He graduated from McGill University in Quebec and is here on a three-year contract." She glanced from Peña to Rick and back again. "Do you not have a file on him too?"

Rick pressed his lips together to keep from laughing. The look on Peña's face made him wish he had a camera in his hand.

Peña, who usually knew everything about everything, had the grace to admit defeat. He sighed. "I apologize. Thank you for the insight."

With a sharp nod, she said, "Apology accepted. Now, let me get these men started on some antibiotics."

The process of hanging the bag of medicine on the IV stand and starting the drip came without any fanfare, but Rick felt like the moment the liquid went into each man's arm became a cause for celebration.

Now to get them well enough to move.

He looked over at Peña. "Go ahead back to camp. Send an update. I'll stick here."

"Roger." Peña tapped his chest over his pocket. Rick could see the bulge of a meal packet. "Need a meal?"

"No. I have one."

Peña left, and Rick stood between the men's beds, looking from one to the other, praying intermittently.

Doctor Myers took vitals, made notations, and ministered to the woman on the cot across the room. Eventually, she approached with a folded metal chair. "Please, sit."

"I don't think that chair will hold me, Doctor. This gear is heavier than it looks."

She nodded. "I know. I took it off your soldiers. I think the chair will hold up. Test it. If it collapses beneath your weight, well then, at least I'll get a good laugh out of it."

Oh, she was a pistol, this one. He spun the little chair around and lowered himself into it backward, crossing his arms over the thin backrest. He wouldn't admit how good it felt to sit down. He checked his watch. Two hours had passed since she'd administered the IVs.

"The medicine is going to need time to work," Doctor Myers said. "They should both feel better by morning."

"Cap?"

He surged to his feet and walked over to Ozzy's bed. "Hey, Ozzy. You about done malingering?"

Ozzy lifted his upper body and rested his elbows on the cot. "Doc, my leg is bad."

Doctor Myers slipped on a pair of gloves. "What's your pain level?"

"Like thirty. And I swear I can feel every heartbeat."

Rick examined Ozzy's face. A sheen of sweat covered his pale skin. Doctor Myers lifted the blanket and cut off the bandage covering his thigh. The skin all around his incision puffed up around the stitches in an angry red color. As she probed, Ozzy gasped and threw his head back. Sweat poured down his face.

Rick felt helpless, powerless. He'd done everything he could do for this man, but it wasn't enough.

"I have antibiotics going," Doctor Myers said. "Let me give you some real pain meds."

Ozzy shook his head.

Rick frowned. "Come on, Lieutenant. No reason to suffer if there's a different way."

"No." Ozzy collapsed back on the pillow and put his arm over his eyes. "I'll be fine," he said, panting.

Rick met Doctor Myers's eyes. She clearly didn't want to concede. Instead, she went into a back room and returned with a wet cloth that she draped over Ozzy's forehead. "I'm going to get you another dose of ibuprofen," she said gently. "It will help bring down your fever and ease some of the pain. If you're not feeling better in an hour, I want you to reconsider."

He pressed his lips together, then said, "Ibuprofen would be great. Thanks."

When she turned to go to a cabinet, Rick followed her. "You can't make an executive decision?" he asked quietly. "He's clearly suffering."

She opened a bottle and counted out four pills. She looked from him to Ozzy and back. "No," she said. "I can't override his express desires. And you shouldn't want me to."

With a frown, he watched as she walked back to Ozzy's bed and helped him prop up long enough to swallow the pills. He probably should not have overheard her question. "Are you an addict, Ozzy?"

Ozzy glared at her but didn't answer. Instead, he lay back and closed his eyes.

Addict? As in substance abuse? Drugs? Ozzy had never indicated anything like that. He didn't drink alcohol, but everyone assumed he had personal, religious reasons for abstaining.

Right now, though, wasn't the time for Rick to ask. Ozzy needed to rest, to escape the pain as best he could.

When Doctor Myers went back to her desk, picked up a clipboard, and started writing, Rick headed in her direction. "I'm going to go back to camp and check on my men there."

She nodded as she finished writing, then set the clipboard down. "If I need you, how can I contact you?"

"I'm just beyond the tree line. A sharp whistle will get my attention."

She smiled. "Just whistle for you, eh?"

Rick nodded. "You know how to whistle, don't you?"

Hands on her hips, Doctor Myers said, "Lauren Bacall said you just put your lips together and blow."

"Got to love the classics." Feeling another blush cover his cheeks, he grinned. "You do that, and I'll come running." Sobering, he checked his watch again. It was almost eleven. "When will you check your email?"

"Three."

"Okay, fifteen hundred. I'll be back here at fifteen thirty. Do you need anything else?"

She paused. "I don't need anything for your men."

He turned without another word and walked out of the clinic.

CHAPTER

★

FIVE

The still, humid air sat heavy around them, making their ballistic vests feel twice as heavy, causing sweat to soak through all layers of their uniforms. Two monkeys screeched and chased each other through the treetops. Rick watched them until he couldn't see them anymore. As he opened a packet labeled "spicy penne pasta, vegetarian," he glanced at Fisher, who finished a communication.

"What's the word, Trout?"

"Chuckie knows we're here," he said, using the nickname they'd given Chukuwereije's men. "They found the truck and the bodies and worked it out. Maybe they had a GPS on it or something."

Rick shoveled three bites into his mouth as he stood. "Right. Police and sanitize this AO. Rendezvous at the doc's in twenty mikes. Pot Pie? With me. We need to go figure out how to transport Drumstick and Ozzy."

"One other thing, Daddy," Fisher said. "They added

an order to our evac." He consulted his notepad. "'Evac Shortstack—identity compromised.'"

Rick's heart started pounding. Moving his men would offer enough challenges. Getting Cynthia Myers to go with them willingly because Chukuwereije had discovered who her father was might prove impossible.

He slung his weapon over his shoulder. The doctor could object to its presence, but playing nice had slipped down his list of priorities. He and Fisher walked through the trees and into the clearing. They paused and scanned the area. Nothing appeared out of order. Cautiously, they crossed the clearing and made their way up onto the dirt road. Four kids ran down it, kicking a soccer ball between them. Rick took that as a good sign.

At the medical clinic, Fisher stayed outside while Rick pulled the door open and stepped inside.

Doctor Myers sat at her desk, a laptop open in front of her. She glanced in his direction. "My colleague has confirmed I'm doing everything right. The rest is going to take time."

He gave a hard shake of his head. "Time's up. We're moving."

She stood. "You can't move them."

"Doctor, I hear you. Now you hear me. Chukuwereije knows we're here. I don't have enough men to hold back a real attack. The safest thing for the innocent people in this village is to pack up you and my men and get to an exfil landing zone."

Her eyes widened. "Me?"

He closed his eyes and said a very brief prayer for guidance and patience. "Chukuwereije knows who you are, and I have orders to evacuate you with us."

As a frown darkened her face and fury filled her eyes, he

held up a hand and said, "Look, Doctor Myers. I'd need your help regardless. I am not a doctor. I don't know what to look for. So whether you were tacked on to my list of duties doesn't change the fact that I really need you to accompany me and provide care to my men until we can hand them over to some military docs."

She glanced toward the beds occupied by his men. "I hate the violence that brought you here. I wish none of this had happened."

"Nevertheless." After a brief pause, he asked, "How can we transport them?"

"How far do you need to go?"

He pulled a map out of his shirt pocket and opened it on the desk. "This location here. If we were going through the jungle, it would be about twenty klicks." He ran a finger along a curving line. "It looks like this road will get us there. It will take more like seventy klicks, but we can do it."

She bent to examine the map, and the faint scent of lavender wafted up from her braided hair. "Yeah. It will get you there." She looked up at him. "Tadeas has a truck we can use. I feel confident he'll loan it."

"A truck would be perfect."

With a bright smile she said, "If you go by truck, you won't need me. You'll be there in a few hours, and then you'll be on a helicopter taking you back to wherever you came from."

He ran his tongue over his teeth, then leaned in closer and said very calmly, "Doctor Myers, I appreciate the advice. However, I have orders. You are now inclusive of my mission. I'm sure there's a representative of the US government you can lodge a complaint to upon our arrival at the embassy."

After closing the lid of her laptop with a little too much

force, she snatched it up and stormed to the door. "I need ten minutes."

"You have five."

He could handle the brunt of her misdirected anger as long as she complied. With the sound of the door slamming behind her reverberating around the room, he walked over to Sanders's bed. "Hey, man," he said, looking into his friend's dark eyes. "How's things?"

"Just a scratch." He looked over at Ozzy. "He's got it rough. Moaning in his sleep last night."

Rick walked over to the medic's bed. "Hey, Doc. You feeling better?"

"Much. Antibiotics are kicking the infection back."

"Good." He looked from one to the other. "I'm afraid we have to move you."

Sanders shook his head. "Don't make me laugh. It will hurt too much."

"Bad guys a-comin'. Give me five minutes and we'll get you loaded up."

"I can walk with crutches," Ozzy said.

Rick snorted. "Yeah. Through the jungle? We're getting a truck. You're welcome to stay supine for the ride."

He walked outside. Near the hut across the dirt road, Doctor Myers spoke to Tadeas. He glanced in Rick's direction, nodded, then set off down the road at a jog.

Rick crossed over to her. She glanced at him but didn't speak before she spun on her heel and vanished into the hut. He paused at the doorway and glanced inside. She had a backpack open and was shoving clothes into it.

When she turned and saw him, she said, "I cannot believe you're kowtowing to the State Department. I'm thirty-two years old. You'd think I would have the freedom to go where I want to go in the world."

He crossed his arms and enjoyed the shade the overhang of her roof provided. "Ma'am, I don't kowtow. But I did raise my hand and swear an oath to protect and defend. Now that your cover is blown, so to speak, this is the protect part. I'll get you to the embassy and you can handle your own freedom from there."

She went to the washbasin, grabbed her toothbrush and toothpaste, and shoved them into the bag. "Oh, I will handle it."

The sound of a truck engine caused him to turn just as Tadeas pulled to a stop by the clinic door. Rick walked across the street. "I appreciate your loaning this to me."

Tadeas got out and patted the truck's roof. "I inherited it from an old fisherman here. We use it for medical emergencies. I'll call this that."

Rick shook his hand and said, "Thanks, brother."

"Do you need a hand?"

"My men have this. Chukuwereije is bound to have men show up."

Tadeas's mouth formed a hard line. "There is evil in this world," he said. "But I know you have been working a few weeks trying to eradicate what you can."

"Won't do any good until we can get the head of the snake."

Tadeas nodded. "He has great power here."

Rick gave a closed-lip smile. "So do we."

A sharp whistle sounded from the tree line. The rest of his team emerged from the jungle. He whistled back and watched as they carried gear across the clearing.

He met them at the truck. What they couldn't carry for

seventy kilometers went into the bed, leaving room for a pallet for Sanders. Fisher and McBride lifted the CRRC, which the team universally referred to as the cricket, into the bed. When they loaded the inflatable watercraft, the ancient, rusted leaf springs on the truck rocked and complained under the weight of its outboard engine.

"Should we leave it?" Peña asked.

Rick opened the map and looked at it again. "If the road is blocked, we can go by river."

Peña ran his finger along the river. "That's a long, exposed journey."

"So's the road." He folded the map back up and slipped it into his shirt pocket, then made a hand gesture. "Let's roll."

Doctor Myers supervised loading Sanders onto a stretcher. Fisher and McBride carried him out and lifted him onto the pallet they'd prepared for him.

Rick hooked his boot onto the rear tire. "How's it going, buddy?"

Perspiration beaded Sanders's forehead. His skin had an ashen color. "Maybe I shoulda died."

Rick's heart twisted. "God's in charge of that."

"Maybe I can get a consultation with Him."

Rick placed his hand on his friend's forehead and said, "I'm praying for you, bro."

He followed the men back into the clinic and found Ozzy standing next to his cot. He clutched the IV stand like his life depended on it. Sweat poured down his face, and his arms quivered, making the IV stand rattle against the tile floor. "I'm not lying down. I'll sit."

"There's no room for you in the back, anyway. I need you to sit in the cab." Rick walked up to him and put a hand on his shoulder. "But you should let them put you on a stretcher to carry you out. I'm not a fan of you putting any weight on that leg."

"Like you read my mind, Daddy," Ozzy whispered. He collapsed onto the cot and gripped the side of it, bowing his head. A drop of sweat dripped from his forehead onto his leg. "This isn't good."

Rick sat across from him and leaned his elbows on his knees. "What can I do?"

Ozzy shook his head. "Get me that bucket. Fast."

Rick grabbed the plastic bucket and met Doctor Myers's eyes as Ozzy vomited. She laid a wet cloth across the back of Ozzy's neck and pulled a syringe out of her pocket.

"I have some ondansetron," she said.

Ozzy nodded. "Four milligrams should do."

She smiled as she pulled the cap off the needle with her teeth, then inserted it into the IV. "Yes, Doctor," she said.

"Sorry," Ozzy whispered.

Rick frowned. "Is that pain medicine?"

She shook her head as she capped the needle. "Anti-nausea."

"You have to give him something."

Ozzy reached out and grabbed his wrist. "Cap, please. Let me be in charge of this." He paused, then let out a breath. "That's better already."

Doctor Myers took the cloth from around his neck and wiped his face with it. She placed it back on his neck, then knelt and cupped his cheeks with her hands. "You may have to make a hard decision."

"If I can get to the embassy, they'll have options that are non-opioid."

"I wish I had a spinal block."

"I couldn't travel with it anyway."

"True." She straightened. "It's going to be a hard ride."

Ozzy nodded. "Let's get it started, then. Sooner we go, sooner we're there."

Cynthia climbed into the back of the truck and crouched near Sergeant Sanders. She put her face close to his and observed the indicators of pain in the tightness around his mouth and the sweat beading on his brow. "How are we doing after the jostling and loading you into the truck?"

"No offense, but next time my chest gets cracked open, I'm going to demand better service."

She patted his cheek and stood just as a rucksack got tossed into the bed. It hit the side of her ankle, sending pain shooting up her leg. She gripped the top of the cab and breathed in through her nose, trying not to lose her patience with the men who simply followed orders as expediently as possible. Once the initial pain faded, she maneuvered her way around the gear and jumped out of the bed.

"I want someone in the back with him to keep any of that gear from landing on him."

McBride nodded and climbed into the back. "I got you, Drumstick."

The door to the clinic opened, and Captain Norton and Sergeant Fisher emerged with Ozzy between them. Ozzy had an arm slung over each of their shoulders, and he used them like crutches.

"What are you doing?" she demanded, rushing toward them. "I thought you were going to use the stretcher. That man should not be upright."

"Tell him that," Fisher said as they maneuvered to the cab of the truck.

When they reached the truck, Ozzy leaned against it, raising his face to the sun. Sweat soaked his shirt. Cynthia stood in front of him and had to crane her head to look up at him. "I feel confident that you have the medical background to understand the damage you can do to your leg if you walk on it."

He panted as he spoke. "Doc, I'm not walking on it."

"You could lose that leg," she snapped, then she let out a breath. "I'd prefer it if you didn't."

He barked a laugh. "You and me both." His eyes grew serious. "I'm not lying in the back of a cab. I'll go down upright."

"Die with your boots on? Something like that?"

He looked down at his feet. "At least one boot."

"You're on the verge of losing my good graces, Lieutenant."

"Yes, ma'am," he said as Fisher opened the door. He clearly braced himself as he prepared to get into the cab. Cynthia admired the delicate way Fisher helped him.

She turned around and found Captain Norton. He had his map open on the hood of the truck and conferred with Tadeas. She hurried forward. "Captain, Lieutenant Osbourne—"

He gazed at her, the hard look in his eyes cutting her off. "Is a big boy." He dismissed her by turning back to Tadeas. "What is this bridge situation like?"

She clenched her teeth together tightly enough that she was surprised they didn't crack. Spinning on her heel, she marched across the street and back into her hut. Her backpack sat on the empty cot. She had filled the small bag with everything she had brought with her into the country. She snatched it up and started out of the hut but stopped in the middle of the room.

"God," she prayed, hands on the sides of her head, "I feel more out of control than I did seven months ago. Please, please help me. I feel so angry right now, and I don't want to be. These men don't deserve angry Cynthia. I like them too much."

Hoping to leave her anger behind in the empty hut, she left the building and crossed the street into the clinic, ignoring the hubbub of activity around the pickup truck.

Ayo was filling a box with prenatal vitamins. Tears streaked down her face. She and Tadeas had spread the word to evacuate the village.

Cynthia walked up to her and put a hand on her back. "Are you okay?"

Ayo looked at her, her dark eyes swimming with tears. "They'll burn it all down."

"It won't be the first time. Maybe it will be the last, though." The two women hugged. "I feel like this is somehow my fault."

"They would have killed us all when they came with the dead man. You don't know what they're like. The American soldiers out there, they've brought more peace to the lives of villagers for hundreds of miles than we've had for a long time."

It felt odd that Ayo talked about the men who had killed people in front of her as bringers of peace. "I think we have different definitions of the word 'peace,'" Cynthia said.

Ayo raised an eyebrow. "I think we have different lots of things, Doctor. Chukuwereije is not the first warlord to terrorize our nation. He is just the most recent. Those men he has? They were once little boys who were taken and forced to kill until they were molded in his image. If your Western soldiers can help our true government gain control of this jungle, then mothers can stop living in fear of the day their village is overrun and their boys are snatched from their arms." She put the lid on the box and picked it up. "Do you know why the entire village is getting into boats and heading down the river? Because no one needs to convince them what Chukuwereije's men will do when they arrive. They know it because they've all lived through it."

Contrite, Cynthia followed her assistant out of the building. A teenager took the box from Ayo and ran it down to the river. The women hugged once more.

"I'll be back as soon as I can," Cynthia said.

"I look forward to that day," Ayo said. She sauntered over to Tadeas. "I have everything."

He glanced her way and nodded, then tapped the map and straightened. "Are you good?" he asked Captain Norton.

He nodded. "I could use your knowledge and experience."

Tadeas shrugged. "I have to get Ayo and her family to safety."

"I respect that."

Tadeas held out his hand, and Captain Norton shook it. "Godspeed, Captain." He turned to Cynthia. "Doctor, it was a pleasure working with you."

"And you. I hope to be back."

He gave a smile that said he didn't anticipate her return though he admired her optimism. "Have a good journey." He picked up the cage of chickens at his feet and walked down to the river.

Cynthia turned to Captain Norton. "I'll ride in the back with Sergeant Sanders."

"I'd prefer it if you rode in the cab."

"I—"

"Have no body armor and a blond head that makes a perfect target for a man with a high-powered rifle. You're also half the size of any of my men, so you'll fit back there. Not everything has to be a debate. Now, we're on a bit of a tight schedule here. So please, Doctor, climb into the back seat."

He turned away from her, clearly expecting her to comply without another word. Setting her jaw, she climbed into the back seat and sat sideways. She glanced through the glass and saw McBride settle in next to Sanders as Fisher jumped out of the bed.

As Captain Norton drove the truck slowly down the road, she looked at the empty huts. No children played. No chickens scratched the red ground. Sadness filled her heart at the ways of man and the kind of evil that emptied an entire village of people, forcing them to flee into the jungle to save their lives.

CHAPTER
★
SIX

Wanting to give the scouts ahead time to assess their situation, Rick drove the truck slowly. When they'd walked into the village this morning, it had been full of life. They'd heard men at the river, fishing. Children played, groups of women gathered together over fires or in circles with younger children. Chickens scratched the ground, and goats enjoyed the grass in a fenced area. Now not even a chicken remained, no fires burned, and every hut stared back at them with empty windows.

After conferring with Tadeas, they had decided to go north, away from Chukuwereije's current base of operations. At a point about thirty kilometers ahead, Rick would go east and drive to the rendezvous point, where the helicopter would meet them.

Doctor Myers had convinced Ozzy to recline his seat. She had enough room to minister to him as needed and had opened the back window to facilitate communicating with

McBride about Sanders. Rick heard her voice but didn't pay attention to anything but her tone. Instead, he thought about what he would do if they encountered enemy resistance. How could he protect the two injured men and the civilian with him?

The wide red road gradually narrowed into little more than a goat path through the jungle. Swanson and Peña walked ahead, cutting back the more oppressive growth so that the truck could get through. Fisher took point about twenty yards ahead of them.

An hour into the journey, Fisher trotted back from the scout position and replaced McBride, who took his turn walking ahead. Peña had gone forward and taken point.

Doctor Myers leaned forward and put a blood pressure cuff on Ozzy's arm. Rick watched out of the corner of his eye while she took the reading, then made a notation on her clipboard. She shifted and spoke out the back window. "Sergeant Fisher, do you know how to take a blood pressure?"

"No, ma'am," he replied. "I can do pulse, though."

"How are you doing, Sergeant Sanders?"

"Better than three-day-old mud on a set of Mickey Thompsons," he said.

Rick chuckled. The more tired or stressed his friend got, the more his Alabama came through.

"I'm calling that good," Doctor Myers said.

Rick glanced in the rearview mirror and saw her smile. So far, she hadn't smiled much around him. The expression softened her face, made her look very young and very vulnerable.

"Hey, Daddy," Swanson said through the radio. Rick could hear the stress in his sergeant's voice.

"Copy," Rick replied into the microphone of his earpiece. "We got a roadblock half a klick up ahead."

"Reassemble," he said, slowly coming to a stop. He looked at Doctor Myers in the mirror. "We have a roadblock ahead."

Her eyes widened. "What does that mean?"

"It means we might be packing stretchers through the jungle," he said. "Inventory your equipment and supplies and prioritize down to must-haves, wants, and wishes." He paused. "Just in case." He angled his body toward his medic. "Hey, Ozzy?"

"Daddy."

"Any chance you could walk? If you had crutches?"

Ozzy's eyes widened, and Rick could tell he contemplated his answer. "If I had serious meds on board."

Rick thought about Ozzy's refusal of opioids. "What does that mean to you?"

Ozzy looked down. He took a deep breath, then met Rick's eyes again. "It means I'll function." He shifted his head back so he could look at Doctor Myers. "Load me up, Doc. As much as you think you can give me."

She narrowed her eyes at him. "You sure?"

"I am."

Tapping the back of Rick's seat, she said, "Let me out, please."

Rick slipped out of the truck and walked to the back. He looked into the bed. "Can you walk?"

Sanders let out a breath. "I can try."

Rick set his weapon on the tailgate and jumped into the truck bed. He and Fisher lifted Sanders until he sat up against the cab.

"Whoa," Sanders said. "I don't know."

"Sit there a spell," Rick said. "I'll be back."

He joined the scouting party as they arrived at their location. Swanson wiped his forehead with his shoulder. "Twenty armed men, six vehicles. They have the road blocked with three, then a few paces back, three more."

"No way to push our way through."

"Not feasible." Swanson pulled a map out of his breast pocket and opened it on the hood of the truck. "They're here," he said, tapping with his fingertip. "We're here. Our rendezvous is here."

Rick saw no way to get to their rendezvous spot without going through the roadblock. They discussed alternate routes.

"We could go by river," McBride said. He gestured at what looked like a large animal path into the jungle. "It's through there, about eight hundred meters." He drew a line on the map with his finger. "Use the river to cut through this way, then when we're here, we're close to the exfil."

Rick nodded, then glanced up at the surrounding jungle. "It's going to be a long eight hundred meters," he remarked, considering the two men, all their necessary gear, and the three-hundred-pound cricket. "Right. McBride, you and Swanson haul the cricket down to the river, then double back and assist. Peña and Fisher, you assist Ozzy. He should be able to one-leg it to the locale." More quietly, his words intended only for his men, he added, "The doc and I will carry Drumstick on the stretcher. I don't know how far she'll be able to go, but we'll get as far as we can. Hopefully you two will be back before she reaches muscle failure."

As they unloaded the truck, Doctor Myers slipped her backpack on, then her medical bag, angling it across her body.

Rick watched McBride and Swanson head into the jungle before he turned to the doctor and said, "You aren't going to be able to carry that weight. I need you to help with Sanders's stretcher."

She nodded. "I'll put the bag on the stretcher, over his legs. It's not a far distance."

He pursed his lips, mentally figuring their odds of success, before nodding. "Okay. I'm going to get rid of the truck. Peña, you're with me."

He made a sloppy three-point turn with the truck, intentionally kicking up a rooster tail of dirt behind the back tires. He drove about a quarter of a mile back down the road, then turned and drove into the jungle, letting the trees close around the truck. He and Peña covered the tracks. The untrained eye would think they'd turned around from the roadblock and headed back the way they came.

After jogging back to where they left everyone, Rick looked at Ozzy, who sat leaning against a tree. "You feel like a walk?"

Ozzy shrugged one shoulder and grinned up at him. "Good as I can be, I reckon."

Giving the morphine to Ozzy had made him uncomfortable, but he'd had to do it. Fisher and Peña got on either side of Ozzy, and he used them like crutches. They entered the jungle.

Rick glanced at Sanders, who had his eyes closed. He directed his attention to Doctor Myers. "We need to walk carefully. Clearly animals use the path. We're going to try to avoid doing anything that looks like a human came this way."

She looked at the path and back at him.

"You good to carry him?" he asked as he tied a bandanna around his forehead.

She laid her medical bag gently across Sanders's legs and nodded. He walked to the head of the stretcher and she stood at the foot. They both crouched and gripped the handles.

"On my count," she said. "One, two, three." On three, they both lifted.

Rick shortened his stride to accommodate her shorter legs. He glanced over his shoulder, noticing that she appeared to handle Sanders's weight with ease. As they entered the jungle, he said softly, "Speak up if you need help. I'll keep the pace slow."

"I'm good. It's not far." Despite her words and her bravado, he could hear the strain in her voice.

His boots sank into thousands of years of jungle floor as the leaves on the trail enfolded them. Despite the cooler air under the canopy, sweat slid down his back. If he hadn't thought to put on the bandanna, salty sweat would blind him right now. He glanced at the ground, not able to identify boot marks in the thick blanket of leaves. Maybe the tire marks he left would be enough of a red herring to send any scouts in the wrong direction.

He didn't like the idea of making their way to the LZ via the river. The exposure out on the water made him think of the shooting-ducks game at the county fair. But if the enemy thought his team had stayed with the truck and turned around, maybe they would waste precious minutes or hours looking for them in the wrong direction.

A mosquito buzzed in his ear, but he couldn't swat at it. He carefully took one measured step at a time, praying for God's protective hand over their little foray into the wilderness.

★ ★ ★

The strain of carrying Sanders first numbed Cynthia's muscles and then made them burn like she had acid in her veins. Leaves brushed her face. Birds whistled above them, calling out to each other as the party of humans passed. She tried not to think about the critters and creatures that watched them walk through their territory and hoped that Captain Norton would be the one to break through any spiderwebs. She could handle a lot of jungle life, but the spiders sent her into a panic.

Sanders made a small sound, and she focused on his face. He lay with his eyes half-closed. "You doing okay, Sergeant?"

He fully opened one eye to look at her before half closing it again. "Just thinking about God's purpose for my life. Wondering if I've been on the right track."

"Been there, done that, sir." She blew at a bug that insistently hovered in front of her nose. "It's how I ended up in the jungle."

"What a coincidence," he said. "Same here."

The brush ahead parted, and Swanson jogged up to them. "Passed Ozzy and company just ahead. They're doing okay," he said. "McBride's rigging the cricket. Clear ahead so far."

Captain Norton nodded, then gestured with his head toward her, instructing Swanson to relieve her. She wanted to put her chin up and tell him she had it handled, but her smaller frame and shorter stride slowed them down, and right now they needed speed more than she needed to prove her ability to carry a man twice her weight through the underbrush.

As soon as Swanson took the stretcher handles from her, she shook her hands to loosen the muscles and get blood flowing back into her fingertips, then snatched her medical kit off her patient's legs.

"Go ahead and get in front of us," Swanson said. "If something happens to you and you're behind us, we'd never know."

She had a feeling he'd intended to tease her with the last line, but he also meant it. It made her chuckle.

Captain Norton stared at her, his expression blank, as if evaluating her as a factor in his tactical calculations. "Pick up a stick or twig or branch or something. Wave it in front of you as you walk. You know. Spiderwebs."

Her eyes widened. She went to break a thin branch from a nearby tree, and Swanson hissed, halting her. "Don't do that," he said. "Pick up something off the ground."

Right. She would have just marked their trail. Feeling foolish, she picked up a small stick, rubbed her shoulder against her sweaty temple, then pushed through the vegetation, waving the stick in front of her like a wand. As she passed Captain Norton, she paused and slapped his cheek.

His eyes hardened, and she held up her palm. "Got it," she said, showing him the smashed mosquito.

"A warning next time would be not only appreciated but highly recommended," he said in a quiet voice. Then he added, "Thank you."

She smiled. "Happy to slap you anytime, Captain."

"Likewise, I'm sure." His beard twitched, and she wondered if he fought a smile. "Careful going, Doc. We're not trying to mark our trail."

She knew that, of course. She understood the logic and the reasoning. Instead of replying, she swiped at the sweat on her brow and carefully moved a large leaf out of her way.

Without her eyes on Sanders giving her something to focus on, her mind wandered to her villagers. Worry rolled through her chest and choked her throat as tears stung her eyes. Would she ever see them again? Would it take removing Chukuwereije from power before she could come back? Perhaps if she used an alias and returned, then the powers that be couldn't use her as a political pawn. It frustrated her to no end to know where God wanted her but to have the people who "handled" her father dictate otherwise.

A few steps later, she heard the river. Knowing their jungle trek would end soon quickened her pace, but when a leaf cut her right ear, she hissed in pain and slowed back down. She dabbed at her ear, then looked at the smear of blood on her fingers. As soon as she had a moment, she'd apply antiseptic to it.

Absently waving away the mosquitoes that circled her head, she stepped out of the underbrush and stopped at the top of the incline down to the water. She dropped the twig as she looked left and right. Dare she mention crocodiles and snakes to Captain Norton? The most dangerous animals in the rivers by far were the hippopotami. Likely, he already knew about them. She'd avoided the water in her months here because of the invisible dangers that lurked below the surface.

Pushing her own fears aside, she approached Ozzy. He and his teammates had also paused at the incline. Sweat poured from his face. Concerned, Cynthia checked his pulse. His heart pounded furiously.

"Can you get him down there?" she asked, looking at the rocks and brush on the slope.

Fisher nodded. "If he would lie down on a stretcher, it would be less risky. That way, if we lose him, he doesn't land on his leg."

Ozzy looked at her with wild eyes. "I didn't take that shot just so you could put me on a stretcher."

"No. You took that shot so you wouldn't scream in pain going through the jungle." She inspected his leg and could see no blood or other seepage through his pants. She took that as a good sign. "Mission accomplished. Next mission: take you down to that big black boat your teammates have so cordially assembled for us. Sergeant Fisher is right. You need to be on a stretcher for that."

He shook his head emphatically. "I'm not lying on a stretcher."

She pushed a finger against his chest. "Then sit on it."

Captain Norton came through the trees just then. He stopped short where they all stood. "Problem?"

Cynthia smiled. "Nope. If you take Sergeant Sanders down to the beach, then bring the stretcher back up here, we can get Lieutenant Osbourne down."

Captain Norton, Peña, and Fisher carried Sanders precariously down to the beach. The steep incline offered no help in navigating. At one point, the ground gave way beneath Fisher's feet. He slipped and caught himself with one hand, never letting go of his end of the stretcher. Cynthia gasped and started to rush forward, but she stopped when he regained his footing and Sanders stayed stable and steady. She didn't even realize she was holding her breath until they reached the boat, and she slowly let it out. McBride stepped forward and helped Sanders aboard the craft.

Cynthia turned and gestured to the ground. "Please sit, Lieutenant Osbourne."

He raised both eyebrows. "Doc, if I get down, I don't know if I'll get back up."

She checked his leg again. She could feel the heat through his pants. She'd love to remove them and check the pulse in his lower leg but would wait until they arrived at the embassy in a few hours.

"Hang in there, Doctor," she said, deeply respectful of his grit. "You'll be sitting in the boat in no time." She looked at the boat and flinched as Sanders tried to sit up. "I'm going to go down and supervise Sergeant Sanders on the boat," she said to Swanson. "I'll leave Ozzy here in your capable hands."

Only when she started down the incline did she realize just how steep it was. How those men had maneuvered a stretcher carrying a grown man down what amounted to a cliff face amazed her. She slipped on the red dirt, and her heel caught on a rock. She went down, landing hard on her rear.

"You okay, Doc?" Captain Norton asked as they climbed back up the hill.

She carefully regained her footing and brushed at the backside of her pants. "I think so."

She continued the semicontrolled descent. At the bottom of the hill, she walked over to the raft. It had looked much smaller folded up in the back of the truck. She climbed in and maneuvered her way over to where Sanders sat, propped up against the corner. His skin had turned very pale, and his face shone with perspiration.

"How are we doing, Bill?" she asked, kneeling next to him.

"I think if I get to sit perfectly still, I'll be okay," he said, panting. He opened his eyes and looked at her. "I'd rather be lying in a warm bed right now."

She winked. "You and me both."

Intentionally not watching the descent of the crew carrying Ozzy, she focused instead on checking Sanders's vitals.

Just as she finished noting his blood pressure, the team arrived. She stepped over the bench seating and worked her way to where Ozzy sat propped in the corner, one leg bent and the other stretched in front of him.

"Okay, Ozzy," she said. "Let's check you out."

He chuckled, and his head rolled back and forth. While the rest of his team worked at loading the boat and casting off, she bent close to him. "I asked you once before, but you didn't answer. It's helpful for me to know. Are you an addict, Ozzy?"

He pried his eyes open and looked straight into hers for several moments before speaking. "Yes. Got hooked in medical school. We just used to play around with it, you know, then one day I realized how often I thought about doing it again. Had to leave my residency. Too many temptations." He laid his head back and looked up at the sky.

"Hey," she said, putting her fingers against his neck, "thank you for taking the morphine today. I know it was a hard decision."

He rolled his head over and looked at the jungle. "I couldn't have made it otherwise. They'd never leave me behind. It wasn't a hard decision. It just sucks. I got my five-year coin a few months back."

They made quick work of loading the rucksacks and weapons into the boat. Peña handed everyone drab-green life vests. As he handed one to Cynthia, he explained, "If you submerge in the water, it should automatically inflate. If it doesn't, pull this cord. If that doesn't work, blow into this tube."

She glanced down, felt the cord, and identified the tube, then nodded.

He handed her two more vests and said, "Can you rig Drumstick and Ozzy? I need to get on the motor."

"Yes. Thank you, Lieutenant," she said, then worked her way over to Sanders. She hated to jostle him and moved very carefully. "I need to lift you just a little," she said after slipping his arm through the hole. "You okay?"

"Better than a skinny tick on a fat deer," he said as he raised up.

She smiled and fastened the vest, taking care not to jostle his chest tube. She held a canteen up to his lips and encouraged him to drink. "Imagine how much better it will be when you're in a clean bed with some pretty nurse tending to you."

"Can't imagine better," Sanders said, then closed his eyes. His color looked good, and his skin felt cool to the touch.

She maneuvered to Ozzy with the other vest as the boat started drifting. "Hey, Ozzy, we have to put this on you."

He rolled his head toward her and opened one eye. "Got any water?"

His canteen sat in his lap where she'd put it, so she held it to his lips, and he greedily drank about half of it. "Okay, let's get this vest on you."

He helped, lifting his arm, moving his body as needed. His skin felt hot, dry. She retrieved her stethoscope from the cargo pocket of her pants and listened to his chest. His heart raced like he'd just run a mile.

She took the handkerchief from around his neck and dipped it in the river. Instead of wringing it out, she just put it back on his neck dripping wet. He sighed and kept his eyes closed.

When she'd done all she could, she carefully worked herself over to where Captain Norton sat. "Sanders is in good shape. Osbourne will be. I'll be happy to have them in actual medical beds by the end of the day." She glanced at his face, trying to read any expression there and getting nowhere. "How long will the boat ride take?"

Swanson answered. "Just over an eight-klick boat ride, then another hundred meters inland to the LZ."

"About five miles," she calculated.

Swanson glanced at her. "Okay."

She nodded. "So not long."

He shook his head. "Not long."

CHAPTER
★
SEVEN

After the truck ride followed by the trek through the jungle, floating down the river felt calm by comparison. They used paddles instead of the motor and stayed close to the shore, which meant they constantly went under overhanging tree branches. Cynthia couldn't help but look up every time to make sure something like a splendid dagger-tooth tree snake or Goldie's tree cobra wasn't about to drop into the boat.

Insects darted around, hovering over the water, then shooting off again. She looked over the edge of the boat and watched a school of little silver fish moving together in perfect harmony. She smiled as they swerved away from the boat.

Several hundred yards from where they'd started, she glanced over and saw a small boat tied to a tree. She recognized it as belonging to one of her villagers. She took that moment to pray again for the people she had grown to love.

Fisher got on the radio and started talking in jargon Cynthia did not understand. It sounded nothing whatsoever like the Hollywood depictions of soldiers using a radio, so obviously Hollywood got it wrong. Captain Norton sat next to him, occasionally jotting notations in a small notebook. At one point, Fisher checked his watch and said, "Fifteen twenty. Roger."

She checked the time. Two more hours and they'd board an American helicopter and fly to the American embassy.

She accepted the offer of a canteen from McBride and took a swallow of tepid river water. She knew they'd purified it, making it safe to drink, but she had to play a mental game with herself. Her village had a well with clear, clean water. No one there drank the river water. In fact, she had been cautioned against it during the mission brief. The water tasted of iodine and smelled like a public swimming pool, but it wet her dry mouth.

Her body ached. Even though she'd come by force, she still planned to check in to the most luxurious hotel Katangela offered and take an hour-long bubble bath. After a long soak, she'd order a rare steak and decadent dessert and maybe take another bath after dinner.

Even though she looked forward to those tiny luxuries, she still had no desire to go back to the DC area. Too much had changed inside of her. Maybe if she couldn't come back here, she could continue medical missionary work somewhere else. People needed good obstetricians all over the world. Just because she'd claimed this little corner of Africa as her own didn't mean she couldn't work elsewhere outside of the US.

That might work. Change her name, travel under an assumed identity, and continue to serve communities that needed her skills.

She observed the team of men that accompanied her. She couldn't help but notice that none of them relaxed as they stayed close to the bank and slowly and quietly moved with the current. They all looked around continuously, finding the source for every noise, searching the trees for every shadow of movement. Their weapons stayed at the ready. She imagined the hypersensitivity to sound and environment they experienced right now. That would exhaust her after a short time.

They came to a bend in the river. Swanson reached up and gripped a thick overhanging branch to anchor them. The branch moved only slightly. Captain Norton caught her eye and silently placed his index finger over his lips. Cynthia felt a surge of adrenaline. What was happening?

Knowing how much she would hate an observer asking questions during a complicated labor and delivery, she stayed quiet and tried to make herself as small and out of the way as she could in the thirteen-foot space.

Swanson opened the map. "The road we were on intersects here," he whispered to Captain Norton, running his finger across the river on the map. "There's a bridge up ahead."

What Swanson left unsaid spoke much louder than his words. If the enemy thought their group might have some means of navigating the river, they may have set a trap on the bridge. They could be lying in wait for them.

Captain Norton nodded. "McBride. Swanson. Use B-7s and swim around the bend and grab some recon. Try not to get spotted." He looked behind him. "Could they be coming up in a boat?"

Peña shrugged. "If they had one ready to go. We moved fast. We didn't have to find a boat. They would also be coming against the current, so we'd certainly hear them approach."

"Check."

McBride and Swanson slipped quietly into the water and inflated their B-7 flotation devices. Cynthia couldn't imagine the strength it took for them to stay afloat and then to swim with their weapons and all their equipment. It took a lot of willpower for her to keep from cautioning about hippos, crocodiles, or snakes like the banded water cobra. These men knew their environment and their jobs. They didn't need her paranoia.

She checked on her patients. Sanders hadn't moved. She carefully maneuvered her way over and crouched by him. When she put her fingers on his neck, his eyes opened.

"Hey, Doc. We're going to have to quit meeting like this," he whispered.

"I can think of more ideal surroundings." His skin felt good. No fever. Pulse rate steady. "If all of my patients could take my treatment like you have, I'd crack ribs open more often."

His lips twitched. "Don't make me laugh, darlin'. I have a feeling it would hurt like a—" His smile faded a little. "It would hurt a lot."

She smiled and nodded. "Understood."

As she turned away, Captain Norton caught her eye. She gave him a thumbs-up and went to the opposite end of the boat. Ozzy had his head back, using the side of the boat like a pillow. When she touched his neck, he didn't move.

She knew how much he must hurt even with the opiates. He'd probably fallen asleep as a defense against the pain. She admired his resolve, and the fact that he'd taken the drugs for the sake of his team and not himself.

His skin felt warm, his pulse thready. She wanted to check

his leg but didn't want to undress him out here in front of everyone or expose the wound to potentially virulent microbes. Just a few more hours and she would have access to medical equipment and a sterile environment.

The rocking of the boat made her gasp, and she jerked around, only to see McBride and Swanson climbing in. She put a hand on her chest to steady herself. She hadn't even seen them arrive, they moved so stealthily.

McBride used his olive-green bandanna to wipe his face. "Bridge is covered. Four that we could see. No way we can get by in the daylight. Not quietly, at least."

A muscle ticked in Captain Norton's jaw. "We don't have a lot of options."

"We could take them out," Fisher said. "Jerry Maguire and Pot Pie can flank them and set up."

Peña shrugged. "Sure. Only we have zero intel. How many more where we can't see?" He sighed. "We're sitting ducks in this cricket."

Swanson spread the map out. "We could backtrack. Cross over to the other bank. Go against the current to this spot here," he said, tapping his finger. "Then take this road over here that will go around to this spot." He glanced over at Captain Norton. "Bird could pick us up there."

Captain Norton shifted the cap on his head and looked at the river. "No time to row it. Current's too strong. Fighting it will take the motor. Might as well send up a flare."

The men sat silent for several moments. Finally, Peña looked at her, surprising her. "Doctor Myers, is there a village close to us?"

She looked at the map, all the while rejecting the idea of endangering another village. Then Ayo's words came to her, about the peace this US Special Forces team had brought to the area. "There is one. It's right here," she said, pointing out the location behind them. "You probably saw the beach."

Fisher nodded. "That wooden boat pulled up under the tree about a third of a klick back."

"That's probably it." Cynthia looked behind her but could only see jungle. "I've traveled there weekly to check on pregnancies and infants. It's a small, isolated village."

Swanson smiled at her. "As opposed to the bustling metropolis you were just in?"

She chuckled. "That was a large village with a church and a medical clinic. This one just has the living quarters and about a third of the population. My midwife, Ayo, likely went there. Her grandmother lives there."

Captain Norton gestured at Swanson, who folded the map back up and stowed it. "We can get to that village, offload Doctor Oz and Drumstick, set up camp. Doc can stay with them. We'll recon the road and bridge and secure them for our use." He pointed at Fisher. "Get with HQ and reschedule the exfil for oh five hundred. Tell them we'll be arriving by truck."

Cynthia appreciated his optimism, even if she felt it a bit misguided. Her doubt must have crossed her face, because he frowned at her. "Doctor, they are spread thin looking for us. Probably have roadblocks set up, bridges covered, all sorts of men looking everywhere. It's not like Chukuwereije's entire army's on that bridge."

"Better for us if it was," Swanson remarked. "Take less time to subdue."

McBride laughed quietly. "I hear you, brother."

"Where will we get a truck?" Cynthia asked, even though she guessed the answer.

Swanson grinned at her. "We have plenty of time to solve that problem."

Even while they joked, they secured the boat to move again. Soon, six of them worked the large paddles against the current to gradually and quietly bring them upstream toward the beach.

Rick watched Doctor Myers slip her medical bag over her head as she prepared to disembark. For the last hour, he'd surreptitiously observed her. He admired her tenacity. Going under the trees clearly frightened her, as if she expected a snake to drop on her head at any moment. A month ago, he'd had the same concern. Since arriving in the country, he'd killed two different species of water cobra. The knowledge of how easily their heads came off their bodies under the blade of his machete had removed the last of his trepidation about them.

He could tell that passing near crocodiles made her uncomfortable, and he wondered how much stemmed from understanding what they could do and how much stemmed from an irrational fear. He imagined that she'd heard stories and possibly even treated victims of the large reptiles. He personally hoped he'd never get on the bad side of one, but he had a feeling they'd leave him alone if he left them alone. His larger concern was annoying some hippopotamus. Hippos would just as soon kill you as leave you be.

Despite all of that, Doctor Myers never uttered a word of complaint—though she clearly wanted to—and his respect for her grew.

On the beach, secured by the overhanging tree, they removed their flotation vests. Rick got out of the raft, then turned and helped Doctor Myers over the side. The water came up to his knees. Walking slowly and carefully, they stepped up onto the beach and into the jungle.

Once the foliage closed in around them, he stopped and turned toward her. She looked up at him in curiosity. "You okay, Doc?" he asked.

Her eyes widened, and she looked down at her torso and examined her arms. "All appears to be in working order, sir." Then her face relaxed into a rare smile that caused the breath to catch in the back of his throat. "I'm sorry. I have a bad habit of defaulting to inappropriate humor whenever I find myself in stressful situations."

He hadn't seen a lot of humor from her, but the statement made him grin anyway. "Good job keeping your sense of humor to yourself until now."

She tapped her temple. "I think the thoughts. I just don't always say the words." She ran her fingers through her hair and lifted it off her neck. "Anyway, I'm fine. I realize you're escorting me to the embassy because it's your job and those are your orders. I just want you to know that I'm only going along with it because your men need constant medical attention, and the rest of your team have other things to worry about besides their injured comrades."

"Appreciate your honesty," he said with a short nod. He started to turn away but stopped again. "It's important you tell me if you're not okay. You're not trained for this type of scenario. We are. Until we encounter certain stressors in life, we really can't know how our brains will react. But please trust that I am doing everything in my power to keep you safe."

"I understand that, Captain." She gestured forward. "Shall we?"

The village lay another fifty yards through the trees. When they reached the edge of the tree line, he put a hand on her shoulder and applied pressure. She got the hint and lowered herself into a crouching position. He took his time observing the village. The huts. The quiet streets. He couldn't smell exhaust from trucks. Instead of tense silence, the village made some noises, and no sound seemed out of place.

"Any idea what hut Ayo would be in?" he said in a low voice.

Doctor Myers nodded. "Her grandmother is the medicine woman. She'll be in the larger hut over there."

Rick's eyes followed the direction of her pointed finger to the hut. He examined it using his binoculars. From here he could see bones hanging from the rafters. He really hoped the skull once belonged to a monkey and not a human.

"Feel comfortable going in there alone?" he asked. "I think you'd draw less attention than me."

Doctor Myers glanced at him. "Captain, I'm five feet tall and blond-haired. I promise that you, in all your gear and with that beard and gun, will draw less attention than me."

With a smile he stood. "Fair enough. We'll go together."

Rick raised his fist and caught Peña's eye about twenty feet to their rear. He made a series of hand gestures, and Peña replied with some of his own. Rick nodded and turned his attention back to Doctor Myers.

"All right. Let's go." They rose to their feet and began to push out into the clearing. He put a hand on her arm before she stepped forward. Looking directly into her eyes, he calmly said, "If something happens, do what I say as soon as I say it. Don't think about it. Don't ponder my motives. Don't second-guess me. You can't argue or reason or try to negotiate. Just do as you're told—if you want to stay alive."

She appeared unnerved by the seriousness of his tone, then smiled. "Sure thing, Daddy."

He caught the bark of a laugh in his throat before it surfaced. With a little shake of his head, he said, "There's that inappropriate sense of humor again."

They stepped out of the trees and onto the orange clay. He looked around, checking all the shadows. From inside a hut came the sound of a baby crying, then a woman's voice singing. He saw no people.

When they reached the hut, they pressed close against the outer wall as they worked their way around to the front. Doctor Myers tapped on the door, and seconds later, Ayo opened it. When she saw the doctor, her eyes widened, and she looked over her head and all around. "Come in," she whispered, "quick."

Inside the hut, Tadeas sat at a wooden table with an old woman who had dark skin and gray braids. She wore a bright-orange dress that wrapped around her frail body and tied together over one shoulder.

Doctor Myers hugged Ayo. "There are roadblocks and bridges being watched. We can't move until nightfall."

Ayo spoke in French to her grandmother, who remained still and stoic. She watched Rick with dark, serious eyes.

Tadeas stepped forward. "Can we help?"

"We don't want to bring danger to your village," Rick said. "We're going to set up a camp in the jungle. But we need intel, if you have it. Have any of Chukwereije's men come through here?"

Tadeas nodded. "They're just looking for you, though. They searched each hut but left without further incident. We worried they'd recognize Ayo or me, but they didn't." He looked around as if assessing their safety. "We hid the boys. One of the huts has a hidden floor. Whenever the men come, we can hear them driving down the road. So far, we've had time to get the boys gathered and into the space."

Rick tightened his fingers on the pistol grip of his weapon. "How often do they come?"

Ayo answered. "A couple of times a year. Sometimes more."

"They never wonder why there aren't any boys?"

Tadeas shrugged. "It's different men each time. They've depleted the male population in hundreds of kilometers in every direction." He put his hand on Ayo's shoulder. "We will provide any assistance we can give to defeat the evil that is Chukuwereije and everything that he stands for."

Rick glanced at Doctor Myers. She stared at him with a thoughtful expression. He would love to know what she was thinking. "We'll stay outside of the village and be gone before daylight." He raised an eyebrow. "Ready, Doctor?"

As they walked out of the hut, Rick glanced around. He could feel eyes on him but couldn't see anything. Briefly, he entertained paranoid thoughts of a sniper in the trees, spies in the village, a hostage situation, but he wanted to believe Doctor Myers would say something if she detected anything not quite right with her people.

Once the leaves of the jungle enfolded them, he relaxed slightly and came to a sudden stop. She nearly ran into the back of him. "Everything seem copacetic in there?" he asked.

Her eyebrows drew together, and she waved a bug away from her face. "As opposed to what?"

"As opposed to not a real conversation because they were hiding something or possibly afraid."

She opened her mouth, then closed it again. Maybe she'd started to knee-jerk a reply but changed her mind and was taking the time to consider the question. "Nothing felt off to me. But this is a very new situation for me, so if it was off, I'm not sure I would know what to look for."

He searched her face and saw nothing but sincerity. "Good enough."

As they walked back to the boat, he thought about his injured men. The weight of the responsibility of getting them to a safe, clean, modern medical environment weighed heavily on his shoulders.

Peña came down out of a tree when they reached the edge of the beach. Rick glanced up. Either McBride or Swanson perched above them, but he didn't see any sign of either one.

"What do we know?" Peña asked.

"Chukuwereije already came through the village looking for us," Rick said. "Tadeas thinks they're spread thin. The villagers have devised a way to hide people if it comes to that. I gathered from the conversation that this village has been terrorized by our favorite warlord for a long time. They'll help us any way they can."

Peña looked from Doctor Myers to him. "Copacetic?"

Rick shrugged. "Beggars can't be choosers."

His intelligence officer shook his head. "Gotta be worse than this before I beg." He gestured toward the river with his chin. "What are we gonna do with them?"

He thought about it. "I'd love to leave them in the boat. Here, safe, and still. No more jostling or moving. But it can't be hidden the same way that a camp can." He looked at Doctor Myers. "What's your medical opinion, Doctor?"

Her eyes widened as if she was surprised he remembered her presence. "I like the idea of leaving them in the boat, especially if it means that at the end, they only have to go another few hundred yards before we reach the extraction point. If that can happen, it will be much better. If not, I will do my utmost to work it out."

He maintained eye contact with her while he considered her response. The hostility he had faced the first time he met her had disappeared. He wondered what had changed for her to have such a reversal of attitude. Maybe she understood their desire to help the people of this country rather than hurt them. He recognized a resilience in her that he respected.

"Let's see what we can do about camouflage," he said. "Then get everyone to eat something while we can."

CHAPTER
★
EIGHT

"Here, Doc, wear this," Swanson said, holding out a brown T-shirt. He gestured at her white tank top and khaki pants. "You kinda shine through the trees."

Cynthia looked at it and briefly wondered when the soiled garment had last seen the inside of a washing machine, but then slipped the T-shirt over her head. The hem brushed her knees. "Thanks," she said. "I didn't get dressed this morning intending to hide in the jungle."

He grinned. "I always dress for just that occasion."

She squatted down next to Sergeant Sanders. He had good color despite the trauma to his body in recent days. He held a metal cup of broth that Sergeant McBride had made out of some bouillon powder. "Are you good here? Do you need to get out of the boat?"

He slowly shook his head. "Sitting perfectly still is the best thing right now. I honestly think sitting here feels better than it did lying in the bed."

She pressed her fingers into his neck and checked his pulse rate. "If you need anything, let me know."

Lieutenant Osbourne lay with his leg propped up on a rucksack. He had his eyes closed but when she squatted down next to him, he opened them. She did not like the color of his skin. When she touched his neck to check his pulse, his skin felt warm. "Are you good in here, or you need to get out of the boat?"

He looked at her blankly for several seconds as if processing what she asked. "The more still I am, the better I am. The idea of moving right now . . ." He shook his head. "Hopefully, that won't have to happen anytime soon."

"What is your pain level?"

"Intense." Hardly a scale of one to ten, but she appreciated his candor.

"Are you hungry at all?"

"No." He held up his canteen. She noticed the tremor in his hand. "But I am staying hydrated."

"I can get you a broth made with bouillon."

"I just need to stick with water right now."

She glanced at her watch, calculating the time until she needed to give him more antibiotics. "I can probably give you another dose of morphine."

He grabbed her wrist, his palm hot and dry. She looked into his eyes. "Please don't offer again. Let me ask."

She studied his face and finally nodded. "Okay."

It helped that her patient knew the extent of his injuries and the care he needed. She could tell from his personality that he had a hard time adjusting to needing help. "We need to get you into a sterile environment and fight off the infection."

He chuckled. "From your mouth to God's ears."

The boat stayed sheltered behind the branches of a fallen tree. Cynthia glanced up, checking to see if any of the branches slithered instead of swayed. She rubbed the back of her neck, wishing she wasn't so squeamish about the local fauna. Though, in all honesty, she only felt uneasy about the wildlife that could kill her.

Peña and Fisher lay on the floor of the boat and pulled their hats down over their eyes. The way they could turn the hypervigilance on and off fascinated her. She wondered how they acted out in the civilian world.

She climbed out of the boat and walked onto the shore, staying in the shade of the trees. She sat on the dirt and drew her legs up to her chest, pulling the hem of the shirt down over her knees. From this vantage point, she could see both patients.

A large ant carrying a white seed ran past her. She moved her legs out of its way, then looked up at the sun, closing her eyes to its rays. It shone in a bright blue sky, and the heavy and humid air blanketed them. In another couple of hours, it would rain, freshening the air and momentarily cooling the world down.

She looked over as Captain Norton sat beside her. He laid his carbine rifle on the ground and wiped his face with a handkerchief. She could see the lines of worry and fatigue around his eyes and wondered what his face looked like without the red beard and the dirt.

"That beard has to be hot," she said.

He absently rubbed it. "Not as bad here as in the desert." He pulled an MRE pouch out of his cargo pocket and held it out to her. It contained more than twelve hundred calories, enough to sustain her for the next twenty-four hours. She smiled as she took it from him.

"Spicy penne pasta, vegetarian," she read out loud. Glancing at him from under her lashes, she joked, "My favorite. How did you know? Was that in my file too?"

He grinned as he opened his own pouch with a long knife. He pulled out all the packets inside one at a time and slit most of them open. When he finished, he held the knife out to her, handle first. She accepted it and gingerly sliced open her own MRE pouch. The blade was astonishingly sharp.

"Just a guess. Didn't feel like getting lectured about eating animal flesh," he answered.

She snorted and imitated his actions, opening all her packets with the knife. She took the long brown plastic spoon out of her pouch, then extended the knife back to him. "I guess I had that coming. Though I'll admit that I was dreaming about a juicy rare steak and something deliciously chocolate earlier."

"Well, this is not that."

She followed his lead, using the plastic spoon to eat the cold pasta straight out of the foil bag.

He chewed and swallowed. "It's not bad, though. You get used to it."

"I like spice." She considered what he'd said about being lectured. "You are one of those people I wish I could go back and redo my first meeting with. Remove the horror and stress, maybe meet in a coffee shop or something. I have a feeling we are both actually pleasant people who wouldn't feel the need to lecture each other constantly."

He chuckled. "You are a likable person, Doctor Myers."

"Cynthia, please."

"Cynthia." He said her name as if savoring the way it rolled off his tongue. She detected an accent and tried to place it. "Rick," he said as he pointed toward his chest with his spoon.

"Rick." She nodded. "Are you Richard?"

"Nope. I was born Rick. My dad wanted me to be named what they'd call me, and he never wanted me to be called Dick or Richard." He slipped the unopened packet of peanut butter and the one labeled bread into his left cargo pocket. "What about you? Were you ever Cyndi?"

"I wanted to be, but my parents would never go along with it. I thought it was the kind of name perky little popular girls had, you know. I could dot the 'i' with a heart and be very feminine and cool." She took another bite. "Alas, Cynthia stayed my name despite my best efforts."

"Still could."

She glanced at him. "Still could what?"

"You still could dot that 'i' with a little heart, right?"

"I did, all through seventh grade. It didn't feel quite as perky as Cyndi would have." The heat from the spices in the pasta sauce slowly sneaked up on her, tingling her tongue. "I think I was destined to be brainy instead of cute."

He folded up the empty packet and slipped it into its outer sleeve. "I think it's all relative," he said. His expression changed, and he looked away from her as his hand covered his earpiece. "How long?" His pleasant look was replaced with dark determination. "Roger." He looked over at Cynthia, then got to his feet and retrieved his weapon. "Stay here."

Seconds later, he disappeared into the trees.

★ ★ ★

Just inside the tree line, Rick met up with Swanson. "How many?"

Swanson gestured with his hand. "Two boats, slowly moving up the river. Checking the banks, under trees, the works."

Rick sighed. As safe and comfortable as they had Sanders and Ozzy, they needed to move them. Quickly. "How long before they get here?"

"They're going slow. Maybe forty-five minutes—an hour tops."

"Okay. Let's get everyone out of the cricket, then sink it. I don't want any trace we were anywhere near this village."

"Roger."

Rick spoke into the mic, giving directions to break down the boat camp and move everyone inland, then he made his way back to the shore where Cynthia waited for him. "We have to move them out of the boat," he said.

Her wide blue eyes reflected every argument she must have thought but didn't say. "Where are we putting them?"

"Just into the jungle for now. Get what you need out of the boat. We have to sink it."

She jumped up and brushed off the back of her pants. "Sink it? It's the best way to transport them!"

As someone who was used to his orders being followed immediately, without question, he clenched his teeth in irritation. "You think I don't know that? That thing is too big to drag through the jungle, and it would leave an obvious trail. I have no way to secure it so that it won't be found. If it's found here, then all your friends in that village become extremely interesting to Chukwereije's men. So you tell me exactly what else I should do based on all your training, combat experience, and wisdom, Cynthia."

As soon as he finished his tirade, he felt guilty. She carried none of the blame for their circumstances. Still, sometimes the way she spoke to him just irked him, generated a defensiveness in him that kept him responding. He sighed at the shocked look that crossed her face, then mentally deflected her fury.

"I know I'm not skilled in combat or evasive maneuvers, Rick." She spat his name like it tasted bitter on her tongue. She lowered her voice to a breathy whisper. "But what I am is a doctor, and your medic is not going to last much longer. I am doing everything I can, but the ultimate goal is to wheel him into a sterile surgical room at the embassy sometime in the next twelve hours. Anything beyond that, I have no more control."

He intentionally softened his countenance. "I know. Sorry. Shouldn't take it out on you. I know you're doing everything possible. Understand that I am too." The sound of a branch moving made him say, "Go with Swanson here. He'll take you to our campsite."

She squared her jaw. "I can help transport the men."

"No, Doctor. You'll be in the way. Meet them at the campsite." He turned, missing the neutral ground they'd enjoyed over lunch. He headed back down to the riverbank as McBride and Fisher carried Sanders out of the boat.

"I can walk," Sanders said. "Help Ozzy."

Instead of acquiescing, McBride looked at Rick.

Rick shrugged. "Just don't let him hit the ground." He briefly wondered if he should have consulted with Cynthia before agreeing to let Sanders walk. He eyed his friend as he took a very slow and cautious step. After three steps, Sanders stopped, sweat pouring down his face. He put a hand on his chest and took another step, and another.

McBride walked half a pace behind him. As Rick passed them on the riverbank, he said in an amused voice, "Looks like he can walk."

Peña and Fisher had Ozzy between them. Hours ago, his medic had tried to walk, had made jokes, had been strong. Now his head lolled back, and Rick could see that he stayed upright only because the two men holding him had interlocked their arms to support him. Cynthia's warning reverberated in his mind.

He made it down to the boat as Swanson jogged up. They unloaded all their gear, then Swanson pulled out his knife. "Sure you don't want to try to hide it?"

Rick put his hands on his hips and looked around. "It's three hundred pounds and fifteen feet long. Given all the constraints, I honestly don't see how."

"It was a yes or no question, Daddy," Swanson said.

They rolled rocks into the boat, then drove their knives into the chambers near the bow. They cut and sliced until no air remained. The cricket sank nicely to the bottom of the river.

"Maybe they'll find it and think we got attacked by a crocodile," Rick joked.

"Yeah."

Rick requested a check-in of the entire team over the radio, then he and Swanson double-timed it to the campsite.

Ozzy lay on a tarp, using a rucksack as a pillow. He had his eyes closed, and his chest moved in a rapid rhythm. Cynthia knelt over him, using a blood pressure cuff. When Rick squatted down beside her, she looked at him but didn't speak until she released the cuff and slipped the stethoscope out of her ears. "BP is falling. I think he's going septic."

Not what he wanted to hear in the jungle. "What do you need?"

She looked up at the sky. "Some way to hang an IV. I'm going to push another bag of antibiotics while we're stopped."

He glanced at McBride. "Can you rig something?"

"Sure. How tall?"

"Not tall," Cynthia said. "Just elevated above him."

"On it."

Rick went over to where Sanders sat propped up on a rucksack. He lowered himself to the ground, and his muscles started hurting. "I'm beat."

Sanders nodded. "No doubt. As for me, I'd have to feel better to die," he said. "I remember being this tired one other time in my life." He watched Cynthia walk by. "Man, she's something, huh?"

The word "something" definitely described her. "And then some."

"She watches you," Sanders said. "I watch her watch you. I can give you my assessment anytime you're ready."

Rick grinned. His friend had an astounding ability to read people. It came in very handy in tactical debriefings of captured enemies. He played the big dumb sergeant, but even if he didn't speak the language, he could tell motivations, moods, who lied and who told the truth, and a host of other things.

"Hit me," Rick said, leaning back as fatigue washed over him.

"She's been hurt, badly. You can see it around her eyes. She doesn't trust men, but she respects strength. It wars inside of her. She's fiercely loyal. She's taken personal responsibility for me and Ozzy and that entire village we left. We could do worse."

Rick made a "hmm" sound as he closed his eyes, thinking about Doctor Cynthia Myers and the reason she didn't trust men. He wondered if her ex-fiancé was still in office and working in the Washington, DC, area. Any man with a shred of class would have made himself scarce. But some men had no class. He couldn't imagine what her father must think of the man who'd done that to his daughter.

He had neutral feelings as far as her father was concerned. The man hadn't run for the office. The president had appointed him. Rick hadn't researched him prior to his accepting the office, and he hadn't had time to think about it since then.

As he dozed off, the last thing he thought about was the smile on Cynthia's face as they'd enjoyed the horrible-tasting MRE. He wanted the chance to make her smile again.

CHAPTER
★
NINE

Cynthia glanced up at the sky as she set a poncho next to Ozzy. The clouds had darkened ominously, and the rain she'd predicted earlier would fall at any moment. She sat next to him and studied his face. The fluids and antibiotics continued to beat back the infection trying its best to kill him. He had better color and looked more alert.

"How's your pain?" she asked.

"Well, I'm not enjoying it very much, to be honest."

She didn't take the bait. "How are you tolerating it?"

He grudgingly said, "If I'm completely still, it's just kind of throbbing."

"On a scale of one to ten?"

The corner of his mouth twitched. "Like forty-two."

It went against her better judgment to withhold the medicine, but she complied. "Try to rest. I know you were fighting the medicine fog before, so you're probably exhausted."

She glanced over at Sanders. She wanted to check him out,

but Rick slept next to him, and some instinct told her if she approached, he'd wake up. The captain looked incredibly relaxed, peaceful. Interestingly, he looked younger too. It made her realize how intense and focused he looked every waking moment. She wondered how much more the burden of not one but two wounded men weighed on him. It also made her wonder about the kind of man he was outside of a combat environment. Did he relax? What did he consider a fun, leisure activity?

Swanson approached and held out a canteen. "Water, Doc?"

"Yes, thank you."

As she handed the canteen back to him, the first raindrop hit her hand. Moving quickly, she spread the poncho she'd set aside over Ozzy and then started to help Sanders, but he'd already covered himself and Rick. Just as the rain let loose, Swanson knelt next to her and covered them both with his poncho.

"Thanks," she said, glad she didn't have to ride out the deluge without protection. "It won't last long."

He looked up. "We've been in country for about a month. I don't think a day has gone by that it hasn't rained."

"Kinda helps make sense of the term 'rain forest,' doesn't it?"

He shrugged. "Better than Fort Benning any day. And anything's better than the desert."

She looked around at the lush leaves of the jungle, the bright pink-and-white-striped flower blooming from a bush, the banana tree bulging with fruit. She could hear the river roaring not far away and thought about the images she'd seen of places like Iraq and Afghanistan. "I imagine it's much different from the desert," she said. "I think I'd like this better too."

His eyes moved around, shining from his dark face. "Except those monkeys. Those critters wig me out, man."

With a chuckle she said, "I used to be afraid they'd climb into my hut at night. It took me weeks to sleep. But it was so hot in my hut with the windows shut. Finally, I just couldn't take it anymore and opened them."

"They ever get in?"

"Nah. They just yell at us for invading their space. They have no desire to invade ours."

He shook his head. "One threw a banana at me."

She laughed. "You must have been in his spot."

"Right. So, what if I'm sleeping in his spot?"

"I guess you'd want to move. You never know what they're going to throw." She'd noticed his accent before, but their time had been spent with more important things. Now she asked, "Where are you from, Sergeant Swanson?"

"Northern Virginia. Alexandria."

"That right? I'm from McLean."

"Ah, a Virginia girl. We played McLean teams in basketball. Went head-to-head with one of the schools for state my sophomore year."

"Unfortunately, I went to an all-girls boarding school in southern Virginia," she said with a grimace. "I'm guessing you didn't play us."

"Can't imagine high school without basketball."

"Oh, we had basketball. It was just all very organized and polite." She glanced across the camp and noticed Rick's stare. The rain must have awakened him. That familiar, serious, and very mature-looking face had replaced the relaxed, youthful look he had while sleeping. She shifted her gaze to Sanders. Humor etched into every line on his face as he spoke to Rick, a grin making his beard move. When he finished speaking, he laughed and nudged Rick. Rick glanced at Sanders, then blinked and smiled as if the joke finally registered.

Cynthia turned her attention back to Swanson. "Did you join the Army right out of high school?"

"Yes, ma'am." He paused. "Well, technically before I graduated. I went to basic training in the summer between my junior and senior year. Drilled with the Guard my senior year. I needed a job, and the idea of flipping burgers held no appeal."

Her eyes widened. "Wow. What were you, seventeen? Your parents were good with that?"

He shrugged. "My dad thought it was the best thing for me. Turned out he was right." Swanson's face hardened, and he looked over her shoulder. For a moment, she thought someone approached from behind her, but then he said, "Roger, wilco," and she realized he was listening to the device in his ear. "Stay put," he ordered, slipping out from under the poncho. Rick joined him, and the two disappeared into the wet jungle.

The *rat-tat-tat* of the rain on the waterproof fabric relaxed her. She bowed her head and closed her eyes and tried to repose as the jungle quieted beneath the downpour. She knew as soon as it stopped, everything would come back to life.

She loved the smell of the rain in the jungle. The water mixed with the decayed vegetation, splashed on blooming flowers, and filled leaves that formed natural cups and bowls, and somehow all of it came together to bring a clean, fragrant smell that she'd never experienced anywhere else.

All too soon, the rain quieted, then stopped. She shifted the poncho off of her as the clouds gave way to the sun and blue sky again. The heat of the sun baked the freshly watered earth, and the humidity started to climb. The cry of a bird above signaled the all clear to the rest of the jungle, and almost immediately, the insect and animal noises returned.

She draped Swanson's poncho over a tree limb, then walked over to Sanders. "Hard to imagine it's winter back home," he said. "Never could abide muggy heat. I'd much rather layer up."

She glanced around at the rich green world with its splashes of color. "Not me. I love not having to keep track of my gloves." She put her fingers to his pulse. "How is your pain level?"

"Maybe three. I feel a lot better."

"Yeah." She sat back on her heels. "Do me a favor and pretend you're still in pain. I want you moving carefully until we get to the embassy."

"Only if it gets me out of guard duty," he said.

"Where is home for you?"

"Sweet home Alabama," he sang. Then he added, "We'll be relocating from North Carolina to Kentucky as soon as we get back."

"That must be hard."

He shrugged. "Not so much. I live in the barracks. I don't own a lot of things, so moving isn't too hard." He sighed. "Harder on the married folk. The move orders got put on hold by this mission. So spouses are just kind of hanging in limbo until we get back."

Her eyes widened. "I never imagined any of you were married. How odd that I never considered it."

He glanced at her. "Peña's married. She's on our team, though. Well, mostly. She consults and is assigned to us often." He pursed his lips. "I think that's all that's here. The other half of us are back at base. A couple of them are married. Gill, Ibrahim."

She gestured at his shirt. "May I?"

"Doc, you almost don't even have to ask," he drawled.

She unbuttoned his shirt and shifted his T-shirt to look at his incision. It looked like it had healed nicely. She prodded around the bullet wound, appreciating the color and feel of the skin. "What about you, Sergeant? Got a girl back home?"

"You offering?"

Her gaze flew to his face, and she saw the teasing in his eyes. "I'm afraid I'm off the market for a while," she said, buttoning the shirt back up.

"Ah, the broken heart."

"Someone break your heart, Sergeant?"

"No, ma'am." A look of stark regret crossed his face. "Afraid I did that all by myself." He shifted and sat up further. "All good?"

"Yep. Very soon, you will not need my care."

Not far from them, Peña said, "Roger," and stood, his weapon in his hands. The nearly relaxed atmosphere suddenly became very tense.

Peña moved to the perimeter of their camp as McBride slung a rifle over his back and climbed a tree.

Cynthia glanced at Sanders. "Do you know what's going on?"

He tapped his ear. "I have no idea. Daddy took my comms so I'd rest."

She bit her lower lip and looked around.

He nudged her shoulder with his fist. "I promise you, you're in the safest spot in this jungle right now."

She glanced at the tree that had consumed McBride and wanted to believe him.

Rick's eyes burned from lack of sleep. Adrenaline would kick in if he needed it and knock back the fog of fatigue, but he would pay good money for four straight hours of undisturbed sleep.

And for a double cheeseburger.

He and Sanders had a tradition that revolved around post-deployment hamburgers. He'd been more ready for a thick, juicy burger a couple of times in his life, but he'd be hard-pressed to name them right now.

As he and Swanson slipped into the jungle, the rain fell in a curtain around them. After the stifling, muggy heat, the rain actually felt good. He took a deep breath through his nose and appreciated the fresh fragrance of the plants and flowers. Their boots moved silently across the wet ground.

"I don't think I've been fully dry since we got here," Swanson murmured.

"Beats the desert," Rick said.

About fifty paces into the vegetation, McBride and Fisher met up with them. Fisher gestured with his hand toward the village. "Three of Chukuwereije's men are in the village," he said. "They're terrorizing the people."

Rick rolled his head back and forth, his mind rapidly sifting through all their options. They could stay where they were, pray that the villagers who saw them earlier didn't tell.

They could capture the warlord's men. They could stop the terror and eliminate the threat.

Right now, getting Sanders and Ozzy to a hospital—preferably without adding to the injured numbers—took the number one slot on his priority list. They could eliminate three Chukuwereije soldiers with little effort. That would also remove the risk of a villager revealing they'd been seen.

"What kind of transport are they using?"

"Small cab, four-by-four." McBride wiped the rain off his face. "I had one like it in high school."

"Piece of junk?"

McBride nodded solemnly. "You got no idea, Cap."

"That could help us tonight." Without the cricket, Sanders and Ozzy would both fit in the bed of a small-cab truck. "Okay. Stealth is called for. Four-man stack, then two by two. Suppressors, blades, or bare hands. Take the men out and secure the vehicle. Stash it away from the village. No traces in the village. None. Clear?"

"Crystal, Daddy."

Rick nodded. "Spread the word."

Fisher took point, and they moved toward the village. On the edge of the tree line, Rick stopped and took a knee, bowed his head, and prayed for strength, speed, and wisdom. Then, in a bounding overwatch military formation, they silently infiltrated the village. They moved like shadows, weapons ready.

That adrenaline rush Rick needed flooded his system, making his nerves tingle and his senses kick into high alert. He heard every sound, saw every shadow, assessed every possible threat.

As they reached the line of huts, he heard a commotion

and gestured for Fisher to sweep around. He and McBride moved forward at a crouch until they got to the hut, then pressed against it. Through the thatch wall, Rick could hear a woman crying and a man yelling in French. He glanced through the window and saw a man holding a Kalashnikov rifle to the head of a teenage girl while her mother cried and begged. A click in his ear told him Fisher was in place. He and McBride silently moved to the front of the hut as Swanson reached the back.

In close quarters, a shot from a suppressed pistol risked collateral damage. A ricochet or a stray round could wound or kill one of the innocent civilians. However, taking on an armed opponent with bare hands came with an even higher personal level of risk. McBride clearly knew this as he dropped his carbine rifle to swing on its sling and swiftly drew his K-BAR fighting knife in the same motion. He sneaked up behind the soldier in three quick steps and neutralized him within seconds.

Rick slid inside the hut and cleared every wall and corner. He held his finger to his lips, begging the women to stay silent. From the hut, he and McBride assessed what they could see of the village. McBride spoke quietly into his microphone, and Fisher and Swanson located and neutralized a man on the brink of assaulting a lone teen girl. Rick could hear her cries in his earpiece and clenched his teeth.

He hated leaving the body of this man in the hut with the mother and daughter, but he had no choice. He whispered to the woman in French, "We'll be right back." He gestured with his chin toward the door. He and McBride left the hut, weapons ready, and moved from hut to hut like ghosts, letting the buildings provide visual cover.

117

They found the last of the three Chukuwereije soldiers at the medicine woman's hut. Through the window, Rick saw Tadeas lying against the wall. He'd taken a beating, according to his swollen eye and bloody lip. Rick watched him through the window, and when Tadeas saw him, he held up one finger. Tadeas very subtly nodded. Swanson slipped into the building and took the soldier down before he even realized what had happened to him. When Swanson uncovered the man's mouth, Rick filled it with the business end of his pistol.

In French, Rick said, "Hello, friend. Nod if there are just three of you." The man glared. Rick cocked the pistol. The man grudgingly nodded. Rick made eye contact with Swanson, who nodded and clapped his hand over the man's mouth as Rick removed his pistol. To Swanson, he ordered, "Make it quick."

The man's muffled scream suddenly and quickly stopped.

Wanting to be certain no more threats hid in the village, they all spent the next several minutes performing a thorough sweep. As the team met back up at the truck, Rick watched about twelve children come out of one of the buildings. He knew the villagers had hidden them under the floor.

"Pot Pie, check the truck. Make sure it doesn't have a tracker. Then go back and get the doc. She's going to want to treat Tadeas. Trout, Maguire, load the bodies. Take their pictures, then drive them to the river and weigh them down. Can't draw buzzards or attention. Then hide the truck. We'll need it tonight."

While his men carried out his orders, he went back into the hut and found Tadeas lying on the bed. Ayo gently cleaned his face.

"You got here just in time," she said, looking up at him with sad brown eyes.

"Were they looking for us?"

She nodded as she rinsed the rag. "They didn't know you'd already been here. They were just looking. They would have killed Tadeas after they made him watch."

He didn't have to ask what they would have made him watch. "I'm sorry to bring violence to your village."

She paused in her movements and looked at him. "Captain, you did not bring the violence. You are working to abolish the violence. We are thankful you are here, doing what you are doing. We are not strong enough to stand up to his men. You are."

"I appreciate that." He gestured at a chair. "Do you mind?"

"No, please. Can I get you some water?"

"Thanks." He sat down and looked at Tadeas. "I have one of my men fetching Doctor Myers. She'll want to patch you up herself."

Tadeas closed his good eye and nodded. "You know," he said in a low voice, "I came here thinking I could make a difference. I'd learned about what the warlords did to the children, to the villages. I thought I'd be bigger and better than them."

Rick shook his head. "One man can't battle an entire army. Chukuwereije is organized. His men are trained from a very young age. Don't beat yourself up because you don't see the difference you're making." He looked around. "If you protect this core family, then you're making a big difference."

Ayo returned with a cup of water. Rick nodded his thanks and took a long drink.

"I'd like to take Ayo home to Montreal with me, but she won't leave her people," Tadeas said.

Ayo sat on the edge of the bed and continued bathing Tadeas's face. "My training is important here. Doctor Myers has taught me above and beyond what I learned in midwifery school. The villages need me for when there are no more Western doctors willing to come here."

Rick scrubbed his beard with both hands. "That's wise. It would be hard to have to choose to leave your home."

Tadeas held out his hand, and Ayo readily gave him hers. A part of Rick's heart tugged at the intimate gesture. "It is not hard to decide to stay," Tadeas said.

Rick started to relax and struggled to keep his eyes open.

"Captain Norton," Ayo said.

He jerked and opened his eyes. Ayo stood before him. Had he fallen asleep?

"You are welcome to rest here until your men get back," Ayo said. She gestured at a pallet on the floor across the room.

He shook his head. "I'll sit here, if that's okay. I think if I lie down, I wouldn't get back up anytime soon." He ended his refusal with a smile so she wouldn't think him rude, though she tempted him with her offer.

"You are welcome here," she said, patting his shoulder.

He intentionally closed his eyes now, relaxing in the chair, hands on his weapon. The next thing he knew, he heard Cynthia's voice. With a struggle, he opened his eyes again. He stood and walked over to Swanson. "Go ahead and head back. I'll escort the doctor."

"Yes, sir."

"Tadeas," she breathed, slipping the strap of her medical bag over her head. "What did he hit you with?"

"Buttstock of his rifle."

"Hope you didn't hurt the rifle," she said as she slipped gloves out of her pocket.

Rick sat quietly and observed her. She was comfortable with these people, at ease. She and Tadeas joked, Ayo anticipated her needs, and Ayo's grandmother interjected comments here and there.

After Cynthia stitched Tadeas's eye, she probed his cheek—"Not broken"—and checked his ribs. "Keep it clean," she instructed, pulling the gloves off. "And watch out for those rifle butts."

The entire time, she ignored the blood of the dead soldier and Rick's array of weapons. He appreciated her restraint.

Finally, she turned and approached Rick. "You need to sleep."

The longest he had ever gone without sleep had been during Ranger School. Compared to that, he could take this. He hadn't even hallucinated yet. At least not that he knew about.

He nodded. "No argument. Plenty of time once my men are safe and you're delivered."

Through his earpiece, McBride reported that they'd returned to camp. "Acknowledged." Rick looked at Cynthia. "Time to go, Doc."

While she gathered her supplies, Rick said to Ayo, "I saw a raft outside against the smaller outbuilding. I'd like to buy it from you."

Ayo translated what he said, and her grandmother waved her hands back and forth. "No, no," she said in French. "I want you to take it. With my blessing."

Rick pulled some money out of one of the many pockets

on his uniform. "Can't guarantee I'll get it back to you," he said in French. He smiled and gestured at Tadeas. "Plus I still owe this one a truck." He handed Ayo some money and then opened the door.

Cynthia paused in the doorway and said to Ayo, "I feel like we keep saying goodbye."

Ayo grinned and hugged her again. "I look forward to saying hello next."

"Likewise. *Au revoir*, then."

"*Oui. Au revoir.*"

Rick opened the door and let Cynthia precede him outside, scanning the streets and buildings, looking for threats both seen and unseen. He breathed more easily when the leaves closed in around them and hid them from view.

"Thank you for letting me come treat Tadeas," she said, ducking under a branch.

He held a large leaf to the side until she passed it. "You care about them."

"Very much. We've worked closely for several months. They're a great team."

"Do they work for the same ministry as you?"

"Yeah. Ayo is a different category. Tadeas and I are funded through our churches and larger religious organizations. Ayo is paid as an employee through the mission versus as a funded missionary."

"Can't imagine the courage it took to come out here alone and unarmed." He glanced her way. "I admire that."

She stopped walking, and he took one more step before turning to face her. "Really? You admire me? I thought you rather disliked me."

She looked up at him with big blue eyes that put the African sky to shame. "Why, Doctor Myers, what *ever* gave you that idea?"

She chuckled and shook her head, then kept walking.

Swanson came out from behind a tree, making Cynthia gasp and step backward.

Rick stopped. "Monitor the perimeter. I'll send Peña when I get back to the camp. Go retrieve the raft that's leaning against the medicine woman's hut."

"Yes, sir."

At camp, he instructed Peña to catch up with Swanson. As he laid out his poncho next to his rucksack, he watched Cynthia check on her patients. Dislike her? Nothing could be further from the truth.

Needing to think about anything else right now, he stretched out atop his poncho and used his rucksack as a pillow. His weapon lay close to his hand. He pulled his hat down over his eyes and stilled, commanding his brain to turn off so he could get at least twenty minutes of sleep.

CHAPTER

TEN

The whispered conversation between Rick, Sanders, and Peña roused Cynthia. They had a map spread open and discussed the details of how they planned to cross the manned bridge. She sat up and scrubbed at her face with her hands, then looked at her watch. She'd slept about forty minutes.

After taking a drink from the canteen someone had set next to her pallet, she got up and stretched, then walked over to where the men sat. As she knelt next to them, Peña looked at her. "Do you drive?"

"Yes."

"A standard? You know, a stick shift?"

She raised her eyebrows. "Yes."

Peña looked at Rick. "Problem solved."

Rick's mouth hardened. "I'm not leaving her defenseless."

Sanders smiled. His black beard framed his white teeth. "Well, now you're just trying to hurt my feelings," he drawled. "I've been called lots of things but never defenseless."

"You were pretty defenseless when that bullet lodged itself in your heart," Rick said. "Two days ago."

"Alabama boys heal like magic," he said, wiggling his eyebrows. Then his face grew serious. "I'm not kidding, Daddy. I got this."

Rick opened his mouth, but Peña cut him off. "He's right, Cap. We're short a body to do this right. Either put her in a tree on overwatch with a sniper rifle or put her behind the wheel."

Cynthia sat back as if pushed, landing on her rear. "Excuse me?"

"It's a good plan," Peña said, as if she knew the plan. "Nothing to worry about."

With glaring eyes, Rick pointed at Peña. "She isn't trained in tactical driving."

"She isn't trained with sniper fire either. But I think she can fake one better than the other."

Cynthia cleared her throat. "Can we please quit talking about me like I'm not sitting here? Exactly what plan are you referencing?"

Before Rick could answer, Sanders said, "You drive Ozzy and me to the pickup location so we can meet the helicopter. If the rest of the team makes it on time, great. If not, they catch the next bird, not having to move with our hindrance."

She needed to drive them? Why couldn't one of the others do it? "By myself?"

Peña shook his head. "Nah, Drumstick and Doc Oz will be with you."

She closed her eyes and shook her head. Maybe she hadn't awakened on her pallet. Maybe through a sleep haze, she could hear them making a plan and had inserted herself into it. She'd

125

pinch herself if it wouldn't make her look like an idiot. "Stop. Please." She chewed on her lower lip. "You're going to trust me to take the wounded soldiers to a helicopter landing site?"

Sanders tapped the map. "I'll be with you. I'll navigate, guide, and protect."

With lips pressed tightly together, she nodded slowly. "And if you lose consciousness?"

Rick pointed at Sanders. "Exactly. Thanks, Doc. What if you fall out?"

"Sir, I feel fantastic. I don't think I could run a marathon, but my energy is returning and my pain is manageable. Getting Ozzy on that bird is the most important mission we have right now." Sanders glanced at Cynthia. "If I lose consciousness, you'll know where to stop because I know exactly how many kilometers it is. We'll pay attention to the odometer in the truck and use it as a guide."

"Great," she said, panic making her voice breathy. "As long as we're paying attention."

"Doctor Myers—Cynthia—if you're not comfortable with this, don't do it," Rick said. "Despite Peña's claims, we can make it work with one less shooter."

Did she need them to, or could she do this? She only had to drive a truck down the road, a distance less than she drove to her favorite restaurant in Bethesda.

She looked at Rick. His face remained stoic, his eyes hard. He gave nothing away. At last, she said, "I can do it."

Something flashed in his eyes, something she couldn't read. Without another word, he nodded and returned his attention to the map. She appreciated that he didn't argue with her and accepted her at her word. Now she needed to make sure she didn't let him down.

"Okay, so you three are in the truck here," he said, pointing. "At our mark, you floor it. Cross the bridge. Keep driving. Swanson scouted ahead and saw no activity. It's just about nine and a half kilometers."

"Nine point four-two," Sanders said.

Rick continued as if he hadn't spoken. "It should take you twenty minutes or less. Right here," he said, drawing his finger along the road, "is a wide field. The road runs right alongside it. This is where the helicopter is going to land." He looked at her again, his green eyes shining with intensity. "Park in the jungle on the other side of the road. If we aren't there by oh four thirty, unload Ozzy and Sanders and get yourselves into the field. Sanders will have the radio, so he'll be communicating with the bird."

She studied the map. It all sounded completely reasonable, provided she discounted the several hundred insurgents in the area. "What do we do if Chukuwereije soldiers come?"

Sanders spoke up. "We kill them, ma'am. As many as we can before they kill us, anyway."

A knee-jerk reaction caused her to pull back. "I don't want—"

"They won't come," Rick said. "They're spread thin. The only men we know about in a ten-kilometer radius are on that bridge." He reached over and put a hand on her knee. "Hey, Cynthia, look at me." She met his gaze again. "Most of them are scared kids. We're highly trained soldiers. They don't have the organization or the foresight to strategically lie in wait for our helicopter in every clearing in the country, and they don't have any way to decode our radio transmissions. They bully villagers, rape, pillage, steal, shoot people without regard. The organization the group has is run from the capital city, and Chukuwereije himself has been losing power daily since we arrived. Besides, the rest of us will be giving them some work to do while you're getting to the LZ. Okay?"

She tried to process what he said. It sounded good, and she didn't think he'd lie to her. Finally, she nodded. "Okay. When do we leave?"

The night vision goggles gave a perfectly clear view of the soldiers on the bridge. Rick scanned the area, seeing no other human activity. As far as they could tell, no one had relieved these men all day. No other traffic had come by via this road. This was a good thing. The soldiers would be bored, tired, starting to think they'd wasted their time guarding this particular bridge. In the back of his mind, he wondered about the river below. His team had observed no activity from this vantage point, but he didn't want to find out that the soldiers had saved a surprise for him.

He climbed down from the tree and quietly made his way to the rally point. The men wore camouflage paint on their faces, making the whites of their eyes shine against the different shades of green paint. Fisher pulled a Chiclet of fruity gum out of his jacket pocket. He popped it into his mouth like a pill and asked, "What's the news, Daddy?"

"Low and slow out there." He glanced at Peña. "What's up with the river?"

Peña lifted his chin, a motion he often did as a precursor to a report. "I swam along the bank to within twenty yards. Saw nothing. Not a great strategic location. No good access to the bridge. No great cover for a craft."

That was what he wanted to hear. He focused on Fisher.

"You and Peña Colada paddle to the other bank. Just like we went over. Jerry Maguire, Pot Pie, and I will meet you in the middle."

The men grabbed their gear and the boat they'd borrowed from Ayo's grandmother, then went into the jungle toward the riverbank. Swanson rubbed his beard. "They're going to exhaust themselves crossing."

"At least they're not swimming," McBride said. "Remember that time in—"

At the snapping of a branch, Rick threw his left fist into the air. The men held weapons ready, hyperalert for any sound. When a pack of monkeys screeched by over their heads, Rick's heart lodged in his throat and adrenaline made his limbs tingle.

"I wish we could put the wildlife to sleep for the next few hours," Swanson said under his breath.

Rick chuckled to himself as he signaled for a report from Sanders, who waited in the truck with Cynthia. After a little bit more deliberation, they'd installed Ozzy in the back on a padded pallet and given him a weapon. Sanders would keep watch while keeping an eye on Ozzy. Rick had felt the temperature of Ozzy's skin as he helped him into the back of the truck. They needed to get to the embassy like yesterday.

Sanders signaled the all clear back to Rick. Now they just had to wait for Peña and Fisher to get into position.

Rick motioned with his hand and led the small team to the edge of the jungle. From here they could see the road and bridge clearly.

"Ah, waiting," Swanson whispered, scanning the area. "Come join the Special Forces. You'll have months and weeks of soul-killing boredom punctuated by mere seconds of concentrated excitement."

"Hold tight," McBride said. "I need to email MEB and see if they'll use that as their new slogan."

"Hey, man, it's what we call truth in advertising," Swanson said.

"I'll give you both more than a few seconds of excitement if you don't cut the chatter," Rick warned under his breath.

Neither man joked again, but McBride chuckled as he examined a tree. "This'll do," he whispered, then slung his weapon across his back and pulled himself up onto the branch. He would provide overwatch cover fire for them. Rick looked up at the tree as McBride maneuvered his way through the branches, finding one that had the right vantage point and with a sturdy enough limb to hold his weight.

Rick didn't like sending his men over the river. They'd scouted the other side just as thoroughly as this side, but an entire river sat between him and them. This was one of the harder parts of leading men into battle—separating himself from them.

He checked his watch. They'd been gone too long. He thought of all the things that could have delayed them, starting with an angry bloat of hippopotami and ending with a giant water cobra out looking for a midnight snack. Just when he thought he needed to send someone to investigate, he got the signal from Peña. They had reached their staging areas.

"Let's rock," Swanson said, slipping the night vision goggles on.

"On my count," Rick said into the microphone.

Between the paranoia of an animal entering her hut and the cacophony of noise at night, Cynthia had had to teach herself how to relax and sleep when she first got to Katangela. As the sun set, the noises in the jungle increased, as if the insects, birds, and animals had to make up for the lack of light. Frogs croaked louder than she could have ever thought possible, insects trilled, night hunters squawked from overhead, and animal sounds she didn't even recognize harmonized with the din. Over time, her brain had conditioned itself to start shutting down and relaxing as the noise increased.

Not so tonight.

Clouds obscured the moon, removing her ability to see anything beyond her hand. She'd never quite gotten used to the blackness of night here. Back home, there was always some streetlight or appliance light or some other kind of light pollution to cut the darkness. Here, there were only the stars and moon.

Ozzy lay in the back of the truck, stretched out on a bed they'd built with their gear. At his request, she'd loaded him up with morphine. They didn't know how rough the roads would be between here and the pickup location, and they had to get him from the truck to the helicopter somehow.

Sanders sat in the seat next to her. For all appearances, he looked fine. He had minimum pain, good blood pressure readings, and a normal temperature. He didn't mind sitting up, though he'd partially reclined the seat. He held a weapon ready, and they had all four windows down so nothing would obstruct his vision or hearing. She couldn't believe she had put her life into the hands of a man whose chest she'd cracked open just two days before.

She did not speak because she didn't want to distract the only guard she had. When she'd taken the driver's seat, she'd promised Sanders and Rick that she would follow all directions immediately when given to her, without question or argument.

Earlier, to her utter shame and embarrassment, she'd stalled out three times trying to drive them to this location. She hadn't driven a standard vehicle since college, and the clutch on this one slipped like hot butter on cold ice. Finally, her muscle memory returned, and she had driven them smoothly here.

Before she could mentally go over the route she'd memorized this afternoon, the sound of gunshots broke through the discord of animal and insect noises. Her mouth went dry and her vision tunneled. She took slow, deep breaths, periodically shaking her hands because they'd started tingling from the rush of adrenaline. She had a hard time sitting still in the truck. Her body wanted to move! To run and jump or hide!

Sanders had tensed next to her, his carbine ready. She knew he wanted to be with his men, and she wondered how he felt about being trapped in here babysitting her.

In the silence of the vehicle, she could hear the sounds coming from his earpiece. Voices yelling, gunfire not in tune with when the sound reached her. It felt like listening to an action movie without seeing the screen.

The gunfire became more sporadic, then stopped just as Sanders said, "Go. Now!"

Ready for the command, she put the truck in first gear, then carefully pressed the accelerator and let up on the clutch. Now that the time of action had arrived, she feared failing on such a level that when the truck started to buck as the gear slipped, she quickly pushed the clutch back in and closed her eyes. "Please, God," she whispered, then went back through the motions. This time, the truck moved smoothly forward.

"Lights," Sanders said.

She found the knob and pulled it, and suddenly the road lit up in front of her. "Thanks," she said, then concentrated on shifting into second gear, then third.

"Faster," Sanders said.

"I don't want—"

"If there were enemy combatants anywhere within a few miles, they heard the gunfire, and their drivers are flooring it to get to this bridge." He put a hand on her knee and pressed down as if trying to control her speed. "Faster. As fast as you can make this pile of rust go."

She'd agreed to do whatever he said without argument. Emotion brought tears to her eyes, and she prayed he couldn't see them.

She pressed down on the accelerator until it touched the floor. The speedometer pushed toward sixty kilometers per hour, then seventy. When she hit the edge of the bridge, the front of the truck went up, causing a feeling of vertigo before it crashed back down.

She never saw Rick and his men. She just drove as fast as she could, hitting bumps and dips in the road like she didn't have a critical patient in the bed of the truck. On straight stretches she drove faster, and as she rounded corners, she slowed and downshifted, afraid to encounter a pack of duikers or a troop of monkeys, or men bent on stopping her truck and killing everyone inside.

It still took almost fifteen minutes to get to their destination. She felt like she'd driven super fast, but she must have kept her speed more conservative than she thought. She backed into the jungle, facing the field across the road like they'd told her to. As she turned the truck off, she heard Ozzy moan.

She glanced at Sanders. "You okay?"

"Finer than a frog hair split three ways," he said, opening his door and speaking into his microphone. "Feet dry."

He got out of the vehicle and leaned against the open door, looking up at the sky. A moment later he said, "Roger." His voice came out weaker than she'd ever have the power to make him admit. She just prayed he could keep up his energy long enough to get aboard the helicopter.

Cynthia got out of the truck and opened the tailgate. Ozzy opened his eyes and looked at her. "Hurts," he whispered.

She touched his face with both hands. His skin burned hot. "We're almost there," she said, checking his pulse. *God, please get us there. Please don't let him die here.*

Sanders walked very slowly around the truck and leaned his hip against it. "Doc, we need to prepare the LZ." He pressed a hand to his chest. "I can't. Can you do it?"

They'd explained it to her, drawn pictures, used vernacular to help her understand. She prayed she could do it. She found the pack and sorted through the equipment, then held up a flare. "This?"

Sanders nodded and slouched onto the open tailgate.

Completely alone, she ran to the field and counted paces to set out the panels.

CHAPTER

★

ELEVEN

As soon as the helicopter touched down, a soldier jumped out and ran to the truck. He conferred with Sanders, then nodded and slapped Sanders's shoulder before turning to her.

"Doctor Myers," he yelled over the sound of the rotor, "I'm Sergeant Waller. Combat medic. I will assist you on the trip to the embassy." He had friendly blue eyes and had to bend down to talk to her.

She nodded. "Nice to meet you, Sergeant Waller. I have Lieutenant Osbourne. He was shot in the thigh. I had to surgically repair his femoral artery. We're just over sixty hours post-op, and I'm pretty sure he's septic. We need to get straight to an OR when we arrive."

"Yes, ma'am. We have a surgeon standing by." They carried the stretcher with Waller in the lead. Together, they loaded Ozzy into the rack prepared for him. As Cynthia and Sanders strapped in, the helicopter started to lift off.

"Wait!" she said. "We're leaving them?"

Sanders shook his head and lifted his hand in her direction. She scooted off her seat and leaned toward him so she could hear over the sound of the helicopter. "There's two more birds. We're going up to provide cover."

That's right—she remembered him mentioning another helicopter earlier. Relief at his words made her eyes fill with tears again. She nodded and buckled into the seat along the wall of the helicopter, then put on the helmet Waller handed her. The helicopters didn't have any lights on. From her vantage point, she had the same view as the gunner, except he wore night vision goggles, and she could see only blackness surrounding them.

She took a deep breath and slowly let it out, exhaustion creeping along her spine. She rubbed her eyes, feeling the grit in them, already imagining hot running water in a hotel room.

The ping of a bullet striking the helicopter pushed all those thoughts away, and her heart leapt into her throat.

When their gunner started firing, she slapped her hand over her mouth to keep from crying out loud. The muzzle flashes lit up the inside of the cabin like silver lightning strikes. Every third round was a tracer and made his fire look like a ray gun, like something out of a science fiction movie. How could he even see down there? How did he know what to shoot at and in what direction his team lay versus anyone else?

She tried to look around him and see the ground, but the blackness covered the land and the muzzle flashes and tracer rounds had dazzled her eyes.

In her helmet, she heard the conversation between the pilot and the medic. "Got room for another patient? We have bad actors in the AO."

"Roger," Waller replied. "We can take him."

They were landing in the middle of the gunfire! Her mouth went dry even as she realized that the gunner had quit returning fire. Logic started to push back her fear.

As the helicopter landed, a feeling of vertigo rushed up her chest and over her neck. It reminded her of descending in the elevator from the top of the Washington Monument. She closed her eyes and breathed slowly and deliberately, desperately hoping she wouldn't get sick. When she heard someone boarding, she opened her eyes.

Swanson helped Rick in, then climbed in himself. "He got hit!" Swanson yelled as the helicopter lifted off again.

Cynthia heard the confirmation that everyone had gotten on board one of the other two helicopters, then felt the machine fly forward instead of just hovering above the ground. Pushing back the vertigo, she grabbed her bag from where she'd secured it and climbed through the group to where Rick sat, blood covering his face. Fear raced through her, making her trip.

She caught herself before she fell, then crouched next to him and pulled a pair of gloves out of her back pocket. "I need light," she said in a harsh voice, taking his face in her hands. Waller shone a flashlight down on Rick's head.

"It's not that bad," Rick said. "Just grazed me."

"I'll tell you how bad it is," she said, pulling a bottle of saline out of her bag. She squirted the saline along his hairline until she found the injury. She had a hard time telling the difference between his blood and the grease paint. It looked like a bullet had cut through his right temple, nicking the tip of his ear. "You need stitches," she said, grabbing Betadine out of her bag. "I can clean it, but I can't stitch it here."

He grabbed her wrist. "I'll be fine. Thank you." He released her hand and strapped himself into the seat. "Just take care of Ozzy."

"Ozzy's as taken care of as he can be," she said. "Let me clean this and I'll stitch you up when we get there."

"I'm sure there's a doc there who will take care of it." He glared at her as if daring her to retort.

She didn't understand why he refused her help, but she wasn't going to beg him to let her put a needle in his head. He was probably pumped up, with adrenaline flooding his thoughts and senses. She wondered how hard he found it to sit still, strapped into a seat, after the last few weeks. It made sense that he wouldn't want someone to poke and prod him right now.

She sat next to Sanders. "How are we doing, Sergeant?"

"Like a blue tick on a coon hound," he said, his voice raspy. She didn't like his color. As she pressed her fingers to his neck to check his vitals, he said, "You did good out there."

She pulled her stethoscope out of her bag. "Your captain doesn't think so."

Sanders snorted. "Yeah, right. He's as proud of you as a beauty queen's mama."

She listened to his heart. Steady, strong. "Why don't you lie down for me? I'm sure Sergeant Waller could set you up."

With an insistent shake of his head, he said, "All due respect, Doc, I'm walking off this bird. I'll go all the way to medical and collapse there, if you don't mind."

The men on this team made rather odd medical choices. "No problem," she said with a sweet smile. She worked her way back to Ozzy. As she listened to his chest, she looked up and spotted Waller watching her. She held his gaze while she analyzed the crackling sound magnified by the stethoscope. She slipped the earpieces out of her ears. "Rales on the right side," she said, running a hand over Ozzy's forehead. "How long is the trip?"

"'Bout an hour."

"Wow. It took me about eight hours to get out here when I first came."

"Did you come by boat or truck?"

"Both. It was faster to do the first leg over land because of the way the river bends."

It was a very odd sensation to look out the window and see nothing but blackness below. It reminded her of flying across the Atlantic Ocean the summer after she graduated from college. She'd left the JFK airport at 9:30 p.m. and flown all night over nothing but blackness. She couldn't even sleep on the flight, afraid she'd wake up swallowed by the dark. She made sure her return trip from London left in the late morning so it would be daylight the entire trip.

"I imagine that was a beautiful journey," Waller said.

She thought back to the day she'd arrived in Katangela. She'd had so much going on inside her head and hadn't really paid much attention to her environment. But after months here, she knew what he meant and nodded. "It was. I was actually looking forward to the return journey."

YAMBULI

Rick never enjoyed reentering civilization after extended time in combat zones. He'd spent too long with his senses on high alert, and civilization tended to have bright lights, lots of noise, and people going about their civilian days without a thought to what went on outside their safe little walls or borders.

The sun started to lighten the early morning sky as the jungle opened below them and they flew over the slums on the outer limits of Katangela's capital city of Yambuli. The city sat where the river met the Atlantic Ocean. Gradually the slums became flat-roofed houses lined up like building blocks in chaotic rows, and eventually they flew over multistory buildings. About fifteen million people lived and worked there, from the world's poorest children beggars to some of the most affluent moguls. The dichotomy between the villages in the jungle and this city fascinated him.

The American embassy in Yambuli contained several buildings inside a walled compound, including a fully staffed medical facility. After they landed on the main building in the compound, medical personnel met the helicopter with gurneys to transport Ozzy and Sanders.

Cynthia didn't even look at Rick as she bent her head and ducked out of the helicopter, then spoke to the nurse at the head of Ozzy's gurney. The medic who had flown with them stayed with Sanders. Fighting the impulse to follow, Rick got off the bird with Swanson and waited for the rest of their team to dismount from the other two helicopters. Together, they made their way to the one-story annex that housed the Special Operations headquarters. Once there, Rick discovered that they could not get barracks rooms.

"Why?" he asked.

The Marine lance corporal at the desk had her black hair pulled back into a tight bun and a scattering of freckles over her brown nose. She had a hard time looking him in the eye, which bothered him.

"We have a detail of DVs here from DC. All the rooms are taken, sir," she said.

"Distinguished visitors. How nice. Where's the rest of my team?" he asked. The five soldiers who'd split from his team had helped another one out on a larger mission. "Where are they staying?"

"They left this morning. We lodged them at a hotel for the last two days." She handed him a packet, her hand trembling slightly. Rick thought she couldn't be older than nineteen. "You have rooms at the hotel. The hotel shuttle will take you. Just fill out this paperwork."

He shook his head. "Lance Corporal, we cannot walk into a hotel lobby looking like this."

She stood and pointed down a hall. "Sir, the gym has a locker room. Grab a shower and get some breakfast at the DFAC, then we'll have the shuttle come for you."

He scrubbed at his beard and thought about the breakfast waiting for them in the dining facility. "Fine."

He turned to the team. He could tell they'd started to decompress. "Get your footlockers out of storage. Shower in the gym and slide into civvies. I'll meet you at the DFAC."

After filling out the paperwork for the hotel, making arrangements for a shuttle, and checking in with his commander and scheduling a debrief for tomorrow at eight, he went to the shower. By the time he got there, everyone had already left. He slathered cold cream on his face and neck to wash away the camouflage paint. The cream felt and smelled good. With it still on his face, he stepped into the shower. He'd take a longer, hotter shower at the hotel, but for now he relished the feel of clean water washing away weeks of grime. The water ran over his head, across his shoulders, down his torso. It mixed with green paint and red blood, making a strange brown color as it swirled down the drain.

By the time the water rinsed clear, he could barely stand up. He dug through the footlocker he'd collected from storage and found a pair of jeans and a T-shirt. He wanted to sleep, but he needed some real food first. The idea of another MRE held absolutely no appeal. He glanced at the big analog clock hanging above the door. Seven ten. Perfect. Only ten minutes since they'd started serving, so they should still have some of everything. Maybe even pancakes. His stomach growled and his mouth watered at the thought.

In the basement of the embassy, Rick found the DFAC. He walked in and smelled classic breakfast scents: meat cooking, breads baking, coffee brewing.

He closed his eyes and just sniffed it in. Ahh, coffee. After grabbing a tray, he loaded a plate with corned beef hash, a cheese and mushroom omelet, fresh fruit, and a stack of pancakes. He added a glass of orange juice and a cup of coffee to his tray, then found his team holding a place for him at a table.

Peña looked up from his oatmeal. "Thought maybe you'd gone to the hotel."

The smell of the food had revived him. "Not until I eat and check in on Ozzy and Drumstick."

Waller, the medic who had flown with them, sat at the end of the group near McBride. "Sergeant Sanders is resting in the medical facility on the fourth floor. I hooked him up with an IV and got some fluids in him. He's doing well. Lieutenant Osbourne is still in surgery."

Rick looked around but didn't see Cynthia. "Where's Doctor Myers?"

Waller frowned slightly. "I, uh, think she's in surgery with Lieutenant Osbourne, sir. Last I saw they were trying to find her some scrubs." He gestured toward Rick. "I can glue up your head for you if you want. You're bleeding onto your food."

He patted his head with a napkin, and to his surprise it came away bloody. He shook his head. "No thanks. It'll be fine." He bowed his head and asked God's blessing on the bounty of food in front of him, then picked up his fork. "Amen." He scooped corned beef into his mouth. When he noticed that he was bleeding down the side of his face, he said, "Okay. Maybe after I eat."

"Check" was all Waller said in response.

"Where's everyone else?" Swanson asked, clearly referring to the other five members of their team.

"They sent them to Djibouti as soon as we boarded the helicopters."

McBride shook his head. "You know Hanson loved that. I bet he's still cursing."

Rick thought about his warrant officer, the perfect right hand for him. "We should hook up with them in a couple of days if all goes according to plan."

The food tasted better than almost anything he'd ever eaten, and it was perfectly complemented by the coffee and orange juice. About an hour later, feeling full and beyond tired, he went to the medical section. He found Sanders crashed out on a bed behind a curtained area.

A nurse came up to him. "He is fine medically, just a little dehydrated and tired. He'll probably be released tomorrow morning when we take out the chest tube."

He turned and faced her. "And my other soldier? Lieutenant Osbourne?"

Her eyebrows drew together in a frown. "He's still in surgery. If you go through that door there, you'll see the signs. There should be a waiting room."

He pushed through the doors, then walked through the corridors until he found a sign that read, "Surgical Family Waiting Room." He stopped short when he saw Sergeant Waller already there.

"How did you get here so fast?" he asked.

Waller held up his ID badge. "Came in through a different door."

"Know anything?"

"I know lots of things." He pulled on a pair of gloves and held up a box. "For instance, I know I have antibiotic ointment and sutures in this box. I know you're going to sit still and let me fix you up because you have now done everything you needed to do, so you can relax."

Resigned, Rick sat down, and Waller stood above him. "I said it was okay."

"You clearly haven't looked in the mirror." Waller held up a syringe. "Want me to numb it, or are you still feeling the need to act tough?"

Considering how bad his ear stung without anyone touching it, he finally relented. "Numb it."

After Waller finished stitching his temple and ear, he settled into an uncomfortable waiting room chair and closed his eyes. The next thing he knew, someone touched his shoulder. Before he could think, he had ahold of the person's wrist and had brought up his other arm to grab a very narrow neck. His eyes flew open, and he found himself staring into Cynthia's shocked face.

Forcing himself to relax, he released his grip on her and said, "Never touch a sleeping soldier."

"I accept your apology," she said in a husky voice, and he smirked. "You'd think I would have learned my lesson the first time," she said and cleared her throat.

He scrubbed his face with his hands and sat up straighter. "What time is it?"

"Almost ten." She sank into the chair next to him as if someone had pulled a plug on her. "In residency, we worked thirty-six hours in a row. My first shift like that, we had so many women in labor they were lined up in the hallway and we were calling hospitals for other places they could go. Some sort of mini baby boom. I know I've been this tired before, but right now I can barely remember it."

He looked at her. She wore surgical scrubs and had her hair stuffed up under a surgical cap. Her eyes were red rimmed and framed with dark circles.

"How's Ozzy?" he asked.

"I did everything I could do, but I am not a vascular surgeon and he really needed a vascular surgeon." She leaned her head back and pressed her fists into her eyes. "I tried to save it, but we had to take the leg."

The breath caught in the back of his throat. They'd had to take Ozzy's leg? He couldn't imagine. His stomach turned as he thought about every decision he'd made in the last few days, wondering if he could have possibly done something different that wouldn't have ended this way. Despite all the denial and worry swirling through his mind, he said,

"Cynthia, he would have died if you hadn't done what you did. You and I both know that. He's gonna live because of you."

"I appreciate that." She wiped at her eyes and pushed herself to her feet. He stood with her. "I do. But the fact is Ozzy would still have both legs if you guys hadn't gotten into a gunfight in the first place."

He gritted his teeth and shook his head. "You know something? I almost convince myself that you and I could be friends, and then you say something like that. Maybe if you kept your mouth shut more often, we'd get along better."

Anger coursed through his body like a current. He felt too tired, too emotionally charged, to have this argument right now. He imagined the same applied to her.

He spun on his heel and stormed out of the waiting room. He needed sleep. Hours and hours of restorative, empty-minded sleep. Instead of taking the elevator, he went down the stairs and exited the stairway into the courtyard of the compound. He crossed to the annex building and slammed the door open. "Get me a ride to the hotel, Lance Corporal."

CHAPTER

★

TWELVE

Cynthia walked out of the waiting room berating herself for her timing in speaking out. She wanted to run after Rick and apologize but knew that both of them needed food and sleep first. She went back through the corridor and into the room where Sergeant Sanders rested. The nurse there directed her to the dining hall.

She stood in the doorway and breathed in through her nose. It was between breakfast and lunch, so most of the serving stations had closed down, leaving brunch selections like cold cereal, fruit, and pastries. But they had pancakes! She loved pancakes. She took a stack of four, covered the fluffy disks with fresh strawberries and blueberries, and added coffee and cranberry juice to her tray.

The tables held only a scattering of people. That gave her a chance to sit alone and try to figure out how she could apologize to Rick and have him believe her sincerity.

"Excuse me, Doctor Myers?"

She looked up and examined the man before her from head to toe. He wore a dark-blue suit with a green-and-blue tie and had a coil coming out of his jacket, leading to the earpiece in his left ear. "Let me guess," she said, taking a drink of her juice. "Secret Service."

"Special Agent Zachary Monroe," he said. "Doctor, your father is here and would like to speak with you."

Her father? What was he doing here? She looked at her tray and the steaming pancakes and smiled up at the man. "Do you mind if I eat first? I haven't eaten anything other than an MRE in a couple days."

A smile came quickly to Monroe's face. "I've had a few weeks like that. When you're finished eating, I'll escort you to the sixth floor and take you to the vice president. If you don't mind, I'll join you for a coffee in the meantime."

"Sure thing."

Monroe walked away to fetch his coffee, and she laid the paper napkin over her lap, then bowed her head. *God, thank You for getting us here, for Ozzy and Bill surviving until now. Touch their bodies with Your healing power. And, God, help me navigate around Captain Norton in a way that keeps me from saying things that hurt him, because I like him. Thank You for this food. Amen.*

While she ate, she thought about Ozzy's leg, inadvertently flinching as she remembered the sound of the bone saw. If they hadn't taken the leg, the infection would have continued spreading until he died. They didn't make antibiotics strong enough to fight it back. Intellectually, she knew that. Emotionally, she wished she could have effected a different outcome.

Then to take it out on the man who bore the responsibility for all the soldiers under him! Only exhaustion and a punchiness born of coming out of a draining, harrowing experience that included a man pressing a gun against her temple, witnessing men die violent deaths up close, a chase through the jungle, bad guys shooting at the helicopter she'd escaped in—only those would make her lash out and intentionally try to goad Rick.

Shame burned in her chest and caused a bitter taste in her mouth that overpowered the pancakes. Why couldn't she just let him do what he did and leave him alone about it? It didn't affect her anymore. Maybe it felt better to push the blame off her shoulders and onto his. If so, what did that make her?

Exhausted.

To top it all off, she had to go speak to her father, the recently appointed vice president of the United States of America, in this exhausted state. Again she wondered why he had come.

Special Agent Monroe returned bearing a cup of black coffee and sat down across from her. He made no attempt at small talk, which didn't surprise her. Cynthia was his detail, not his guest or his friend.

After finding where to drop her tray, she followed Monroe up to the sixth floor. A Secret Service agent met them at the elevator landing. "Hello, Doctor Myers. I'm Special Agent Newel."

Cynthia's response came out unintentionally abrupt. "I was told my father wanted to see me."

Clearly unruffled, Special Agent Newel gestured and said, "Right this way, ma'am." She led Cynthia through a corridor and swiped a security badge to scan them into the next section of the floor, then took her to an office. She tapped on the door twice before opening it and stepping aside so that Cynthia could enter in front of her.

Her father, Vice President Randal Myers, rose from behind the desk and approached her. He was average height, lean, with silver hair and bright-blue eyes. The last time she'd seen him, he'd sported a silver goatee. Today he had a clean-shaven face. Some focus group must not have liked the facial hair.

His voice naturally boomed when he spoke. "Sweet pea. I can't tell you how good it is to see you." He held his arms out, and she readily stepped into them.

"It's good to see you too." She stepped back and looked up at him. "Mr. Vice President." She grinned and superfluously straightened his tie. "Last time I saw you, you were only a senator. My, how you've grown."

He smiled a little uncomfortably. "Obviously it was in the plan, but not this way. I'm sorry you missed out."

She thought of her mother and how she loved entertaining and throwing parties. "I'm sure Mom threw a party to be reckoned with in the annals of history."

"Unrivaled. You know her well." He gestured toward a leather sofa. "Need to have a conversation with you."

She stopped and stood firm. "Daddy, I am completely exhausted. The journey here was very stressful, and I've been awake since six yesterday morning. The way you say 'conversation' makes me think I should probably sleep first." She looked at the sofa. "And I'm afraid if I sit on that, I'm gonna fall asleep right here."

He smiled. "At least then I would know you were safe." He slipped his hands into his pockets. If he'd driven himself here, he would jingle his car keys. But he probably hadn't driven himself anywhere since taking the oath. "Would you like to have breakfast with me up here tomorrow?"

"I'd love that." She looked at her watch. "I'd say dinner, but I don't know if I'll be awake by dinnertime."

With a shake of his head, he said, "I have to do a dinner with our ambassador tonight and a state dinner with Katangela's president tomorrow. I'm afraid my new title comes with some responsibilities that don't give me complete freedom of travel."

She looked up at him. "I'm really proud of you, Daddy."

"Thank you, sweet pea, but like I told your mom, save it for when I win the office in an election." He patted her on the shoulders. "There's a car downstairs to take you to the hotel." He pulled a card and a lanyard out of his pocket. "Here's all the numbers to reach me and your credentials to move around my area of the building here. Get some good rest, and I'll see you in the morning."

She started out of the room but paused and turned with her hand on the doorknob. "Is eight good?"

"Uhh . . ." He walked around to the desk, picked up a slip of paper, and glanced at it. "Could you make seven thirty work?"

"Seven thirty is fine."

After Rick checked into the hotel, he managed to toss his room key near the television and drop his kit bag on the floor before he fell facedown on top of the bed. The next thing he knew, he was waking up in the same position, but the night sky now replaced the bright morning sunlight that had streamed through the big window. He lifted his head long enough to see the clock. Eight thirty. His stomach felt like it could eat itself out of his body. He hoped the hotel restaurant stayed open late.

He rolled out of the bed and went into the bathroom. Tropical flowers floated in a sink full of water. It took a moment to register why, and he realized it was designed to impress the hotel guests with luxury. He considered the running faucet and clean water more than luxury enough.

He washed his face, then stared at himself in the mirror, pressing his fingers against his red-rimmed, puffy eyes. He ran his hands along the sides of his face, scratched at his beard, then scrubbed it with some soap that smelled like hibiscus, digging out the rest of the camouflage paint. He would be glad to get home and shave the beard off. He turned his head and studied the stitches in the top of his ear and the bandage along his temple.

It annoyed him that he'd gotten shot. He'd gotten stabbed once in a hand-to-hand fight with an insurgent in Afghanistan, but never shot. The stab wound had hurt a lot more than this graze to his temple. But his ear throbbed, and he hoped Waller had known what he was doing when he stitched it.

His body hummed with energy and exhaustion all at once, like he needed to jog for three miles and sleep for three hours at the same time. His mind felt fuzzy, fatigued, dull, as if stubbornly lingering between asleep and awake.

When he went back into the bedroom, he saw a light flashing on his phone. He pushed the button for messages and listened to Fisher's voice. "Hey, Daddy. We had them just send this to your voice mail so we wouldn't wake you. It's eighteen hundred and we're going to eat. We slipped a note under your door with all our room numbers."

If they'd eaten at six, he didn't think he'd find them in time to join them. He walked through the bedroom and into the next room. He had barely paid attention to his environment when he came in hours ago. The room had a couch, a desk, and a television stand. A fruit bowl sat in the middle of the coffee table. It held some bananas, oranges, and figs. He grabbed a banana and ate it in three bites.

After he slipped his key into the back pocket of his shorts, he dug through his kit bag and found his wallet, checking to make sure he had a credit card and, for anonymity on the outskirts of a war zone, no military ID. Then he left his room. If the hotel restaurant wasn't open, he would walk until he found someplace that was. On the way here, he remembered seeing a KFC next to a Starbucks. The presence of Western fast-food joints in the most remote corners of the world always amazed him.

Before he went to the restaurant, he stopped at the front desk. A man in a maroon suit smiled brightly at him.

"English or French?" Rick asked.

"English, sir. My English is good."

Rick smiled. "Good, because my French is *très* terrible. Do you have a laundromat here?"

The clerk nodded. "There is a laundry service. You put your clothes in the bag, put the bag in the hallway. A maid, she will gather them and return them by morning."

Rick shook his head. "Is there a place where I can do my own laundry?"

The man frowned, obviously translating the question. Then he smiled and nodded exuberantly. "Ahh, yes, sir. On floor five, there is machines. Use your room key. No problem."

"Do the machines take money?"

The man opened a drawer and held up a token that reminded Rick of the video arcades in movie theaters back home. "I can give you tokens and charge them to your room. No problem. You need soap?"

"How many tokens do the machines take?"

"One, sir."

"I'll take two, please. And soap for two loads. Is the restaurant still open?"

"Yes, sir. No problem. Open until ten. Hot meals. Very good. The bar is open all the time. You can get cold food in there all the time."

"Thanks."

"No problem. I am Hodari. You need anything, ask for Hodari."

Rick walked through the empty lobby and found the restaurant. The woman at the host stand perked up when she saw him. "Good evening, sir. Just one?"

"Just me." He gestured toward the big bay windows. "Could I sit by the window?"

"Of course, sir. Follow me."

At this hour, few guests visited the restaurant. He followed the hostess along the mahogany floor, past tables lit with low lamps and adorned with tropical flowers. Three men sat around a circular booth, all with open laptops and chatting in Italian. Over at a corner table, a couple sat close, leaning toward each other and talking quietly.

When they reached the two-top tables that sat along the window looking out over the river, he spotted Cynthia. She sat alone, staring outside with a pensive look on her face.

He halted and considered the tactical situation. He owed her an apology for raising his voice, at the very least. He allowed himself a small sigh and gestured toward her table. "I'll join her." He took the menu from the hostess. "Thank you."

He stood there for a moment watching Cynthia before he stepped up to the table. She looked rested, relaxed. He had never seen her this way. It made her look younger, smaller, vulnerable.

He approached the table. "May I join you, Cynthia?"

She jumped, possibly unfamiliar with the sight of him in civilian clothes with clean hair and skin. Then the relaxed look slid from her face as recognition dawned and her guard came back up. "Of course. Please."

He sat down. A clean place setting was in front of her, so she hadn't yet eaten.

She held up her cell phone. "I've been reading texts I've missed for the past five months. So much life happening in such a short amount of time." She studied his face. "You look better. How is your head?"

He touched the bandage. "Sergeant Waller insisted I get stitches, despite my objections."

She smiled with closed lips. "I think I told you the same thing. When someone with my training insists that you need stitches, best guess is that you probably need stitches."

He could tell she wasn't reprimanding him but teasing him. He glanced at the menu. "What did you order?"

"Something with chicken and rice. There's a lamb dish on there that sounded good too. I almost ordered both."

The waiter arrived. Rick ordered the lamb dish with double meat and a bottle of water. When the waiter left, he looked out at the river. The moonlight reflected on the surface of the water.

"Doctor, I owe you an apology," he said.

Her eyes widened. "Me?"

"Yeah, earlier today—" He sighed. "I shouldn't have said what I said. I was exhausted and still a little amped up. Coming back from a mission is always a little hard on me. Knowing that about myself should have kept me from saying anything at all. Instead, I raised my voice at you, and I said things I didn't mean."

"Well," she said, picking up her water, "at least I know you want to be friends."

He chuckled. "You're an amazing woman. I've seen you in action, so I know. And I do respect your feelings. I do." He liked the way the blush covered her cheeks.

"I owe you an apology too," she said.

His heart gave a slight tug when he remembered her words. "That right?"

"Yes. What I said about Ozzy's leg—that was truly horrible. I know I was starving and exhausted, but please know that I believe you did everything in your power to get us out of there."

He appreciated her candor and decided to let the matter rest. "Let's start over."

"I would love that." She visibly relaxed.

He smiled. "What did you do before you came here?"

She took a small sip from her glass before she set it down. "I worked a year in a private OB-GYN clinic my aunt started. I'd done my internship at Johns Hopkins, and when I finished a residency program, it felt like the clinic was the next logical step. But now I'm sitting here trying to remember what my days looked like." She crossed her arms over her chest and sat back in her chair. "What about you? You said you went to the Citadel. Are you from South Carolina?"

"Me?" He raised his eyebrows. "No, ma'am. I'm from Kentucky."

"Kentucky? I thought I detected an accent."

The waiter brought a platter of flatbread with dipping sauces. He set it on the table and poured sparkling water into Rick's glass, then set the bottle down beside his glass.

After the waiter left, Rick extended his hand toward Cynthia, palm up. She glanced at his hand, then at his face, before straightening and laying her fingers lightly in his palm. They bowed their heads. He prayed, "Father, thank You for this food. Please bless it to the nourishment of our bodies and bless our bodies for Your service."

He ripped a piece of bread in half and dipped it in hummus. Cynthia chose the green dip that looked like tabbouleh.

"What kind of a degree does a Special Forces officer obtain from the Citadel?" she asked.

He swallowed before he answered. "I always wanted to be a soldier, so I formed my degree around my desired career. I have a degree in strategic intelligence with a minor in political science."

"So, he's super smart too." She washed a bite of bread down with some wine. "That doesn't surprise me." She dipped another piece of bread into the green dip, so he tried it. The flavor of parsley and garlic married well in his mouth. "Do you like Kentucky?" she asked.

"Let me put it this way. Heaven is a local call from Kentucky. I come from a small town in the most perfect location in the continental United States. My soul longs to be back home whenever I'm away."

With a soft smile she said, "I don't feel that way about Virginia. I think about going home and I just feel deflated."

He stared at her in the low light for several seconds before he said, "That's understandable. You left in the midst of pain and humiliation. Even though it's home, the last feelings you had there still cause warring emotions."

She raised an eyebrow. "Rather insightful, Captain."

"It's not like it's a mystery, Doctor." He grinned. "Although that's about as deep as I dare delve into the intricacies of the female psyche."

"Very wise."

A few moments of silence passed as they chewed their bread. She broke the silence with a tone of reflection in her voice. "Still, don't really want to go back. I have another contract ready to sign to stay here. I can't believe I only have a month left of my original six months."

"Ready for you to sign? But not yet signed. Does that mean you were trying to decide?"

"Maybe. The day everything happened at the village, I had decided to sign it. I think my father's going to tell me I have to go home."

Knowing what kind of dangers the jungle would bring her, he wouldn't disagree with her father, but he'd never say that to her. "You'll have to call him first thing in the morning DC time. Think you can stay awake?"

She shook her head. "He's here. I already saw him at the embassy. I was just too exhausted to do more than say hi. I'm having breakfast with him in the morning."

Rick sat up a little straighter. "Your father is here in country?"

"That's what I said."

"You probably shouldn't have told me that. Told anyone, I mean."

"I trust you, Captain," she whispered. "Besides, he has a state dinner tomorrow night, so the press already knows."

Rick took a long, deep swallow of water. "So, what if he says you have to go home? What then?"

"Then I'll have to tell him no for the first time in my life. I don't know how he'll handle that."

He used the small spoon on the serving tray to spread hummus onto his bread, then topped that with tabbouleh.

"Do you have family in Kentucky?"

As he chewed, he thought about home. He hadn't let his mind go there while on mission. Now that he was relaxed, sitting in a restaurant eating flatbread and hummus across from a beautiful woman, he thought of his grandfather's farm with the railroad trestle along the back edge of the property, and his father's hardware store in the small town of Charula. "I do. My parents are both alive and both have siblings, so I have a county full of first cousins."

This time her smile lit up her face. It did strange things to the rhythm of his pulse. "The quintessential Small Town, USA, boy next door. I bet they're very proud of you."

He gave a sheepish grin. "They are proud of me. My parents have always supported me."

The waiter appeared with their plates. Seconds after he served them, he disappeared without a word. For a few minutes, they both concentrated on eating. Rick enjoyed the spices with his perfectly prepared medium-rare lamb and the flavor of the rice. Cynthia, who had only taken delicate bites of the bread, dug into her chicken and rice as if it were a contest. He liked watching her eat.

They chatted about family, college, travel. As the waitstaff cleared their plates and replaced them with a fruit plate, Rick brought the topic back to her father. "How long did it take you to find out you were the daughter of the VP?"

She shrugged one shoulder. "I used that satellite connection to check email once a week, so I found out four days later. His party put him on that path when he was a junior senator from Virginia."

"So, he was part of that corrupt nanny state government?"

Cynthia swallowed and nodded. "That's how I know the scope of it. Daddy fought it hard the whole time. Sent three people to jail. A drop in the ocean. He's always had ambitions of high office. He wanted to fix things from the top down. He has the charisma to pull it off too. Especially now that he's the VP. His name is more well-known now—he's more in the public eye."

Rick chuckled. "He seems to have earned a lot of respect. From all public accounts, he's a man of integrity. That's high praise these days."

"He absolutely is." She shook her head. "However, I do not ever get involved. I am not a politically minded person. I've seen a lot in the background that makes me rather disgusted with the entire system and both parties."

The waiter arrived with the check, and Rick asked him to split it in two.

Cynthia picked it up. "I've got it."

"No, ma'am, you don't." Even while she scribbled on the check, he said to the waiter, "Put my charges on my room."

"What room, sir?"

"Four zero five."

Cynthia held up the bill. "Already taken care of, Rick."

The waiter took the bill from her and disappeared.

"You don't need to buy my dinner, Cynthia," Rick said. "This meal is paid for. If you pay your taxes every year, you've already bought my dinner."

She gave a brilliant smile. "You're welcome."

That made him laugh. They stood and walked together to the elevator. He used his key card to access the floor, then pressed the number four. He looked at her. "What floor?"

"I'm actually down the hall from you." She put her hands behind her neck and stretched her back. "I slept all day, but I feel like I can sleep all night."

"Good. Do it. You'll be better for it."

She looked at her watch. "How is it ten thirty already?"

Ten thirty? They had just spent the last two hours talking, and it felt like five minutes. "I have to be back at the embassy at eight."

She nodded. "I have breakfast with my father at seven thirty."

The elevator opened on the floor. "You should ride with us."

She looked up at him and batted her eyes. "Still in protective mode, Captain?"

They walked down the hall until she stopped in front of room 411. As she accessed the room with her key card, he leaned against the doorframe. "I think I'll always be in protective mode with you, Cynthia."

"Well, that just sounds exhausting." She opened the door and held it open with her shoulder as she turned toward him. "Thank you for joining me for dinner. I enjoyed getting to know you better."

"Likewise." He paused. "We'll leave at seven, if you want a ride."

She stepped farther back into her room. "See you at seven."

He waited a few moments after she shut the door. He didn't know why. Maybe he hoped she would open it again. Maybe he listened to make sure there were no sounds to indicate foul play inside. When nothing happened after several moments, he straightened and walked down the hall to his room.

CHAPTER

★

THIRTEEN

Cynthia's alarm surprised her. She'd expected to wake up in the middle of the night and not be able to go back to sleep, but somehow, she managed to sleep until six.

She lay in bed, gazed at the ceiling ornately decorated with what looked like carved pineapples and pomegranates in the crown molding, and thought back to dinner last night. A silly smile covered her face as the image of Captain Rick Norton in shorts and a T-shirt crossed her mind. Compared to his face and arms, his legs looked very pale, but his entire body rippled with muscles.

After a long, hot shower, where she pampered herself with the amenities offered by the hotel and lathered her hair with shampoo and conditioner, she put lotion on and then her last clean outfit. She bagged her dirty clothes and set them in the hallway for housekeeping.

At seven, she went down to the lobby and found Swanson

and Fisher sitting in the red chairs that flanked the fountain. They wore shorts and T-shirts. "Good morning. I hardly recognized you without your, uh, other outfits on."

"Morning, Doc," Fisher said. "We have uniforms back at the embassy. Unfortunately, the boots have to go back on."

She glanced at his feet. He wore leather flip-flops. "I don't imagine those sandals would serve you well in your line of work."

Swanson gestured toward a different restaurant than the one where she'd eaten last night. "There's breakfast in there."

"I appreciate that. I have to go have breakfast with my father."

Swanson raised an eyebrow. "Your father's here?"

Rick spoke from behind her, startling her. "Her father is the reason we had to suffer through staying in this luxury hotel instead of sleeping on thin mattresses in the barracks at the embassy. His entourage took our place."

She smiled as she turned to face him. "You sound really put out about that."

He shook his head. "You have no idea." Unlike his men, he wore his uniform. It was different from the one he'd worn in the jungle. That uniform didn't have a name tag or all of the skill badges that this one displayed.

"What does your father do?" Fisher asked.

Cynthia raised her eyebrows. "Seriously?" She looked at Rick. "I thought you had a file."

"Only Peña and I read it." He looked at Fisher. "He's Vice President Randal Myers."

Swanson whistled under his breath. "No wonder Chukuwereije wanted to have a 'chat' with you," he said, using air quotes.

Feeling a little uncomfortable, she cleared her throat. "Well, he wasn't the vice president when I came out here."

McBride and Peña arrived. Peña looked toward the restaurant. "Do we want to eat here?"

Rick shook his head. "I walked through the breakfast about an hour ago. The DFAC at the embassy has a better spread."

"Will we have time to hit the DFAC?" Peña asked.

"Yeah. Debrief is at eight. Plenty of time built in." He held up a set of keys. "I rented a van."

Fisher stood. "Let's do this."

Rick led the way. He'd parked the van in front of the door. He opened the passenger's door and made eye contact with Cynthia. She got in, and he shut the door and walked around to the other side.

As he started the van, he said, "I'm surprised your father didn't send a car for you."

She angled her body toward his. "My father no longer sends me cars. On my insistence, of course, but he respects my wishes."

He headed out into the traffic. "You don't like taking advantage of the luxury his high office affords?"

"I don't like pomp and circumstance. Much sound and fury signifying nothing."

He nodded. "Yeah, but now that car would be for security purposes."

"True. But with your team, I don't think I could be safer."

He grinned at her. "That is probably accurate."

She studied him. He had not shaved, and his woolly beard and longish hair looked completely wrong now for some reason. The chest of his uniform was adorned with wings, wreaths, lightning bolts, and bayonets above the words US

Army. She even saw what appeared to be a diving helmet. "You managed to get a lot done since dinner last night."

He turned left and onto a main road. "I washed my uniform. It didn't take long. While it was drying, I made arrangements for the van. I think I was asleep by midnight."

"I can't believe how much sleep I got yesterday."

"It comes from a lack of quality sleep and a high-stress environment. Yesterday your body was exhausted and your mind was decompressing. Sleep is how God designed restoration."

It didn't take long to arrive at the embassy's parking lot. Rick pulled up to the guard shack and handed the armed guard a piece of paper and everyone's ID cards, including Cynthia's credentials. After a glance at all the items, the guard handed them back. Moments later, two sets of gates slid open one at a time.

Once they had parked, the team climbed out of the van. Rick slipped his soft cap on and said to the men piling out of the back, "Eat before you change. Brief at oh eight hundred in the CHU."

Cynthia slipped her bag over her shoulder. "Thanks for the ride, Captain."

His beard moved with his smile. "Enjoy your breakfast."

Inside the building, she handed her ID and the pass her father had given her to the security officer. who instructed her to let the pass be seen at all times. She slipped the lanyard over her head and followed his directions to the elevators. On the sixth floor she found the same Secret Service agent she had spoken with yesterday.

Cynthia smiled. "Good morning, Agent Newel. I am here to have breakfast with my father."

"Right this way, Doctor Myers."

At the door to her father's office, Special Agent Newel tapped once then opened it, gesturing for Cynthia to go inside. Her father looked up from his desk and smiled as he slipped his reading glasses off. On the table by the window sat platters of bagels and cream cheese and lox. A silver-plated coffee service sat on a small tray next to the table for two.

"Good morning, Daddy," she said.

"Ahh, sweet pea, you look much more rested than yesterday." He came around his desk, and she easily went into his arms for a hug. "It does my old heart good to see you."

They sat at the table, and her father asked the blessing on the food. When they raised their heads he said, "So, tell me. How are you feeling today?"

She poured steaming coffee into a china cup lined with pink primroses. "Good. Back to myself. I'm afraid I was a bit of a zombie yesterday. I slept about twenty hours total since the last time I saw you."

He raised an eyebrow. "You *were* exhausted." He piled a bagel with smoked salmon and capers. "Understand you had some trouble."

She spread a thin layer of cream cheese on her bagel and added a slice of smoked salmon. "The Special Forces team was in a firefight with the warlord not far from my clinic. Things got a little hairy after that."

Her dad sat back, holding his cup and saucer. "Did you have any trouble like that before then?"

"Not to that extreme. The warlord has been growing in strength for the past five years or so. He's amassed a rather large army and wants to instigate a coup on the government here. But we were really remote. We'd get the occasional truckful of warlord bullies, but the locals have that pretty well handled."

They ate in silence for a few moments, and then her father said, "I've been following the politics here pretty closely, for obvious reasons. Unfortunately, my new position puts you and your mother in the spotlight. When Chukuwereije found out your connection to me, you were extracted for your own safety."

"I know that. But I'm doing really great work here, Daddy. I have women from four villages who sometimes travel an entire day to come to my clinic. I plan to sign another six-month contract."

Her father's face maintained a pleasant countenance. "That would have been ideal, but I'm afraid it won't be possible. You can easily be captured, then used as a pawn in this political game. You need to go back home where it's safe for a while."

She took a sip of her coffee, appreciating the rich flavor. "I am happy to work under an assumed name. I don't need to be Cynthia Myers here."

He shook his head. "Too late for that. Your face is all over the news. You're on magazine covers and the front pages of newspapers. The incident with Andrew made you an unfortunate focus of media spotlight for a while and provided quite a bit of fodder. Now, here, it simply isn't safe."

She carefully wiped her lips with a napkin and put it on her plate. "I appreciate your concern, Daddy. I get it. But I am not going to give in to the threat of violence. I am on a mission sanctioned by a Christian organization, and I am doing humanitarian work that needs to be done. The political maneuvering here has nothing to do with me." She stood. "It was really good to see you, Daddy. I'm really proud of you, and I love you very much."

As she started to walk from the office, her father said, "Cynthia, do not make me force this."

She turned and faced him. "I'm thirty-two years old. I'm a grown woman. You raised me to be strong, independent, and make my own choices. What can you possibly do to force anything? Come to think of it, why would you want to?" She blew him a kiss. "Be safe going home."

Colonel Jenkins sat in a recliner and glanced at Rick's team. He preferred to do his debriefs in the rec room. He felt that with everyone relaxed and in a nonthreatening setting, they would be able to remember more details and feel less intimidated by rank. Rick had always thought him a rather odd man. Eccentric. Despite that, he was a great leader and always had their backs.

The colonel had a broad chest, long limbs, and large features. He kept his head shaved and sported a West Point alumni ring over his wedding ring. As usual, and in defiance of a few military regulations, he toyed with an unlit cigar while he spoke. "I looked in on Lieutenant Osbourne this morning. He seems in good spirits."

Rick had looked in on him as well. He knew Ozzy well enough to see the shadows in the corners of his eyes. But he didn't correct the colonel. "He's a fighter." He paused and then added, "We might want to make sure a chaplain checks in on him pretty regularly."

Colonel Jenkins nodded. "When we received the report of

the extent of Lieutenant Osbourne's injuries, we went ahead and had a new medic assigned to your team. You met him yesterday. Timothy Waller. Staff Sergeant. He was dying on the vine out at Carson. As of now, he's OPCON to you with orders to PCS him to our unit soon to follow."

Rick thought about the tall blond man who had stitched his head. He hoped he wasn't too green. He didn't feel like breaking in someone who had joined Special Forces because the recruiting posters made it look cool. "Yes, sir."

The colonel pointed his cigar at him. "He's also from Kentucky," he said, as if that made everything right. "You guys might have something in common."

Peña chuckled. "Yeah, Daddy. Because Kentucky."

Colonel Jenkins continued. "Sergeant Sanders will rejoin the team as soon as he gets clearance from the doctor. At this time, I don't see a need to replace him. Any objections?"

"Sergeant Sanders is irreplaceable, sir," Rick said.

"Tell me what kept you in the jungle. I read the reports. Give it to me fresh from your perspective."

Peña interjected. "All due respect, sir, the reports *are* our perspective."

The colonel waved his cigar like a wand that could erase Peña's words. "I get that, son. I've heard from you and from Captain Norton. I'd like to hear it from the entire team. You guys are the best we've got, so I need to get a sense of the entire picture."

McBride spoke up. "The only issue we had was the fact that we were in a jungle and we needed extraction by helicopter. There's only so many places a helicopter can land in the jungle, sir."

Fisher nodded. "Ozzy was hurt bad, Sanders was hurt.

With only half a team, we felt the loss of those two. Add the complexities of the terrain and the threat factor—suffice it to say our movements were restricted to the extreme."

"And we didn't know who to trust," Swanson added. "The bad guys aren't wearing uniforms."

"We had Chukuwereije, sir," Rick said. "He was boxed in. Katangela soldiers were coming at him from the city, and we were closing in on him in the jungle. His losses were massive. We confirmed the kill of his son. But as soon as we had to pull back because we had two injured, they scattered like cockroaches. It's like we lost an entire month of work and he threw off our operational tempo."

Colonel Jenkins shook his head. "It's a chess game. You lost your rook." He tossed his legal pad on the little table in front of the couch and stood, slipping his unlit cigar into his breast pocket. "Intel claims Chuckie is back in the city now." He had never been able to pronounce the warlord's name and had nicknamed him Chuckie in their first briefing. "There are all sorts of rumors on the streets. Langley can't pin down any real information about location, but general area is a certainty."

Rick paced to stand behind the couch where McBride, Fisher, and Swanson sat. "I do not want to get into a fight with that man inside the city. The kind of collateral damage that could happen here is too much to risk. Thoughts?"

"I don't think that is how this will go down. But it isn't up to us." Colonel Jenkins waved his hand toward the window. "That's up to people much higher than us. Our mission was to end Chuckie's reign of terror. I doubt that the powers that be here in Katangela want CNN putting an urban firefight up as their lead story."

McBride surged to his feet. "Let them. Give us an embedded reporter, and we can show them the holes people dig in their huts to hide their sons, the women Chuckie butchered so that they can't feed their babies, the villages he burned to the ground, and everyone in them who died because that's how he exercises power."

Peña scowled. "The joint chiefs lent one team to Katangela to aid in eradicating Chukuwereije. They did that so we could do this covertly. Remember that word? Covert?"

Rick spoke up. "Which leads us back to a firefight in the streets of the capital city. I don't see that being a good thing." He looked at Colonel Jenkins. "What are your orders now, sir?"

"We'll know by tomorrow. Make sure all your reports are complete. Take it easy. Get good chow and good sleep. Try to stick to embassy grounds and the hotel. Like you said, we don't know who to trust. On that note, try not to look like an American SF team when you're in public. If you see something, say something. All of you update each other." He looked at Peña. "Lieutenant, I want you to confer with the intelligence office here at the embassy. Get a read on real-time info on Chuckie that doesn't have to go through me first, and if anybody gives you static, call my cell directly. I'll unstop any stops if I have to kick the ambassador's door down to do it. Get me? They're expecting you at ten thirty."

Peña nodded. "Yes, sir."

Colonel Jenkins released them. Rick gave some brief instructions to his team, then sought out Sergeant Waller. He found him at a Navy corpsman's computer terminal in the little Marine sick bay near the back of the embassy grounds.

"Colonel Jenkins tells me you're from Kentucky."

Waller looked up from the computer screen, and his hands slid off the keyboard. "Sorry, sir. Didn't hear you come in. I was emailing my wife." He stood. "I'm from Charula. Probably never heard of it."

"Charula? Really?"

"Born and raised."

"Ever been to Norton's Hardware?"

Waller's eyes skimmed Rick's name tag. "You kin?"

"My father is the Norton."

Waller grinned and crossed his arms. "That a fact?"

"Small Army, huh?"

"Small Army." Waller gestured toward the computer with his head. "My wife is from there too. We were high school sweethearts."

"Go, Mighty Eagles," Rick said. He held out his hand and Waller took it. The other man's grip was strong and sure. "Welcome to the team."

"Thank you, sir. It's an honor to be a part of it." He gestured toward the hospital area. "I went to AIT with Ozzy. I'm thankful to have the opportunity to serve in his unit."

Emotion filled Rick's throat, and he cleared it. "He's a good man."

"Yes, sir."

CHAPTER

★

FOURTEEN

As she skimmed the notes on Bill's chart, Cynthia pulled the wheeled stool close to his bed and perched on it. "You'll need to go home for a little while," she said. "Your body has to heal."

"I feel fine," he said. He picked at the sheet covering his lap. "I can't stand being cooped up like this."

"Sergeant—"

"Bill."

She paused and then said, "Bill, you had a bullet enter your chest and park itself next to your heart. Then someone who is not a heart surgeon cut you open, removed said bullet, and patched you back up. I spread your ribs open with a metal tool so that I could reach the bullet. That was four days ago. I'm sorry you're feeling cooped up. You have to let your body heal or your career as you know it will cease to exist."

He stared at her with a stern look on his face. Finally, he

lay back against his pillow and huffed out a breath. "Fine. Why can't I go back to base? Why do I have to go home?"

"Bill, do you not want to go home?"

"I don't want . . ."

She waited and then said, "To be replaced?"

He glared at her. "I am irreplaceable. My home is a single wide in Pelham, Alabama, that my mother usually shares with her man of the month. I'd prefer to convalesce elsewhere."

She remembered their conversation in the jungle. "In North Carolina, you'll go to barracks?"

"Yes, until it's time to move to Kentucky."

"How about Germany? One of the doctors here mentioned it."

He smiled and held up both hands as if to shrug. "Germany, Bethesda, or Walter Reed. I'm not picky."

She patted his shoulder and stood. "I'll see what I can do. But I want eight solid weeks from you. That's how long it's gonna take your chest to heal."

"Deal."

She made a mental note to ask the doctor about his transfer. "Okay. I'm off to see Ozzy."

She walked to the end of the room and peeked around the curtain that shielded Ozzy's bed. He sat with a book in his hand. He looked up at her with blank eyes.

"Looks like the infection got kicked back," she said as cheerfully as possible. "It's good to see you sitting up."

He looked at the bed, his eyes pointing in the direction where his leg should be. "I imagine I'll do quite a bit of sitting in the future."

She slipped her hands into the pockets of her skirt. "This

will sound like a platitude, but it's not. The advancements in prosthetics are remarkable."

He snarled. "I guess it's good I lost my leg now instead of earlier, then, right?"

"Ozzy, I did everything I knew how to do." Her voice cracked, and she put her hand over her mouth to keep from sobbing. Forget trying to be cheerful. She just needed to keep from becoming a puddle.

His face softened. "Doc, you and I both know I'm alive because you did what you did. I don't hate you for it. I imagine if I'd been birthing a baby, you would've been a rock star."

With a grin she said, "That would've been something to see."

His face turned serious again. "I understand the psychology. I know I have to go through the stages of grief over losing my leg. I'm edging out of disbelief and pushing toward anger. You might want to just let me be for a little while."

The curtain moved, and she glanced up as Rick peeked his head around. "You up to visitors?" he asked.

"No, sir."

"Okay." He looked at Cynthia. She could see the worry in the edges of his green eyes. "Can I buy you a cup of coffee?"

She chuckled. "Big spender. The DFAC coffee is free."

"That mean you're buying?" His face remained poised, stoic. He would have made a great vaudeville straight man.

"Not like you're likely to let me go anywhere besides here or the hotel," she said.

"Don't judge me based on the limitations of my environment."

Ozzy scowled. "Why don't you make your environment somewhere I'm not? Some of us have major surgery to recover from."

Rick held the curtain aside for Cynthia. "Want anything special from the DFAC?" he asked Ozzy. "I could bring you something sweet. They might have key lime pie."

"No." Ozzy closed his eyes, then said, "A leg would be good."

"If only I could." He let the curtain swing shut. On their way out of the bay, he stopped at Bill's bed. "Want anything from the DFAC?"

He shook his head. "Nurse already smuggled me in a bowl of bread pudding."

Rick chuckled. "Took you less than twenty-four hours to get them eating out of your hand."

"Southern charm, brother. You should try it sometime." He winked at Cynthia. "Ain't that right, Doc?"

Heat flooded her cheeks, and she followed Rick to the dining facility. Soon, they each had a cup of coffee. She studied Rick's face, trying to imagine what he looked like without the beard. He took a sip of coffee, then looked up, catching her staring.

"What?" he asked, running his hand along his beard. "Did I get crumbs in my beard?"

"I had a really good time last night," she blurted out. She paused and took a sip of the hot drink. When she spoke again, she slowed down a little. "Thank you for joining me."

"I did too. It was nice to get to know you better."

She toyed with her watch strap. "What's next for you?"

"Next?" He shook his head. "We aren't done here."

"No?"

"Our mission is to eradicate Chukuwereije and his organization. Unless the higher-ups have changed the plan, it's still what we're doing here."

She processed that. How could he go back out there after his time here, with no one shooting at him, good food to eat, good water pressure in a warm shower? It felt like they should let him and his men go home permanently and maybe send someone else back.

"So, you're going back into the jungle?"

His smile didn't meet his eyes. "Doctor Myers, I cannot discuss that with you." Then he winked and asked, "What's next for you?"

She didn't feel chastised, though a few days ago she would have bitten back with something mean and sarcastic. She wondered what had changed. "I don't know. My father is trying to get me to go back to the States. That was what our breakfast was about."

"That would certainly be safer."

"Of course it would. That's not why I'm here though, is it? Safety is not my motivation." She ran her thumbnail down the waxy coating of her cup. "Two weeks from tomorrow I'm supposed to go to Yambuli and get on a boat that will spend the next month floating down the river. It's a rather large vessel that has a dentist office, a pediatrics facility, and a pharmacy. Medical professional volunteers from all over the United States are going to come and begin the slow float down the river to hit village after village, cleaning teeth, immunizing children, and meeting basic medical needs." She took another sip of coffee. "That's why I'm here. Safety has nothing to do with it."

"But it does now, doesn't it?" He drank some coffee, then

looked into the cup instead of at her. "Now that people know who you are, those who would use you, threaten you for political gain—don't you think that would interfere with your mission?"

"Of course it would." She sighed. "I can change my name. I can dye my hair. This is a big jungle. There's no reason for me to leave."

He smiled. "I imagine your father has different opinions."

"My father," she said, crossing her arms on the tabletop and leaning forward, "basically told me to choose to leave or he would force me to do it. And since I'm thirty-two years old, I can't imagine how he'll force me. It's not like he can take away my car keys."

With a chuckle he said, "I bet you were a fun teenager."

"Like he would know. Unless he conferred with the headmistress of my boarding school." She huffed out a breath and sat back again. "Sorry. I'm not going to keep ranting about my father. I actually love him very much."

"It's hardly ranting."

They sat in silence for a few moments, then Cynthia said, "Bill asked me to intervene on his behalf. Can you help me do that?"

His face grew serious. "Intervene?"

"He doesn't want to go back to Alabama. He said the environment there is not conducive to good healing."

Rick barked out a laugh. "Was that the word he used? Conducive?"

"No, he used words like single wide and man of the month."

"That sounds more like it."

"He doesn't want to go home. He wants to go to Germany, and he mentioned Bethesda and Walter Reed."

179

Rick nodded. "He and Ozzy will both go to Germany first. That's kind of the staging hospital. I'll ask Colonel Jenkins if there's a way to let Bill stay in Germany then rejoin the mission."

"Do you need me to write anything medically?"

"I know you want to help, but I don't think you'd carry any kind of authority over the docs here or in Germany. He needs what, eight weeks? I don't see them needing to send him home for that. But I'll ask Jenkins and let you know if you can help."

Her coffee had started to cool. "Where's Ozzy from?"

"Miami."

"Does he have a support system in place there?"

"That would be something for Ozzy to say, wouldn't it?"

She raised her eyebrows. "Sorry?"

"Bill talked to you and gave you information. Ozzy did not. There is a difference."

She pressed her lips together and nodded. "Fair enough." When he opened his mouth, she held up her hand and said, "That wasn't sarcasm. I understand, Rick." She paused. "What does the rest of your day look like?"

He drained his coffee and crushed the cup. "Take care of my men. I need to secure washing machines and get the men access to computer terminals. We have weapons to clean, gear to replace. They're meeting me in the ready room in about twenty minutes."

She gave a soft smile. "Thank you for the coffee."

He pulled a slip of paper out of his shirt pocket and slid it across the table. "That's my cell number. If you need anything, call me. Don't text me. I really hate that." He stood and picked up both their cups. "See you later, Doc."

The smell of gun oil, known as CLP for cleaner, lubricant, and preservative, filled the room. Rick's team pulled tables and chairs from other offices into the room, and each of them found a spot to disassemble their M4s. Rick also cleaned Bill's. Waller had joined the team and took care of Ozzy's. After Rick examined his bolt carrier and made sure it had no cracks and the spring to ensure it moved well, he used a brush to clean the inside, then rubbed a thin coat of CLP onto it.

Fisher had finished cleaning his weapon and reassembled it. Now he had out a ceramic sharpening rod and a leather strap to sharpen his knife. The sound of the blade scraping across the rod in rhythmic motions blended in with the smattering of conversation.

"I went and saw Ozzy today," Swanson said. "His spirit is dark, man."

Fisher examined his blade and ran his thumbnail over the edge of it. "Wish we could do something for him."

Rick nodded. "Pray for him. Pray with him. That's what will lift Ozzy. Nothing else we can do."

"Yeah," Fisher said. He went back to the ceramic rod.

Swanson pulled his machete out of his bag and started unwinding the tape from the handle. "Where you from, Waller?"

The medic looked up from his work. "Kentucky. Charula."

"Can-tucky? Just like Daddy here."

"Same high school."

Swanson glanced at Rick with a grin. "You ganging up on us, Cap?"

181

"Something like that." He pointed his CLP-slicked finger toward Waller. "He deployed with Third Group."

"And Tenth," Waller said.

"I was in Tenth. Three years ago," Fisher said. "Colorado was not my favorite."

"No? Altitude mess with you?" Waller asked.

"Yeah, man. Never did feel like I could breathe right. It was a relief to PCS from there even if it was to Bragg." Fisher slid the bolt into place on his weapon. "When were you there?"

"Now. My wife's busy dealing with packers and movers this week."

"Waller, Waller," McBride said. "Kentucky. Isn't there a bourbon called Weller?"

"I believe there is," Peña said, laughing.

"Perfection. Waller, you are Kentucky Bourbon." He pointed at his chest. "I'm Jerry Maguire, because I happen to have the first name of Gerald." He pointed at Swanson. "Daniel Swanson, also known as Pot Pie."

"I can't imagine how you made that leap," Waller said dryly.

Everyone laughed as McBride continued. "Travis Fisher, but he is better known to us as Trout." Finally, he pointed at Peña. "Jorge Peña. You two can hang together, Kentucky Bourbon, because he is better known to us as Peña Colada."

Waller nodded and smiled. "Ironic how I always get the bourbon name."

"Do you mind?"

Waller shook his head and answered with a straight face. "Not a drop."

Rick enjoyed the conversation as background noise while

he thought about Cynthia. He'd never met a woman who invoked such extreme reactions from him. She could make him so angry, and then that shifted to a desire to protect her and shield her from any and all harm. He admired her skill as a doctor and wanted to soothe her after the way she took Ozzy's prognosis so hard. In the end, though, her perspective of what he did for a living, of the passion God had placed in his soul for this life—he didn't think he could ignore something like that. He figured she couldn't either.

So why, while sitting here cleaning weapons she abhorred, was he unable to get her off his mind? He needed to just dismiss her altogether. He'd gotten her back here. Safe. Alive. Mission accomplished.

When they finished cleaning their weapons and he inspected them, he left everyone logging onto computers to call or write home. Given the time zone differences, that would close out their day.

He went back to medical. Bill reclined on a mountain of pillows with his head back, eyes closed, and headphones on. Rick tapped his toe as he pulled the stool close to the bed.

"This was just getting to the good part," Bill said, sliding the headphones off.

"What book are you listening to?"

"Murder mystery set in New York during World War II. Pretty good." He looked at his screen. "Written by Violet Pearl. They have a nice library here. All ebooks and audiobooks, but that's cool. Pot Pie brought me my phone out of my locker."

"Doctor Myers told me you don't want to go to Alabama."

A shadow fell across Bill's face. "Rick, don't."

"I'm not lecturing or 'shoulding' or anything. I'm letting

you know that Colonel Jenkins is going to make sure you stay in Germany. Then when you're medically released, you'll come back here or hook up with us wherever we are."

Relief filled his brown eyes, making them shine. "Appreciate it."

Rick slapped his knee and stood. "You need to go home and visit your grandmother. How about I go with you next Christmas?"

Bill shook his head. "No way. Not Christmas. All the crazy comes out then. How about Easter? She leaves Meemaw alone at Easter so she won't have to go to church."

"It's February. We won't be home by Easter."

Bill grinned. "Even better. Easter next year."

"We'll work something out." Rick started out of the area and turned on his heel. "You good?"

His best friend tapped his chest. "I'm good, bro."

CHAPTER

★

FIFTEEN

Cynthia secured a computer terminal inside the embassy. She could have done it at the hotel, but she liked being around the people here, so she stayed at the embassy even after checking on her patients. With data and electricity so precious in her village, she just stored emails to answer whenever she returned to civilization. Consequently, she had about five months of catching up to do.

For two hours she looked at pictures, read messages, replied. She smiled, laughed, cried with friends. It felt so good to get back in touch.

Her best friend, Dahlia, had sent a weekly email, telling Cynthia about her life and her toddler, Theo. Cynthia ran her fingers over the picture of his face on the screen, remembering the day she'd delivered him like it was yesterday. He had grown so much since she'd left!

She typed a moderately detailed email and promised to call her friend as soon as she could. As she pressed send,

Secret Service Special Agent Zachary Monroe appeared at her elbow. "Doctor Myers?"

She glanced up and frowned. "Yes?"

"The vice president has asked that you join him tonight at a dinner in the home of the president of Katangela."

A state dinner? She really didn't enjoy those on a good day. So much pomp and press and everything done for the sake of show. She shook her head. "I'm afraid I don't have anything appropriate to wear for a state dinner with me."

He nodded. "Yes, ma'am. I've been instructed to escort you to your hotel. You have several articles of clothing from which to choose for tonight waiting on you there."

Annoyance brought a sarcastic retort to her lips, but she pressed them together. This man had nothing to do with the decision-making process that had brought the two of them together for this conversation. "I guess I don't have an excuse, then, do I?"

Monroe didn't respond to her words. He didn't smile. He simply said, "I have a car out front whenever you're ready."

She understood that to mean that he expected she would be ready right now, because the vice president had deemed it so. With a sigh, she logged out of the computer and stood, slinging her backpack over her shoulders.

Monroe handed her down into the car and shut her door but did not join her inside. The car held a standard detail of two agents, neither of whom she recognized. She didn't feel like making small talk, so she sat in the back of the small sedan and endured the five-minute ride in silence. When they pulled up in front of the hotel's main entrance, she let herself out of the car before someone could open her door and paused at the window of the driver. He lowered it.

"What time does this event begin?" she asked.

"Eight."

She looked at her watch. "I have four hours. You don't need to wait for me. Just please be here at quarter to eight."

"We'll wait here, ma'am."

"That's certainly your prerogative, but I'm not coming down until 7:45."

He nodded. "Yes, ma'am."

She chewed on her bottom lip as she crossed the lobby. At the front desk, the smiling clerk beamed in her direction. "*Bonjour*, mademoiselle."

"*Bonjour*." Speaking French made her suddenly miss Ayo and Tadeas. "I was told some dresses were delivered to me."

She gave him her name and room number, and he clicked and clacked on his computer. "Ah, yes, they were delivered to your room."

"My room?"

"*Oui.*"

After thanking him, she headed up to her room, trying to decide how she felt about the fact that a dress delivery waited for her inside an area she had locked and secured. Her father claimed that danger hung over her to the point that he wanted to force her to leave the country, yet someone on his staff had presumed to enter her personal space here.

As she entered her room, she eyed the garment rack standing next to the couch. She discovered four complete outfits, each one tasteful and simple in a way that matched her personal style. She had her choice of red, silver, black, or blue. Her mother had obviously had everything to do with the choices. She settled on a rich, royal blue sheath that had wide shoulder straps and fit tight all the way to the floor. A slit up one leg reached just above her knee. Silver embroidery formed an elaborate design along the neckline and down the V-shaped opening in the back. The material glittered and shone in the light when she moved.

On the table, she found bags and boxes that contained jewelry and hair and styling accoutrements. She wouldn't need any jewelry with this dress because of the appliqués.

After she took a long shower, enjoying the hot water with good water pressure, she dried her hair and secured it in a simple French twist. She dug around in her bag and found some makeup that she hadn't touched in five months. Looking through the boxes of shoes, she found silver heels. As she slipped her feet into them, she wondered if she'd even be able to walk in heels all night after months of wearing boots. The matching blue clutch held her cell phone and room key with just a little space to spare.

At 7:40, she walked down the hallway. As she approached the elevator, it opened and Rick stepped out. When he saw her, his steps faltered until he just stopped moving. He looked at her with wide, unblinking eyes and a stoic expression.

She nervously ran her hand down her stomach, then brushed at the skirt. "Hi."

He nodded. "Hello." The rich baritone of his voice hung in the air.

"I, uh, have to join my father for dinner at the president's home."

His beard moved with his smile. "And here I was hoping you'd gotten all dressed up for me. I would have loved to have dinner with you again tonight."

Her heart fluttered. "I would too. Unfortunately, the Secret Service whisked me away this afternoon." She nervously

188

pointed toward her room. "I don't know who did it or how, but I had clothes and shoes waiting on me. It's all incredibly interesting. Well, annoying really, but also interesting."

He looked toward her room and narrowed his eyes. "They went into your room?"

"Yeah." She cleared her throat. "I wish they'd left it with the front desk or something. It would have been less creepy."

He glanced around, then frowned. "Will you do me a favor?"

"Of course."

"When you get back tonight, will you call my room from the lobby? I'll meet you and walk you to yours."

"Uh, sure." After a pause she asked, "Why?"

He grinned. "Do I need a reason to ask a beautiful woman to call me?"

She blushed. People had called her all sorts of things—*short* usually at the top of the list—but never *beautiful*. "I'll call. But now I have to go, or they'll definitely come up here looking for me."

"Have an amazing time tonight, Cynthia." He pivoted to watch her make her way to the elevator.

She paused at the elevator and smiled at him over her shoulder. "I'll try."

She wore a silly grin the entire ride down. Something about Rick Norton made her feel capable, worthwhile. Rather the opposite of how Andrew, her philandering former fiancé, had left her feeling. As she floated across the lobby, someone whistled. She glanced over and spotted McBride and Swanson.

"Looking good, Doc," Swanson said. "No offense."

McBride nodded. "Careful, Doc. You'll break hearts walking around looking like that."

With a giggle and a wave, she breezed through the doors and out of the hotel. Immediately a car pulled up. A different agent than before got out of the passenger's side and opened the back door for her. As she slid into the car, she saw her father.

"Daddy," she said. "I didn't expect you here."

He put down the paper he was reading and focused on her. He had on a black tuxedo with a white vest and white bow tie. "Ah, you chose the blue. I told Margaret that was my favorite."

Margaret had worked as her father's assistant for twenty years. "She always has good taste."

"She always listens to your mother." He patted her knee. "Tonight will be fun. I'm glad you're my guest."

They rode in silence for a few moments. She tried to relax so he wouldn't see how tense she was.

Finally, he said, "I don't appreciate having to make you heed my caution."

Startled, she looked at him. "I beg your pardon?"

"I wanted you to choose to leave. Now I have to play the bad guy."

With eyes wide, she asked, "How will you do that?"

He fiddled with his tie before he said, "Katangela will revoke your visa effective the end of this month."

She gasped. "Why would you do that?"

"You forced my hand. You could have made a different decision—the right decision."

Anger boiled in her chest, and she clenched her hands. "I'm willing to risk it. It's a big jungle. They're not going to come looking for me to deport me."

His face turned hard. "They will if I ask them to."

He had never forced his hand with her. Even in her most rebellious, attitude-driven teenage years, the two of them had shared a special bond. She didn't even know how to fight with him.

They glared at each other for several moments before he said, "I won't hesitate to ask them to revoke the privileges of your entire organization from this country if it means getting you out of here. Don't test me."

She sat back in her chair and turned to look out the window. Tears burned in her eyes, but she would not shed them. Fury rippled through her, compounded by the fact that he chose to give her the news right now, on the way to an important state dinner. She looked at her dress. He knew she didn't approve of the pomp and circumstance that came with high-level politics, didn't like shows of wealth and privilege, and absolutely hated having cars sent for her when she had other means of transportation. Tonight, she'd set all of that aside to spend time with him, a man she loved and respected and had missed.

She ran her hand down her skirt and swallowed tears. He'd chosen an expensive way to make his point that she would compromise her standards for him. She'd risk his wrath on her, but she couldn't risk his wrath on the mission she worked for. That would affect hundreds of missionaries and thousands of people—including Tadeas and Ayo. Obviously, her father knew this or he wouldn't have threatened it. He had a tendency to keep his promises.

"It's wrong of you to do this. I can't believe you're betraying me this way." She looked at him again. "I've spent my entire life seeking purpose. In my little clinic a hundred kilometers away, I could feel God's pleasure in what I was doing. There are ways you can help me be here clandestinely. That would take way less power than what you're wielding to force me to go home." She looked back out the window. "I do not want to be on your arm tonight."

He stayed silent as the car slowed to turn into a long drive. It stopped at the wrought-iron gate, and armed guards approached either side of the car. The driver spoke to one of the guards, and they waved the car by as the gate slid open.

"I'm sorry you feel that way," her father said. "You are my priority, and I'm only keeping you safe. One day you'll thank me. But one thing is certain, you won't embarrass me tonight. Please get out of the car with a smile on your face when we arrive."

She glared at him. "Or what?"

"Or your mother will be humiliated, because the press will see you and stir everything up again. This is what I'm calling your soft launch back into the world. I love you and I'm trying to make it easier for you."

Her teeth ached as she clenched her jaw and focused her gaze on the mansion that came into view. It housed the president who ran a country from his elaborate home while villages without electricity or plumbing or even basic medical needs were terrorized by rebels. If it wasn't for the mission groups who came in and dug wells, inoculated children, and installed generators, then those children would never have been inoculated and villagers still wouldn't have clean water.

But her father was a clever man. First, she'd never do anything to humiliate her mother. She'd seen too many children in her parents' circles who manipulated and connived and embarrassed on a regular basis. That would never be her.

Second, this *would* work as a soft launch. It would put

her in the sights of the press without the framework of the northern Virginia/Washington, DC, society. It would put her in a position of authority on her father's arm in lieu of her mother.

"Fine," she spat.

The car slid to a halt, and a man in an emerald-green uniform with gold adornment opened the door. As she got out of the car, she thanked him in French and stood to the side to wait for her father.

Rick sat back in his chair at the head of the table and laughed at a joke that Swanson made. He took a drink of sparkling water and looked at his team. They'd invited Waller to join them in the hotel restaurant. Rick had done some checking up on the young medic and decided he fit perfectly. He thanked God for bringing him to the team. He hated to lose Ozzy, but this would end up as a good thing for his unit.

He thought about the way Cynthia had looked tonight. Maybe if he'd known he would encounter her dressed like that, he would have had more control of his reaction. She'd taken his breath away until his mind fogged up and everything around him stilled. It amazed him that he'd even had the faculty to speak.

Swanson held up a piece of meat on his fork. "I don't know what this is, but it's amazing."

Peña laughed. "It's probably hippo."

Rick shook his head. "It's goat. Staple meat here."

Swanson put it in his mouth and spoke around it. "I'm good with that."

"Beats an MRE any day." Fisher took a bite of his own food.

They'd ordered a family-style meal. Platters of meat and vegetables, breads and sauces filled the long table. Rick noticed a dish that looked similar to the one Cynthia had eaten last night and added that to his plate. He enjoyed the flavor as much as he thought he would.

McBride reached across Peña and grabbed a piece of bread from the basket. "Did anybody read about the Super Bowl today?"

"I did," Fisher said. "Can't believe they made it."

As the conversation moved to sports, Rick's mind floated back to Cynthia. He did not like that anyone had taken the liberty to enter her room without her permission. It had taken true restraint not to go in himself, to search for bugs or cameras or any kind of hidden threat.

Suddenly, it occurred to him how much she had dominated his mind, and he wondered why. Maybe because of the way she'd looked in that dress, the way it made his mouth go dry? Or maybe the way she moved in the heels that gave her a little bit of height? Or the way she smelled, like a lavender field after a summer rain . . .

"Hey, Captain," Peña said, interrupting his thoughts. "Do you still have the van? The rec room at the embassy is really nice. Thought we might want to go shoot some pool."

He patted his pocket and felt the keys. "Yep. Let's get out of here."

By orders from Colonel Jenkins, they could go only to the hotel or the embassy. His team desperately needed some decompression. Better the rec room at the embassy than the hotel bar on the next level. Rick would gladly drive them.

They paid their bill and went out to the parking lot. The heat from the day still clung to the pavement. For the first time since they had come into the country, it hadn't rained once today. The air felt heavier, hotter.

It didn't take long to get back to the embassy. Soon, both pool tables had tournaments going, and Rick sat back in an easy chair with yesterday's newspaper. He skimmed headlines, read a couple of articles, and contemplated going up to medical to check on Ozzy and Bill when his phone rang.

It took a couple of seconds for him to dig it out of his pocket. It wasn't a US number. Expecting it to be a wrong number, he answered in French. "*Allô?*"

"Rick?" Cynthia's voice came through in a frantic whisper. "You have to help us."

CHAPTER

★

SIXTEEN

Even though she had attended several events with her father as the senator, the scaled-up version that came with the title of vice president surprised Cynthia. Her father was the focus of attention, the highlight of the evening, and everyone wanted to speak with him or be seen speaking with him. Private paid photographers wandered around snapping pictures while news reporters in a cordoned-off area filmed the event from afar.

Early in the evening, President Akinjide had introduced his daughter Zalika to Cynthia. Zalika was tall and thin and wore a turquoise-and-orange sheath with patterns that reminded Cynthia of peacock feathers. The colors provided a striking contrast against her dark skin.

"Zalika just returned to us from Cambridge," President Akinjide said in English. "She is a doctor like you."

Cynthia smiled. "It's nice to meet you. What kind of medicine do you practice?"

"I have a degree in infectious diseases," Zalika said. "I hope to help the people of my country." She and Cynthia stepped into a quieter corner. "I understand you have been here for several months."

"I have. In a village about a hundred kilometers from here. I had an obstetrics clinic, but we also treated general medicine needs." Cynthia stopped a passing waiter. "Do you have sparkling water?"

He nodded and left them.

"I would love to talk to you some more and learn of the medical needs you saw away from the city." Zalika sighed. "Of course, the needs of this city could consume all of my time and energy and I'd never make a dent."

Cynthia thought of the conversation she'd had with her father. "I'm afraid I won't be here much longer. My father's new position makes it impossible for me to remain."

"I understand. Our country is in a very tenuous place right now."

"I'm happy to correspond with you, though. I've been here for five months and treated people from several villages."

Zalika smiled warmly. "We will have to make sure that our information is exchanged."

The waiter returned with a silver tray bearing a single glass of sparkling water with a slice of lime on the rim. She smiled and thanked him. As she reached for the glass, she noticed what looked like blood on the cuff of his white shirt. With a frown, she nonchalantly tried to look closer and thought she saw the edge of a burn mark on his wrist. When she looked back at his face, he still had a pleasant expression.

"*Merci*," Cynthia whispered, taking the glass from the

tray. He nodded and turned away. She turned back to her new friend. "Zalika? Who hires the staff for your father's events?"

Zalika looked around. "He has a security officer who is in charge of that. Everyone is carefully screened."

Should she call Rick? And tell him what? That she was likely suffering from some form of post-traumatic stress and thought the waiter served in Chukuwereije's army? That she had mentally transposed the edge of a burn on his wrist into Chukuwereije's brand? Besides, pulling a phone out during a state dinner was the height of rudeness. She glanced in the direction of the press area. She'd suffered enough at their hands. No way would she intentionally give them fodder.

Her father beckoned her from across the room with a single lift of a finger, and she set her water down, untouched, and joined him. She met the First Lady and her son, smiled for several photographs, and stepped to the side again as her father took the podium and spoke about the US support for the people of Katangela. He made no mention of the Green Beret team down the road who had come to aid in fighting the people bent on insurrection.

The constant flashes of the dozens of cameras dazzled her eyes, so she looked down or to the side, trying to avoid their strobes.

Finally, they went into the dining room, escaping the press and the cameras and the yelling of questions that went unanswered. Cynthia found herself seated next to Zalika on one side and the minister of the Cabinet of Health on the other. The wide table prevented her from conversing comfortably with the First Lady across from her.

As they served the first course, Cynthia tried to look at the wrists of the servers but never managed to catch a glimpse.

Nervous energy hummed up and down her spine. What should she do?

Out of the eye of the press, she slipped her phone out of her purse and set it in her lap. As discreetly as possible, she powered it on and waited. She could feel it go through the various vibrations as it booted up. Five minutes later she had a break enough in the conversation and accessed her contacts, pulling up Rick's number.

"Is everything okay, Doctor?" the health minister asked.

She smiled over at him. "Certainly."

He gestured with his spoon. "Is the asparagus soup not to your liking?"

As much as she didn't want to even try to eat, she picked up her spoon and took a small sip of the soup. "Mmm," she said with a closed-lip smile. "Delicious."

He nodded and turned the other direction. Cynthia stirred her soup to make it look as if she were eating. When a waiter appeared at her elbow, she jumped and dropped her spoon. It clattered against the side of the bowl. "Sorry," she said. He took the dish away, and someone else placed a plate of horse mackerel in front of her.

She flaked off a small bite, then carefully chewed. Her stomach protested the presence of food, so she slowly sliced another piece off and just ran it through the sauce.

Zalika engaged her in conversation. She tried to pay attention to it, but every time she felt movement behind her, she held her breath. Finally, she closed her eyes and took a deep breath in through her nose. *Please, God, help me relax.*

As she opened her eyes, everything suddenly felt like it had decelerated to slow motion. The waitstaff wheeled in carts with trays covered in silver domes. She glanced down the table at her father, who wore his polite, "I'm at an important dinner" smile and nodded at the president as he took a drink of water. Her gaze went back to the carts. Before she could even process what she saw, the waiters lifted the domes, and pistols sat where the food should be.

She gasped and opened and shut her mouth, unable to form a sound. With shaking hands, she swiped at her phone screen and hit the button to dial Rick's number as the armed men circled the room.

A loud explosion shook the room. Her gaze flew to the two men on her father's detail as they spun toward the sound of the explosion.

"No!" she yelled when two waiters shot the men in the backs of their heads. They fell to the floor, their hands on weapons that never cleared the holsters.

Immediately, she dove under the table before the rest of the room even knew what had happened. "Come on, come on," she whispered, listening to the screams of the people at the table.

On the fourth ring, Rick answered, "*Allô?*"

"Rick?" she said in a frantic whisper, so relieved to hear his voice that tears started streaming down her face. "You have to help us."

"What happened?" His voice took on the hard tone she recognized from the jungle.

"Chukuwereije." A hand grabbed her from behind and dragged her up. As she dropped the phone, she yelled, "Hurry!"

★ ★ ★

They arrived at the president's mansion thirty-two minutes after Cynthia's call. They'd had to change into their uniforms and gear while conferring with leadership. While the Department of Homeland Security, which controlled the Secret Service, and the Department of Defense, which controlled Rick's team, argued with the US State Department over details like precedence and jurisdiction, Rick had his men secure weapons and ammunition so that when Colonel Jenkins gave the go, they would go with no delay. The entire time, Rick thanked God that they had all stayed together, that half of his team hadn't abandoned them for the hotel bar, and that they'd invited Waller tonight. So many different things had gone right to bring everyone into the same room in proximity of weapons and gear that he could only believe God had arranged it so.

They saw no movement at the big iron gate. He put the van in park as the large SUV carrying the remaining Secret Service detail pulled up. Technically, legally the Secret Service had the lead on this mission due to the danger to the vice president. However, their boss and Colonel Jenkins agreed that since Rick's team's original mission was to capture and subdue Chukuwereije, and since they had specialized training in urban assaults, they would take the lead until the Secret Service could secure the vice president.

McBride and Fisher leaped out of the van, making surprisingly little noise for their size and weight, and investigated, finding the guards dead. Fisher figured out how to open the gate and initiated that, then the two rejoined the team.

Rick was grateful the van he'd rented was an older model and he could turn off all the lights. He didn't drive all the way to the front door. Instead, he parked just out of view of the house, and everyone quietly got out. They didn't bother shutting the doors behind them.

Weapons ready, they stayed low and hugged the shadows, spread out tactically more than ten feet apart with overlapping fields of fire, and prepared to meet any threat.

The Secret Service had given Colonel Jenkins the schematics of the house, and as far as Rick could reckon in the precious minutes he'd spent studying the layout, he decided they'd breach the front door as a team. He didn't have enough shooters or time to reconnoiter or split them up.

They encountered no resistance. Clearly, the enemy did not expect anyone to challenge them from the outside. The front door stood slightly ajar. At Rick's signal, Fisher pushed it open and kept a grip on the large iron door handle while sweeping the room at knee level with the pistol grip of the M4. Behind him, McBride swept the room at eye level. Moving his weapon in the opposite direction, Rick sought targets at waist level. They'd practiced breaching rooms like this for hours in places like Fort Bragg, Fort Benning, and improvised tactical shoot houses on forward operating bases all over the planet.

They entered an empty foyer. Swanson walked backward into the room, covering the team's back with sweeps of his carbine. Beside him, Waller alternated facing forward and backward, protecting their left flank, while Peña did the same on their right. The six men covered every inch of space around them and moved as if they were a twelve-legged beast, in perfect concert.

Moving silently, the team glided across the span of the room, communicating only with hand signals. Rick looked up at the tall ceiling in the foyer as he moved soundlessly on the tile floor. He and Waller went into the first room on the right, one of them automatically aiming high and the other low. It appeared to be a library. Full bookshelves rose three stories up. They went back into the hall, walking carefully, listening for every sound.

Another room to the left revealed a wall full of hunting prizes. A lion frozen in midroar, a zebra, a rhinoceros. Elephant tusks hung over the mantel, and the scent of tobacco hung in the air. Rick's lip curled in distaste.

As they moved back into the foyer, a gunshot sounded from a room at the end of the hall. They moved toward the sound, more alert and ready than before. They turned like the hands on a clock, rotating through the hallway, checking every corner and every shadow as they rolled up to the door.

Another gunshot. Perhaps seven seconds had passed since the first shot. As they came to the room from which the gunfire had originated, a third shot sounded.

Rick faced back in the direction they had come. At his signal, Swanson kicked the door open, and the team went in, weapons ready. In a swift, almost singular movement, Peña and McBride shot the two men who raised guns in their direction. They collapsed in front of a roped-off area confining perhaps twenty people.

The hostages all knelt on the ground, facing the wall, their hands laced behind their heads. They sobbed, cowered, and cried. Three people lay dead. It looked like Rick's team had stopped an execution of the entire group.

"Stay put," Rick told them in English as they swept through the room. No one said a word, no one picked up a camera or a cell phone. Apparently, they were all frozen in shock at what had almost happened to them.

Waller faced backward, covering the hallway. Rick and the remainder of the team moved past him in a flash. Rick crouched with his back to Waller while Peña and McBride swept right and Swanson and Fisher swept left. When Peña and McBride got close to the men they had shot, they each put four more bullets into the supine forms—two shots to the head and two to the chest—before raising their weapons to scan for further deadly threats.

Seconds later, Swanson and McBride both yelled, "Clear!"

Remembering the map, Rick sprang to his feet and took in his surroundings. They had entered the central ballroom. A podium stood near a wall with stage lights pointing at it. The people behind the ropes must be the press corps.

"Dawn!" Waller yelled.

A Secret Service agent in the hallway answered, "Zulu!" and Waller lowered his weapon as the Secret Service agents entered.

Rick approached the hostages and asked, "Where is the vice president?"

A woman wearing a badge bearing the logo of a major American news agency pointed at a corridor. "The dining room, through there." As he turned away, she said, "The waitstaff did this."

In his peripheral vision, he watched two Secret Service agents approach the press corps with weapons drawn. He knew they'd all be questioned and vetted before the agents released them.

After a low whistle and a circling motion with his index finger, Rick's team moved as one again to the end of the room. The corridor branched off in two directions. He sent Waller, Fisher, and Swanson to the left toward the kitchen to neutralize anyone they found there. He, McBride, and Peña went right.

They paused at the door and waited for the report about the kitchen. After several minutes, Swanson's voice came quietly over their comms. "Had to secure a couple of hostiles. There's a door here to the dining room. We're ready."

Using his hands to direct the two with him, Rick spoke into the mic. "On three. One, two." Steeling himself for what he might find on the other side of the door, he said, "Three!"

CHAPTER

★

SEVENTEEN

The man who dragged Cynthia out from under the table hauled her by her hair and all but tossed her into a corner. She went to Zalika, who had blood pouring down her face. She cupped the woman's face in her hand and tilted her head, trying to see the gash on her temple. "What did they do?" she asked.

"Hit me with a gun."

Zalika needed stitches. A man standing next to them had a handkerchief in his tuxedo pocket. "May I?" she asked, pulling it out of his pocket before he replied. She pressed it against the wound. "Keep pressure on it."

She knew she should feel scared, but she was angry—and focused, looking for someone who might need medical care, trying to pay attention to everything that was happening around her so she could act when the time came.

The waitstaff had separated them into two groups. Those her father would call civilians—spouses, companions, and such—huddled together, while the government officials knelt on the floor on the other side of the table. The waitstaff had shed their jackets and held everyone at gunpoint, staring at them with steely eyes and hard mouths.

The sharp smell of gunpowder hung in the air, reminding Cynthia of burning orange peels. She glanced up and saw the holes in the ceiling that had come from the men firing their weapons in the air. A woman sobbed somewhere in her group. Cynthia looked around and spotted her in the arms of a man in traditional Katangela dress.

A man in an olive-green military uniform strolled through the door. He had salt-and-pepper hair, a close-cut gray beard, and nearly charcoal-black skin. Two men with Kalashnikov rifles flanked him. He walked directly up to where her father knelt next to the president and asked in French, "Mr. Akinjide, do you know who I am?"

The president glared up at him. "You are Chukuwereije. Your men have terrorized my people for years."

Chukuwereije nodded to a man standing with him, who stepped forward and punched President Akinjide in the cheek with a gloved fist. Zalika gasped. The sound of the punch sickened Cynthia. The man had probably supplemented his glove with something like steel shot.

"You mean your starving people? The poor and destitute who live out in the jungle? People who travel for days just to get basic medical care provided by Western pigs?" Chukuwereije tapped his chest. "I have not been the one terrorizing your people. They are yours to terrorize after all."

President Akinjide straightened, his cheek split and already swelling. "You have killed innocent people, maimed mothers, stolen children. You are an evil man."

Chukuwereije nodded again, and the soldier punched the president in the abdomen. The president fell forward and didn't immediately straighten.

The terrorist focused his attention on a man next to her father. "You are Apst Gatawwa, minister of the interior."

The man in the white jacket with gold flourish nodded and raised his chin. "I am Minister Gatawwa."

"Minister Gatawwa." Chukuwereije gestured in his direction, and the soldier behind the kneeling officials walked up behind the minister. "For crimes against your people, I find you guilty."

Before Cynthia could think, the soldier shot the minister in the back of the head, and the man slumped forward. She gasped as women screamed, and another official in the line with her father started to cry. President Akinjide roused, saw his minister lying near him, and tried to reach out to him, but the soldier grabbed him by the back of the collar and hauled him up. He demanded the president put his hands behind his head.

Cynthia could see her father's arms trembling behind his head. He couldn't hold that position indefinitely. She prayed for strength for him to endure whatever came next. He looked at her, his eyes calm, his expression unreadable.

Zalika had her arms wrapped around herself, and even though her entire body trembled, she made no sound. Would Chukuwereije go after the daughters of the two men, or would he leave them alone?

Her answer came much too soon. Chukuwereije gestured at Zalika. "You will come to me."

A soldier stepped forward and grabbed Zalika's arm, hauled her to her feet, and pulled her over to stand in front of the warlord. He roughly grabbed her chin in his hand and twisted her face to one side, then the other. "The doctor has returned to her own country. How much did it cost the people of Katangela to educate you in the West?" He sneered. "My men are looking forward to you. But first, you must kill your father."

Cynthia gasped again and covered her mouth. *Please, God*, she silently begged. *Please end this.*

Zalika lifted her chin. "I will not."

Chukuwereije barked an order, and a soldier approached Cynthia's group again. He grabbed a woman in a blue-and-white dress and threw her on the ground in front of him, ignoring her cries as he put the muzzle of his weapon against her head.

"You will kill him, or I'll kill her," Chukuwereije said.

Zalika looked at the woman. Tears filled her eyes, then streamed down her face. "You can do that, and you probably will. That makes you a killer of another person, yet it won't force me to kill my father."

"Then I'll go through everyone, one at a time, until they're all dead." He put his nose against hers. "And that will be your doing, Princess Akinjide."

Cynthia admired the woman's courage as she replied, "It's Doctor Akinjide. And it will not be my doing. Their blood will be on your hands, and my father's blood will never be on mine."

Clearly, Chukuwereije did not usually encounter someone brave enough to contradict him. He grabbed Zalika by her hair and twisted her around. She stood at an odd angle, pain registering all over her face. Then he pushed her toward a tall man near the kitchen door. "Do what you will. Perhaps by the time you've finished, she'll feel more compliant."

"No!" The strangled cry ripped itself out of Cynthia's throat as Zalika fought and scraped against the two men who dragged her toward the kitchen.

The warlord focused on her. "Ah, Doctor Myers," he said in English while wagging a scolding finger. "I have been looking for you."

Before she could process his words, two men grabbed her arms and dragged her to stand in front of him. She looked him in the eyes. They were so dark they were nearly black, cold. She could see no empathy or kindness in them at all—just an emptiness that caused a chill to go down her spine.

"I found my son's body. He'd been dumped like a dead pig. But you know something? Under his body was a glove that could only have come from your clinic." He grabbed her by the throat, moving as fast as a cobra striking. "Tell me, Doctor, how you let my son die. Explain it to me."

Her breath hitched. "If he'd been on the steps of the best emergency department in the world, he would have died from his injuries. I hadn't even examined him when he took his last breath."

"So you didn't even try to save him. Just as I thought." Even as he talked about his dead son, she saw nothing on his face—no sorrow, no regret. He snatched her hair and turned her toward her father, then lifted his gun to her father's head. "I wonder how hard you will work to save your own family."

★ ★ ★

Rick's team breached the door. Rick saw President Akinjide kneeling next to Vice President Myers along with four other men in formal African dress. They all had their hands laced behind their heads. Akinjide had sweat pouring down his face. Next to him, a man lay facedown on the ground, apparently shot in the head.

In his right hand Chukuwereije had a pistol pointed at the back of the vice president's head, and he held Cynthia by the hair with his left hand. Two soldiers stood to one side of him, and another stood next to a group of people in formal dress. The corners of the room appeared empty, and he saw no one under the table.

All of this information he processed in the split second it took him to enter the room and raise his weapon. "Got him," he said into the mic as he squeezed the trigger without any hesitation and fired a single shot. His bullet hit its mark, and Chukuwereije went down, dragging Cynthia with him. She cried out and clawed at her hair.

He waited until his men had followed protocol by ensuring their respective targets had departed from the land of the living. All he wanted to do was rush to Cynthia. Vice President Myers had turned around and taken her into his arms. She had her arms around his neck, sobbing.

Rick radioed base to let them know they had taken out Chukuwereije and all of the soldiers present. From the kitchen door, the woman Swanson had identified as President Akinjide's daughter came running. She headed straight for her father, whose aide had helped him to his feet.

"Are you okay?" the president asked her in French.

"*Oui*, Papa." She pointed at Waller. "He saved me before . . ." She cleared her throat. "Before anything could happen."

Waller nodded to the president. "No thanks needed. It was my pleasure, sir."

"Thank heaven," he exclaimed. He turned to Rick. "Thank you. How did you know?"

"Doctor Myers called me." Unable to stay away another second, Rick went over to Cynthia and her father.

The vice president looked up at Rick, unshed tears in his eyes. Rick read no condemnation for his killing of the warlord.

"Are you hurt?" he asked, kneeling with them.

She looked up at him, her face streaked with tears and once more with blood that was not hers. "Thank you," she said, then released her father and threw her arms around him. "I knew you'd come."

He helped her to her feet but didn't let her go. The feel of her in his arms was too perfect to just relinquish right away.

Four Secret Service agents ran into the room and straight to the vice president. Two of them stood behind him, and the other two moved a little farther back and into the crowd of people.

Vice President Myers held out his hand. "Captain," he said, "thank you. How did you know to come?"

Rick squeezed Cynthia close. "Your daughter called me, sir."

With a quizzical look, the vice president asked her, "How?"

"The waiter out in the ballroom had the Chukuwereije scar on his wrist," Cynthia said. "At least, I saw the edge of it and thought that's what it was. So I wanted to call Rick—I mean, Captain Norton—but didn't because I thought I was being paranoid. You know, kind of a post-reaction to everything happening."

He raised his eyebrows. "And?"

"And I watched the waitstaff really closely. I kept waiting for one of them to, I guess, do what they did. I kept my phone in my lap and had Rick's number ready."

Rick was so proud of Cynthia's insight and the way she'd trusted her instincts. As much as he didn't want to, he reluctantly let her go and looked down at her. The shadows in her eyes had started to dim. She looked more in control, less terrified. "You going to be okay?" he asked gently.

She gave a closed-lip smile and brushed at his uniform jacket. "I am now."

President Akinjide approached. "Mr. Myers, I cannot express my horror over what happened tonight," he said. "I feel like apologies will never be enough."

The vice president held out his hand. "None required, Mr. President. I'm thankful for the quick response of my team here."

"As am I, sir. As am I." He turned to Rick. "We owe you and your team our lives."

Rick didn't know how to respond. He didn't often come face-to-face with presidents of countries where he'd been assigned. "We're thankful for the quick thinking of Doctor Myers that allowed us to respond quickly."

The door burst open, and the members of the press corps descended.

Rick spoke into his mic. "Exfiltrate through the kitchen. Try to keep from getting your face photographed on the way out." He looked at the vice president. "We can't be here with the press, sir. With your permission, I'll get my men back to the embassy."

The vice president nodded and rubbed Cynthia's shoulders before he turned toward the group crossing the room.

CHAPTER

EIGHTEEN

The rapping on her door made Cynthia's breath catch in her throat. Heart pounding, she tiptoed across the room. With her back to the wall, she stared at the door on her left, waiting.

Waiting for what?

Shaking her head, knowing she still suffered from a reaction to tonight's events, she quickly looked through the peephole, her eyes widening when she saw Rick. She covered her heart with her hand, taking a deep, steadying breath, then put on a bright smile, threw the lock, and opened the door.

"Hi," she said.

He held up a bakery box and slowly lifted the lid. She saw a chocolate tart dotted with fresh cream and raspberries. How did he know her favorite dessert?

"Mind if I come in?" he asked.

"Please do," she said, stepping back. She looked at the clock. It was nearly one in the morning.

"I was saving this for tomorrow, but I saw you on the balcony when I got back to the hotel, so I knew you were still up."

She cleared her throat. "I tried to sleep, but my mind won't shut off." Taking the box from him, she asked, "How did you get this?"

"The chef at the embassy gave it to me. Apparently, your father had ordered it for you."

"My mother takes care of those kinds of details. It's his favorite too."

He pulled two forks out of his pocket. "Would you like some?"

They sat on her balcony. The warm breeze carried the scent of the river. "Rick, promise me something," she whispered. "Never admit to my father's event coordinator that we ate this directly out of the box while drinking hotel coffee out of paper cups."

He grinned. "My lips are sealed." He kicked the leather flip-flops off his feet, settled back in the chair, and propped his ankles up on the balcony railing. "How are you feeling?"

"They didn't hurt me." A quiver went through her stomach and came out through her shoulder blades as a shiver. The physical response to his question surprised her, though it shouldn't have. She understood the psychology of post-traumatic stress. She'd just never experienced it before. "My dad told me the minister of security's wife had been taken captive by the warlord. They found her dead in the middle of the street. The minister admitted to allowing the men onto the estate in exchange for her life."

He shook his head. "You can't bargain with people like our man Chuckie. She was dead the minute they decided to use her as a bargaining chip."

"I think Zalika knew that." She took a shuddering breath. "She was so brave. She wouldn't play his game, and he didn't know what to do with her. Then he gave her to his men—" Her breath hitched.

Rick pulled his legs down and put a hand over hers. "Hey," he said, "they didn't even touch her. My men were in the kitchen when she came through the door. They probably never even knew what hit them."

Tears filled her eyes and streamed down her face. "He was going to shoot my dad. If you'd been twenty seconds later . . ."

"But I wasn't." He shifted the little table that held the cake to the side and turned to fully face her, rubbing his hands up and down her arms. "God made sure of that, didn't He? Everything was arranged. I was actually thinking about that tonight."

He made sense. Clearly, God had intervened. The tears stopped almost as quickly as they'd started. Swiping at her cheeks, she said, "I'm, like, the biggest hypocrite in the world."

He settled back and propped his legs back up. He almost lazily asked, "How so?"

She shrugged. "The first conversation we ever had, I put you down for using a gun, for perpetrating violence. My life wasn't worth the lives of the three men you killed." She picked up her cup and settled back in her chair, taking a small sip. "And then I call you tonight to come save my dad, knowing what that would entail."

He sat quiet for several moments. "You're not being a hypocrite, I don't think. You still don't think those lives were worth your own. But your father was in danger. You were saving

216

him. I think you realized the slaughter of all the people in that room wouldn't be prevented with a pacifistic approach." He sipped his coffee. "Less hypocrite and more enlightenment."

She forced a grin. "My perspective has not changed."

Rick nodded. "I know that. I just struggle with the why of it."

Cynthia studied him long enough to understand that he meant it. "Well, I have no doubt that Christ could have killed thousands with maybe just a wave of His hand. But think about it, Rick. Christ our Lord said, 'Blessed are the peacemakers, for they will be called children of God' in Matthew 5:9. And soon after, in verses 38 to 48, He declared, 'I tell you, do not resist an evil person,' and 'Love your enemies and pray for those who persecute you, that you may be children of your Father in heaven.' The children of Israel wanted the Messiah to return as a conquering king who exacted violent retribution on their enemies. Christ defied them without violence. He went with the soldiers peaceably from the garden of prayer and ultimately laid down his life. Should we Christians not be Christlike in all things?"

"I believe I do seek to be Christlike," Rick said.

Cynthia's eyes widened. "That's not what I meant—"

Rick raised a hand to forestall her rebuttal. "What I mean is that I have accepted that as a Christian and a soldier for the United States Army, involvement in armed conflict and warfare is a necessary part of life until Christ returns. I know that God called many, many people—from Joshua to Deborah to David—to commit acts of warfare in His name, from Jericho to Jerusalem. I also believe that when Christ the peacemaker returns, He will bring the wrath of God and judgment with Him. Scripture assures us that His robe will

217

be dipped in blood and a sword that will strike down the nations will proceed from His mouth, if you care to read the nineteenth chapter of Revelation starting at about verse 13."

His hand felt so good when it covered hers. With a grin she asked, "Why do I feel better when I'm with you?"

He glanced in her direction, and the look on his face made her heart rate increase. "That's a question we both ought to analyze." He looked back out over the river. "All through the steps I had to take tonight—reports, debriefs, making sure my men were okay—all I could think about was checking with the kitchen about some kind of dessert and getting back here. I've never been so distracted from my job before."

They sat in silence for a few moments. She wanted him to continue to analyze why she took up his thoughts and stayed on his mind, why he wanted to be here with her instead of with his soldiers, but she didn't know how to encourage him to speak. Instead, she asked, "So, what's next for you? Isn't your mission now concluded here?"

He didn't answer right away. They watched a riverboat glide past the hotel, the light reflecting on the water. Finally, he said, "We will likely go back and join up with our group in Djibouti. I don't know what happens after that." He glanced her way. "Most of the time I can't answer those kinds of questions. Please understand that."

She nodded. "I didn't mean to overstep."

"I didn't think you did." He laid his head back and closed his eyes. "What about you? Now that the immediate threat has passed, do you still have to leave?"

Emotion made her chest ache. "My father seems to think I will always be in danger here. He's using his influence to force my hand." Fresh tears filled her eyes. "I've never felt more fulfilled than I have in that little clinic. I don't know how I'm going to just walk away and leave Tadeas and Ayo and all the people I've come to know and love."

"You don't think he'll change his mind? Have you talked to him since everything happened tonight?"

"He's made it clear he isn't going to change his mind. The best thing for me to do is to leave with him tomorrow and readdress it back home. It was hard enough to convince him that I would be safe in the hotel instead of with him at the embassy."

"Ahh. That explains all the Secret Service around."

"Secret Service? He didn't send Secret Service with me. Well, he had someone drive me. But they didn't stick around."

Rick chuckled. "Cynthia, there are Secret Service in the parking lot, down on the riverbank in full view of this balcony, and in the lobby. How did you not see them?"

Heat flooded her cheeks. "I guess I wasn't looking for them."

"They've been here since we got here."

"Well, color me not surprised." Her neck muscles tightened almost painfully. "Should I feel embarrassed about that?"

His eyebrows drew together. "Embarrassed? Why?"

"Because I am not their detail."

He sat up straight and turned his body toward hers. "Not entirely true. He is their detail, and you were already picked as a pawn. Protecting you while he is secure inside the embassy behind Marine guards protects the interests of the country. I imagine if you had stayed at the embassy, your movements would be under much less scrutiny."

Suspicion about why he'd come to her room tonight darkened her mood. "Are you part of that scrutiny?"

He looked at her for several moments with disappointment on his face before he said, "No."

"So, you weren't approached by my father or some member of his team to help keep an eye on me?" She could hear the edge of hysteria in her voice and wondered if he could too.

Again, he simply said, "No."

She looked back out over the water. Did she believe him? Of course she did. He had never once given her reason not to. She took a deep breath and slowly let it out. "Sorry."

"Understandable." He turned back around and propped his feet up again. "You *were* my mission, once. I completed that mission when I got you to the embassy safe and alive. Now, you are no longer my mission. You are just my problem."

She grinned. "Your problem, huh?"

The sound of a woman's laughter reached them. "I am here entirely of my own volition," he said. "But you let me in, so maybe I'm your problem too."

She held her hand out, and after a pause he took it. The feel of his strong grip chased away all the remaining fear and angst that had swirled in the back of her mind. "Thank you. I didn't realize how much I needed you to be here."

They sat like that until the sun started to break over the horizon. Maybe she dozed off here and there, but for the most part she simply enjoyed chatting with him and holding his hand.

As the sky lightened to pink, a gray parrot flew up onto the railing of the balcony and squawked at her, twisting its head right and left. Before she could react, it flew away.

Rick seemed to take that as a cue. He stood and said, "I have to get back to my room."

She'd love to have the night never end but knew he was right. She stood as well and walked him to the door. Gripping the handle, she looked up at him. "Do you think I'll ever see you again?"

He cupped her cheek. She leaned into his hand, enjoying the warmth, the feel of the rough calluses on his palm. "Goodbye, Cynthia. It was a pleasure some of the time— when it wasn't a big problem."

As she opened the door for him, she laughed. "Goodbye, Captain Norton. Thank you for saving my life a couple of times."

He paused and looked back at her. "Not a problem." With a wink he walked down the hall.

After Cynthia watched the sun rise, she finished packing. At nine o'clock, a Secret Service agent would knock on her door and take her to the airport.

She left the dresses hanging in the wardrobe and called the front desk to have them returned to the store where her father had purchased them. She had only her backpack in the way of luggage.

Before she left, she wrote a letter to Ayo and another to Tadeas, who had a postal box in Yambuli, explaining what had happened the night before and her father's demands that she leave the country. She promised to pray for them and try to find a way back. She asked Ayo to pack what was left of her belongings and have them sent to her. Even as she wrote it, she imagined that the Chukuwereije soldiers had burned the huts down. Anything she had left would have been destroyed.

She didn't see her father before or after she boarded the Boeing C-32, the jet modified until it was worthy of the call sign Air Force Two whenever her father was aboard. He stayed secure in his office inside the plane, and she chose not to approach him. She remained in a secluded area, away from the press corps but not mixed in with her father's staff.

His aide handed her a garment bag and said, "It's twenty-two degrees in Maryland, Doctor. Your father thought you might not have appropriate apparel."

She glanced in the bag and saw a thick sweater and a wool coat. She thanked the aide, then hung up the bag in the closet near the bathroom.

Not long after taking off, she ate a perfectly prepared steak for the first time in five months, accompanied by a pile of steaming scrambled eggs and some rye bread. A flight attendant helped her turn a bench of seats into a bed. Full, exhausted, sore, and emotionally empty, she had barely lain down when she fell asleep. The next thing she knew, a different attendant woke her, explaining that they would be landing soon. She had slept for more than eleven hours and still felt tired all the way to her bones.

She found a seat by the window and looked out as the coastline came into view. They would land at Andrews Air Force Base soon.

Hearing movement behind her, she turned her head and saw her father approaching. Before she could escape, he sat down across from her.

"The press will be there in droves when we land," he remarked.

She glared at him. "That is the first thing you have to say to me in the last thirteen hours?"

"I assumed you didn't want to talk about anything else. And then you were sleeping."

As she examined his face, she noticed the fatigue lines around his eyes and his unusually pale skin. "I'd love to discuss me getting back to work in my clinic."

With a sigh, he closed his eyes and rubbed the bridge of his nose. "Cynthia, this is not the time."

She leaned forward. "This is the only time. This is just you and me, and you have no escape, no meeting to attend, no function waiting on your presence."

"You aren't going back," he snapped. Then he relaxed and said, "I'm sorry. It's just . . ." He took a deep breath. "What happened to us did nothing but solidify my belief that you made the right decision and the best place for you is in the States."

She crossed her arms. "You coerced my decision. I didn't have the freedom to actually decide for myself."

"Well, clearly that was wise on my part, or else you'd still be there."

"You understand, don't you, that you seriously damaged our relationship."

"I'll take a daughter mad at me over having to bury her."

Jaw set, eyes steady, she waited for him to speak again. Finally, he broke eye contact and looked out the window. She heard and felt the landing gear deploy.

"You might want to go run a brush through your hair, maybe slap on some lipstick," he said. "If your mother sees you disembark like that, she'll be embarrassed."

"I don't want to meet the press," Cynthia said.

"You don't get to choose. They were there last night. It's already news. They'll be waiting for us." Her father leaned forward and took her hand. "I love you, sweet pea. I'm sorry my career has interfered with yours."

Hot tears sprang to her eyes. "It doesn't have to."

He shook his head. "I'm afraid that isn't up to me."

With a deep sigh, she said, "I guess I have something to get used to."

"Guess so."

After a moment, she asked, "Will I have my shadows with me in the States?"

"The Secret Service?" He chuckled. "Afraid so."

She raised an eyebrow. "Is that absolutely necessary?"

With a nod he again said, "Afraid so."

She looked out the window and watched the ground rise up to meet the airplane. Deep in her heart, she knew she had only one decision to make: to forgive her father, accept the demands of his new position, and figure out what was next for her life. As soon as the plane securely touched the ground, she grabbed her bag from the seat next to her and stood. "I'll go do what I can with my appearance."

Once she'd retrieved the garment bag from the closet, she slipped into the bathroom. After changing into a pink turtleneck sweater and a pair of gray slacks, she put on some light makeup and ran a brush through her hair. In the bottom of the garment bag, she found a box with a pair of gray leather ankle boots.

The plane came to a stop just as she came out of the bathroom. She didn't see her father anywhere, so she put everything back into her backpack, left the empty hangers and shoebox in the closet, and sat back down, waiting for instructions. She still had to learn all the protocol and didn't want to go the wrong direction or out of order.

It didn't take long for an aide to retrieve her. He took her bag from her and said, "We'll put this in the car, but you'll want your coat."

While she stood near the door, he helped her into her coat, then held out a pair of gray leather gloves and a soft pink hat.

"You're acclimated to the warm jungle," he said, smiling with impossibly white teeth. "This will help."

She glanced at her father as he approached. Someone, another aide or a member of the flight crew perhaps, brushed the shoulders of his black wool coat, then helped him put it on.

"Daddy, it occurred to me that you had to purchase these clothes in the States. You weren't getting wool pants in Katangela."

He accepted gloves from an aide and looked at her out of the corner of his eye. "Your mother sent them. She handles those details."

"You never even thought about leaving me there. You always intended to bring me home."

He put a hand on her shoulder and squeezed. He would never have this conversation in front of his staff. Contrite, she turned and waited for someone to tell her when to walk down the steps and where to stand at the press conference.

Rick pulled up the news site on his laptop and accessed the video of the vice president's arrival at Andrews Air Force Base. He barely recognized Cynthia standing beside her father. She wore winter clothes, makeup, and a fuzzy pink cap.

She looked very calm, very regal. Vice President Randal Myers stood at the podium, and she stood to his right. He answered questions about the incident the night before using generalities and little demurs. Rick wondered if he would mention his team or if they would remain top secret.

"Mr. Vice President, news staff present at President Akinjide's home claim that US military were the rescue force. Can you comment on that?"

Myers impressed Rick with his answer. "The exact location and movements of any US military unit is not a topic I would discuss in a press briefing."

Basically, none of your business, reporter.

Myers's staff had requested no release of any photographs or videos of Rick's men on the site. So far, he hadn't come across any. He appreciated them accommodating the request. Their enemies had access to the same kinds of media outlets he did. He'd rather his team not be identified.

Even when someone directed a question at Cynthia, her father answered on her behalf. Had they set up that process ahead of time, or was he instinctively protecting his daughter from people who likely did not have her best interests at heart? Eventually, a question came that he couldn't deflect, and Cynthia stepped closer to her father to answer it.

"Doctor Myers, can you tell us how you felt during the incident at President Akinjide's home?"

She spoke clearly and calmly. "It's hard to put into words. A warlord trying to stage a coup attacked us. People were killed in front of me, and I was powerless to do anything about it. Some brave men died, and some brave men saved us. The reign of terror created by a terrible warlord who spent years terrorizing the outer villages, stealing children, killing fathers, and maiming mothers has been put to an end. I'm not quite sure what my feelings are, but I think the friends I left behind in Katangela would use words like relieved. Likely thankful. Perhaps even overjoyed."

Rick smiled. Cynthia had no fear. He heard no hesitation in her voice. Despite her views on meeting violence with violence, she didn't hesitate to say that putting an end to Chuckie was the right thing to do. He appreciated her honesty and her self-evaluation that came from that.

As she walked away from the podium next to her father, he looked at the clock. It was past midnight and he'd been awake for close to two days straight. What was he doing? He needed to sleep because tomorrow he and his team would travel back to their base in Djibouti and prepare to end their deployment. They'd been in country for five months. Everyone felt eager to get back to the States and relocate the unit to Kentucky.

But he stayed awake, stealing glances at the video of a press conference that had nothing to do with him. The woman standing next to the vice president of the United States was so far out of his league that he couldn't even pretend to belong inside her orbit. He needed to put all of this aside and get back to work.

He thought back to the dossier he had on her. Her ex-fiancé's actions had driven her to Africa in the first place, and he wondered if the fallout still lingered in her social circle.

She didn't have anything to do with him, though, did she?

He lay on the single bed and stared up at the barracks ceiling. The vice president's departure had freed the barracks rooms for his team's use, so they had checked out of the hotel this morning. But now, instead of sleeping, he kept imagining Cynthia's bright blue eyes staring up at him as they argued their way through the jungle of Katangela.

With a huff, he rolled over onto his stomach and willed his mind to shut down and give him some rest.

CHAPTER

NINETEEN

Cynthia slipped her credit card out of the leather folder and signed the bill, then sat back against the wooden chair. She'd stretched out this lunch as long as she could. Going back to work held no appeal to her. She'd been back in civilization for four weeks and still felt so out of place. How could she continue to do this?

She grabbed her coat and purse and left the restaurant, ignoring the ever-present Secret Service shadow assigned to her. In the four weeks since she'd returned, they'd been less invasive than she thought they would be, and she felt thankful for that. However, the day she didn't require their services anymore would make her very happy.

Back at her office, she slipped on her lab coat and grabbed the tablet, accessing the patient's chart as she walked into the exam room. "Good afternoon, Ms. Ibsen. I'm Doctor Myers."

The woman sat in a comfortable recliner, her three-thousand-dollar purse on the table next to her. She brushed her black hair out of her face as if to make sure her enormous diamond ring caught the light just so. Cynthia almost rolled her eyes.

"I have to say I'm not happy to be handed over to a new doctor."

"I can appreciate that. Doctor Ennis was covering for me while I was away. He was a temp." Cynthia scrolled through the last appointment. "How are you feeling? It looks like you're entering the second trimester."

She made a face. "I am quite done with this entire experience. My clothes no longer fit. I don't have the energy to shop for more. It's rather distressing."

Cynthia set the tablet on the counter and patted the exam table. "Let's take a look, shall we?"

Ms. Ibsen huffed out a breath. "Is that absolutely necessary?"

With a smile Cynthia replied, "Absolutely."

Very gracefully, the woman stood on four-inch heels. She sat on the exam table, and Cynthia touched her shoulder. "Lie back, please." As she examined her, she said, "You should be feeling less fatigue now that you're in the second trimester. This is a good time to go ahead and supplement your wardrobe with maternity clothes. I'm afraid you can look forward to quite some time before your clothes will fit again."

"Can I schedule my induction today?"

Cynthia frowned. "I didn't see anything in your record to indicate the need for an induction."

"I plan to have the baby on August second."

She waited and then asked, "Why?"

"Fashion week in Milan is in September. That should give my body time to heal and get back to work."

Cynthia pressed her lips together and finally said, "Ms. Ibsen, August second is more than three weeks before your due date. It might not be safe for the baby to be born that early."

"It will be fine. My housekeeper's baby was born earlier than that, and she was perfectly healthy."

"I don't think—"

"Doctor Ennis agreed. He was extremely supportive."

"Excuse me," Cynthia said. She snatched up the tablet and left the room. After instructing the nurse to go ahead and make the next appointment for her patient, she walked down two hallways and into a private suite of offices.

The young man at the outer desk smiled at her. "Doctor Myers, I don't think you have an appointment."

"She'll live," Cynthia said, pushing through the door to her aunt's office.

Aunt Kate hung up the phone and looked at her with wide eyes. "Did you not have back-to-back appointments this afternoon?"

Cynthia threw herself into one of the chairs in front of the desk. "I can't do this anymore."

Her mother's sister raised a perfectly manicured eyebrow. "Do what, dear?"

"Cater to these pompous, spoiled women."

Aunt Kate chuckled. "You've only been back to work for a week. I'm sure it was different in the jungle."

"You're right. It was entirely different. Women traveled for days sometimes to come to my clinic. Some of them from the more remote regions would camp out in the jungle near their due dates to be sure to have access to my clinic so their babies could be born safely. My midwife would take a week every month and hit the remote villages, teaching and delivering vitamins. And here I have Ms. Ibsen demanding an induction three weeks before her due date so she can go to Milan in time for a fashion show. Are you kidding me?"

"Cynthia, dear, you cannot compare a supermodel to an African villager. It's not fair to either one of them."

"I know." She put her head back and looked up at the ceiling. "I just don't think I can work here right now. I probably needed a longer reintegration time."

Aunt Kate stood up, walked around her desk, and sat in the chair next to Cynthia. She reached out and took her hand. "You need to stop for a while. The last nine months have been extremes, and you've never once given yourself time to grieve the loss of your relationship, understand the immense differences in culture, and process what happened to you the last few days you were there. It's a lot to take in. Maybe you jumped in with both feet too soon."

Cynthia chewed on her bottom lip. "Maybe I've just seen too much now to be this kind of doctor. Maybe I need to be where I'm needed and worth something."

"You are worth something to these patients too. They're just unable to recognize it."

As she got to her feet, she said, "I love you, Aunt Kate. Go ahead and hire a permanent replacement for me. I'm sorry to disrupt the staff this way."

"No reason to be sorry, child. Go take some time to yourself. Mourn, pray, heal. Then look at everything and decide what you want to do next." She stood and pulled Cynthia into her arms. "It won't be working here, I know that, so expect a negative answer if you come asking."

Cynthia chuckled. "That was the nicest firing ever."

"You quit first. Don't forget. Besides, Doctor Ennis just called, checking to see if I could add him to a regular rotation. He'll be thrilled." She cupped Cynthia's cheeks. "Go on, then. Tell your mom I'll see her tomorrow."

★ ★ ★

DJIBOUTI

From the back of the briefing room, Rick watched the sergeant major and colonel go over the details of a mission for a more select team. Because his team had been back in Djibouti for only a few weeks, they would provide support for a fresher team from here on base rather than in the field. Rick wasn't going to complain. The battle rhythm of combat operations was intensely stressful. His team needed a less demanding operational tempo.

Just as they concluded and released everyone, the phone in the pocket of his uniform vibrated against his leg. No one outside of this room would call him on this phone. He never took it into the field with him, and no family in the States had the number. The last time it rang, Cynthia had called from the Katangela state dinner.

Stepping into the hallway, he glanced at the screen. The 202 area code made his heart skip a beat.

"Norton," he said.

"I wondered if this number would even work now," Cynthia said.

He hadn't heard her voice since the press conference. He couldn't stop the grin that came from deep inside him. "It's amazing the technology we have these days. The first time I deployed, we relied mostly on emails." He stepped outside and into the alley between two buildings. The sun beat down on his head. He put his cap on and found some shade. "What time is it there?"

"Three a.m."

Her voice sounded husky. "What has you calling Djibouti at three in the morning, Doctor Myers?"

She paused, then said, "I quit my job yesterday. So now I'm homeless and jobless."

"Homeless?"

"Well, technically, I'm staying with my parents."

"Wow. Vice presidential residence. Fancy schmancy homeless shelter." He looked up at the sky. A puffy white cloud hung in the air against the perfect blue background. "Why did you quit your job?"

She sighed. "A supermodel asked me to schedule an induction weeks before her due date so she could get her body back before the Milan fashion week. I just stood there, thinking about my patients in Katangela and how desperate they were to have healthy babies who survived the first two years. So I quit." After a long pause, when he thought they'd lost the connection, she said, "I'm out of place here."

He understood what she meant. He had a hard time reentering society after deployments. The military had a system in place, the chaplaincy had programs that helped, counselors were readily available, and training about integration happened. But her father had ripped her away unwillingly, she'd had to face reporters hours later, and then she was expected to just get back to work.

"What will you do about it?"

"I don't know. My choices are kind of limited right now."

He barked out a laugh. "Really? I understand not getting to come back to Africa. But you have a big, wide country you're a part of. It isn't all Maryland high society, Doc. You feel like you need to keep serving? Then find a way to serve. Need doesn't begin and end in Katangela."

After a few heartbeats she said, "I knew if I called you, you'd kick me in the behind."

"You're welcome." McBride came out of the building. "I have to go. It's time for chow. This number isn't the best way to connect with me. I have it off most of the time. Let me email you."

"Well, thank God you had it on tonight. Clearly, He knew you needed to lecture me."

"Go to sleep, Doc. Rest your mind. Hand it all over to God. Rest your spirit."

He hung up the phone and turned as Peña came out of the building and found him. His intelligence officer looked pointedly at the phone in his hand. "Who's calling you on an unsecure line?"

"Doctor Cynthia Myers."

Clearly, Peña hadn't expected that answer. "Really? She okay?"

"A little lost. They kind of threw her into the fray. She'll make it, though."

"And she called you?" Peña looked him up and down. "Good thing we're due to go home soon, eh, Daddy?"

He actually felt himself blush. "It isn't quite like that."

"If you say so." Peña slapped him on the shoulder. "Time for lunch. Then Colonel Jenkins wants to see us. Something about our report of the attack on the president's home."

He sighed and rolled his neck. "Okay. I wonder what's on for chow today."

"Armpit of camel, from the smell of it," Peña said as they walked toward the chow hall.

"Oh, good. My favorite," he said, thinking of a thick hamburger from his favorite bar and grill. He rarely counted down the days until he made it back home, but this trip he found himself looking at the calendar every day, antsy to be back on American soil.

★ ★ ★

WASHINGTON, DC

At seven in the morning, Cynthia sat at the breakfast table and idly stirred cream into her cup. Her eyes burned with fatigue. She glanced up at the door as her mom came into the room.

Annalise Myers had gone to law school with Cynthia's dad. They met at a campus political rally for Annalise's father, a congressman from Maryland, and got married a year later. She practiced law until Cynthia's birth, then threw her energies into raising Cynthia and supporting her husband's political aspirations. She managed his staff and his campaigns and closely monitored his speech writers. Navigating the Washington, DC, social circle had come easy to the Maryland native. She thrived in her position as the vice president's wife.

Her blond hair fell in waves that framed her face. She stayed fit with a daily workout in their home gym. And she never, ever walked out of her personal space without perfectly applied makeup and all the proper accessories.

This morning, she wore a cotton-candy-pink pantsuit with a sage-green belt and matching heels. Thick gold hoops adorned her ears and matched her chunky gold necklace.

"Good morning, love," she said, going straight to the coffeepot. "How are you?"

Cynthia hadn't seen her parents for a few days, so she decided not to discuss nightmares and the fear of falling asleep. "How was San Francisco?"

"It rained every day. Didn't get out to any of the vineyards. Took some of the fun away." Her mom sat down across from her. "Katie called."

Aunt Kate had probably called before the office door even shut behind Cynthia yesterday. "Oh yeah? Are you to intervene?"

"Nothing like that." She carefully took a sip of her coffee. "Want to talk about it?"

She let out a long sigh. Her mom had not come in to reprimand her. She'd come to love her and counsel her. "I'm okay, Mom. I'm just out of sorts. Nothing here feels right to me."

After a moment's pause, her mom asked, "And what would make it feel right?"

"That is certainly the question, isn't it?" Cynthia pushed her cup away. Exhaustion made her a little dizzy, and she didn't think the caffeine buzz would help. "I think I'll contact Hands and Feet and see if they have any domestic missions."

"That's a great idea." Her mom reached over and grabbed

a banana out of the fruit bowl. "You could also talk to Uncle Nathaniel. He might know of something."

Uncle Nathaniel had been serving for a long time as a minister in a DC church. He had put her in contact with Hands and Feet nine months ago. Contacting him would definitely be the right decision.

Cynthia put her elbow on the table and propped her chin in her hands. "Daddy was wrong to bring me home, Mom."

Her mom did not answer until she had peeled the banana. "It wasn't about you. There is a bigger picture here, and unfortunately, you're very much inside that picture frame. I'm sorry about that, but we're making sacrifices right now. It won't be forever."

"I know." She straightened. "Doesn't it seem like we've been having this conversation my entire life?"

Her mother's smile didn't meet her eyes. "It certainly does. You'd think we wouldn't have to have it for a while." She followed the veiled hint with a petite bite of banana.

"Cute, Mom. You know I support you both. But I think there's going to come a time when it gets to be about me."

Her mom sighed. "Many things have been about you, dear. The only thing you're prevented from is working in a country with a tenuous political system that led to violent outbreaks. Other than that, you're rather unencumbered. Open your mind and remove the blinders that are giving you tunnel vision." She patted Cynthia on the cheek. "We are very proud of you and know God will do good things with you, even under these restrictions."

Cynthia slipped out of the chair. "I'll call Uncle Nathaniel." She stopped by her mom's chair and hugged her, breathing in the familiar smell of her vanilla body scrub. "In the meantime, I'm going to go jogging."

"Have fun, dear," she said, pulling her phone out of her pocket.

Cynthia went into the kitchen and rinsed out her cup, then went up the back stairs to her room and used the landline there to call the Secret Service detail. "This is Doctor Myers. I'm going to go for a run in twenty minutes."

After she changed, she sat in a wingback chair near the fireplace to put on her tennis shoes, and her cell phone rang. When she saw the incoming number, her stomach fell. Immediately, her mind went back to that dinner at the White House. Andrew, late and drunk, had arrived with some tall, curvy daughter of a diplomat on his arm. When Cynthia tried to pull him aside to confront him, the woman pushed her and started screeching at her. She grabbed a drink off a table and threw it in Cynthia's face, which made Andrew laugh and laugh until he fell over and into a table, glass and china breaking everywhere.

Cynthia stood there in total shock, a gin martini stinging her eyes and stripping makeup off her face. Someone swooped in and escorted her out of the room, but by then the damage was done. The incident, filmed by an eager cameraman without a sense of decency, had played on an almost continual loop on the twenty-four-hour news shows and had become the source of much laughter on social media platforms.

Andrew, a young congressman from Illinois, hadn't tried to contact her since the morning of that incident. Why would he call her now?

With shaking fingers, she declined the call and blocked the number. She didn't care what he had to say. She hoped his antics that night made him lose the next election and he could go back to his law firm and stay out of her life—and out of her city.

She tied her shoes and secured her hair. A check of the temperature had her also grab a knit cap out of her closet and slip it on over her ears before she bounded down the stairs. A Secret Service agent wearing a pair of sweatpants and a hoodie met her at the door. She knew another one already waited outside.

The cold air stung her face. She looked up at the gray March sky and wondered when spring would beat the cold away. She had loved the weather in the jungle. Perhaps she needed to go to a tropical climate, get away from the city.

As she jogged, she contemplated her options, thinking again of Uncle Nathaniel. At an intersection, she pulled her phone out of her pocket and shot him a quick text, asking if he was free. She glanced over at her companion. "I'm going to the parsonage for Capital Christian."

He nodded and said something into his radio. Instead of waiting for the light, she turned right and picked up her pace. About twenty yards later, her phone vibrated. She glanced at the screen and saw her uncle's confirmation.

Two miles later, she paused outside of the gate, looking up at the green two-story house next to the parking lot of the old church. She wiped her face on her shoulder and opened the wrought-iron gate. Her legs felt a little rubbery, and sweat poured down her back. Before she'd made it to the second step, the door opened, and her uncle stepped out onto the porch.

Uncle Nathaniel was her father's older brother by twelve years. He was tall and athletic with bright-blue eyes and gray hair that had once been reddish-brown.

"Well, hello, niece. What a surprise," he said, grinning.

"Hey, Uncle Nathaniel." As she approached him, he held out his arms, but she put her hands up, palms toward him. "I'm super sweaty."

"Bah." He grabbed her and pulled her close. "It is so good to see you. I'm having dinner at your house tomorrow."

"Really? I guess I could have waited instead of bothering you."

"Nonsense." He gestured inside. "Let's get you out of the cold before you get sick." He looked at the two men with her. "You too."

"No, sir. We'll stay here."

Nathaniel led her to the little sitting room off the foyer. Here, he met with parishioners, keeping them out of the deeper, more personal portions of his home. This room led to the dining room, and through that was the kitchen.

She had always loved this charming and comfortable room. Tall bookshelves held all sorts of faith-based family and marriage counseling books, some Christian fiction, and some doctrinal texts. Light-blue couches flanked a fireplace that warmed the room. Yellow and dark-blue pillows brightened the space.

Cynthia perched on the edge of the couch. "I quit my job yesterday."

"Well, so much for small talk, I guess." He smiled as his housekeeper, Frances, came through the dining room carrying a tea tray. She set it on the low table in front of him. "Thank you, Fran."

After she left and Cynthia held a steaming cup, she continued. "Something inside of me changed in the jungle. I can't continue to work in private practice."

He settled against the corner of the couch, a cup and

saucer balanced on his crossed leg. "I know it was hard on you to come home."

She pursed her lips. "It's my duty as a daughter. I get that, even if I want to pout. Daddy worked his entire life for this position, and for the next one up. I understand that. I'm upset and I think he made the wrong choice, but I love him and support him."

"He knows that. He really struggled with the decision to bring you home. He and I spent some time in prayer over it."

"It's done now. And like a friend reminded me, Katangela is not the beginning and end of mission fields. I just need to decide where to go." She added, "And pay isn't a barrier."

"Your skills and education are worth pay, even if it's a stipend compared to what your aunt Kate paid you." He studied her face. "Now, favorite albeit only niece, tell me about how God worked on you for the last six months. I can see it in your face, I want to hear your words." He cocked his head slightly. "Or explain why you look completely exhausted."

Hot tears sprang to her eyes. She could talk to him. He would keep her confidence, and he would pray with her and for her. "I've been having nightmares," she whispered. A tear slid down her cheek, and she closed her eyes. "They're so vivid that I put off going to sleep so I don't have any more."

He reached for her hand. "Let's talk about that."

CHAPTER

★

TWENTY

FAYETTEVILLE, NORTH CAROLINA

Rick stood on the corner of Maple and Sixth and looked up at the sign for the Hammerhead Bar and Grill. His mouth watered and his stomach growled. He glanced over at Bill. "Ready, brother?"

"As ever."

The two of them had spent eight years in the military together. The Army had assigned them to the same units at the same times, they had deployed together, and they had returned together. Whenever they arrived at a new military installation, they always asked around for where to find the best burger, then on Fridays they would go rate them. Whenever they returned from deployment, they always had that first meal in the States at the best burger restaurant.

This deployment, Bill had returned home from Germany a week ahead of Rick's return from Africa. He'd waited for Rick to get that burger.

Rick had no words to express the happiness that filled his heart when he saw Bill standing, joking, and moving like a twenty-nine-year-old and not a ninety-year-old. He didn't realize how much stress he'd carried over Bill's injury until he saw him recovered, ready to get back to work.

They sat at their usual table, waiting on the fully loaded burgers cooked medium-well. "So," Bill said, "Peña Colada said you got a phone call last week."

An uncomfortable feeling, almost an embarrassed anxiety, filled Rick's chest. "Yeah? What's the point of the scuttlebutt?"

Bill sat back, crossing his arms over his chest. "Dude, her dad is the vice president. Now that she's back with her own kind, she isn't going to be into a grunt, unless you have a silver spoon hidden away somewhere I don't know about."

He intentionally relaxed his jaw. "I assume you have a point?"

"I love you, man. You are the epitome of reliable and dependable. Great for getting a damsel in distress out of the jungle, for example. Not needed so much back in public society. I'm just watching your six."

Bill had always had an issue with the perception of class. He'd grown up poor—poorer than most—and saw people with any kind of status or wealth as the enemy. Rick had tried to point it out to him in the past, but Bill didn't even realize his bias.

Regardless, Rick didn't consider this topic any of his friend's business. Yes, he felt some pretty serious attraction toward Doctor Cynthia Myers. Yes, if they lived within driving distance of each other and she showed even the slightest inkling of interest in pursuing a relationship with him, he'd be hard-pressed not to ask her out.

Reality didn't include any of that.

"I appreciate that, but you can get off my six. She called me exactly once after coming home. She was struggling with reintegration." He gave a shrug saying that things like struggles with reintegration were self-explanatory and came with the job. "Never heard from her again."

His friend stared at him for several moments before he nodded. "Good." As the waitress set their plates in front of them, he clapped his hands together and rubbed them. "Ahh, here it is. You ready?"

Bill bowed his head, and Rick looked at him for a moment before he followed suit and said, "Thank You, God, for the safe return home, for Bill's healing, and for this food. We love You."

Rick took a juicy bite, and the flavors mingled in perfection on his tongue. As he chewed and swallowed, refusing to hurry that first perfect bite, he considered his best friend. He'd shaved his beard, but he hadn't shaved today, so he had a thick shadow of black hair on his cheeks. His dark eyes shone under a University of Alabama-Huntsville ball cap.

Bill sliced into his burger to dissect it into two even halves. "It only matters because of next week."

The team had been ordered to go to the White House so that the president could personally give them awards for their part in saving the vice president. Rick had fought the idea, but Colonel Jenkins—who fully understood why Rick and his team had no desire to receive awards from the president— got his orders from a general with a lapel covered with stars who gave them no choice.

"Next week?" Rick asked innocently. "Not sure what you mean."

Bill chuckled and took a drink of Pepsi. "You better tread carefully, bro. If someone were to draw a diagram explaining the term 'out of your league,' it would be a picture of Doctor Cynthia Myers."

Rick released a deep, annoyed sigh. "You're not telling me something I don't already know. Quit worrying about it." Bill opened his mouth as if to speak again, and Rick held up a finger. "Enough."

He'd managed to go most of the morning without thinking about the fact that he would see Cynthia again in just a few days, but Bill had brought it back to the front of his mind. He tossed down his napkin and went to rub his beard, then remembered he had shaved already. Instead, he ran the back of his hand over the stubble on his chin.

Bill dipped a french fry in some mayonnaise. "Heard from Ozzy?"

"I have." Rick nodded. "He'll be there in DC with us."

"Tried to call him last night. He kept me on the phone for all of about fifteen seconds." Bill didn't disguise the concern in his voice.

Rick thought about the dark look in Ozzy's eyes as the medics had loaded him onto the aircraft bound for Germany. He'd had little to say the entire time they'd been in Katangela at the embassy. Rick had sent several video recordings to encourage Ozzy and show his support, and since coming back to the States he'd called and texted, but he couldn't get through to him.

"Everything he ever set out to achieve suddenly got ripped away," he said. "Now he has to rediscover who he is."

"Think he'll go back to surgical work?"

"He had to leave it for some reason." Even though Rick

suspected why, he would never openly speculate. "Don't know if he can go back or not. I guess we'll see."

They ate in silence for a couple of moments before Bill asked, "You taking leave after DC?"

"Yeah." Rick sat back, full of good food. "Did I tell you that the new medic is from Charula?"

"Yeah, man. They know how to make them in Kentucky."

"He was good. I'd go back into combat with him."

"Like I said." Bill tossed his napkin onto his empty plate and took a chug of his drink. "I gotta tell you, Rick, I never experienced the kind of fear I experienced when I got up from my hospital cot and headed into the jungle. I was sure I was going to die when we began the journey."

Rick tried to process what his best friend meant. The fear he'd personally felt reared up inside him. He had to intentionally push it back down. "And?"

"All those hours of lying still, fighting back the pain, it was just me and God, man. And suddenly all of that fear and trepidation about it just dissipated into nothing. I'm not ready to leave this earth and meet God face-to-face. I mean, who is at our age? But now I know I'm not afraid to either."

Rick thought over his job, of the times when he didn't know if he would live to see the sun go down. "I can't imagine someone who is afraid of death doing our job."

"No. But it's nice to have the affirmation."

He nodded. "I can see that." He drained his glass. "It's the fear of living that has me concerned. I don't want to turn my life into a cycle of waiting for the next deployment. Starting to think I want more."

"A family?"

"Yeah. 'It is not good for man to be alone,'" Rick said, quoting Genesis. "Feeling that in my soul lately."

"Do we really have the kind of career that's conducive to a happy marriage?" Bill asked after a few moments.

"Depends on the wife," Rick said with a grin.

"Four little words." Bill pointed a finger at him. "Out of your league."

★　★　★

WASHINGTON, DC

What color did one wear to a military awards ceremony? Did she go all patriotic or keep it subtle?

"Ugh," Cynthia said, finally settling on a blue dress. She wrapped a red-and-white belt around her waist and slid into a pair of red heels. She laid out a red sweater in case it got cool at the venue.

As she started from her room, she paused. Why had she put so much effort into her clothes? Would it show? Should she change into something a little more neutral?

Putting her forehead against the doorframe, she chided her nervousness. "Come on, silly," she whispered. "He's not going to even look twice at you." If he'd had any interest in her, he would have called by now. His unit had arrived back in the States two weeks ago. For the first week, she'd jumped like a nervous kitten every time her phone made a noise. She'd given up waiting for him to call a week ago.

She went downstairs and grabbed a yogurt out of the refrigerator. While she ate, she skimmed the national news magazine that had her father on the cover. In it, she read an article about the need for qualified doctors in military hospitals. That gave her a niggling idea. Maybe a military hospital wouldn't be a bad thing. Maybe that environment would be safe enough for her to practice medicine without fear or publicity.

After she tossed the empty container in the trash and washed her spoon, she used the kitchen stairs to go back to her room and passed the cook coming down. "Morning, Mabel," she said.

"Morning, Doctor Myers. Luncheon will be ready at one o'clock. Your father asked me to confirm the time with you."

Cynthia paused and turned. "Lunch?"

"Your father has the Army guests coming." Mabel stopped at the bottom of the stairs and looked up at her. "Will one o'clock be satisfactory?"

Her heart started beating a little more rapidly. "Great. One is great."

She continued up to her room. Had her mother intentionally not told her? Maybe her father assumed her mother had told her, and vice versa.

Rick and his team would come here for lunch? It was one thing to be present in an orchestrated and scripted ceremony along with other people before the microscopic inspection of the press. It was quite another to have the men unscripted in her home with just the Secret Service, her, her parents, and their private staff.

As she put on makeup, she applied some concealer to hide the shadows under her eyes. The constant nightmares had started to annoy her. She should be stronger than this. Why had her experiences affected her this way? What, subconsciously, did she still fear?

She sat back in the chair and closed her eyes, intending to rest for a moment. Suddenly, she heard a gun cock in her ear. Her eyes flew open, and she met the black eyes of Chukuwereije. "Tell me, Doctor, how you let my son die," he hissed.

Cynthia gasped as she woke up, her heart pounding. The president's quarters in Katangela faded away. She sat at her makeup table in her parents' home. The warm April breeze came in through her open window, making the curtains flutter.

She looked at the clock and saw she'd lost seventeen minutes—just long enough to fall into the beginning of REM sleep. Pressing her fingers below her eyes, she willed the panic away. "God," she whispered, "I need You. Chase these demons out in Christ's name."

The maid had left a bottle of water on her nightstand. She drained half of it, refreshed her lipstick, and called down to let the Secret Service know she was ready to go to the White House.

CHAPTER

★

TWENTY-ONE

In the East Room of the White House, Cynthia stood next to the president as he awarded medals to the members of the US Army Special Forces Operational Detachment Alpha. He read each citation and secured the medal, then personally thanked each man, spoke a personal message, and moved on to the next soldier.

Cynthia barely recognized their clean-shaven faces as they stood in their dress uniforms. She spoke to each of them, then introduced them one by one to her father, who was on her other side. Each man had something personal to say that made her smile or laugh or want to hug him.

Lieutenant Osbourne brought tears to Cynthia's eyes. He leaned on crutches, his uniform pants folded up over his stump. When he got to her and she looked at the Purple Heart and the Bronze Star clipped to his uniform, she almost lost the tight rein on her control at the stoic expression on his face.

When he finally met her eyes, she said softly enough that

only he could hear her, "I'm so sorry I couldn't save your leg, Ozzy."

For the first time, his eyes warmed, and he held out his hand. When she placed hers in it, he pulled her close and wrapped his arms around her, despite the obstacle the crutches presented. His raw strength surprised her, though it should not have.

He spoke low in her ear, his words only for her. "Doc, if you ever need anything, no matter what, I'm here. No matter what."

She brushed her lips over his cheek and said, "Thank you."

As Ozzy made his way back to his seat, she turned to Bill, who was next in line. She grinned and held her hands out to him. "I cannot tell you how happy I am to see you up and moving," she said.

"Well, ma'am, I can't tell you how happy I am to oblige." She hugged him, and he added, "I won't gripe about the scar on this auspicious occasion. I'll catch you on that subject next time."

Thinking about the size of the incision she'd had to make, she laughed. "I think I'd be afraid to see it."

She opened her mouth to continue, and he held up a hand. "If you're about to apologize, stow it. I'm walking and talking, shiny as grease on a pig. You owe me no apology."

She smiled and nodded. "God bless you, Bill."

"Doc," he said, and moved to her father.

After she introduced him to her father, she turned and found Rick standing in front of her. Immediately, her heart started pounding and her breath fled from her lungs. All she could manage was a breathy, "Hi."

Without his beard, she could see his entire face. He had

a strong, square jaw, full lips, and a Roman nose. His green eyes shone. Freckles she'd never noticed before were sprinkled across his nose. "Hi, yourself," he said, grinning.

She put her hand in his, and he clasped it with both hands. Instead of standing there shaking his hand like a civilized human being, she stepped closer and hugged him. For a moment, he didn't move, then his arms came around her.

She took a deep breath, breathing in the lemony scent of his aftershave. "I'm so happy to see you."

After squeezing her tight, he stepped back. "The feeling is mutual." As she looked up at him, his eyes narrowed. "Why the shadows, Doc?"

She waved a hand in front of her eyes to combat the tears that suddenly appeared. "Nightmares. They'll go away, I'm sure. I'm doing all the things." Before he could say anything else, she turned to her father. "Daddy, you remember Captain Norton."

"Yes, of course. We met briefly that night of the dinner. Captain," her father said, putting a hand out, "it is a pleasure. I am thankful for another opportunity to speak to you in person. I know you were fundamental in keeping my daughter safe. I cannot thank you enough."

"Sir, it was a pleasure to get to know her. She is an incredible woman, and you should be proud of the way she handled herself in the midst of crisis after crisis."

Heat filled Cynthia's cheeks, and she put a hand on her father's arm. "I can assure you that half of my handling myself was arguing with him." She smiled. "I'm sure I could have made his job a little easier."

Everyone went to their seats, and the president spoke a few more words. After he finished the ceremony and left the room, Cynthia sought out Rick. "I understand we're having lunch as well," she said without preamble.

He turned from talking to Peña and said, "So I've been informed. At least there isn't a ball in our honor," he teased.

Unsure what to say, she waved a hand in the general direction of her father. "I have to ride with the motorcade. See you there?"

"Hey, Doc," Peña said, stepping around Rick and taking her by the arm. "Is there room in that motorcade for one more?"

She blinked and processed his question. "Of course! Do you want to ride with me?"

He wiggled his eyebrows. "I would, but I think Daddy would be better served to accept that honor."

As he walked away laughing, she turned to Rick. Heat flushing her face, she cleared her throat and asked, "Would you like to ride with me? Us! Would you, um, ride with us?"

When he smiled, dimples appeared in his cheeks. His beard had covered those. "I'd be honored."

They walked behind her father and his team. "Nightmares, huh?" he said.

She rubbed her arms and nodded. "I'm at the point that I'm afraid to go to sleep."

"Have you talked to anyone?"

"My uncle is a pastor and a counselor. I've spoken to him a couple of times."

"I'm sure he's great. But you might be better off working with a counselor trained in war-related PTSD, which is what you're suffering from. Your mind is processing everything that happened and compensating for the horrors of what you experienced and witnessed. There are people specially trained who can help you process and learn coping mechanisms to keep the nightmares at bay."

"I'm a doctor, Rick. I know the psychology." They reached the car, and she tried to convey that she wanted this to be the end of the conversation. "Isn't it good that I'm having nightmares?"

He nodded. "It would be tragic if you were not." He stood by as she got into the car. When she looked up at him expectantly, he leaned in and said, "On second thought, I better ride with my men. See you there." He looked at her father. "Sir."

As the door shut, she huffed out a breath.

Her dad raised an eyebrow. "Did you want him to ride with us?"

"Of course I did," she snapped, then relaxed. "Maybe he thought it wasn't appropriate to ride with you."

"Well, sweet pea, it wasn't. So, good on him for not." He looked at his watch. "They're scheduled to arrive at our quarters in twenty minutes."

She looked out the window and watched the familiar buildings roll by. "I really like him," she said.

"I couldn't tell." When she glanced at him, he winked. "There is going to be a pretty tall barrier for him."

"Meaning you."

"No. No, sweet pea. I don't have a problem with that man, and I have always trusted your judgment in matters of romance. Once, and not so long ago, to your detriment, in fact." He lowered an eyebrow, apparently at the very thought of Andrew. "I mean, he's a captain in the Army of the United States, and I am the vice president of those very same United States."

She pressed her lips together and tried to word what she wanted to say. Finally, she just said, "So?"

He chuckled. "My darling daughter, he's going to have a problem with that. He obviously already does."

"Do you?"

"Again, I do not. Of course not." When the car rolled to a stop in their drive he added, "But I'm one heartbeat away from becoming his commander in chief. That may be an issue for him or his chain of command."

The door opened, and Cynthia slid out. They walked side by side into the residence. "It shouldn't," she said.

"You're right." Inside the door, he pressed a kiss to her temple. "See you at lunch," he said before he headed into his office.

It took all she had not to hover in the foyer and wait for the cars to arrive. Instead, she wandered into the dining room and found her mother looking at a clipboard. She smiled at Cynthia. "How was the ceremony?"

"How to describe a ceremony in the White House. Surreal? It was good to see everyone again, though."

Her mom walked forward and cupped her cheek. "You look more relaxed and happier today than I've seen since you got home." She looked back down at her clipboard. "Is there someone I should know about?"

Heat rushed to Cynthia's face and tickled the back of her throat, making her cough. "Mom!"

She grinned and nodded. "Aha! I thought so."

"You and Dad both. How is that even possible? I didn't think you guys paid that much attention."

"Darling, we pay all the attention." She checked next to a line item and straightened a fork. "Now, go freshen up. They'll be arriving soon."

The cherry trees outside the residence gleamed in the sunshine like flocks of fattened flamingoes propped atop toothpicks. Rick stood next to the window and watched one of the trees dance in the wind. Pink petals floated down like falling feathers.

He heard Cynthia's approach, identifying her from the heels that she wore. He steeled himself for the way she looked in her blue dress, for the way her eyes shone and the way her lipstick made her lips look lush and full. Properly prepared, he turned and looked at her. She hesitated slightly before she came all the way into the room.

He'd sat next to her at lunch. They'd chatted with everyone around them, but this was the first time they'd found themselves alone since her hotel room the day she left Katangela.

"I'm glad you were able to come to lunch," she said. "It's good to spend so much time with you."

He silently agreed. This moment made all the formality of the morning worth it. "How have you been settling back in?"

She shrugged. "I feel lazy. This is the idlest I've been since high school. I'm ready to get back to work."

She fidgeted with her feet, rolling her heel back and forth. He wondered if she realized it. He met her eyes and said, "So, last time I talked with you, you'd quit your job. Have you found something else? Somewhere to serve?"

"No. I'm working on getting my mind and heart back to normal before I try a new job."

He appreciated her wisdom. He looked back out the window. "This is it for us. We go on leave starting tomorrow."

She stepped closer to him. "Where will you go?"

He glanced at her out of the corner of his eye. "Home. Kentucky. It's been too long."

She rested her hip on the window seat. "Do you have a hard time going home?"

He shook his head. "No. It's my refuge." He thought about his parents' brick house two blocks from his high school. Even though the little town changed every time he left it, it always still seemed the same. "It's the place where I let all of this go. Nothing chases me there. I relax, connect with friends, family. It's like a haven from the rest of the world."

A shadow crossed her face. "I don't know what to do to capture that."

"You're not in your home. You're with your family, but I imagine it would be different if you'd come home to a house you know." He turned and sat next to her. "Above that, there's a process of acceptance. You experienced this extreme event, and now you feel this way. Human beings aren't supposed to experience events like that, but you did. And then you develop coping mechanisms for the times when it overwhelms you."

She smiled up at him. "I hear you speaking from the voice of experience."

"We've been involved in a war somewhere for my entire career. I don't think you want to understand my experience." He grinned. "Besides, you're a pacifist, remember? I'd hate to ruin my chances with you."

"I'm still a pacifist," she said. "But I think it has morphed into an understanding. I think I now understand the occasional necessity for an appropriate application of force, even if I would personally prefer that it wasn't ever necessary."

He leaned toward her, bumping his shoulder against

hers. "You just described every member of my team." Dropping the lighthearted tone, he added, "None of us want it. Each of us feels remorse when the deeds are done. But we do not abjure violence. 'Those who abjure violence can only do so because others are committing violence on their behalf.'"

"Someone has been reading his Orwell." Her face grew serious. "I can understand that. I can."

For several quiet moments, he waged an internal debate, hearing the countering opinions of Peña and Bill. He finally screwed up his courage and asked, "Would you be free to join me for dinner tonight?"

Her eyes widened, and he feared she would flat-out turn him down, laugh in his face, demand to know what made him think he could ask such a thing. Instead, a smile lit up her face. "I would love to."

He gestured behind him. "How does that work with your chaperones?"

He could tell she hadn't considered them. After a moment, she said, "I think I'll be safe enough with you. I can tell them not to join us tonight."

He frowned. "Is that safe in itself?"

"I think you can handle anything that comes at me." She stood. "You've not let me down yet."

His attention focused on the weight of the Silver Star hanging from his chest. He wanted to touch it but didn't want to fidget in front of her. "I will do my best not to let you down, Cynthia."

She blinked. "You don't have to tell me that. I know."

He looked at his watch, having a hard time believing it was already three. "What time is good for you tonight?"

"Let's say seven. I want the sun to still be up. Dress casually." She started to walk away but spun on her heel. "Do you have a car?"

"I have a car."

"Great! I'll see you here at seven."

Long after she rushed out of the room, Bill strolled in. "You ready, brother?"

He looked at his best friend. "Yeah."

"We're all talking about doing one of those walking tours tonight."

"Sorry. I already have plans."

Bill put a hand on his arm. "You aren't serious."

Rick turned to face him fully. "I am dead serious."

Bill tapped a finger against his chest. "You are out of your mind. Do you know that? Did you not listen to a word I said?"

"Relax, Bill. Even Peña thinks it's a good thing. And it's his job to keep us on the straight and narrow path." At the black look that crossed Bill's face, he realized something. "You're jealous."

His friend took a step back. "Shut up."

"You are. Of course. You had a lot of personalized attention from Cynthia. And since some misplaced propriety has kept you from asking her out, you think I should be bound by the same rules." He stepped closer to Bill. "I can't believe you're being that selfish."

Bill's eyes narrowed. "You're not good enough for her. None of us are." He held his hands up. "Look at this place. This is where she's from. This is her world. How do you plan to fit in here, Kentucky boy?"

"I've never put stock in environment, Bill. I know you

do." He stepped close enough that the toes of their highly shined boots almost touched. "I'm sorry you didn't feel good enough to ask her out, but it's not going to stop me."

"You need to take a step back." Bill looked pointedly at Rick's rank insignia and said, "Sir."

They glared at each other for several moments before Rick stepped back. "Sorry, brother. Let's get everyone rounded up."

CHAPTER

★

TWENTY-TWO

When Cynthia opened the door at seven, it pleased her to see that Rick had listened to her about casual clothes. He wore jeans and a light-blue button-down shirt that turned his green eyes almost sea-blue. She had on a loose-fitting sleeveless green top and a pair of white jeans.

She grinned widely at him. "Hello! Right on time."

He stepped to the side as she walked out onto the porch. "I don't have to come in and go through some ritual conversation with your parents?"

She raised her eyebrows. "I'm hardly a teenager, Rick. No ritual conversations required."

He led the way down the steps to his car. She got in and he shut the door. As he climbed into the driver's seat, he asked, "Where to?"

She gave him the address. He loaded it into his GPS, and she settled back in the seat as he maneuvered through the downtown Washington, DC, traffic. "I did a takeout order.

I remember you and Bill talking about finding the best hamburger. I thought I would give you a taste of my favorite."

He grinned as he glanced in her direction. "That sounds like a perfect date."

About forty-five minutes later, they sat under a blooming cherry tree in Yards Park. Spread before them on the table sat four different kinds of burgers. She'd ordered a bison, a lamb, and two kinds of beef. She also had toppings, grilled veggies, and condiments.

"Sorry if I went a bit overboard," she said. "I should have just let you order."

He cut all the burgers into quarters. "This is better than ordering myself. What a good idea."

As they made their plates, she asked him, "How did the burger tradition begin?"

He smeared mayonnaise on a bun. "It seems to be the thing that other countries can't do well. I love exploring different food cultures and always try to immerse myself in local spices and flavors, but I only eat burgers in the States. I think I've become a bit of a snob that way."

She laughed. "What is your favorite culture for food?"

He sprinkled some black pepper on a Parmesan cheese fry. "There was a place we stayed at in Kuwait that had this incredible buffet. It was magazine perfect every night. It wouldn't break my heart to live there and eat only that for the rest of my life."

She picked up a sweet potato fry and pointed it at him. "As long as you come home to get a burger?"

He winked. "Exactly." He looked up and pointed at the pink blossoms on the tree. "The cherry trees are incredible."

Cynthia looked out at the park, at the sea of pink trees

and the paths turned pink from falling blossoms. "I'm so happy you were able to come while the blooms are at their peak. It's truly the best week of the year."

After a few quiet moments he said, "After what happened with your fiancé, tell me what caused you to run away from everything and go to the jungle."

Her eyes widened, and she thought back to standing among all those people with gin running down her face. "Why?"

He shrugged. "Because I only know what the report said. I don't know what happened to you. I'd like to hear it from you."

As she contemplated his request, she chewed a small bite of lamb burger. "He was a junior congressman in the opposing party. My father was the majority leader. I think Andrew was trying to humiliate my father through me. The worst part of it is that my father thought so too. And I didn't listen to him when he tried to warn me about him."

Rick raised his eyebrows. "Really? I got none of that in the report."

"Yeah, we had this whirlwind romance, and Andrew proposed to me. I'd just turned thirty-two and was watching friends from college getting married, starting families, and all I could think of was that time had let me down. So here was this dynamic, handsome man who swept me off my feet. No man had ever looked twice at me, much less shown me so much adoration and attention. Then in front of the entire cabinet during the president's sixtieth birthday, he made a public spectacle of me. In the end, I realized I was just a political pawn." She took a sip of her sparkling water. "Much like in Katangela. Just a little less violent."

After several silent moments, he said, "I'm so sorry. I wish

I could erase that for you." He reached over, took her hand, and sandwiched it in his. She could feel the strength radiating off him. "Cynthia, I want you to hear me. I don't care about politics or who your father is."

She started to chuckle as if he joked, but he squeezed her hand and with serious eyes said, "Hey. Listen to me. I don't know your father. I know you. I want to get to know you better. Understand?"

With tears in her eyes she said, "I understand." She softly cleared her throat. "Here's what came to life inside of me during the months in the jungle: it was an experience that's part of what has molded me into who I am today. God's Word promises us that He will take all things and make them good. Even the horrible things."

He smiled and broke the serious moment, then picked up another quarter of a burger. "So far, the bison is winning. Let's try this one, shall we?"

After they ate, they packed up all the leftovers and put them in the cooler the restaurant had provided, then walked around the park. The sun had just started to fade, bursting the sky with pinks and oranges, making the colors of the trees look like glowing Japanese lanterns. They chatted about God, life, and college. The conversation flowed over to Ozzy.

"I know he's getting counseling by people trained to handle cases like his, but that doesn't stop me from worrying about him." Rick leaned against the trunk of a cherry tree. "He closed himself off from me."

Cynthia looked up at the darkening sky. "I've taken my share of psychology courses and did my rotation in psychiatric care during medical school, so I understand a little bit of the psyche that he's struggling with. The fact is, you're not the one to help him. I know that probably hurts you."

He frowned. "Why?"

She didn't know how to word it without being blunt. "Because you're in his old world, the world he can never be in again. One day, seeing you won't destroy him. Right now is not that time. Keep in touch with him, love him, pray for him, but don't expect your presence to be any kind of healing balm. He's angry, and he's facing a life he never would have picked for himself."

A muscle ticked in his jaw, then he sighed and looked up at the sky. "You're right."

She laughed. "I often am."

"I'll remember that." He straightened. "This was really nice."

As they turned to stroll down the path back to the car, she slipped her arm into his. "It was. How long are you here?"

"I am officially on leave."

She glanced up at his profile. "For how long?"

"Ten days." He looked out over the water. "I'm planning to get home to Kentucky at some point."

"You said that today. Home to your refuge." She leaned into his arm. "Do you normally spend your entire leave at home?"

"Sometimes. After my first deployment, I needed some headspace, so I drove from Washington State to the Florida Keys. Took my time. I did stop in Kentucky for about five days, but then I kept going. I needed that."

"Is that how you process deployments? Time alone?"

He shrugged. "I don't think about it. It was what I needed to do that time. Other times, all I can do is think about getting home and sleeping under my parents' roof, sitting in my home church, helping my father with his store inventory."

"Ah, your normal. Sometimes your mind craves normalcy in the aftermath of horror you shouldn't have to be a part of."

He glanced down at her. "Another psych rotation insight?"

With a smile she said, "Possibly."

He slowly stopped walking and turned to face her. He put one hand on her shoulder and cupped her cheek in his other hand, gently running a thumb under her eye. "Maybe you should apply some of that learning to yourself," he said quietly. "Tell me about your nightmares."

She tried to pull away, but he held her still. Images flashed through her mind faster than she could stop them.

"Jungle?"

"No," she whispered. "I was never afraid in the jungle. Well, I mean, other than the time you had me drive two wounded men like their lives depended on it."

He grinned. "You were too angry to feel fear."

"You're right." She tried to smile, but it wouldn't form. She licked her lips. "Can you let me go?"

Immediately, he released her. "So, it was the night of the dinner?"

Wrapping her arms around herself against the sudden shiver that went down her spine, she nodded. "Why was I not afraid when I had a gun to my head at my clinic, but when they invaded the president's home and it was never about me, really, why can't I get that out of my head?"

After a moment, he said, "Because it was never about you. It was about your father. If we hadn't arrived when we did, he would be dead now. Plain and simple. If you hadn't called us, he would be dead, and you would have spent the entire time they kept you alive suffering unspeakable horrors until they finally killed you."

She pulled her sweater tighter around her neck and wrapped her arms around her middle. "I don't understand."

"He would have killed every person in that room, and deep down, you know you couldn't have stopped him. It was the lack of power that's making you afraid in your psyche. Hurt you? Fine. Hurt other people? Use you? Not so fine."

"Now who's doing a psych rotation?"

He slipped his hands into his pockets. "I just know the things that scare me. Facing God after my death is not one of them, but seeing people I love hurting or in danger—that can scare me."

They continued walking. She stepped closer to him, enjoying having him by her side. When they reached the car, she felt like they'd arrived there way too soon. "You never answered my question. How long are you staying in DC?"

He leaned against the hood of the car. "I guess that depends on whether you'd like to have lunch with me tomorrow."

With a grin, she looked up at him. "I think I can manage that."

"Then I'm here at least through tomorrow." He looked over her shoulder. "Someone has been following us since we stopped by the water. It's not Secret Service."

She closed her eyes and sighed, trying to release the sudden irritation at the invasion of their privacy. "Probably press."

"Ah." He shifted, slipped a pair of sunglasses out of his shirt pocket, and put them on. He opened her door. "Then let us depart, Doctor Myers. The last thing I want or need is my picture in the paper, especially without a beard."

As he drove away from the park, she glanced at his profile.

"I'm sorry about the press. It's something I've gotten used to since I came home. It never used to be a thing. At least, not until the president's sixtieth birthday. Now I think Daddy's position has compounded that."

"It's not anything you have control over." He glanced behind them as he shifted lanes. "I imagine outside of the district, it's a less likely occurrence."

"Probably. I guess it depends on what's going on in the world at the time. It fascinates me, the things people are interested in news-wise."

He checked the rearview mirror before taking his sunglasses off.

She gestured toward him. "Were the glasses to block your identity?"

"Yes."

"Like the beard?"

"Exactly. Facial profiling makes anonymity a necessity in my line of work. Partly for my family's safety, and partly for the purpose of clandestine operations."

"Wow." She propped her elbow on the armrest and leaned toward him. "Impressive, Captain Norton."

"Yeah, well, impressive is what I'm always striving to achieve." His grin was quick and easy.

He pulled up to the gate at her parents' residence. When he rolled the window down, a man's voice came over the intercom. "Yes?"

"Captain Norton, bringing Doctor Myers home."

"One moment."

Before the last syllable died off, the gates silently swung open. Rick eased the car forward.

"I've contemplated finding my own place," Cynthia said,

"but I haven't quite decided I want a Secret Service companion, so I've put it off."

"Well, at least you have all the amenities here," he said with a smile.

"Ha!" she said. "And then some."

"Your old hut would probably fit in that gatehouse over there," he remarked as he put the car in park.

"Twice." She slipped off her seat belt. "Please take the leftover burgers to your guys. They'll probably enjoy them."

"You assume I'm willing to share." He slid out of the car and walked around to open her door. She took his hand and let him help her up. He did not move back. She stood secure between him and the door. Gently, he picked a cherry blossom out of her hair and then held it up, letting the wind catch it. "Thank you for going to dinner with me, Cynthia."

"I enjoyed it. It was nice to spend time with you on American soil." She reached up and brushed her fingertips across his cheek. "To see your actual face."

He smiled briefly, then stepped aside. "Where do you go to church?"

"I go to my uncle's church." She told him the address.

"You'll be there tomorrow?"

"I will be there at ten."

"Great. See you then."

CHAPTER

★

TWENTY-THREE

Rick sat in the back of the church on an old wooden pew and watched people filter in. He'd spotted Secret Service in two different locations. He wondered if the level of security was always this high or if the incidents in Katangela had heightened it. Had more threats been made against the vice president because of the death of Chuckie? Unless Rick himself had something directly to do with the threats, he would never know.

He'd texted Cynthia to let her know which pew he was in but wondered if she would sit with her family. She had not replied by the time they stood to sing the single chorus for the call to worship. As he sat down, he smelled the faint scent of lavender and glanced over as Cynthia slid into the pew next to him.

"Sorry I'm late," she whispered. "Slept in."

He nodded. "Slept?"

With a wide grin she said, "Six full hours and no nightmares."

"Then you are completely forgiven."

After someone welcomed them from the podium, the congregation stood to sing. While the instrumentalists played the opening chords, he leaned close to her and put his lips near her ear. "Maybe we need to have dinner every night."

She looked up at him, and he saw the red flush across her cheeks. Then she winked and smiled and started singing.

For the last six months, the closest thing he'd gotten to a church service was with the chaplain in a tent. He liked worshiping in a 150-year-old building, a place where generations of followers of Christ had gotten married, raised their children, fellowshipped together, and prayed together. He wanted to dig into the records of the church and discover any hidden gems. History inspired and encouraged him and helped him see the world through different eyes. He loved the fact that churchgoers and church planters had provided the foundation for building this country.

Cynthia's uncle preached a solid sermon. It held no surprises, but it also didn't contradict Rick's own faith. The man was obviously intelligent and spoke as if he was having a conversation instead of lecturing from a podium.

When the service ended, Cynthia turned to face him. "I'd love for you to meet my uncle. Do you mind waiting?"

He shook his head. "I'm happy to wait."

It didn't take long for the church to empty. Soon, her uncle approached and held out his hand. "Hello, I'm Nathaniel Myers. My niece told me you would be joining us today."

"It's nice to meet you. Rick."

Nathaniel put a hand on Cynthia's shoulder. "Cynthia

told me about what happened in Katangela. Our family owes your team a great debt."

Praise like that always made him feel the need to fidget and dismiss it. "No, sir. I just appreciate the ability to do a job and the talent to do it well."

Her uncle laughed and slapped him on the back. "Join us for lunch."

He glanced at Cynthia, who smiled broadly. "I would enjoy that."

"Frances always cooks a chicken on Friday and leaves it in my refrigerator. So we have cold chicken and potato salad. It's nice out. Why don't you guys meet me in the parsonage yard?"

"You don't need any help?" Cynthia asked.

"Nope. Go enjoy the trees."

Rick let Cynthia lead the way. She didn't go through the main doors of the church but out a side door and down a corridor to an exit. They ended up in a courtyard that had basketball hoops. She gestured toward a wrought-iron fence covered in ivy. "This way. There's a gate you can't see."

At the corner of the fence, she reached through the ivy, and he heard the latch click. The gate swung open, and they stepped out onto a brick patio. Cherry blossom trees created a pink canopy above and the pink carpet below.

Cynthia gestured toward a table and chairs and sat in one of the chairs. "This is my favorite place this time of year. Especially if it's warm enough to be outside."

He winked. "It's rather pink."

Her laughter floated on the breeze. "All different shades." She stretched her legs out and crossed her ankles. "I scoured the papers this morning but didn't see any pictures of the two of us. I think you spotted him before he did any damage."

"That's good." He crossed his arms and looked up at the trees. "Is your uncle married?"

"Widower. She's been gone a long time. I never met her."

"So, Frances is . . ."

"His housekeeper. She's worked for him for twenty-seven years. She lives here Monday through Friday, then goes to visit her sister on the weekends. It's an interesting setup."

"What does your uncle think about his brother?"

Cynthia grinned. "He constantly prays that my father won't slide into the darkness." She sighed. "But seriously, they have a great relationship. I think my father is steady and strong partly because of his brother's steadfast support."

"So, your uncle is running a DC church, and your father is the former senator from Virginia. I conclude you're from this area, right?"

"Yes. My great-grandfather helped build the West Wing of the White House in the thirties. His son, my grandfather, was a judge in Alexandria. That's how my dad ended up in law school. My mom's father was a congressman from Maryland. He was a career politician, and she met my father at some law school rally that had to do with her father."

He nodded. "Impressive."

"What do your parents do?"

With a smile he said, "My dad owns a hardware store and my mom's a kindergarten teacher."

She grinned. "I love that! A kindergarten teacher! She must have the best days."

"She has good days and bad days. She could fill your ears with stories."

"I bet!"

The door to the house opened, and Nathaniel came out carrying a stack of plates and a tablecloth. Cynthia stood and took the tablecloth from him. She brushed the petals off the table, then spread the cloth on top of it.

Nathaniel set the plates down. "I have unsweetened tea and diet soda."

"Tea would be perfect," Rick said.

"Can you give me an extra hand?" Nathaniel asked Cynthia.

"Sure!" She glanced over at Rick. "I'll be right back."

After they left, Rick watched a black ant crawling along a blossom-covered brick. He wanted to define whatever he had going on with Cynthia, but he didn't know how to—or even if he ought to. The constraints of time pushed against him and made him feel like he needed to move faster than he normally would. Maybe he needed to leave tomorrow with the rest of his team and connect with her another time. But the idea of generating physical distance between them right now didn't appeal to him at all.

The door squeaked open, and Cynthia walked out carrying a tray with a tea pitcher and three glasses. "Sometimes Uncle Nathaniel lets his tea sit for a few days. I just tasted it. It should be good."

Before she could finish unloading the tray, Nathaniel came out with a platter of chicken and a bowl of potato salad. Rick stepped forward to relieve him of the platter and set it on the table. Once they had everything arranged, Nathaniel clapped his hands together and said, "Let's pray."

Rick bowed his head and listened to the prayer of thanksgiving for the food. He silently prayed for God's wisdom to guide him in managing this budding relationship with Cynthia.

★ ★ ★

Long after her uncle went inside to rest before evening services, Cynthia and Rick continued to sit in the courtyard. They talked about family, sports, friends, travel, and their relationship with God.

"What was your journey to mission work? I assume your uncle was a great influence," Rick said, brushing at a cherry blossom petal that had fallen onto the tablecloth in front of him.

Cynthia chewed on her bottom lip and focused her gaze at her nearly empty glass of tea. "That's the kind of question I wish I'd been prepared for."

He smiled. "Paul told us to always be ready to share."

"True." She took a deep breath. "I was raised by godly parents who brought me to this church my entire life. And even though I understood and believed, it wasn't until I was humiliated and broken and standing in the middle of a village in a remote jungle that I truly began to see my place in the kingdom of God. I always had faith, and I always followed, but nothing was ever clear before."

He nodded, letting the words sink in. "Why do you suppose that is?"

"Hmm." She ran her finger down the outside of her glass. "Maybe because I never stopped in my forward momentum to listen to God speak."

"Ah, that whole 'be still,'" he said with a smile. "I understand. After my first deployment, I told you I drove across the country. I had a similar experience. Suddenly, in the silence of being alone, with no schedule or responsibilities or training or anything else on my mind, emotionally and spiritually struggling with what I'd seen and done, I found God. But not until I was in that stillness." He stretched his legs out in front of him and laced his fingers behind his head. "Unlike you, though, I received affirmation and confirmation. Sounds like you received conviction and change."

"Yeah." She picked up her glass and raised it in a toast. "Here's to change." They laughed together at her sarcasm. When she set her glass down, she folded her arms on top of the table and leaned toward him. "I imagine it's hard to get established in a church, having to move and then deploy all the time."

He thought about his spiritual walk. "It is, which is why I personally use the post chapel services. The congregants are either military or retired and know the lifestyle. It allows for the people who are new to the area to come in and be enveloped into the fold without having to establish themselves. I love it."

"Is that what you all do?"

He shrugged. "Bill always finds a little country church. He never has a problem integrating. He's a more outgoing individual in a crowd than I. It isn't hard for him to feel like he's at home in a new church." He considered the rest of his team. "Among those of us who are Christians, maybe half go to one of the various chapel services, and the other half find civilian churches."

She looked around. "I grew up here. Not coming to church here was one of the harder parts of boarding school."

"I always love going home to my parents' church as well."

They shifted topics to hometowns, sports, favorite movies. Rick never wanted to leave that spot. Occasionally, pink blossoms fluttered by in the breeze. Birds sang and squirrels ran across the branches. The light shifted, changed colors, sometimes highlighting Cynthia's hair like a halo and sometimes making her eyes shine.

Eventually, though, she looked at her watch, and he knew their respite from the world had ended. His face muscles ached from smiling and laughing, and still he grinned as he stood. "I need to head back. I'm having dinner with the team tonight before everyone disperses on leave."

She stood with him and held out her hand. "You have a good vacation in Kentucky."

When he put his hand on hers, he didn't know who moved first, but somehow, she ended up pressed against him, his arms wrapped around her. He rested his cheek on her hair and breathed in the scent of lavender, closing his eyes to savor this moment. He wanted more than anything to kiss her, but something held him back. So he simply relished the feel of her against him, his arms around her.

He didn't know how long they stood there, but eventually, he relaxed his arms and stepped back. "Can I walk you to your car?" he asked.

She cleared her throat and gestured over her shoulder. "I'll go in and hang out with my uncle for a bit, then stay for evening services. My parents are supposed to come."

They said their goodbyes, and he slowly walked through the gate and toward his lone car sitting in the empty parking lot. After he got in, he closed his eyes. "God, I need Your help. What to do? What to do?"

He encountered heavier-than-expected traffic for a late Sunday afternoon, then remembered the Cherry Blossom Festival had started yesterday. It had taken some pretty heavy lifting to get their hotel rooms in the midst of the influx of tourists, and he couldn't extend his stay.

In the lobby, he found McBride and Swanson. "Hey," he said as he approached, "where's everyone else?"

"On their way." Swanson looked at his phone. "Trout's in Ozzy's room trying to get him to come with us. No luck, though."

Rick nodded, thinking about what Cynthia had said yesterday. "Tell him to leave but ask if Ozzy wants us to bring him back a steak."

"Roger," Swanson said, typing into the phone.

Eventually, everyone else joined them, including Sergeant Waller and his wife, Leanne. Rick had met her before the ceremony yesterday but hadn't spent a lot of time speaking to her. She'd attended his high school several years after he graduated, and now she worked in search and rescue.

"I imagine going back to Kentucky won't hold the same adventure as Colorado did," he said.

Leanne shrugged and smiled. "I didn't suffer from a lack of adventure in Kentucky."

"Oh, right, you worked there too."

"I did, and your mom was my teacher. When Tim told me about you being from Charula, your name resonated with me. How serendipitous, eh?"

Peña snorted. "You Kentuckians with your big words." He lifted his chin toward the restaurant. "I made reservations. Food's really good and we don't have to figure out transportation."

"Perfect."

He enjoyed dinner with his team. He led a strong group. It was nice to have them all together again, and to add Waller to their group. They bonded, worked well together. They'd faced some losses that almost staggered their morale, but they'd bounced back. He knew that for the rest of their lives, wherever they went and whatever they did, the band of people they'd served with on this team would always have a special place in each of their hearts.

Back in his room, he took a long, hot shower, still relishing the modern plumbing and clean water. He wondered if he would ever take such amenities for granted again. He slipped on a pair of gym shorts and sat in the desk chair, looking out at the Washington Monument that stood sentry behind the White House. He thought about Cynthia's great-grandfather helping build the West Wing ninety years ago, and how he sat here now. Leanne Waller's word came back to him: serendipitous.

He glanced upward and said, "You're pretty amazing, God. Thank You for half of my team being at the same table tonight. Keep them safe as they travel for leave. Help the Wallers find a good house. Let me rest and recuperate at home. Please give me a sign as it pertains to Cynthia Myers. I'm drawn to her, and I feel like that's Your fault. Amen."

Another hour passed, and finally he got up from the chair. He picked up his phone and set it back down. He picked it up again and hit the call button. He probably should have looked at the time first. How was it after midnight? He quickly hit the end button.

Seconds later, his phone rang, and Cynthia's number crossed his screen. "Hey," he said as he answered. "I started to call you, then realized how late it is."

After a slight pause she said, "Is everything okay? How was dinner?"

"Everything is great. Dinner was good. I tried to extend my hotel stay, but it's impossible because of the festival. I'm going to head home tomorrow."

"Thank you for spending the day with me. I had an amazing time."

"It was that." He cleared his throat. "Listen, if you're up to it, Kentucky is, uh, a beautiful state. Have you ever been?"

"No. Never." Silence filled the line, and he looked out at the White House. Finally, she asked, "Are you asking me to go to Kentucky with you?"

Heat rushed to his cheeks, and sweat beaded on his upper lip. "Uh, I just thought that maybe you'd . . ." His voice trailed off. "Never mind."

"Rick." She took a deep breath and slowly released it. "I would love to see Kentucky. Especially in the springtime." Another pause. "Let me see what I can work out."

His pulse picked up speed. "Really? Great," he said on a breath. "I'm leaving in the morning, but let me know. Call anytime."

"I will."

After he hung up the phone, he looked at it for several minutes. Why had he just done that? What had prompted him? Then he remembered his prayer and chuckled.

"Well, God, I sure hope that's what You had in mind," he said, heading into the bathroom to brush his teeth. "I'm game if You are."

CHAPTER

★

TWENTY-FOUR

Theo toddled toward Cynthia with his arms raised, so she knelt down and scooped him up. His bright brown eyes danced in his face, and he patted her cheeks with his plump little hands. She pressed her lips against his black curls and inhaled the smell of baby shampoo while she looked at his mom.

She and Dahlia Nonaka had gone to medical school together. Now her friend worked as a substitute urgent-care doctor for just enough hours to keep up her skills while devoting as much time as possible to Theo and his coming sister. Dahlia had grown up in St. Thomas and met her husband when he traveled back there to help a friend open a sushi restaurant. Now he owned a restaurant in Alexandria. Dahlia had creamy brown skin, black hair she wore in braids that brushed her shoulders, and light-brown eyes.

"Let me tell you," she said, her island accent more pronounced. She sat against the arm of the couch, took a sip of her tea, and pointed at Cynthia. "You need to get on a train or a plane or in a car and get thee down to Kentucky."

Cynthia gasped. "You've never even met this man."

Dahlia shook her head. "True. But I've seen the look on your face when you talk about him. And he sounds very sexy."

Cynthia put her hand over her mouth. "That is the craziest thing I've heard in a long time."

"Crazy doesn't always mean bad."

A giggle escaped before she could contain it. "True."

"Plus he rescued you." Dahlia put a hand over her heart. "You have to admit that is so romantic. And romantic can make all the difference." As Cynthia opened her mouth to reply, Dahlia put a hand up. "Don't you try to deny it or I'll call you a liar."

She chuckled and thought about Rick. What Andrew had done to her had ripped away her ability to trust. The long conversations she and Rick had in Katangela and here had been the best ones she'd ever had with anyone. They made her want to believe she could trust him. "I don't want to be swept off my feet again."

"It doesn't sound to me like the two men are even remotely similar." Theo went after Cynthia's earring, so Dahlia reached forward and plucked him out of her arms. She carried him over to a little toddler-sized kitchen and stood him up next to the stove. "Be like Daddy," she said. "Cook me something good." She came back to the sofa. "Andrew came after you in a planned, strategic attack. You had no hope and not enough experience to see it coming. Rick sounds like someone who is very careful, very methodical, and who would probably cut off his arm before he did anything to hurt you. If he invited you to Kentucky, it's because he wants to spend time with you and wants to give you an opportunity to get to know him in his environment."

Dahlia accepted a plastic banana from Theo with a smile and a kiss. He giggled and ran back to the kitchen. She slid forward and took Cynthia's hand. "Go to Kentucky. Have fun. Take a picture of a racehorse for me."

Heat spread from her chest over her cheeks. "Dahlia, I don't know. What will people think?"

"Sister, I am a Black doctor married to a Japanese chef. Since when have I ever cared what people think?"

That made Cynthia chuckle. "You're right. I know you are." She sighed. "The problem with me compared to you is that I tend to attract reporters lately. So no matter what happens, someone will find out that I went and Rick's reputation might be hurt."

Theo carried over a little plastic skillet containing a rubber fried egg. "Oh, yum," Cynthia said, taking it from him. "Thank you." He squealed and toddled back to his stove.

Dahlia sipped from her teacup and coyly said, "You could travel as Mrs. Nonaka."

Cynthia looked at her with wide eyes, contemplating the thought. "How would that work when I checked in?"

"I can check you in with my phone. You can use the app for the hotel and access a digital key. You'd never have to even go near the front desk."

Could that possibly work? How lovely to travel incognito and surprise Rick! "That's a great idea," she said.

Dahlia clapped her hands and snatched her phone off the end table. "Where are we going?"

★ ★ ★

Cynthia stayed for lunch at Dahlia's, then headed home. In her room, she wrote a check for the coming hotel bill and put it in a thank-you card. She addressed the envelope to Dahlia and found a book of stamps in her desk drawer.

She emailed the head of the Secret Service detachment and let him know she was going out of town but didn't want a detail to accompany her. If anything, that would definitely bring the press.

She'd have to drive because she didn't want to fly under her real name. If she left at four in the morning, she'd arrive by twelve or one.

After she got her suitcase out of her closet, she set it on the bed and thought about what to pack. What did one bring for a clandestine trip to small-town Kentucky? Finally, she settled on mostly casual clothes, one outfit suitable for church, and a little black dress. Out of habit but with the hope that she'd never need it, she grabbed her medical bag.

She carried the bags downstairs and put the card to Dahlia in the outgoing mail tray, then went to her mother's office. The door stood open, so she tapped on the frame as she walked in.

Her mom sat at her desk, signing letters. She looked up and slipped her glasses off. "Hello, love." As she stood, she set her pen on the stack of papers. "I'm replying to elementary kids who wrote me last week."

Cynthia grinned and walked into her mother's hug. "That's a lot of letters."

"They were all very sweet." She led them to the window seat. "So, tell me, what's on your dance card this week?"

How did she explain this? "Captain Rick Norton asked me to join him in Kentucky. He's there on leave in his hometown."

Her mother's eyebrows rose. "I see. And how do you feel about him?"

Wanting to answer the question honestly, she said, "Well, at first I really didn't like him. Every conversation we had ended in an argument. He was everything I did not like. But as we spent time together in the jungle and then in the capital city, my respect for him grew. He's a man of integrity and honor."

After a silent moment, her mom said, "So, in response to my question of how you feel about him, you reply with, your respect for him has grown."

Heat spread up Cynthia's chest and into her face. "I really like him, Mom." She clenched her hands in her lap. "I like talking to him. I like being with him. I want to get to know him more."

"And going to his family home is how that will get accomplished?"

With a shrug she tried her best to explain. "His job is super intense. He told me once that none of what he does for a living travels with him to Kentucky. He allows himself to completely unwind and relax. I'd really like to see him like that, to know the man under the uniform."

Her mom smiled and surprised her by saying, "Wonderful. Have a good trip. Don't make dumb decisions. But please do something for me."

Cynthia hadn't come in seeking her mother's approval, only to inform her of her plans. But getting her approval released a tension that she didn't even know had gripped her until it disappeared. "What?"

"Reinstate the Secret Service detail."

She gasped. "I sent that email to them like twenty minutes ago!"

"And they forwarded it to me like nineteen minutes ago." Her mom put a hand on her shoulder. "Please just let them be present. They don't have to be invasive."

She thought about it for a moment, then nodded. "Fine. They can be in the same town. But I better not ever see them."

"Fair enough. I'll make sure they know that." Her mom cupped her cheek. "I love you. I hope Rick Norton is a good thing for you."

"Thanks, Mom."

The smell of gunpowder mingled with blood burned Cynthia's nose. Her stomach rolled as she rushed to her father's side and put her arm around his shoulders. Before she could speak, the sound of a gun cocking in her ear made her blood freeze.

"Tell me, Doctor, how you let my son die," Chukuwereije said in her ear, his breath hot against her cheek.

Cynthia opened her eyes. Even though she found herself in her own room, her nose still burned with the acrid smell. The taste of fear still filled her mouth. As she sat up, she realized that her tears had soaked the hair at her temples.

Unwilling to try to sleep again, she took a shower, dressed in denim leggings and a loose white T-shirt, and grabbed her suitcase. She left the house at three in the morning. As she drove out of the compound, she saw the flash of headlights in her rearview mirror and knew that her detail followed her. With a sigh, she thought about living in a world that required a security detail to follow someone going on a trip. Sorrow filled her heart as she thought about the violence that drove some people.

To see the world full of such pain, such hate, made her wish she could fix it. She wanted the power to make it all go away, to heal the nations and bring love and peace to all the lands. Even though she didn't have the ability to affect the entire world, she did have the power and the gifts to affect small portions of it. Maybe pouring herself into work would help her psyche heal from the fear that had bruised it recently.

She had always loved visiting Aunt Kate at work, seeing the waiting room full of pregnant women, knowing that her aunt helped them through their entire pregnancies to have healthy births and healthy babies. She'd observed Aunt Kate during family functions, accepting phone calls, leaving because she had to do a delivery, regaling her and her mom with stories and anecdotes.

Before she'd even begun high school, Cynthia knew what she wanted to do for a living. Her interest in politics began and ended with her father, but medicine called to her, spoke to her heart like a longtime friend. Obstetrics had been her obvious choice, but going through rotations in medical school, she'd seen the beauty in all the practices. She only wanted to help people—help women—bring healthy babies into the world.

As the sky lightened, she stopped at a fast-food restaurant in West Virginia and got a cup of coffee and a fried chicken biscuit. Her mouth watered at the smell of the freshly brewed drink mingled with the buttery smell of the biscuit. It transported her back to her residency. After a twenty-four-hour shift, one of the residents had made a run for chicken biscuits and coffee. Cynthia was so exhausted but so pumped at the work she'd done. With burning eyes and an aching back, she sat in the doctors' lounge and enjoyed the breakfast instead of going home and crashing. She didn't realize how hungry she felt until her first bite of biscuit. She'd eaten two that morning, then managed to get home and sleep for about ten hours.

Her mind roamed over the friends she'd made back then, the ones she still had now. She took the time to pray for them individually, thankful for the good people God had placed in her sphere.

She crossed the Kentucky border in late morning and made it to Charula at lunchtime. The hotel didn't allow check-in until three, so she drove around the town square.

If someone had asked her to outline the quintessential small town, she didn't think she could come close to the perfection that she discovered in Charula, Kentucky. Main Street ended at a river park, where a statue depicting emergency response heroes stood under a giant American flag.

She saw a diner, the police department, an ice cream shop, and a coffee shop around a traffic circle. A flower shop had springtime flowers spilling out onto the walk, and a sewing shop displayed beautiful quilts. She found a parking space in front of a dress shop that had lovely retro-style dresses in the big picture window.

As she got out of the car and stretched, she spotted a historical marker. She wandered over to it and read about the county that split almost evenly during the War between the States.

She slipped her sunglasses off and looked around. Her heart lodged in her throat when she spotted Norton's Hardware. With a dry mouth and a pounding heart, she crossed to it. As soon as she got to the parking lot, she recognized Rick's car. After propping her sunglasses on her head, she walked into the store. A bell above the door jingled, announcing her arrival.

A woman in her twenties with brown hair in two braids worked behind the counter, making a key. An older man in blue coveralls with a large belly waited. The clerk made eye contact with Cynthia but did not speak—she just smiled and went back to her task. Cynthia wandered down the aisle and pretended to inspect yard sale signs when she heard Rick's voice coming from the back of the store. She followed the sound and found him chatting with an older man packing a box of PVC piping.

He must have heard her approach because he glanced in her direction and stopped speaking midsentence. Almost instantly, a grin covered his face, lighting up his eyes. She bit her lip and stepped forward. Before she knew what happened, they had moved toward each other and his arms came around her.

For a moment, she just stood there, wrapped up in his strong arms, her cheek resting on his chest. She closed her eyes and relished the feel of him. Then she stepped back slightly and looked up at him. He brushed his fingers down her cheek, his gaze roaming over her face. When his eyes met hers, her breath caught in the back of her throat. His face had a serious expression, his eyes burning with emotion she couldn't define.

She opened her mouth to say something nonsensical like, "Surprise." But before a sound could escape, his lips covered hers.

Everything around them dissolved into nothing save the feel of his soft lips, the brush of his rough hands, the smell of his skin. She stepped forward even more, tilted her head, stood on her toes—anything to get as close to him as possible. Her fingers ran through his short hair, brushed over his ears. She pressed her hands against his cheeks, the rough stubble tickling her palms.

He gripped the back of her head, stilling her. He slowly lifted his lips from hers and pressed his forehead against hers. She closed her eyes, tried to catch her breath, and with every intake of air, she smelled his aftershave. Her head spun, and she licked her lips.

"I was worried you didn't really mean to invite me, that you didn't want me here in your safe place," she whispered.

"There's absolutely nothing I ever wanted more." He turned. She remembered the man he'd been speaking to and felt heat rush over her face.

The man stood there, his arms crossed over his chest, one shoulder leaning against the shelf, just grinning.

"Dad, this is Doctor Cynthia Myers. Cynthia, my father, Harold."

His father? What must he think of her? She put on her best smile and held out her hand. "It's very nice to meet you."

"Well," Harold said, "this is definitely a nice surprise." He shook her hand and then slapped Rick on the shoulder. "You go on now. I'll see you later."

"Not going to argue with the man." Rick took her hand and led the way out of the store, pausing at the doorway to speak to the woman behind the counter. "See you, Darlene."

She stopped polishing the key that she had just cut and nodded at him. "Okey dokey."

Outside, Cynthia slipped her sunglasses back on her face. "I just drove in. I parked across the street near the park so I could stretch my legs a little bit."

He gestured toward a bench in front of the coffee shop, and they sat. "Why didn't you let me know you were coming?" he asked.

She ran her teeth over her bottom lip. "Honestly, I wasn't entirely sure I would come."

"What, you might have driven eight hours and then changed your mind?"

She shrugged and looked at the green paint on the bench. "I might have turned around. I don't know. What if you got home and everything became clearer?"

"It definitely did." He took her hand. "In spades."

She opened her mouth but didn't know what to say as he ran his hand up and down her arm.

"I can't believe someone who went into the jungle of Katangela by herself would be afraid to come to Charula, Kentucky."

She smiled. "Well, I just wanted to give myself an out if I felt like I needed to take it. I haven't had experience in anything like this. Well, except the . . . I mean—"

"I meant what I said, Cynthia." His face grew serious. "I am not looking for anything from you for my own gain. You can trust me."

Desperate to change the subject, she gestured toward the store and asked, "I didn't take you from anything important, did I?"

He shook his head. "I wasn't working there today. My father doesn't usually need my help. I was just chatting with him while he handled some inventory." He turned and scanned the businesses around them. "Where are your babysitters?"

She glanced around too. "My mom convinced me to let

them come, provided I never see them. If I can pick them out of the crowd, I get to send them home."

He raised an eyebrow. "Are you allowed to have that kind of say?"

She shrugged. "I can deny protection. Besides, I'm incognito here. My friend Dahlia made me a hotel reservation in her name, and I should be good."

"Clever girl. What hotel?"

"The big one over by the—"

"Over by the river." He glanced at his watch. "It's probably too early for you to check in."

"Yes—three o'clock. I have time to get lunch."

He gave a broad smile. "Perfect! Let's go to Betsy's."

"Ah yes, the diner you talked about. That sounds like perfection to me."

CHAPTER

★

TWENTY-FIVE

Rick opened the door to Betsy's Diner, and the familiar smell of grilling meat, fresh bread, and coffee greeted him. He led the way to a booth against the wall and instinctively slid into the seat across from Cynthia with his back to the wall and a view of the entrance.

He gazed at her, amazed she'd come. When he hadn't heard back from her in a few days, he assumed she had thought better of the idea and decided she didn't want to see him again. He'd spent the entire day driving home feeling sorry for himself, analyzing their last conversation over and over to see where he had gone off track.

Kissing her had come so naturally. Before he'd realized it, his lips were on hers. If he could freeze that moment in time, he would. He probably should feel at least slightly embarrassed for kissing her in front of his dad like that, but quite frankly, the emotions that overwhelmed him right now left no room for embarrassment.

"If you enjoy a good diner, this place needs to be on your map," he said, pulling a menu out of the stand and handing it to her. He didn't need it. He knew what he wanted.

While she read the menu, he studied her. He could see the fatigue on her face, but it did nothing to detract from her beauty. She must have felt his stare, because she glanced up at him and a blush covered her cheeks. He thought again about their first kiss and wanted to reach across the table just to touch her. "I'm really glad you're here."

She smiled and reached for his hand. He easily placed it in both of hers. "Me too."

"Well, if it ain't the prodigal," Betsy said from beside the table.

Rick glanced at her and smiled. The townspeople of Charula considered Betsy as much an establishment as her diner. At seventy, if she didn't dye her hair with cheap black dye, it would be snow-white. She was five feet one, skinny, and wore heeled boots and bright-red lipstick.

"I got in yesterday. Came here as soon as I could and brought a friend."

She screwed her face up into what passed as a smile. "If you got here yesterday, you did not get here as soon as you could. I reckon you were waiting on your lovely friend to arrive." She looked in Cynthia's direction. "And you are a genuine beauty. I'm certain there's a story there."

He released Cynthia's hand as he chuckled, then remembered something. "Hey, Betsy, do you know Timothy Waller? His parents have a farm out off 15. His wife was an EMT here. Did search and rescue too."

She sucked at her teeth for a moment, then nodded.

"Yes. Ain't seen much of him since high school, but he was stationed here at the Army post for a couple of years recently."

"He's in my unit now. He's my new medic."

"He's a good boy. You should ask him about his wife and him one time. Talk about a story. Not mine to tell, mind you." She looked at Cynthia again. "I'm Betsy, since this one here is too rude to do the introducing."

Cynthia smiled and held out her hand. "Cynthia. Rick told me all about this place. It's nice to meet you."

"Well, at least he's telling somebody something."

Rick narrowed his eyes at her. "Are you about done being nosy?"

She gave him a bright red smile. "For now. What can I get you?"

Cynthia ignored the exchange as she said, "I will take a tuna sandwich and an unsweet tea."

Betsy nodded and looked at him. "Well?"

He smiled sweetly at her. "Patty melt."

When she walked away, Rick cleared his throat. "Betsy is my great-aunt. My grandmother's sister. She is a bit abrupt with family."

Cynthia looked in the direction of the kitchen. "She is certainly a character. I'm glad I knew a little bit about her before we got here."

He shook his head. "When did we talk about Betsy?"

"It was one of those conversations where we talked about a thousand things." She sat back and crossed her arms over her chest. "So, Captain Norton, how do you spend your leave days?"

Once again, his mind roamed to kissing her in the plumbing aisle of Norton's Hardware. He was figuring out what he'd like to do with his leave.

He cleared his throat. "I visit friends and family. Hang with Bill."

"Bill? Sanders?"

"Yeah, he'll be here tomorrow night."

She tilted her head slightly to the right. "I don't mean this to be rude, but why does he come here on leave? Doesn't he live in Alabama?"

Rick thought about Bill's family dynamics and shook his head. "He lives where the Army sends him. We've been friends since we were both young soldiers, so he always comes home with me on leave. This time, he went with Swanson to his parents' home before coming here."

Betsy brought their drinks to the table but didn't speak. He winked at her anyway, and she snapped at his shoulder with her towel.

Cynthia peeled the paper off her straw and jammed it into her tea. "Bill doesn't approve of us, does he?"

Her insight surprised him. "Where do you get that?"

She shrugged one shoulder. "It was just some undercurrent when you two were in DC. I guess I didn't make a great impression on him, huh?"

Shaking his head, he took her hand in his. It looked very small in comparison. "He thinks you're out of my league. One day you'll wake up and realize it, and then where will I be?"

She raised her eyebrows. "What do *you* think about that?"

With a slow, languid grin, he said, "I think that I really enjoyed kissing you earlier and hope we get to do that again soon."

A smile lit her face. "Yeah? It wasn't planned or anything."

"Says you." He let her go and sat back as Betsy set their plates in front of them.

"Thanks, Aunt Betsy," he said, making a kissing motion in the air.

"Humph," she replied, then stomped off.

Cynthia looked at her retreating back, then at him. "What made her so angry?"

"Betsy takes pride in knowing everything about everyone. Her ear is always to the ground. She never shares it. She just knows it. She didn't know about you."

"Ah. Gotcha. If your mom had met me first or something, word would have gotten to her and she wouldn't have been surprised to see me."

His eyes widened. "How do you understand small town gossip?"

She snorted. "Please. I know Capitol Hill. Nowhere on earth tops that gossip pit."

He bowed his head and thanked God for the food and for Cynthia's safe travels. After she said, "Amen," they started eating.

In between bites, they chatted about each of their drives from DC to Kentucky. "How come you didn't get here until yesterday?" she asked before biting the corner off a potato chip.

"I went home via North Carolina. I had to pack, make some arrangements."

"And you go back there from here, or to your new place?"

"There first. We'll go back and get ready to move to Fort Campbell, Kentucky."

"Fort Campbell?" Betsy said from two tables over. "Well."

He grinned over at her. "Better than Bragg."

"That ain't very hard, from what I hear."

His grin turned into a smile. "Fair enough. But Campbell's in Kentucky."

"Ain't most of it in Tennessee?" she said as if she meant it as an insult.

He chuckled. "Not the part I'll be in."

"Humph."

Cynthia took a bite of her sandwich, then brushed the crumbs off her fingers. "Why do you have to move?"

"Our entire team is moving. There are twelve of us. There's a strategic reason we're going from Bragg to Campbell, but it's not really up to me to guess what it is. I just go where they tell me to go and sign in the day I'm supposed to sign in." He could see the questions on her face. "It's part of the military culture."

Her expression relaxed. "Understood. So, twelve? I only met seven."

"We'd been split in Katangela. Half of my team got folded into another team of twelve to do a bigger mission. They got back to Yambuli about a week before we did. They would have just stayed and waited for us, but your father's detail kind of took up the space. As soon as we got on those helicopters, they took off."

"They were waiting to make sure they didn't need to come help you?"

"Pretty much. Knowing Chief Hanson—who you haven't met but he's my assistant commander—they were sitting on the tarmac waiting for the green light to head into the jungle." He wiped his fingers on a paper napkin and sat back.

"Is Fort Campbell the Army base I saw driving here?"

He thought about the route she would have taken and shook his head. "No. The installation here is Fort Breckenridge. I use the PX and commissary sometimes, but I've never been stationed here. Not sure how I'd feel about that." He took a bite of his patty melt. "Campbell is on the border of Tennessee not far from Nashville. In fact, the post is split between the two states. I'm looking forward to being there for a couple of years."

They ate in silence for a moment, then she said, "Bill told me Peña's wife works with your team."

He nodded. "Emma. She's a contractor with some pretty fantastic language skills. That's how they met. She was providing translation services." He thought about Emma Peña. "She has an interesting story. She fit right into the team, and every time I can use her, I do."

Cynthia pushed her plate aside and rested her elbow on the table, propping her chin in her hand. "You love them."

Eyes widening, he said, "Them?"

"Your team."

He processed the thought, analyzed his feelings, and then tried to put them into words. "They call me Daddy for a reason. At any given time, their lives, their livelihoods, rest in my hands. I have the authority to tell them when and what to eat, when and where to sleep, and who or what to kill. They trust me implicitly, and I trust them. Together, we're a finely tuned instrument."

She smiled. "You love them."

"Yes." He chuckled and tossed his napkin onto his empty plate. "You finished?" He looked pointedly at her half-eaten sandwich.

"I ate a big chicken biscuit a few hours ago. I'm good."

★ ★ ★

After lunch, they walked around the town square. Rick pointed out landmarks, businesses, and points of interest. They strolled down one road and ended up at the riverside park. Rick went into a little coffee shop and got them coffees, and they sat side by side at a picnic table, their backs to it, watching a barge slowly make its way down the river.

Cynthia felt relaxed and a little sleepy. Content to sit next to him, she didn't feel the need to fill the silence. She scooted closer, and he put his arm around her. She leaned into him, closing her eyes and savoring his presence.

A horn blaring startled her, and she jerked up.

"Well, hello there," Rick said.

Confused, Cynthia looked around. The light in the sky looked different. "Did I fall asleep?"

"You did. I'm going to have to say something to Lizzy about her coffee."

Embarrassment spread heat up her cheeks. "How long was I asleep?"

"Oh, a good hour." He rested his arm on the table and leaned toward her. "I'm not complaining, Doc. I kind of liked holding you while you slept."

Energy hummed through her muscles, and she jumped up. "I, uh, need to go check in." She picked up her phone to check the time and saw a text from Dahlia.

All checked in. You have a digital key on your phone. Have fun.

She held up her phone. "Dahlia checked me in. I have a key."

"Cynthia, you don't need to escape."

301

She slowly lowered herself back down. Her embarrassment at falling asleep started to fade, and her flight response stilled. "I don't sleep well anymore," she said, feeling the need to explain.

Concern etched a frown into his face. He brushed a thumb under her eye. "Still nightmares?"

Tell me, Doctor, how you let my son die.

"Yes."

"Have you talked to anyone?"

"Just Uncle Nathaniel." She ran her teeth over her bottom lip.

"I really think you need to speak to a professional counselor." The idea of trying to put into words how she felt to make someone understand held no appeal. "I appreciate the thought." She stood again, slower this time. "I'm going to go to the hotel and freshen up."

"Sounds good." He gestured with his chin toward the coffee shop. "Your tail has on a blue T-shirt. He's been sitting at that little table on the patio staring at his phone for the last hour."

"He's probably not the only one."

"No. There's a car across the park."

"As long as it's not the press." She put her foot on the bench and leaned toward him. It felt good to stretch her legs like that after sleeping at an odd angle. "How do you feel about my companions?"

Amusement glinted in his eyes. "I feel like they better be ready to do their job if it comes down to it."

In a bold move, she put a hand on his cheek and leaned closer to him, lightly brushing his lips with hers. "Give me an hour?"

"Sure. I'll text you my address."

"I'll meet you there." She straightened and brushed her hair away from her face.

He stood. "I'll walk you to your car."

She easily slipped her hand into his, and they gradually made their way back to the town square. "I love this town," she said. "It's exactly perfect."

He squeezed her hand. "I'm glad you came."

"Me too." At her car, she pulled her key fob out of her pocket and unlocked it. "I'll see you in about an hour."

He stepped forward and brushed her cheek with his fingertips. The vibration of his touch radiated down to her toes. He looked down at her for what seemed an eternity, his green eyes growing ever darker. Finally, he lowered his lips and gave her a gentle kiss. The butterflies woke back up and started fluttering in her stomach.

"I'll see you in about an hour," he echoed as he raised his head and opened her door for her.

Thankfully, Cynthia was just a few blocks from the hotel. She grabbed her suitcase out of the trunk, pulled up the hotel's app on her phone, and used the login Dahlia gave her, accessing the room number and digital key. She kept her sunglasses on as she strolled through the lobby, thankful she didn't have to stop at the front desk, and went straight to the elevator and then the third floor. When she got to her room, she heard the lock disengage.

As soon as she unpacked, she called Dahlia. "I had no issues. Thank you again." She could hear baby Theo in the background, squealing at something.

"How did it go?" Dahlia asked.

A silly grin covered Cynthia's face. She put a hand against her cheek. "He kissed me. As soon as he saw me."

"Girl! I expect details soon!"

"You bet."

She hung up and rolled her head back and forth. While she waited for the shower to heat up, she wandered over to the window. Her room looked out over the river. She looked to the left, pressing against the glass to see as far as possible, and spotted the park where they'd had coffee this afternoon. Well, Rick had coffee, she had a nap. Such a small amount of time together and she'd wasted it sleeping!

She got into the shower, determined to wash away the fog of exhaustion. After drying her hair, she reapplied makeup, then slipped on a pair of gray jeans and a shirt the color of burnt copper. Not knowing the evening temperature in early April in Kentucky, she grabbed a sweater just in case.

Rick had texted her his parents' address, and a quick check told her she had about a ten-minute drive. She looked at her watch. She should get there right at the hour mark. With a smile, she let him know she was on her way and headed out of the hotel.

She drove through the charming town and out of the downtown area. Here, she found some chain restaurants and larger nationally branded stores, a hospital, and a sign pointing to a high school. Just beyond the sign, she turned into a neighborhood and soon parked in front of a brick ranch-style house with white shutters and a flower bed full of yellow and white daffodils.

As she got out of the car, the front door opened, and Rick filled the doorway. He'd changed into a pair of dark jeans and a light-blue long-sleeved T-shirt. He slipped a hand into one pocket and raised the other in a greeting.

"Looks like you found it okay," he said, approaching her car.

"Yeah. Not hard to find at all."

When he reached her, he paused, then slipped a hand behind her neck, giving her a soft kiss. She could smell his lemony aftershave and brushed the backs of her fingers over his smooth cheeks.

"You shaved again," she said when he lifted his head.

"Observant and beautiful." He used his thumb to point behind him. "I bet my mom's standing in the doorway."

Cynthia glanced over his shoulder and saw a woman step through the door and onto the front stoop. "She is," she said, suddenly nervous. "Is it okay that I'm here?"

"Are you kidding me?" He kissed her forehead, then turned and took her hand, leading her up the drive. "Mom, Doctor Cynthia Myers. Cynthia, my mom, Dorothy."

Rick's mom had straight, gray-streaked brown hair cut to her shoulders and laugh lines around her bright-green eyes. "Oh, please. The only person who has ever called me Dorothy was my seventh-grade science teacher." She stepped forward and held out her hands. "I'm Dottie. Welcome to our home."

Cynthia put her hands in Dottie's, and the woman pulled her close for a hug. She smelled like vanilla and cinnamon. "Thank you. I'm so happy to be here."

Dottie gestured to the door. "Harold normally gets home about seven thirty, but he was going to see if Monty could close for him tonight. Come in, come in. I have dinner about to go into the oven."

CHAPTER
★
TWENTY-SIX

Cynthia stretched her legs out in front of her and leaned back against the chair. The temperature had soared into the midseventies, and the sun beat down, warming her skin. She sat in a picnic area in the gardens on the grounds of the Creation Museum. All around her, flowers bloomed in a beautiful rainbow array. She watched a dragonfly hover over the water of the little creek that ran through the garden and thought about having to go home tomorrow.

"Rick's coming," Bill announced, setting a bottle of water on the table next to her. "He's waiting for the food up in Noah's Cafe."

She picked up the bottle. "Thanks."

Bill had arrived yesterday, Friday. Rick had convinced him to join them on their visit to the Creation Museum, but it had taken some persuasion.

Bill had an intensity about him with such depth of perception that Cynthia worried he saw something wrong with her that she didn't know existed. It created a little undercurrent of anxiety in her that she hadn't felt around him in the jungle.

He sat on the other side of the table, so she swung her legs around and faced him. He watched her with his dark eyes, his face serious, and finally asked, "What are you doing here, Cynthia?"

The question caught her off guard. She decided to be literal. "Eating lunch after spending the morning in a museum dedicated to the scientific evidence supporting the biblical account of creation."

His smile did not reach his eyes. "What are you doing here with Rick, Doctor Myers?"

Putting her chin up, she said, "Spending time with him. Getting to know him. Why do you care?"

His mouth hardened. "Because I care about him. You made it clear how you felt about what we do for a living. Except it's not just his occupation, you know. That's who he is."

She frowned. "What do you mean?"

"I mean he's not someone who is going to fit into your elite circle in the nation's capital. He's the commander of a US Army Special Forces ODA. It's a big deal. He's a big deal. What he does is highly specialized. It has taken him fifteen years of education and training to be one of the best at what he does."

She respected that about Rick. After a beat she said, "And?"

"And this here—this relaxed time in the sunshine and the flowering garden—is the exception to the rule. The man you met in the jungle, that's who he is at his core. If that's not something you can deal with, then you need to step away now before he falls for you any further."

In the time she'd spent with Rick in the hotel in Katangela, in DC, and here, she'd learned that Rick was so much more than the team daddy of a Special Forces A-Team. She knew Bill understood that and wondered why he chose to pinpoint-focus on that aspect of Rick's life. She narrowed her eyes. "And if I *can* deal with it?"

He studied her face for several moments. "Marriage isn't for men like us. Divorce is more our style."

"Why's that?"

"Because we can't let something like a wife and kids at home affect decisions we make in the field. Do you understand what I mean?"

Never one to be bullied, she said, "There are married men on your team."

Before he could reply, Rick approached carrying two trays of food. He set them on the table.

"Ooh, perfect," she said, grabbing a grilled chicken salad. She determined to put Bill's words away and not let them affect her mood. She leaned into Rick's arm while he prayed over the food and afterward, intentionally refusing to meet Bill's eyes.

While they ate, they talked about their experience in the museum. Cynthia loved the logical layout of the exhibits that showed the scientific evidence of a Creator, how God's plan brought humanity out of the garden of Eden and into Christ's arms, and how to process the bad things that happen in the world.

"I didn't actually learn anything new," Bill said as he pulled an onion off his sandwich, "but the way everything's laid out really affirms what I already know."

"Likewise," Rick said. "I think I'm going to bring Mom

and Dad out here next week. Maybe take them to the Ark Encounter too."

"I'm surprised you've never been here before," Cynthia said. "You're only a couple of hours away."

He shrugged. "Normally when I come home, I'm completely focused on decompressing. I don't usually look for something to do."

She thought about Bill's words again. Trying to push them out of her mind, she dipped a piece of grilled chicken into some ranch dressing and said, "Well, thank you for bringing me. I will definitely come back another time."

They'd taken separate cars. Bill left from the museum to go visit with Sergeant Waller, who had arrived in Charula to visit his family. In the car with Rick, Cynthia reached over and took his hand.

He glanced over at her as he got on the interstate. "I'm going to miss you."

She brought his hand up and pressed her cheek against it. "I'm going to miss you too. Too bad you won't be stationed in my area."

"Right? No Green Berets in those parts."

She looked in the side mirror and saw their tail. "Do you think the agents enjoyed the museum?"

He chuckled. "I think they only had eyes for their job. I doubt they even looked at one exhibit."

"Maybe they saw enough that it sparked an interest and they'll go back one day. It's possible that going today will affect eternity for one of them."

He squeezed her hand. "I like that thought." As she yawned, she covered her mouth. He glanced at her again. "You going to be up to driving tomorrow morning?"

"Yeah. If I go in the morning." She'd had a few nightmares this week, but nothing like before. "When I drove here, I left at three and I was fine. But I wouldn't have been at three in the afternoon."

"You can stay longer if you need to."

"I know." She glanced at a horse farm as they drove by. A beautiful chestnut-brown mare had a new foal that stood next to her on skinny little legs.

They chatted the rest of the way to her hotel. When Rick parked in the parking lot, they got out of the car, and she stretched her hands above her head. "I need to walk off the ride."

Hand in hand, they strolled to the river and walked slowly along the path, knowing that at the end of the walk, they would have to say goodbye.

Bill's words rolled through her mind. He could read people like a book. Rick had mentioned that several times. He relied on Bill to help him determine fact from fiction when questioning assets or prisoners, and to give him insight into the mental health and well-being of his team in more stressful situations. What did Bill see that had him constantly bucking against Rick and Cynthia pursuing a relationship?

At one point, she stopped walking and looked up at Rick. He had an attractive presence and was such a confident leader. Courage and authority radiated from him. She imagined a roomful of men would all turn to him for direction if the need arose. She looked at her reflection in his sunglasses, trying to see in her what he apparently saw.

"Do you really love what you do?" she blurted out.

He raised an eyebrow, and his face remained stoic. "I believe I'm doing what God has for me to do."

"That doesn't actually answer my question."

He shrugged. "I'm gifted and trained. When I'm in the field, I feel like I'm truly me. Everything I do and say and feel is a culmination of natural talents, instinct, and the best training in the world."

Emotion surged into her throat. She remembered the Rick she'd first met, the one who had moved with a weapon like it was a part of him. "So, you feel more like you when you're pointing a gun at someone than when you're with me?"

He snatched his sunglasses off. "Whoa. Where did that come from?"

She looked up at the purple and orange hues of the sky reflecting the setting sun. She remembered her gloved hands covered in Bill's blood as she dug a bullet out of his chest, the sound of the saw in the operating room removing Ozzy's leg. For the first time since the hotel in Katangela, she faced the truth about herself, about what she'd experienced and what scared her right now. "I don't think I can cope well after having a front-row seat to watching you do your job."

Her gaze shifted to his face. Emotions swirled in his eyes. "Cynthia, you can't mean—"

"Stop. Don't tell me what I mean." She took a step back. "I believe I could fall in love with you. I probably already have. But I can't be some wife who waits for you to come home. I've been there. I've seen it. I've dug a bullet out of a chest and amputated a leg!"

His eyes narrowed, but not before she saw the panic in them. "So, this is it?"

"Does it have to be? Can't you do something else?"

He flinched like she'd hit him. "Do something else?"

"Yes. Get assigned to DC. You wouldn't have to deploy.

You could do something different for the Army. Or leave it entirely. Get a consulting job or something. Surely someone with your training could find a good job."

After several long moments he said, "I don't have a job, Cynthia. This is what I do. Just like being a doctor isn't your job, it's what you do. I would never dream of asking you to stop being a doctor, but somehow it's perfectly fine to ask me to stop being a soldier?"

She spoke so quickly she had no idea where the words even came from. "It's not the same. I save lives. I bring newborn babies into the world. It's a miracle, you know? Those brand-new lives? Every one of them is a miracle. Your job literally means you have to end lives and put yours at risk. I've seen it."

A muscle in his jaw clenched. "So that's what you think." She started to speak, but he held up a hand. "Like I said, I'm doing what God would have me to do right now. When I'm doing it, I feel the most complete. We're the same that way. I don't look down on what you do or who you are. Clearly, you don't reciprocate. You don't respect what I am."

"It's not a lack of respect, Rick. It's a depth of understanding that invokes terror."

He shook his head. "You can't mean this. After everything—" He took a deep breath and put his hands on her shoulders. "After the way we've connected, opened up, loved . . ." He closed his eyes and then opened them again. "Tell me you don't mean this."

Hot tears pricked her eyes. "I can't," she whispered. "Please . . ."

"Please what? Please submit to your conditions? Please change everything about who I am to become the man worthy of your conditional love?" He let her go and took a step back, checking behind his shoulder. "Your detail's just around that bend. I'm going to leave you in their capable hands now." He turned on his heel and walked back the way they'd come.

Panicked, she rushed after him. "Rick!"

When she grabbed his arm, he spun back around, jerking free. "Stop it. You don't get to just suddenly drop this on me. Go home, Cynthia. Thanks for coming to visit. It's been very edifying."

This time when he walked away, she didn't go after him.

★ ★ ★

FORT BRAGG, NORTH CAROLINA

As he went into the headquarters building, Rick slipped his green beret off his head. The specialist manning the desk said, "Morning, sir."

"Specialist." He didn't recognize the man. The unit replacing them here at Fort Bragg had started arriving during Rick's leave, and he guessed the specialist belonged to them.

As he passed Colonel Jenkins's office, he glanced in and spied the empty desk. He turned right down a hallway and went into the ready room, where he found the colonel standing at the podium, typing on a laptop.

"Morning, sir," Rick said.

Colonel Jenkins glanced up. "Captain. You headed out to Campbell?"

"Tomorrow morning, sir. Clearing out my desk today."

He'd driven back to North Carolina the day after he last

spoke with Cynthia. He'd spent the last several days packing up his house, spending as much time as possible trying not to think about Cynthia and what she'd said.

"See you there next Tuesday." Colonel Jenkins gestured at the screen behind him as it lit up with a slide presentation. "I have the new team coming in today. Going to give them the post briefing."

"Yes, sir." Rick headed to the outside courtyard, putting the beret back on. Over his left eye he lined up the crossed arrows and sword atop the crest, while he draped the beret over his right ear. The movement looked effortless despite the hours it took to shape the wool berets into submission.

He found Bill playing basketball with a man he didn't know. "Hey, Drumstick. Got a sec?"

Bill shot and missed from the three-point line, then turned toward him. "Yes, sir!" He slapped the man on the shoulder as he jogged toward Rick, then held out his hand. "Good to see you, brother." He stopped at a bench and picked up a towel and a bottle of water. "You headed out today?"

"In the morning."

Bill downed half a bottle of water in a few gulps, then asked, "You okay?" They sat on the bench, and he mopped his face with a towel.

When Rick left Charula, Bill had stayed behind, taking up the spare bedroom at Rick's parents' house, visiting with Waller and letting Rick's mom pamper him and mother him after his injury.

"Cynthia and I broke up," Rick said.

"Oh?" Bill slowly lowered the towel. Rick thought he tried to look surprised. "Want to talk about it?"

"No."

Bill nodded. "Good."

Rick sighed. "Yes."

Bill waited, looking about as uncomfortable as when he'd had a bullet lodged in his chest.

Finally, Rick said, "She can't bear to think about what it's like when we're deployed since she has firsthand knowledge of it."

Bill nodded. "Figured. She and I chatted briefly about it."

Rick had guessed, but he wanted Bill to confirm. "Chatted about what?"

"About the differences between leave and active time."

Rick felt his anger stirring. "Took that on yourself, did you?"

Bill narrowed his eyes. "Look, brother, this was going to come from her now or at some point in the future. Don't you think you were both fooling yourselves into thinking it would work? Your worlds were never meant to do anything but collide."

Rage tinged the edges of his vision. "And yet they did more than collide. What do you think that means?"

"I think it means you had to rescue her, and she had some misplaced attraction for you that came from that. As soon as the dust settled, she would have realized it. Breaking up now just saved your hearts from future destruction." He stood and tossed the empty bottle into the trash can next to the bench.

"What do you know about it?"

Bill snorted. "There was this girl in college. Man, she lit up a room just walking into it. I couldn't wait to go to class just to be in the same room with her. We dated for a couple of years, but I broke up with her before she could realize we couldn't possibly be together."

Rick raised an eyebrow. "I see. So you think I need to be as miserable as you? That it?"

"Me? Miserable? I'm finer than a hog in fresh mud." He picked up his bag and slung it over his shoulder. "You want to go get some chow?"

Rick's hand fisted, but he reminded himself that he wore his uniform, Bill was his subordinate, and they stood on military grounds. He would not do anything to affect his career.

Even though he'd love to stand up and take his fist and . . .

"No."

Bill started to turn away but paused and looked at him again. "I didn't tell her to break up with you. Our conversation was barely two minutes long. If you're trying to pin her decision on me, you're looking in the wrong place."

"Maybe you put the thought in her head," Rick said, his jaw aching from clenching it.

"Maybe. Or maybe it was already there and something I said made her aware of it." Bill started to walk away and tossed over his shoulder, "I'll see you in Kentucky tomorrow."

Rick didn't reply. He didn't even watch Bill leave. He just sank into his own mind, analyzing the conversation with Cynthia. Should he have reacted that way? Should he have talked to her more?

He shook his head. Any compromise would have been entirely on him. She wanted him to give up what he did, what he was designed to do, to completely change his career path and go live where she lived. He couldn't do that. Right now, what his team did, how he led them through it, and what his country required of him served as his sole purpose. He couldn't just leave it behind. He couldn't even imagine a compromise that would work.

Perhaps Bill had a point. Maybe figuring all of that out now would save him extra heartache in the future.

The door opened and Peña stuck his head out. "Colonel wants a word with you, Cap. Chief Hanson is already in there."

He took a deep breath. The fresh air didn't help. Work would help. That was where he needed to focus right now.

"Thanks," he said, standing and walking toward him. Peña had on a pair of jeans and a T-shirt with an alligator on the chest, so he obviously wasn't on duty. "When are you headed out?"

"In a few. McBride is riding with me. We're hauling his motorcycle behind my truck. He's loading it right now."

"You're not helping him?" Rick asked.

"Sure I am. I'm hauling that gaudy hog about eight hundred miles behind my truck."

Rick chuckled. "Okay. I'll see you Monday."

"Yeah. See you, sir."

Back in the ready room, Rick shook hands with Hanson. His assistant commander was tall with olive skin and dark eyes. His mother and father had met when his father was stationed in Okinawa. He could speak Japanese fluently.

"Hey, Chief. How was leave?"

"I put on seven pounds."

"Having eaten your wife's cooking, I can understand."

Hanson laughed. "It's like I didn't have any control over the hand that put food in my mouth."

Colonel Jenkins finished talking with a lieutenant from supply and approached them. "Gentlemen. Hate to make you hit the ground running, but we have a situation in Syria. Looking for the man responsible for those hotel bombings yesterday. Intelligence thinks they've pinpointed a possible locale. I emailed you a link on SIPRNET, and you can review the files in the SCIF," he said. "I'll be at Campbell next Tuesday. Be ready for a briefing."

"Yes, sir," Rick said. "Do you want us to say anything?"

"No. We'll know more then. Let the team get settled without the added stress."

"I was going to stay, sir," Hanson said. "Our movers aren't scheduled to come until Monday."

Colonel Jenkins smiled, his eyes crinkling at the corners. "You know I understand, Mr. Hanson, but we need the full team. I'll have my wife call your wife. The support system will be mobilized. She can do it without you."

"Yes, sir."

After the colonel left, Rick turned to Hanson. "You good?"

"Sure. Until I talk to my wife." He laughed and shook his head. "She'll be fine. I'll be there all day today and tomorrow. I'll drive tomorrow night and give myself Sunday and Monday to review these files. I can access the SCIF at Campbell."

"Good." Rick gestured with his thumb. "I need to go finish packing my desk."

"Yes, sir. See you Sunday."

"Yeah. After chapel?"

"Roger."

Rick left Hanson in the ready room and went to his cubicle. He had left a cardboard box on a chair, so he started tossing things into it. A bottle of Kentucky bourbon autographed by the master distiller and some other notable people sat on top of his filing cabinet, so he wrapped it in some bubble wrap and set it gently in the box. His nameplate, box of pens, and personal stapler followed. Soon, he'd stripped everything personal away.

While he worked, he tried to process Bill's involvement with Cynthia. As his brother in Christ, he shouldn't have done something that hurt Rick so deeply. Unless, of course, he'd only intended to help him avoid the inevitable hurt.

His stomach growled as he hefted the box. On his way out of the room, he looked at the clock. It was almost one, so he'd missed eating in the chow hall. He would put the box in his car and hit a fast-food place on post.

As he opened his car door, his mind wandered back over the days spent with Cynthia in Kentucky. Emotion tightened his chest and made his eyes burn. A part of him wanted to rail at Cynthia, make her hear what he thought of her feelings on the matter, but he wouldn't ever do that. Instead, he'd focus on work and just keep operating the way he always had.

CHAPTER

---- ★ ----

TWENTY-SEVEN

Stirring the caramel into the melting vanilla ice cream was almost hypnotizing. Cynthia felt riveted watching it. It reminded her of the whirlpool at the base of the waterfall she'd seen in Kentucky. A tear slid down her nose and splashed into the bowl.

Her dad had walked in on her crying at the kitchen counter and sent the staff away. He'd pulled off his tie and kicked off his shoes. Now they sat at the kitchen island among the remnants of chili dogs and all the fixings. The ice cream container sat open, the scoop slowly sliding down into the melting dessert.

"What do you think you want to do?" her dad asked.

What a good question. "I think I want to go back in time two weeks and change a conversation."

For several moments, he watched her, then finally asked, "With a certain Army captain of our acquaintance?"

"I really messed that up, Dad. I thought . . ." Her breath hitched.

"You thought . . . ?"

"I thought I could be important enough for him to change what he does." She shoved the bowl away and leaned against the stool back. "Why did I think that?"

He stared at her with serious eyes. "I think the more important question is, why would you want to?"

She studied his expression. "What do you mean?"

"I mean, he is who he is. I happen to know a lot about him. Probably a lot more than you. The second you were under his care, I had his file."

She should have guessed that. Her father's world worked that way. "What do you mean, he is who he is?"

"I mean, he is the man you were attracted to. The man who rescued you not once but twice. The man who put himself between you and an enemy bent on hurting you, at risk of his own life and limb. The man who came the second you called from the dinner, bringing with him the full force of his team, without question or hesitation. He is who you were attracted to. Not someone else. Not someone who would leave that to be with you."

She pondered that. She *had* fallen in love with Captain Rick Norton, leader of a Green Beret team, who did hard, amazing things, made tough decisions, and took care of the people on his team like they belonged in his family.

That did not detract from the truth, though. "But I know what it's like. I was there. I experienced it with him. How can I possibly live with that? Every time he left, I'd know what he was doing and the danger he was in."

"Sweet pea, you have to understand that he's going to be

in that danger doing those things whether you're with him or not. So do you want to be the one here, sharing his downtime with him, loving him through the hard times? Do you want to be by his side, supporting and praying for him, serving God with him?" He reached over and covered her hand with his. "Or do you not want to be that person for him? You cannot think about the what-ifs like that. Statistically, he's as likely to die from a car accident. Would you never want him to drive again if you knew what an accident is like?"

Needing to move, Cynthia pushed off the stool and paced to the other side of the counter. "It's hardly the same thing."

"It is exactly the same thing." He pointed at her. "It's just a different perspective. You have never liked violence. You've always taken a pacifist approach. That's fine. I respect that, and oftentimes you and I have similar views. But understand that there is evil in the world, and sometimes what protects pacifists are soldiers willing to meet that violence with equal violence. You and I both have seen that play out in the real world. In the last several months I've observed our president making decisions that one day I hope to have the wisdom and courage to make." He walked over to her and put his hands on her arms.

Tears streamed down her face. "What if something happens to him?"

"Then you call us and we'll mourn him with you. We'll support you supporting him, whatever that looks like." He pulled her into his arms. Despite the fact that he held the title of vice president of the United States, he also held the title of daddy. He smelled exactly the same as he had when she was five. He kissed the top of her head, then stepped back. "Why don't you go take a hot bath? Pray about it.

Sleep on it. Pray about it some more. Your mom and I are here if you need us."

"Thanks, Dad." She gestured at their debris. "Do you want me to clean up?"

"No. I'll get it."

Her father walked to the sink and turned on the water as Cynthia walked up the back stairs. She headed into her room with the intention of taking the recommended bubble bath, but she ended up on her knees by her dressing stool. Tears slid down her cheeks. She laid her forehead on her folded arms and sobbed. She wanted to pray, to cry out to God to help her make the right decision, but she couldn't form the words. Instead, she relied on the promise that Romans gave, that the Holy Spirit would intercede on her behalf and take the cries in her heart to God.

She knew without a doubt that she loved Rick Norton with all of her heart. By the time she'd finished praying, no longer kneeling at her stool but lying on the floor in a fetal position, her sleeve thoroughly soaked by her tears, she knew that the love she felt for him would be enough. She would support him and his job, wherever that took him. She would serve by his side the same way her mother had served with her father all of their marriage.

She got up, went into the bathroom, and turned on the cold water. Splashing it on her face took her breath away, refreshed her. She washed away all the tears, and when she felt like she could talk without sobbing, she dialed Rick's number. It went straight to voice mail, and she hung up without leaving a message.

Had he blocked her number? That didn't seem like something he would do. He would face her head-on. So either his battery had died or he had his phone off for some reason. She would try again in the morning.

Her gaze fell to the laptop on her desk. On impulse, she sat down and opened the lid. She chewed on her lower lip, then opened a search engine and typed, "How to apply for an Army hospital position."

Hours later, her résumé updated and her references lined up, she accessed the government jobs board and typed "Fort Campbell" into the search engine.

CHAPTER

★

TWENTY-EIGHT

SYRIA

Rick stood at the village limits in Syria's Idlib province and looked at the shell of the building. His nose itched with the smell of burning rocket fuel and RDX high explosive from the warhead. The remaining fuel in the missile had nearly doubled the effect of the main warhead, amplifying and spreading the destructive force at impact. The concrete building next door had collapsed in on itself. Concrete lay in chunks, and exposed steel rebar stuck up out of it, twisted in weird angles. One of the concrete slabs had completely crushed a car.

He looked down at his civilian clothes, feeling odd and out of place in them and a bit annoyed at the lack of pockets and load-bearing equipment. He rubbed his chest, his fingers running over the ballistic vest atop his shirt.

They'd been in the country for a week, trying to find the

terrorist leader Gamal Khalil, who had dispatched five suicide bombers into US-owned hotels in Egypt and Kuwait three weeks ago. Fifty-two people had died in the mass attacks, including fourteen Americans.

Rubbing his eyes, he went farther into the building and found Emma "Selah" Peña sitting across from Naeem Qassim. The missile engineer had offered intelligence on the terrorist leader Gamal Khalil after Khalil used his technology to bomb a civilian hospital.

Jorge Peña stood guard next to the table, watching over his wife as she interviewed Naeem. Emma wore a long-sleeved, floor-length dress and a hijab. She had been born in Afghanistan, but when her father aided the Americans in 2001, it put her family's lives in danger. When she was ten, they fled the country and relocated to Texas. In the culturally diverse American school, she discovered her gift for languages, and her parents couldn't get her lessons fast enough. She graduated college at twenty-one with a degree in international affairs and fluently spoke six languages.

After serving in the military for six years, she'd gotten a job contracting for the Department of Defense and worked as a translator for units all over the Middle East because she spoke all of the languages in the region without a trace of an accent. Over the years, she'd developed skills from observing interrogations, or what the military euphemistically called "tactical debriefings." Often when she was assigned to Rick's unit, he allowed her to take the lead. Her husband spoke Arabic well enough to get by and to guide her in the interview if needed.

Emma, whose code name became Selah after she and Peña got married, had drilled Naeem for the last two hours. The man was starting to look fatigued. Rick watched with anticipation as she changed tactics and came at Naeem from a different direction, then switched again. He couldn't understand all her words, but he understood enough and had worked with her long enough to know her facial expressions, mannerisms, and tactics.

Rick watched the fight go out of Naeem, and he started talking. Peña perked up, and Emma nodded. Finally, she looked up at Peña and said, "I have coordinates."

"Is it guaranteed that Gamal Khalil will be there?" Peña asked.

"He is confirmed." Emma spoke in Arabic to Naeem, then stood up. "He says we've just killed his family."

"Not us," Rick said. "Khalil will." He made a circling motion with his finger, and the team started packing up. "If this intel pans out, we'll get him and his family to Jordan. That was the deal."

She spoke to Naeem again, and he covered his face with his hands and nodded.

Rick looked at Fisher and said, "Get HQ a SITREP."

Hanson came from the back of the room. "Old man's back. He wants us there."

"Roger."

Rick's team dispatched Naeem with instructions to collect his family and take them to the address he had given. Their contact in Jordan would help him with the relocation.

They got in their vehicles and drove through the streets. Rick couldn't believe the destruction. Not a single building stood without at least some damage, and more than half the buildings had been bombed to annihilation. People picked through the rubble. He wondered what they searched for. Sentimental objects? Food? Clean water? Survivors?

Back at their base, they changed into uniforms, and he and Hanson met up with Colonel Jenkins.

"What time is the meeting?" Colonel Jenkins asked, looking at an aerial view of the coordinates.

"Twenty hundred hours," Rick said. "Selah is finalizing her report. She said she'd email it to you on the high side as soon as she finished."

Someone tapped on the door. At the colonel's bidding, Emma came into the room holding a folder with a red cover sheet that red SECRET in large block letters. "Colonel Jenkins, here is my full report and the transcript of the interview. I also emailed via SIPRNET, sir, but thought you might want it soonest."

Colonel Jenkins chuckled. "Interview. That's a nice word." He took the folder from her. "How'd you get the transcript so fast?"

"I have a program." She'd changed out of the hijab into Western-style clothes—khaki pants and a red golf shirt—and had her black hair bound into a tight bun at the base of her neck. She glanced at Rick. "Captain," she said with a smile, "looking forward to you showing us around Kentucky."

His eyes widened. "You finally going home?"

"Yes, sir. My assignment ended a month ago. I only stayed for you."

He couldn't hold back a grin. "I am not the one you stayed for."

A dimple appeared at the corner of her mouth. "Touché."

The colonel finished skimming what she gave him. "Excellent work, Selah. If all goes well, this will prove true and we won't need your services for this assignment anymore."

"Thank you, sir." On her way out of the room, she said to Hanson, "Housewarming party at your house the Saturday after you get back, according to your wife."

Though his face remained stoic, his voice betrayed his pleasure at hearing the news. "Wonderful! It's been too long since we've all been together."

"It has. Be safe. I'll see you all soon."

The colonel turned to the map on the wall. "How do you want to do this tonight? The objective is capture, not kill. Khalil is too important an intelligence asset, and Washington wants him."

Rick knew this, but he'd also seen the destruction the man had wreaked on the town. It wouldn't hurt his feelings if the mission had a little more finality to it.

They discussed strategy and mapped out the plan, then brought the entire team in to go over it.

On their way to the mess hall to eat dinner, Rick walked next to Hanson. "Can I ask you something?"

Hanson glanced at him out of the corner of his eye. "Of course, sir."

Rick stopped outside of the mess hall and stepped off the path, leaning against the wall. "How distracted are you about home when you're here?"

Hanson narrowed his eyes. "There a problem with my performance, sir?"

"Not at all. It's not about you." He pondered what to say. "I've been distracted during this mission. I don't relish the thought of this being my new normal."

"Ah! Okay." Hanson's face relaxed. "Best advice I can give you is to compartmentalize better. Save thinking about that girl back home for the downtimes, then let the thoughts come. If you're in the middle of something else, push back the thoughts, put a lid on them, but then intentionally open that lid when it's safe. Make sense?"

Rick nodded and scrubbed at his beard. "Not easy."

"Not even a little bit. It's a learned skill."

"Thanks. Anything else?"

Hanson shrugged. "Having my wife back home, knowing how much she cares about me, makes what I do so much more important. It makes me a better soldier because I want to get home to her. I wouldn't care as much if she weren't keeping the home fires burning, I don't think. I can't explain it, but it's true."

"Appreciate your candor." Rick gestured to the door. "Let's get something in our stomachs before we go to work."

★　★　★

FORT CAMPBELL, KENTUCKY

Cynthia dialed Rick's number for the third time this week, but it went straight to voice mail again. For the first time, though, she decided to leave a message. She took a deep, shaky breath and said, "Hi. It's me. I'm here. At Fort Campbell. I, uh, would really love it if you would call me back when you can."

As she disconnected the call, she sighed and surveyed the empty living room of her new house. She couldn't believe that only three weeks had passed since sharing ice cream with her dad. Within a week of applying for a job as a physician at the Blanchfield Army Community Hospital at Fort Campbell, she'd accepted an offer to work in obstetrics.

She'd started her new job a week ago and, so far, loved it here. The doctors and nurses she worked with had accepted her without hesitation. Navigating the military hospital system presented the biggest learning curve for her, but her supervisor stayed available to answer questions and guide her through the process.

She stayed at the Turner Guesthouse for a few nights, but because of her position at the hospital, she was able to rent a little house on Fort Campbell itself. In a rare coincidence, she was able to move in almost right away. That saved her having to battle the traffic coming in through the gates from Hopkinsville and Clarksville. Living on the base also made her readily accessible to her patients the nights she was on call and helped her convince her parents that she no longer needed protection. With Chukuwereije dead and the media buzz having moved on to something new, her parents agreed to relinquish the security detail with the caveat that they could reinstate it if something happened. She'd agreed.

Now she had an empty house to furnish and her first day off in a week. She'd wanted a completely fresh start, so she came with nothing but her bed, clothes, and books. Every day she'd added to her list of ideas and needs for the house. Even if Rick completely rejected her, she felt like God wanted her living here and working in this hospital.

She decided to go to the chapel service. The first weekend here, she'd gone to the contemporary service. She'd looked for Rick but hadn't seen him in the crowd. In fact, she hadn't seen anyone she recognized from his team. In all fairness, though, the Memorial Chapel was full of young families and single soldiers. She could easily have missed someone.

This morning, she would attend the traditional service. As

she put on a light-pink dress and tan sandals, she wondered what she'd say to Rick when she saw him.

Hi, Rick. I love you. Please forgive me and love me back. She groaned out loud. How could she do this?

Determined to go through with it, she grabbed her Bible and walked out of her house into the warm May morning. Honestly, at this point, what choice did she have but to go through with it? She'd moved all the way out here for this purpose. Caving in to insecurity would make all of this for nothing.

Instead of the Memorial Chapel, this service was held in the Liberty Chapel. As she walked up the path, she noticed the older crowd. Inside, the person who handed her a bulletin looked to be in her seventies, and the choir members at the front were all easily grandparents. She did see several younger families in the congregation. But not Rick.

Sighing, she sat in the back so she could examine the people in attendance, watch who came and went. She really enjoyed this service. It reminded her much more of Nathaniel's church. The chaplain who gave the sermon had a rich, booming voice that carried the message with an almost poetic quality.

After the service, they all joined together for lunch in the annex. Every person she made eye contact with greeted her warmly, and by the time she sat down at a table with a sub sandwich and a bottle of water, she felt completely at home.

"Doctor Myers?"

Hearing her name, she spun around and spied Leanne Waller. She'd met the woman during the awards ceremony in Washington. Her heart started beating furiously. Leanne would know how to get in touch with Rick.

"Mrs. Waller," she said, standing and holding out her hand. "Please call me Cynthia."

"Leanne." The red-haired woman stood several inches taller than Cynthia. She wore a sleeveless dress and had well-defined muscles in her arms. Cynthia remembered that she worked as a search-and-rescue operator.

They shook hands warmly, then Leanne asked, "What are you doing here? Or can I ask?" She set her plate of food next to Cynthia's and pulled out a metal chair.

As they sat down, Cynthia said, "It's not a secret. I took a position here at the hospital. In the OB ward."

Leanne grinned. "That's fantastic. Tim said something about you being in Charula when we were there visiting Captain Norton. Sorry we didn't see each other." She unwrapped her sandwich. "He didn't say anything about you moving here, though."

Cynthia felt herself blush. "As far as I know, Rick doesn't know I'm here."

Leanne gasped. "You're kidding!"

"No. I've been trying to call him, but he never answers."

Leanne looked around and leaned close to her. "They're not here right now."

"Where are they?" Cynthia asked before giving it a second thought.

After a moment of puzzled eye contact, Leanne said, "Somewhere with no cell service."

Suddenly the stress of Rick not answering his phone drained out of her. "Oh." She looked at her sandwich. Not here meant deployed, on a mission, and the way Leanne delivered the message gave her the impression that they wouldn't discuss the details. Why hadn't she thought of that?

It should have occurred to her the longer he went without answering. "Well, I guess that explains it, then."

Leanne studied her for several seconds. "How come you didn't know that?"

Cynthia cleared her throat. "We, uh, had a bit of a breakup. I moved here as part of a hope of reconciliation." She felt a little foolish. "Now I'm beginning to wonder"— she took a deep breath to steady herself and looked Leanne in the eye—"if I did the right thing. I did try to call him and tell him I was coming."

A slow smile spread across Leanne's face. "I love this." She took a bite of her sandwich, then wiped her lips with a paper napkin. "Look, they'll be back in a few weeks if all goes well." She leaned close again and said quietly, "They kind of come and go without much word or warning."

Cynthia opened her water and took a long drink from it. "I can wait."

Leanne grinned and raised her own water in a salute. "Welcome to the world of waiting. It's just part of the life."

Cynthia enjoyed lunch at the chapel. Leanne was new too, so it did them both good to have the company. Afterward, Cynthia went to a furniture store, settling on a gray couch and matching chair. At a home store, she found turquoise and yellow pillows for the couch, and a gray-and-turquoise rug with yellow accents to tie it all together.

She got home, unloaded the items she'd purchased, marked in her calendar the date the furniture would be delivered, then called Rick's phone. "Hi, it's me again. I just found out you're not here. I'm glad you're not just blocking my calls or something. Anyway, I'll be waiting until you get back. Please call me when you get this." She paused. "I love you."

CHAPTER

★

TWENTY-NINE

Weary to the core, Rick let himself into his house and pulled off his beret as he tossed his keys on the kitchen counter. He moved into the living room and lay on the couch. He knew he had to take his boots off, and he really wanted to take a long, hot shower. But right now, he needed sleep.

When he opened his eyes again, bright sunlight poured through the bare windows. He blinked and looked around, disoriented. Moving boxes filled the room. His flat-screen television hung on the wall, and the cords dangled loose below it. He'd had enough time upon arriving at Fort Campbell to sign for his quarters and unload the moving truck before his team had to leave again.

They'd spent the last two months in Syria. They'd done good work. But his heart hadn't been on the mission, and his mind felt chaotic and distracted the entire time.

Hanson had given him sound advice, but he didn't relish thoughts of Cynthia like Hanson did his wife. Putting the metaphorical lid on her and opening it when he had time to focus on her did not appeal to him. Nothing about thinking of her gave him much joy or peace. It physically hurt his heart whenever she crossed his mind. He wanted to stop thinking about her altogether.

He got off the couch and went to his bedroom. On the way, he ran into a box and uttered a mild expletive as he rubbed his shin. His mattresses sat stacked against the wall, and the bed frame lay in pieces. He needed to get moved in.

In the bathroom, he stared at his face in the mirror, noting his bloodshot eyes. He silently thanked God for having the next four days off. He needed to rest, restore, and unpack.

After taking a long, hot shower, he dug through boxes in the bedroom and found a pair of jeans, a T-shirt, and tennis shoes. He retrieved his duffel bag and rucksack from the car and took them straight to the laundry room. Once he had a load of uniforms in the washing machine, he shaved off his beard. He ran his hands over his smooth chin, opening and closing his mouth. Much freer.

As he ate, he surveyed the open boxes and the chaos around him. He started with unpacking the kitchen, always the easiest room because everything had a place.

After he poured a cup of tea, he pulled his notebook out of his duffel bag and started making a shopping list. He ought to check his messages and voice mails, but he didn't have the energy. He also should probably go to chapel. He never missed unless he had to. But this morning he didn't feel like it. Instead he headed to the commissary and the PX to fulfill his shopping list.

His phone chirped as he parked his car. He saw Bill's number. Bill hadn't deployed with them for medical reasons.

They'd shared a couple of emails, and over time Rick had let go of any resentment he had toward Bill. In doing so, he discovered that he'd really missed his friend.

"Hey," Rick answered as he got out of his car.

"Hey. You up for dinner?"

"No, man. Can we do it tomorrow instead?"

"Sure. I have to report at oh seven, but I should be free about seventeen hundred."

"That will be perfect." He slipped his sunglasses off as he walked into the PX. "It was strange being in the field without you. Didn't realize how much I relied on you."

Bill scoffed. "It was weird being here without you. For about the same reason." When he spoke again his voice lacked any humor or irony. "My meemaw died."

The breath went out of Rick. "I'm so sorry. I can change plans. We can meet tonight."

"No, dude. Tomorrow is good for me. It's been a few weeks."

"If you're sure."

"Sure like a squirrel with a peanut."

With a grin Rick said, "Whatever that means."

"Yeah. That's a fail. See you tomorrow."

Rick grabbed a cart and rolled into the PX. He needed shower curtains, bath rugs, and garbage cans—the things he always replaced with a move. On his way to the home section of the store, he passed a candle display. The smell of lavender suddenly assaulted him, and he froze in his tracks.

He'd managed to go about three hours without thinking of Cynthia. An ache suddenly manifested in his chest, and he rubbed it with a fist, trying to make it go away. When would this end? It had been months and it just never stopped.

After clearing his throat with a harsh sound, he went to the furniture section to price rugs. Then he worked his way back through the store and found the rest of the items on his list. Once he checked out, he headed to the food court.

While standing in line at the chicken place, he heard the musical sound of laughter, and his whole body froze. His hands turned cold and his heart started pounding.

He couldn't think of a single logical reason for Cynthia Myers to magically appear in the Fort Campbell food court. His tortured mind had just made her up in the wake of the lavender candles he could swear he still smelled.

After placing his order for a dinner box, he picked up his cup to take it to the drink station and heard the laughter again. Closing his eyes, steeling himself for the disappointment of turning and not seeing her, he shifted his gaze in that direction, the whole time telling himself not to look.

Cynthia sat at a table with three other women in pink and blue hospital scrubs. She had her hair pulled back into a messy bun and sunglasses perched on her head. How?

"Sir?"

Startled, he looked behind him. The cashier at the chicken place held out his bag. Mutely he took it, then walked over to Cynthia. She had a smile on her face and listened intently to the woman in front of her. But as he got close, she looked up and made eye contact with him. The smile slowly faded from her face, and she stood up.

"Hi," she said on a breath. "Wow. Hi."

The other women at the table fell silent and watched the two of them with the intense concentration of the audience at the final round of Wimbledon.

"Hello." He didn't know what else to say. He didn't want

to look away from her in case she disappeared, so he kept his eyes locked on hers.

Cynthia cleared her throat. "I look for you everywhere, so I shouldn't be surprised to see you, but I am."

"What?" He tore his gaze away from her long enough to take in the other women, to take in her scrubs again. She didn't belong here, yet here she stood. Heart pounding furiously, he asked, "What are you doing here?"

She blinked as if processing his question. "Didn't you get my voice mail?"

He shook his head.

Gesturing at his food and his shopping cart of bags, she asked, "Were you headed out?"

"I still have to hit the commissary." He set his food in the toddler seat of the shopping cart. "But I'm leaving here."

"I'll, uh, walk out with you." She picked up her food tray and turned to the other women. "Thanks for having lunch with me. Good work today. I'll see you later."

He didn't want her to walk out with him, but he didn't say so. They went out to the parking lot, and he mutely loaded his bags into the trunk of his car. She stood silently by, watching. When he put the last one in, he shut the trunk and said, "Well, it was great catching up."

He started to walk away, but she said, "Rick, stop, please."

Ignoring her, he walked over to the cart corral and used a little more force than necessary to push his cart into the line. When he turned back around, Cynthia still stood there.

"What voice mail?" he asked as he ripped his car door open.

"The one I left you weeks ago."

He shook his head. "I've been out of the country since mid-April. I just got back to Kentucky last night."

"I knew that." She rubbed the back of her neck. "I just assumed you'd listen to your voice mail when you got back."

With a frown he demanded, "What did it say?"

"Could we get together somewhere private? I'd like to talk to you somewhere other than the PX parking lot."

He mulled over his response. So many options came to him. Finally, he said, "Do you have a car here?"

"Yes."

"Is your number the same?"

"Yes."

"Come over for dinner. I'll text you my address."

The relief that crossed her face twisted his heart in a physically painful way. "Okay. I can do that."

★ ★ ★

Dahlia frowned into the phone's camera. "Why are you going to his house? Why can't he come to yours?"

Cynthia leaned forward and carefully applied her lipstick. "Because," she said, pressing her lips together gently and then rubbing them, "he doesn't know I have a house here. That's part of that conversation." She sat back and primped her hair. "How do I look?"

"Like a million bucks. You're going to knock his poor socks off."

She stood and twisted in the mirror. She had on a pair of plum-colored pants and a black tank top. She'd left her hair down and loose and wore a pair of black dangling earrings. "You think I should have gone for the red dress?"

"Nah. Too dressy. Save that for when he falls back in love with you and takes you out somewhere for dinner."

She picked up the phone. "Kiss Theo for me. Thank you for your help."

"I'm just happy to see it finally coming together. Call me. Not tonight. In the morning!"

Cynthia double-checked the address on her phone. When Rick had sent it to her, she couldn't believe it. He lived just a street away from her. She wondered what he'd say when he found out about that.

She grabbed her purse and went out through the back door, crossed her backyard and into the next yard, and came out onto his street. Standing there, she could see Rick's car about four driveways down.

Little nervous flutters began in her stomach. What would he say to her?

Putting her chin up, she refused to be afraid. He'd listen to her and let her talk. She believed that. Otherwise, he wouldn't have asked her over. Then his answer would be either yes or no. At least she knew the possibilities.

With purposeful steps, she walked down the sidewalk and then up his drive. She rang the doorbell right at six. Within a second, he opened the door. He looked at her, then past her. "No car?"

"Not tonight." She smiled up at him, her heart beating so painfully fast she could feel her pulse in her neck. He looked tired, but it felt so good to lay eyes on him.

He stepped aside and she walked in. Through the doorway of the kitchen, she could see steam coming from a pot on the stove. He led the way past the kitchen and into the living room. He had moving boxes stacked everywhere.

"They didn't even give you time to get unpacked?"

He shrugged and gestured to the sliding door that led to the back patio. "Sometimes you can't control the timing of things. I have some meat ready for the grill."

She followed him outside. On the concrete deck he had a glass-topped table that he'd set with plates and forks. She sat down in one of the chairs as he picked up a platter wrapped with aluminum foil and walked over to the grill. Heat waves radiated from it, distorting the evening air.

"Hope salmon is all right," he said, using tongs to put a salmon fillet on the grill. "It sounded really good."

"Grilled salmon will be amazing." She nervously clutched her hands together and waited for his full attention.

He put the platter down and took the seat across from her. "I listened to my voice mail. I'd just like to know one thing."

Her mouth went dry, and she ran her tongue over her lips. "Anything."

He studied her face for several seconds before he asked, "Why?"

She took a shaky breath. "Because by getting a job at this military hospital, I'll be in the system and should be able to find jobs wherever you go." Deciding not to beat around the bush, she said, "Because I love you. I love you, and I want to love you on your terms, not mine."

It fascinated her how he didn't move a single muscle as he processed what she said. He sat perfectly still and perfectly stoic. Eventually he asked again, "Why?"

She'd spent months wording this as carefully as she could. "Because loving you on my terms would require you to change, and I don't want that. I want you, Rick Norton. I want who you are, who God designed you to be, whatever that looks like."

He tapped the top of the table with his index finger. She wondered if he even knew he was doing it. "What about your coping skills? What about all that intimate knowledge of what I do and how I do it and how dangerous it is?"

Tears clogged her throat, and she cleared it to try to speak around them. "I am not going to love you any less if I'm away from you. What you do and how you do it isn't going to change, whether I'm with you or not. I would rather be here, supporting you, praying for you, loving you, than separated and always wondering."

He stood and walked over to the grill. Using a large metal spatula, he flipped the fish over and shut the lid. She could smell the savory aroma, and it made her mouth water.

He stood for a moment, gripping the handle of the lid, his back to her and his head slightly bowed. Finally, he walked back over to the table and set the spatula down, then held out his hand. She paused before putting hers in it and letting him pull her to her feet.

He reached out and brushed her hair off her forehead, then cupped her cheeks. "You better mean it." He spoke in a harsh whisper that moved through her, penetrating her heart, throwing wide the doors she'd tentatively cracked open.

Savoring the feel of his hands against her skin, she closed her eyes as tears slid down her cheeks. When she opened them, she gasped at the intensity in his eyes. "I mean it with my whole heart," she whispered.

Before she finished the last word, his arms came around her and his lips covered hers. She could taste her own tears and smell his familiar scent. His cheeks felt smooth under her hands, his palms burning through her shirt. She stood on her tiptoes, desperate to get closer to him. Finally, he ripped his mouth away and pulled her tightly against him. She wrapped her arms around his neck and held on, crying, smiling, thanking God that he believed her.

When he loosened his hold, she stepped back and framed his face with her hands. "Please take that fish off the grill before it burns," she said with a smile. "That would be a shame."

CHAPTER

★

THIRTY

Rick rang the doorbell to Cynthia's house and stepped back. She'd put purple mums on either side of her front porch. The November evening air had a crisper feel to it than just a week before.

After about ten seconds, Cynthia answered the door. She still wore her scrubs and had deep circles under her eyes, so he knew she'd just gotten home. She'd clipped her hair up off her neck, which gave him a view of the curve of her neck where it met her hairline.

"Get any sleep?" he asked, stepping into the house that was a mirror of his own.

"No. So many babies. I bet if we worked backward about thirty-eight or thirty-nine weeks, we'd discover a large unit that came home."

He followed her into the kitchen. She picked up her electric kettle and added water to the coffee in her French press.

"We didn't have plans, did we?" she asked. "I can't imagine making plans knowing I was on call last night."

"No. We didn't." Nerves danced up his spine and made his stomach clench. What if he'd misunderstood everything up until this moment? "Did your parents share their Thanksgiving plans with you?"

She pulled a coffee cup out of the cupboard and held it up. He nodded, so she pulled another one down. "For some reason they did not. It was very frustrating. They just told me to cancel my plans to come home."

They took the coffee to the living room and sat on the couch. He set his cup on the table in front of them without taking a sip.

"Listen, something came up," he blurted out. "I have to go somewhere very soon."

She raised her eyebrows. "Somewhere?"

"Yeah. Not really something I can talk about."

"Oh, right." She took a sip of her coffee and smiled. "I'll catch on. Just tired."

"It's fine. I'm just not allowed to say." He leaned forward and took the cup from her hands. Holding it had warmed her fingers. He shifted off the couch until he knelt on one knee next to her. "Cynthia, I don't know how long I'm going to be gone, but I do know I really would like to marry you before I leave."

Her mouth opened and closed, and her fingers squeezed his. "Marry me?"

"Yes." He pressed a kiss to the backs of her knuckles. "I love you. I want to live the rest of my life with you. But if I go and something happens to me, I want you to be my wife. Not my girlfriend, not my fiancée. My wife."

Her eyes searched his face, her expression almost one of fear. For a moment, his entire future hung suspended on her answer. At last, she smiled and nodded through her tears. "Yes, of course I'll marry you."

After he kissed her, he pulled the ring out of his pocket and slipped it on her finger. The square-cut diamond sat in a platinum setting. He'd chosen a simple design because simple suited her. She leaned forward and put her arms around his neck, pressing her lips against his. He closed his eyes, breathing deeply, just taking in being with her like this.

Putting his hands on her hips, he set her back from him. "Your parents are meeting us in Charula in two days. We're getting married there, in my parents' church." He paused. "If that's okay with you."

"My parents?"

"I called your dad this afternoon."

"Well, that explains the canceled plans," she said with a grin. "You being all sneaky behind my back."

"I just prayed you'd say yes."

"How could I not say yes?" She put her hand against his cheek. "How long do we have?"

He sighed and thought back to yesterday's briefing. "December first."

She blinked. "You're leaving a week after we get married?" She rubbed her face with her hands. "Wait. I have to start planning if we're getting married in two days."

He pressed a kiss to her forehead and stood up. "No. You'd better get busy sleeping. You're exhausted. Call me when you wake up and we'll talk everything through. We can wait too."

She didn't want to wait, but she'd tell him that after she woke up so he would know she'd had time to process the idea. She walked him to the back door and kissed him good-bye. "Are we seriously going to be married in two days?"

He winked at her and slid the door open, then crossed her backyard.

Cynthia took the coffee cups into the kitchen. She looked through the window and watched Rick cross the backyard. When she couldn't see him anymore, she headed to the bedroom.

In two days, they wouldn't have to say goodbye at the back door anymore. He'd move in here or she'd move in there—she honestly didn't care which—and they'd live together as husband and wife, one in the eyes of God.

She put her hands against her cheeks and looked up at the ceiling. "Thank You, God. Thank You for courage and conviction and for aligning everything to put me in that jungle at that time."

Before she lay down, she snapped a photo of the ring on her hand and texted it to Dahlia.

> You better be in Charula, KY, day after tomorrow. Love you.

Then she called her mom, who answered before a single ring could go through. "Well?" her mother asked.

Cynthia put her head back and laughed. "Well, I guess I'll see you in two days. At the church. Where I'll become Mrs. Rick Norton."

She could hear the smile in her mom's voice. "You sound so happy. We can't wait to see you."

Discussion Questions

When Cynthia is taken hostage by Chukuwereije's men, she realizes that she is going to die and believes that she is prepared to. However, when she is rescued, she's very angry at the loss of lives.

1. Do you feel her anger is justified? Why or why not?
2. In that kind of situation, was it right for the soldiers to kill the men in order to save the people of the village—and, in that moment, Cynthia—or should they have found a different way? Why?

When we first meet Rick, he is a praying man but also a leader in battle. He has a firefight with the Chukuwereije rebels, and later he wishes the mission capturing Khalil had "a little more finality to it."

3. Do you think this dichotomy fits? Can a praying man fight in a battle where he is directly responsible for the death of the enemy? Why or why not?

4. Do you think Christ's words about loving our enemies mean that we should not fight in a war? Explain.

5. In Matthew 24:6, Christ says that there will always be wars and rumors of wars but that we should not be troubled by them. Does that mean we should not be engaged with them as well? Why or why not?

We live in a fallen, broken world. Though Katangela is fictional, there are countries where state-sponsored violence, rape, torture, destruction, starvation, and misery exist.

6. Do we have an obligation to ease the suffering by confronting that evil like Rick and his team do, or is our obligation only to nurture those who are suffering, as Cynthia and her team do?

The first commandment with a promise is to honor your father and mother so that your days will be long upon the earth (Exod. 20:12). Cynthia's father tells her that she will have to leave Katangela just as they arrive at an event, as if knowing she'd avoid making a scene.

7. Do you think he is at fault for forcing her hand in a situation where he knew she'd honor him even if she was angry? Why or why not?

8. Did that situation warrant dishonoring her parents? Explain.

Rick is drawn to Cynthia, but Bill believes that because her father is the vice president of the United States, she outclasses the two of them.

9. Do you think that is a viable excuse? How does that perception work inside the body of Christ?

Cynthia breaks up with Rick because she had firsthand knowledge of the violence and danger he faced in doing his job. She was willing to sacrifice her future happiness rather than live with that knowledge while waiting for him to return from missions.

10. Do you think she underestimated God's ability to show how He could work it all out? Do you think His hand was in it all along, paving the way for her to see what she needed to do with her own career first?

Cynthia's time in Africa changed her. Seeing the poverty and need there made her opulent life much less attractive, to the point that she no longer felt the desire to minister to the wealthy in her aunt's practice.

11. Has anything you've experienced completely shifted your perspective about your quality of lifestyle? If so, what was it?
12. What in your life could be sacrificed for you to turn around and minister to those in need in your community?

Recipes

If you followed my Hallee the Homemaker website years ago, you know that one thing I am passionate about is selecting, cooking, and savoring good whole, real food. A special luncheon goes hand in hand with hospitality and ministry.

If you're planning a discussion group luncheon for this book, here are some suggestions to help your talk be a success. Quick as you like, you can whip up an unforgettable meal that is sure to please and certain to enhance the discussion and your special time of friendship and fellowship.

——— The Ultimate Hamburger ———

Rick and Bill are always on the hunt for the best hamburger. I have tried many recipes and discovered that the ultimate best burger ever is so very simple.

> Use ground beef with a low fat content—ground chuck at 80/20. Take ¼ pound (4 ounces) of meat and form it into a ball. Line a small plate with waxed paper. Place the ball in the center and top

with another piece of waxed paper. Using another plate, press the beef into a patty. This will compress it and help it hold together.

Season each side with salt and pepper to taste. Cook on high heat in an iron skillet until your desired temperature:

Medium-rare: 130° to 135° F (55° to 57° C)
Medium: 140° to 145° F (60° to 63° C)
Medium-well: 150° to 155° F (65° to 68° C)

Just before you're ready to remove the burger from the pan, top it with a slice or two of cheese. I love Swiss cheese or sharp cheddar. Mix them up!

Serve with the Ultimate Hamburger Bun and top with your favorite burger toppings.

—— The Ultimate Hamburger Bun ——

3 tbsp	honey, divided (pure, raw, local honey is always best)
1 cup	warm water
2¼ tsp	dry yeast (1 packet)
3 cups	flour, divided (I use a combination of fresh-ground hard red and hard white wheat—if you don't grind your own wheat, unbleached white flour is good)
¼ cup plus 2 tbsp	powdered milk
1 tsp salt	(kosher or sea salt is best)
3 tbsp	butter, melted

Lightly grease a large bowl to use for rising the dough.

Mix 1 tbsp honey with warm water. Add yeast. Let stand for 5 minutes.

Place 2 cups flour, the powdered milk, and the salt in a large bowl. Blend until well mixed. If using your stand mixer, turn to speed 2.

Add 2 tbsp honey and the water/yeast mixture. Add the melted butter. (If mixing by hand, mix well.)

Add 1 cup flour ½ cup at a time until the dough is no longer sticky. (You may not end up using all the flour.)

Knead with the stand mixer for 2 minutes, or knead by hand for 10 minutes.

Once the dough becomes smooth and elastic, put it into the greased bowl. Turn it once and cover with a light towel. Let it sit in a warm spot until it doubles in size. It will take about an hour.

Punch the dough down. Separate it into eight equal pieces and roll them into balls. Lightly press them flat. Place them on a greased cookie sheet and let rise about thirty minutes, then turn the oven on and let them continue to rise as the oven preheats.

Bake at 350° F (180° C) for 25 minutes.

Remove the bread from the pan and place on a cooling rack. Slice in half and serve with the Ultimate Hamburger. Top with your favorite toppings.

———— Homemade Potato Chips ————

russet potatoes (medium size)
canola oil (organic or non-GMO is best)
sea salt

Wash your potatoes really well. No need to peel them!

Put about two inches of oil in a pan. Heat to 375° F (190° C).

While the oil is heating, use a mandolin or sharp knife and slice your potatoes thin—about ⅛ inch.

Gently slide the potatoes into the oil one slice at a time. Don't overload your oil—just do 6 to 8 slices at a time. The oil will immediately bubble all around the slices. As they cook, they will curl up and start to crisp.

Once the slices curl up, turn them over (some don't make it over—that's fine) and keep cooking until they start to brown.

Remove slices from the oil with a slotted spoon and place on a paper towel. Sprinkle with sea salt.

LOVED THIS BOOK?

Turn the page for a **SNEAK PEEK** at the next in the series, *WORD OF HONOR*.

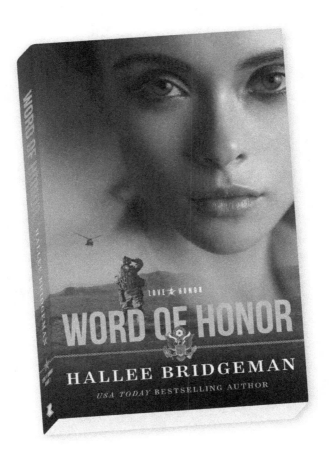

CHAPTER
★
ONE

ANCHORAGE, ALASKA
MAY 27

Even in the late-spring night with the hint of light still in the sky, the headlights did little to cut through the fog. Lynda Culter used a penlight to try to read the paper map, something she hadn't had to do since field-training exercises at Quantico. The mobile signal had disappeared about two miles back, so the GPS offered no help.

"You turned the wrong way back there," she said.

"Nope. Turned right like you said," her partner, Jack, said.

"No, I said turn left. You asked left, and I confirmed."

"With the word 'right'!" Jack pulled over to the side of the mountain road. "Give me that," he said as he snatched the map out of her hands.

Frustrated, she tossed the penlight at him. It hit the steering wheel and bounced, dinging him above his right eye.

She slapped her hand over her mouth. "Jack!" she said on a breath. "I'm so sorry."

He hit the overhead light, then rubbed his eyebrow and turned to glare at her. Soon, though, the glare turned to mirth, and he beckoned her with the crook of his finger. "Come here," he said.

She slipped her seat belt off and shifted her body.

"Kiss it better."

"Jack!" she said again, laughing, then pressed her lips to his eyebrow. She breathed in the familiar scent of his after-shave and then sat back, running her fingers through his soft brown hair. "All better?"

"For now." He reached down and retrieved the penlight from the floorboard, then held it out to her. "I should keep this. Spoils of war and all."

With a grin, she took it from him. She admired his profile as he studied the map. He had a thin face with a long nose, and his sharp cheekbones were offset with a thin beard. His features had helped him blend in during the five years he worked in deep cover with the Russian mafia. He came to her FBI branch in Anchorage just months after finishing his assignment. It didn't take her long to fall head over heels for the charismatic, charming man from Philadelphia. So far, they'd kept their relationship quiet. Neither one of them wanted to be separated. Jack had convinced her to wait until after this weekend to make it official.

She glanced at her phone. She'd just put the picture on her lock screen of the two of them in a café that afternoon. In a clearly intimate pose, they leaned against each other, heads touching. Her dark auburn hair caught the lights of the restaurant, highlighting her lighter red streaks, making her brown eyes shine. His smile brought the dimples out in his cheeks. They looked happy.

"Too bad that warrant came through," she said, thinking of the Memorial Day weekend in front of them. "Who knew a judge would sign a warrant tonight?"

She worked as an analyst, so serving warrants didn't typically fall under her purview. However, she and Jack had been nearby, about to check in to a mountain retreat. Waiting for another agent to come from Anchorage would have taken a couple more hours out of their weekend.

"I told you to wait until Tuesday to submit it." He set the map on the seat between them. "I'm going back," he said, putting the car in reverse.

"Probably wise," she replied, giving a sweet smile. "Since you made a wrong turn."

He turned the light off, but not before she saw the clench of his jaw a split second before he smiled. After backtracking to the intersection, he continued in the proper direction about four miles before they saw the marker that indicated the turn onto the dirt road.

As Jack slowly navigated the terrain to avoid kicking up dust, she said, "I wonder if we should have arranged for backup. No signal out here."

"These people aren't killers," he said. "They're just protesting the oil pipeline. The threat they made isn't even proven."

"Allegedly." She glanced at her phone again as if willing the signal to give her just one bar, enough to complete a call.

Jack slowed the car down and turned off the headlights. They came around a corner and saw the shadow of a house through the fog. Light glowed from two windows. An all-terrain vehicle sat parked next to two pickup trucks. Jack slowly came to a stop, then killed the engine. Lynda glanced at her watch. It was already ten thirty. They didn't have a lot of daylight left.

They got out of the car and met at the trunk. The temperature had dropped into the midforties. It felt good to put on their FBI ballistic vests and jackets. Jack slipped on his cap and held hers out. She shook her head, then pulled her hair back into a ponytail. She hated anything on her head. Jack tossed it back into the trunk, then quietly closed it. Lynda made sure her 9mm pistol had a full magazine. She bent and secured her knife in her ankle sheath.

As they walked toward the house, Lynda mentally prepared herself for a long night ahead. After they apprehended the leader of this organization, they would have to question him. Once they had him in custody, they had only twenty-four hours before they had to bring formal charges. So much for the romantic weekend. Of course, even after twenty-four hours, they could still get a day or two at the spa.

"I probably should call for backup," Jack said, pulling out his phone.

"Wise." She didn't add "like I said," because he wouldn't find that funny. She bit her lip to stop herself from smiling.

Stepping carefully, they walked up onto the wooden porch. Lynda ducked under the window to the other side, and they both peeked through the window. She could make out three people sitting at a table—a blond man, a black-haired man, and a man with long brown hair pulled back into a ponytail. She held up three fingers, and Jack nodded. He stayed where he could see them while she knocked on the door. He lifted his chin in her direction, communicating that someone inside was approaching the door. She stepped back slightly.

The door opened, and the tall blond man who had sat at the head of the table asked, "May I help you?"

Lynda pulled her leather wallet out and flashed her gold badge and ID. "FBI. We're looking for Damien Cisco."

His face relaxed, and he smiled. "Ah, I figured you must be lost. This is not exactly the place where we normally have people come to the door." He came out onto the porch, and she moved back to keep an arm's distance away from him. "Damien lives on down the road about a quarter mile." He took a step and lifted his arm northward. Lynda took another step back and looked in the direction he pointed. "His driveway is hard to see."

Before she could reply, pain exploded in her left ear. Her vision closed down to a pinpoint of light, then nothing at all.

Lynda's head pounded. Nausea rolled in her stomach. Why did she feel so terrible? She tried to roll over, to get more comfortable, but couldn't move her arms. What in the world? Some of the fog lifted, and she realized she wasn't in her bed. Instead, she sat on a hard chair.

In little flashes, she started to remember. Driving up to the house. Asking the man who answered the door about Damien Cisco. The flash of pain. Then . . . nothing. Her heart beat faster. Sweat beaded on her upper lip. With a rush of adrenaline, she pushed the grogginess to the background and every sense heightened. What to do now?

She kept her eyes closed and tried to assess anything that she could in her environment. The smell of damp earth in the cold air assaulted her nostrils. Something sharp and unyielding cut into the delicate skin of her wrists, keeping her hands clasped behind her. Maybe a zip tie? Her shoulders ached from the position of her arms. Shuffling noises came from her left, the click of a switch a split second before a flood of heat. Behind her eyelids, she could see a bright light.

Footsteps. Low voices coming from her right.

Movement behind her, against her.

Her arms were tied to someone else. Jack? It must be Jack. Relief almost made her cry out. She wasn't alone. Praying desperately for courage and wisdom, she tried to listen to the low voices, tried to make out words. Jack started struggling, making her bindings dig deeper into her wrists. She fought back the discomfort and worked against the tight restraints to turn her hand, pressing her palm against his. He stilled at her touch.

Digging into her reserves for courage she didn't know for certain she possessed, she finally lifted her head and opened her eyes. It looked like they sat in the middle of a barn. She could see bales of hay in a loft, wooden beams, a concrete floor. The doors stood slightly open to the dark night outside. How long had she been out?

"Well, that took a while. I was starting to get bored."

The man who had opened the house door sat in front of her. He smiled. "I wonder how many training procedures you ignored tonight. No backup, turning your back on the men in my house. Tsk, tsk, tsk. It seems like the Federal Bureau of Investigation should train their agents better than that."

"You're wrong about the backup," she said. "We called them." She could hear movement behind her but kept her eyes on him. "Damien Cisco, I presume?"

He raised an eyebrow. "So you know my name. You get

the prize." He gestured at the tall black-haired man who had come into her line of sight and carried a camera on a tripod. She had seen him inside the house. "You're going to read a statement from Green War." He walked over to the wall and picked up a foam board leaning against it. Words were written on it in black marker, but from this distance she couldn't tell what they said.

Jack's muscles bunched behind her. He must have just come awake. He gave a small moan, and then his body stiffened.

Cisco walked around to face him. "Well, Agent Haynes. Good to see you. I wondered if maybe Antoine had hit you too hard."

"This is a mistake," Jack said, his voice hoarse. "You need to let us go right now."

Cisco chuckled. "I love how the fascist agent of our government just hands down orders to private citizens as if they're going to be obeyed." The humor left his voice. "Right now, you do what I say. I don't do what you say. You might do well to remember that."

"We have backup on the way. I called them before you attacked us."

"Yeah. There's no signal out here and you know it." Cisco walked back into Lynda's line of sight. She tilted her head to look up at him. "You're going to read this statement on behalf of Green War."

"We are federal agents. You need to let us go." She tried to keep the fear out of her voice. "This will only end badly for you."

He leaned down and put his nose close enough to hers that she could feel his breath. "You really need to quit worrying about my well-being and start worrying about yours."

Terror flowed through her limbs. She could barely breathe. Nausea swirled in her stomach. Her wrists hurt and her shoulders ached, and to her humiliation, her eyes filled with tears. She looked down, hoping Cisco wouldn't see her distress.

"Leave her alone!" The chair rocked as Jack struggled against his restraints.

She wanted to cry out to him to stop moving because of the pain. To her relief, Cisco moved out of her sight and said to Jack, "Fine. Let's focus on you, Special Agent Jackson Haynes of the Fascist Bureau of Investigation."

A man with wire-rimmed glasses that shone against his dark skin came from behind her. She didn't recognize him from the house. He picked up the light stand next to her and moved it. Suddenly, the light no longer blinded her, the heat no longer made her feel like she couldn't breathe. She closed her eyes, a hated tear slipping down her cheek, and tried to figure out what to do next.

"Now, I have a statement here that you're going to read," Cisco said to Jack. "Only, don't call yourself Lynda Culter, because that would be embarrassing. Just replace that with Jackson where appropriate."

"Jack," she said. "Don't—"

He leaned back as if communicating with her, telling her he could handle it. "Fine. I'll read your statement."

"Jack!" she said again.

"Shut up, Lynda."

"Yeah, Lynda, shut up or I'll shut you up," Cisco said.

She looked all around, desperately searching for . . . what? She sat with her hands tied behind her. So far, she'd identified three men in this room besides Jack. Possibly more. She still hadn't seen the man with the ponytail, so that made four combatants. What did she think she could possibly do?

The light when cast onto Jack created a strange contorted shadow of the two of them tied to the chairs. "I am Jack Haynes, an agent of the United States government. I'm here under that authority, and you can all bite my—"

The sound of a hard hit and cracking bones came a split second before Jack's howl of pain. Lynda sobbed, wishing she could see what was happening.

"You really shouldn't improvise," Cisco said. "Shall we go again? You have another kneecap."

Lynda thought she had felt fear before, but it didn't compare to what she felt now. When Jack responded with an expletive and they hit him again, little white dots appeared in front of her eyes and her mouth went completely dry. Then she heard a splash, smelled the undeniable odor of gasoline. Some of it landed against the back of her hand. When she realized they'd doused Jack with gasoline, she started struggling against the restraints, ignoring the cutting pain in her wrists.

"Read the statement. Word for word."

Another expletive from Jack brought a scuffle behind her.

"No! Not in here," Cisco said.

Something cold and metal bit against her skin seconds before her hands fell free. With relief, she brought them forward, rubbing her wrists one at a time. The other two men dragged Jack past her line of sight.

He looked at her as they went by. "Don't give in, Lynda!" he yelled.

They went through a door into another room. Cisco followed. He paused near the doorway and picked up the shotgun leaning against the wall. The men who carried Jack threw him to the ground. He tried to get up but fell again, likely from his busted kneecap.

Cisco stood in front of the open door and lifted his gun. "You're going to read a statement on behalf of Green War."

"Make me."

Lynda struggled, but they had secured her ankles to the chair. Sobbing, she bent over, fumbling to access the knife sheathed against her ankle. She could barely feel her numb fingers, and she couldn't lift her pants leg because of the zip tie securing it. "Jack!"

Cisco chambered a round in the shotgun. Somehow, she could hear the sound through the roaring in her ears. "Last chance. You will read a statement on behalf of Green War."

"Here's my statement, you dirty—"

The room exploded with the sound of the shotgun blast. Lynda froze, unable to believe what had just happened. Cisco turned back toward her. Jack lay just outside the door, unmoving. She could see only his legs and feet. One of the other men lit a match, fired up a hand-rolled cigarette, and tossed the match on Jack. His body went up in flames.

A sound came from Lynda—a scream, a yell, a guttural moan.

Cisco strode across the room toward her, aiming the shotgun at her face. He stopped close enough that she could see the wild look in his eyes. "Now, Agent Culter. Let's have a conversation."

Red and white lights strobed from her right. Through the open barn door, she spotted police cars coming their way. A sob of relief had her close her eyes and bow her head. She didn't know if the man would kill her before help arrived, but at least she and Jack wouldn't die out here where no one would know what had happened to them.

A sharp whistle from the black-haired man made everyone scramble. A thick, bound stack of papers landed at her feet.

"That's our manifesto," Cisco said. "Goodbye for now, Agent Lynda Culter. We'll meet again."

As two police cars pulled into the yard, a door slammed behind her. Sobs tore through her, feeling like they'd rip her body in half. The smell of gasoline-laced smoke filled her nose, burned her eyes, became all she could taste.

"Jack!" she screamed.

Hallee Bridgeman is the *USA Today* bestselling author of several action-packed romantic suspense books and series. An Army brat turned Floridian, Hallee and her husband finally settled in central Kentucky, where they have raised their three children. When she's not writing, Hallee pursues her passion for cooking, coffee, campy action movies, and regular date nights with her husband. An accomplished speaker and active member of several writing organizations, Hallee can be found online at www.halleebridgeman.com.

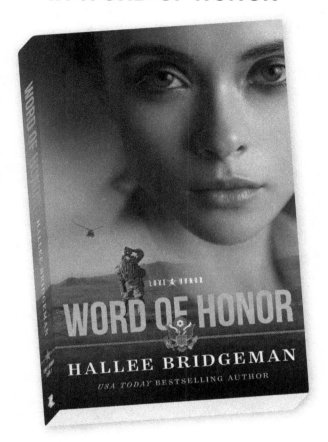

MEET
HALLEE BRIDGEMAN

HALLEEBRIDGEMAN.COM

authorhalleebridgeman

halleeb

halleebridgeman

CPSIA information can be obtained
at www.ICGtesting.com
Printed in the USA
LVHW101627200922
728848LV00003B/163